VOICES FROM THE
OTHER SIDE

VOICES FROM THE OTHER SIDE

DARK DREAMS II

EDITED BY BRANDON MASSEY

KENSINGTON PUBLISHING CORP.
http://www.kensingtonbooks.com

CONTENTS

Introduction   1

Harlem by Eric Jerome Dickey   3

Breath of Life by Lawana Holland-Moore   31

The Share by Terence Taylor   39

Sucker by B. Gordon Doyle   59

Wilson's Pawn & Loan by L. R. Giles   71

The Light of Cree by Chesya Burke   87

Deadwoods by Brandon Massey   95

Smoked Butt by Brian Egeston   115

Our Kind of People by Michael Boatman   123

Natural Instinct by L. A. Banks   131

Lord of All That Glitters by Anthony Beal   163

Leviathan by Christopher Chambers   169

The Arrangements by Patricia E. Canterbury   187

Good 'Nough to Eat by Rickey Windell George   209

Milez to Go by Linda Addison   235

Black Frontiers by Maurice Broaddus   253

Upstairs by Tananarive Due   269

About the Contributors   285
About the Editor   291

VOICES FROM THE OTHER SIDE

INTRODUCTION

The trailblazing continues.

Dark Dreams: A Collection of Horror and Suspense by Black Writers was the first book of its kind: an anthology of original, creepy short fiction, following no particular theme, written exclusively by black writers. Published in trade paperback in the fall of 2004, the book sold well, garnered wonderful reviews and, best of all, opened a lot of people's eyes to the fact that black writers are as capable of bringing chills and thrills to the page as anyone else.

But as good as it was, one book could not possibly express the breadth of the collective imagination of our community's dark dreamers.

So, like the little girl cried in *Poltergeist II*: They're back!

Here, in *Voices from the Other Side: Dark Dreams II*, I've been fortunate enough to entice back to the stage many of the favorite writers from the first collection. Tananarive Due is back with a suspenseful, disturbing tale of innocence lost in "Upstairs." In "The Share," Terence Taylor pens a startling, original story of love and heartbreak that takes place in an otherworldly Brooklyn apartment. L. R. Giles returns with "Wilson's Pawn & Loan," a wicked account of a man who inherits a family business that isn't quite what it appears to be. "The Light of Cree," the entry from Chesya Burke, chronicles the experience of a girl who comes into her womanhood—and her special power. Speaking of power, Linda Addison returns with "Milez to Go," a sequel to her story from the first collection, "The Power," in which she introduced us to two adorable and gifted girls, now all grown up and caught in another dangerous, extrasensory adventure.

Rickey Windell George, known for his visions of "extreme horror," is back, too. His harrowing story, "Good 'Nough to Eat," flips black-male sexual stereotypes upside down—and tears them inside out. Further exploring the themes of the outer limits of sexuality and the supernatural we have "Lord of All That Glitters" and "Sucker" by Anthony Beal and B. Gordon Doyle, respectively. And L. A. Banks delivers an unforgettable tale of primal lust and sensuality in the world of werewolves in "Natural Instinct."

Other returning writers transport us to other places—or even other times—in their stories. Christopher Chambers casts us onto a slave ship in "Leviathan" to face a legendary creature of the deep. In "Breath of Life," Lawana Holland-Moore takes us into the world of a mystic in Senegambia who is charged with the responsibility of protecting his village from an ancient evil. Patricia E. Canterbury, back here with "The Arrangements," takes you into a mysterious realm of ageless women and their strange, lovingly tended garden.

But we've got some new players on the team, too. Eric Jerome Dickey, one of the reigning kings of contemporary African-American fiction, takes a stroll on the dark side in "Harlem," a story of insanity, deception and desire. Michael Boatman, an actor perhaps best known for his roles in *Spin City* and *Arli$$*, demonstrates in the unsettling "Our Kind of People" that he's packing some literary chops, too. In "Black Frontiers," Maurice Broaddus takes us to the Old West, to face myths and monsters. Brian Egeston serves up a delicious dose of macabre humor in "Smoked Butt."

Once again, we've got chills and thrills galore. Have fun.

But keep your night-light on, just in case . . .

Harlem

Eric Jerome Dickey

One

People called me Harlem.

I dubbed myself after that dangerous neighborhood that I'd never seen.

A place not everybody knew about.

A place most people didn't want to know about.

I read life is rough in Harlem and a black man isn't expected to live to see twenty-five. Before twenty-five, a brother is almost guaranteed death, by either drugs or violence. Usually at the hand of another black man. Statistics of Harlem.

So that name fit me perfectly, described me to the hilt.

I was twenty-three.

The clock was ticking.

Another reason I took that label was because one of the nurses at the hospital, Daphane, was from there. She was the first one that was nice to me. She never forced my medication on me. Always brought me some books to read. Snuck me in some extra dessert after hours. Plus she told me what was going on on the other side of the double-locked doors. On the outside. Liking her helped me like being Harlem. She understood where I was coming from.

Daphane. She looked a few weeks shy of twenty but claimed she was around twenty-four. She came here right after I was boxed up and shipped here. A sweet, cute, caramel-flavored, thin sister who always gave a sincere smile back at me when I sent an earnest smile toward her oval face and light brown eyes. She'd always wink and speak when I passed by her on my way to therapy. Whether I was handcuffed or not. My fat-assed, cigarette-smelling, Grizzly Adams–bearded, Bozo-bald counselor never smiled. He talked down to me in a slick sort of way. I hate that Doc Brewster with a passion. First chance I got he would be my next one eighty-seven.

All the rooms were white. White walls. In the corner, a white, twin-sized bed with white sheets sat next to a white porcelain sink that had white fixtures. Like they were trying to make this hellish place seem like it was somebody's Ku Klux heaven. Nothing up in here but southern white nurses in white uniforms. Me decked out in a white hospital prisoner uniform.

Daphane and Phyllis were the only women of color in this joint. Heaven and hell.

Two

Again, I just woke up in a heated sweat, calling out for them to stop. In my nightmare, my little arms struggled with the police as they pulled me away from the paramedics. As I woke, my eyes stung from the salty blood. It took me a few minutes to realize that I was a grown man and not still that terrified child. That it wasn't still that day my soul died.

I kept having the same nightmares. If you were religious, you could call them a recurring set of visions. So I called them nightmares. My mother beating me. My father beating my mother. Me finding my father's body after my mother stabbed him in his sleep. Me crying daddy's gagging on his own blood as he tried to find strength to pull the steak knives out of his neck, back and chest. Me running into the front room and finding my mother's faceless body after she put a shotgun under her chin and pulled the trigger. Me sitting at my father's feet and looking him in the face as he took his last breath. Me getting his cigarettes off the kitchen table and putting them next to his dead body, just in case he wanted to take a smoke. Me balling up into a psychological knot and being quiet, not speaking a word to anybody for almost two years. Me living the life of the Unwanted. Molestations. Me being shipped from place to place to place like unclaimed luggage. Me trying to kill two sets of argumentative, abusive foster parents. More beatings. More molestations. By then I was what they called an "incorrigible" twelve-year-old.

The dreams didn't bother me at first, because I kept my secrets to myself. All I did was read. Closed myself off from the world with newspapers, Shakespeare, Iceberg Slim. But reading let me escape only until my eyes got tired. My mind stayed awake and reminded me of what I had done. I knew I was to blame for it all.

The cigarettes.

When I became violent, they said visions like these were the reason. That I was reenacting what I had seen. I could've told them that. They said I had shit pent up and repressed inside and that was the only way I knew how to release it.

Three

Today, Doc was trying to get inside my head and find out why I killed the people at the inconvenience store. That was the day I got caught. Silent alarm. I made it barely two miles on foot. Police helicopter chased me. It was live on three news channels simultaneously. Had higher ratings than Seinfeld. They showed me running, jumping fences and whizzing through brush. Great stride. I should've run track or something. They played the tape of me shooting the guy.

Damn, I looked good on tape. Great profile.

That was my fifteen minutes of fame.

Should've been an actor.

"Why did you kill those people in the Seven-Eleven?"

"One." I flipped my middle finger. I had to sound harsh and remind Brewster. "I killed only one. Damn, why you always exaggerating? I only wounded the others."

"But you killed eight others. Three women. Four men. One child."

"That's between me and you." I chuckled. "Patient-client confidentiality. And I already know the 187 count."

"It's between me and you."

Daphane cleared her throat. "Why did you shoot him? The Caucasian man at the Seven-Eleven. He wasn't bothering you. He was only twenty-four. He had a family. A pregnant wife."

"So I heard. He was smoking a cigarette."

Brewster asked, "You killed because of a cigarette?"

Daphane asked, "Why?"

"Dunno. I was just in one of those moods, I guess."

Brewster asked, "How did you feel when you shot him?"

"What do you mean? I felt like I needed to reload."

"What Doctor Brewster is asking is," Daphane said, again clearing her throat, "did you feel any remorse for shooting an innocent man?"

"Nope. He tried to keep me from getting away. That's a no-no. Plus, his arrogant ass didn't want Habib or Abdul or whomever to give up the money. And like I said, he shouldn't've been smoking. Cigarettes kill."

Heard the 7-Eleven guy's wife of three weeks had a nervous breakdown when they told her. Miscarried on the spot. She was too screwed up to come to the trial to watch me get ruled insane, then to watch me giggle and blow kisses when they took me away.

Why did they think I was crazy? I was sane. Their idealistic view of the wretched world made them crazy.

Four

I appreciated solitude and darkness. They both echoed what was inside me. So at night, I wanted to stay awake so I could appreciate myself by myself. But no matter how hard I tried, I wouldn't. The medication left me weak, wore me down.

Five

They said jacked-up memories were trapped in my mind and had to be released if I was going to survive, if I was going to make it back to their version of sane. If I was to get normal again. I never talked about them: my insignificant black secrets. They stayed in me, sheltered from the rest of the nonchalant world. Now I was supposed to "let them out to play." From the darkness into the light. From "slavery to freedom." Why did they use racist terms like those to try to persuade me? Were those psychological clichés supposed to be so damn appealing to my blackness?

Six

I had very few memories, and no positive memories of my mother or father. Not one, and I always hated that. I wanted to celebrate Mother's Day with her, Father's Day with him, birthdays with both. But the jacked-up memories had me trapped. Hey, they happened, right? Reality was a real mutha, for ya.

"Daphane, hand me the green folder on Harlem's parents."

"Yes, Doctor Brewster."

"You want to talk some more about your mother, Harlem?"

"My mother? Let's see, where should I start? Alcoholic. Liar. Alcoholic. Child abuser. Alcoholic. Selfish. Alcoholic. User. Alcoholic. Chain smoker. Did I mention alcoholic?"

Daphane rubbed her neck, then sighed. "Yes, you did."

I heard Brewster's frustrated breathing. I started to nod off.

"Harlem, can you hear me?"

"Yeah, Doc. Unfortunately, I'm still with you."

"I'm going to take you back."

"Been there, done that. But go right ahead. I'm ready for another depressing déjà jacked-up vu. My day was going too good anyway. And we can't have that, can we?"

"Start counting backwards . . ."

"From a hundred. Why can't I count up to a hundred?"

"If you wish, you—"

"It was a joke, Doc. Yeah, yeah. Don't matter. I know the routine," I said. "Daphane?"

"I'm right here," Daphane said. I loved her smiling voice.

"Thanks, Daph. One hundred. Ninety-nine. Ninety-eight."

I drifted to another horizon, went to a place where I was asleep and awake at the same time. I was here and there.

"What do you see?" Daphane asked. "Look around."

"Lots of trees. Daffodils, and bumblebees looking for food. Close-cut grass. Sunshine. Lots of nice sunshine. Warm. It's . . . damn . . . it's beautiful."

"Anybody there?"

"Me."

"How old?"

"Maybe five. I believe about five, because I don't have a memory of school. I'm in South Memphis. Ain't it funny how black people always live in south something or on the south side? You want to find the ghetto, go south, young man!"

"Tell me everything," Doctor Brewster interjected.

"Clock-watching MF. Brewster, you a punk."

"Harlem," Daphane said, her voice having that nice smile. "Pretty please?"

"Sorry, Daphane."

"Tell Doctor Brewster what happened."

I exhaled. "Okay. Anyway. I'm five. My mother. We never bonded. When I was fresh out the vagina, she dropped me off with some old Mississippi folks who lived down the street, and didn't make it back until I was six years and some change. I guess she forgot, or maybe something more important came up at the racetrack. Maybe she just couldn't hang. I wasn't a terribly atrocious child, so I know it wasn't because of my looks. I wasn't too dark, which was fashionably incorrect according to some stupid black folks back then. Nobody wanted a black-ass baby that looked like it came from deep, deeeep, deeeeeep ju-ju country in Africa.

"Anyway, I'm mind-rambling again."

"That's okay," Brewster said. "Let your thoughts flow."

"Sorry. I'll try to stay focused."

"Try not to get upset, okay?" Daphane said.

"Okay, Daphane."

Seven

Doc Brewster was trying this hypno bullshit on me. I was supposed to regress, go way back into my past, and see what else has me so jacked up that I behaved the way I did now. He kept calling me Ronnie, and they knew how I felt about that name. If I didn't have these thick leather straps on my arms, I'd choke the life out of him. But I couldn't, because the whatever shot they just gave me left me too weak. I was fading.

"Ronnie?"

"My name is Harlem. Can't you remember? Harlem. H-A-R-L-E-M. Harlem."

"Right, right. I apologize, Harlem. I'm sorry. I was reading off your charts."

"That's alright. I'm sorry for going off in front of you, Daphane."

Daphane smiled. "That's okay, Harlem. Don't be too mean today, okay? I had a rough night last night. Just do what Doctor Brewster asks, and I'll sit down with you and we'll look at yesterday's newspaper."

"You save me the business section and the funny papers?"

"Yeah. I've already circled your investments. One of the stocks you picked out went up a whole point from yesterday."

"Thanks, Daphane. I appreciate it."

"When is it?" Doctor Brewster asked. "Can you see yourself?"

"I can't really tell. It's kind of foggy." My head dropped. Closed my eyes. "I hear voices. Screams."

"What do you see?"

"Magnolia trees. Four-leaf clovers. Weeping willows. Dandelions. Children my age. We're young and happy. Then all of a sudden I'm not. Shit is happening."

"Why?"

"Because of hell."

"Hell?"

"Yeah. Hell showed up."

"Explain."

"That's irrelevant. When it happened, it didn't seem that important. It wasn't obvious to me. My naïveté. My ignorance."

My drunken father stormed across the playground and snatched me away. He beat me in front of all the other children. I didn't know why. I couldn't ask because he was too busy hitting me. My substitute teacher, Miss Bailey, tried to stop him but got pushed to the ground.

"Why is your daddy beating you?" Brewster asked.

"Yesterday," I started, but my throat tightened with fear.

My eyes watered. My voice sounded like that of a child. "Yesterday evening, he sent me to the store to get him a pack of cigarettes. I brought back the wrong brand. He wanted Kool. I brought back Salem."

My daddy walked away. Left me on the ground. Kids laughed and pointed at me. I wished I was bigger so I could hurt him back. I wished him dead.

The memory played over and over in my mind. Each time my daddy hit me, I twitched in my chair. I felt each slap, every kick. I convulsed in pain, almost as if I was in an electric chair.

By the time Daddy got back home, the school had called my mother. They argued and fought. That night, they both died. The cigarettes.

Eight

An everlasting Pine-Sol smell. Echoing words. Rubber soles screeching on the saintly floor, walking in from the hollow hallway. Electronic doors being buzzed open and closed. The rattling of medication bottles as somebody walked by pushing a wobbly cart. Keys jingled like Christmas bells, then my door opened. Somebody from the outside world came into my hell. I smelled sweet perfume, the fragrance of my only friend.

"Harlem?"

I didn't move.

"You asleep?"

"Nope. Just checking my eyelids for cracks."

"I brought you the newspaper. Sorry, I didn't get it to you earlier, but I had the last two days off."

"Away from this beautiful place? What were you doing? Giving up the poonie?"

"You are so nasty. Here's your paper. I'll read it to you."

"Thanks, Daphane. Could you loosen up this strap so I can get some more circulation in my hand?"

"I can't untie you, Harlem," she said sternly. "You know that's against regulations. I could lose my job."

"Please? I'll be a good boy, baby."

She unstrapped the leather bindings on my wrist, and my hand was free. With one hand loose, I could easily knock her out of the way and set myself free in a matter of seconds. The doors to this place are a joke, and the security's no threat to a brother as big as me. I flexed my wrist and pulled Daphane to me.

I kissed her on the ear and whispered, "Thanks."

I would hate it if she lost her job. If she was fired, I'd have nobody who understood me. The loneliness would kill me.

She giggled and slapped the side of my head. "I told you I'm married, so quit flirting with me."

"Let's run away together."

"Tomorrow."

"But tomorrow, my sweet, tomorrow never comes. It's always today."

"I know. Tomorrow never happens. Some people have no tomorrow."

"So live for today."

"Shut up."

She kissed my cheek, then we made small talk as she massaged my arm, restarting the circulation. I told her it felt better, then she put the restraint back on. This time it was more comfortable. She sat in front of me on a stiff plastic chair and read the stock market reports to me. She always educated me on what trends to look out for and where to put my money, if I ever got out and got any money.

She wanted me to get cased and go straight. Most of the time I didn't understand what she was talking about, but I liked to hear her talk that smart talk.

She'd invested some of her own money. Overtime money that she kept stashed from her dumb-ass, cheapskate husband, just in case. She had made close to eight thousand dollars over the last six months. I was very interested in what she did. I encouraged her, and she encouraged me. Through me, she was gaining more autonomy in her life. Through her, I maintained a freaking life. If I weren't so messed up inside my head, I'd want to love her forever and a day. I know I could, if she'd let me.

"You know I love you, don't you?"

"Shut up with that nonsense," she said, then flipped her hand at me. "Your medication must be kicking in."

After we joked a little, she read me the entertainment section, then the comic strips. "The Family Circus" always cracked me up. But it made me sad, too, because it makes me wish I had a family. People who cared. I bet the people in the cartoon strip had relatives to turn to when they got to the end of the road.

"How's your sister?"

"Fine," Daphane said. "I showed her the picture you gave me. She wanted to know what a fine-ass brother like you was doing locked down in a shit hole like this."

I laughed. "Couldn't afford Club Med."

"Who are you?" Daphane asked sincerely.

I smiled. "Harlem."

"No. I mean, who are you?"

"I'm the sum of all of my experiences. I'm the culmination of a series of events that have allowed me to arrive at this moment. Even, quite possibly, driven me to this moment. I have controlled some, but most have led me. There is no other identical to what I have become. None. I am me."

"Har de har har." She smiled, then gave me a serious look. "Harlem, really. Who are you?"

I closed my eyes and cried. Daphane wiped the tears from my face.

I whispered a frustrated, "I don't know."

For years I had been shipped from place to place, had wandered from place to place, and I'd never found me. In one session, Brewster told me to look inside myself to find me. I did. Nothing was there.

Nine

Brewster had started to work my last nerve. This nowhere session had run a little over thirty minutes. Daphane didn't come in today, so he brought along Phyllis, the funny-shaped sister with the atrocious, rough skin that made her look like a nappy-headed Gila monster. Her ugliness could run the T-Rex out of Jurassic Park. She put me in a mood.

"Harlem," Brewster said in that monotonic, patronizing voice I fucking hate, "tell me about the girl. After we talk about it, I'll let you get your rest."

"She was a woman. A woman."

"I apologize. Tell me about the woman."

"Why you always apologizing?"

"I'm sorry. I thought I offended you."

"Doc," I said, exhaling. "You're a spineless, punk-ass piece of shit. Now, you want me to apologize?"

"Do you want to apologize?"

"Punk you."

Phyllis just watched and listened. They wanted to know about Patricia. I hate it when they bring that shit up, which is why they don't do it too often.

"Patricia was your first girlfriend?" Phyllis asked, her brittle voice equally as patronizing.

"Yes. I was fourteen; she was fifteen. Right before I dropped out. I was a virgin; she wasn't."

"Did that bother you?" Brewster was scribbling as he talked. "Her, eh, experience?"

"It bothered me that she fucked Charles."

Phyllis said, "She made love to another—"

"No, she fucked him. She loved me."

Brewster cleared his throat, probably as a signal for Elephant Woman to shut up, then said to me, "And he's your best friend?"

"Was my best friend."

"So you tried to kill them?"

"I didn't try. If I wanted to, I could've. That's why I did what I did and walked away. Every time the bastard takes a step, his limp'll remind him of me. Every time that bitch sees her face, or what little I left, she'll see me."

Phyllis cleared her throat. Shifted. "Then you raped Charles's girlfriend?"

"It wasn't rape. He went inside my woman, so I went inside his. Eye for an eye. Retribution. It's in the good book. Look it up sometime, why don'tcha?"

Brewster repeated, "Retribution?"

"She came over to visit. I always knew Greta wanted me, especially after we found out Charles and Patricia had fucked us over. The first time, yeah, I held her down, tore her shit off and took some from her. Not much, just some. I'd been violated, and I wanted to pass it on. You know, keep it going like a chain letter. She shouldn't've met me up at the park after it got dark. Hey, two days later, she came back and gave it to me. So she must've liked it. So it wasn't rape. Next question."

"She killed herself after that," Phyllis said.

"Why're you giving me old information, huh?"

"You forced yourself on her, right?"

"Don't even try to Perry Mason me, bitch."

Her notes dropped from her lap when she jumped up. "Who're you calling a bitch?"

"Who answered?"

Phyllis's rookie ass exploded. I must've struck a nerve. As Brewster struggled to get control of the session, she growled herself calm. When the room quieted, after she'd picked up all the junk she'd dropped, after Brewster had taken out his handkerchief and wiped his sweaty forehead dry, I smirked a dark, Jack Nicholson-ish "Gotcha."

Phyllis jumped up again. First her face convulsed, then her mouth dropped open. Nothing came out. Either that, or it was at a pitch so high, only dogs like her could hear it. She stormed over her dropped stuff and left. Couldn't hang. Brewster stood and called her name a few times before he glanced at me. He shook his head and massaged his beard before he slowly picked up her stuff, then marched out a couple of seconds later. He knew he might as well go because I never said shit to his smoke-smelling ass unless somebody else was in the room. And if he wanted an easy session, that somebody had better be my Daphane.

Session's over for today.

Ten

Three days went by. No Brewster, no Daphane. No ugly-ass Phyllis. Just some skinny, short-haired, nameless, young Hispanic-looking intern guy dropping off food and giving me medication. Then again, he might be Chinese. Anyway, he gave me the bland crap they called food. He didn't actually give me my medication; he just watched me take it and made sure I swallowed it. He'd check back a few minutes later to make sure I didn't throw it back up after he left. He'd speak politely, but I never looked up or said anything back to him. I think his name was Billy. Or Jesus. Or Wang. Or Epstein. Maybe Bubba. Anyway, I didn't give him a problem either.

Eleven

On the fourth day, Daphane came in carrying a food tray. No newspaper. No smile. Shades. Blue long-sleeved sweater over her milky-white uniform.

I grinned. "You been on vacation again?"

She removed her glasses, and I saw her blackened eye.

Daphane said, "No. Sick leave."

Her husband had hit her again. She wouldn't show me, but I

think she had body bruises. All the beauty that lived and radiated in her speech had been killed. She sounded like one of them. In killing the life in her, he'd killed the life in me.

She told me it wasn't the first time he'd hit her. I told her it wouldn't be the last. She didn't answer.

"He went through my stuff and found out about the extra money, and when I wouldn't give it to him, he went off. I told him I was saving for our future. He didn't give a shit. I couldn't come to work looking the way I looked at first. You know, too many questions and looks and whispers. But I can't afford to be off. They frown on absences. Especially us nurses."

Daphane sat in her favorite plastic chair and watched me eat. They unstrapped me three days ago, so now I could walk around the room unsupervised. There was nothing life-threatening in this cell, so I wasn't no threat to myself or to anybody in here. Daphane came in unescorted because they knew I'd never touch her in a bad way. Outside of her and the food guy, everybody else came in paired or tripled up.

"Other than that time, have you ever hit a woman?" Daphane asked.

"Yep. Girl I used to do named Cassie."

"That's awful," she said.

"But she hit me first. Don't dish it out if you can't take it."

"That didn't make it right."

"That made it a left hook."

Daphane kept on watching me pig out. When I'd look up at her, she'd grin. All you could hear was the sound of my plastic fork scraping against the Styrofoam container.

Daphane quieted for a moment. She said in her fragile tone, "I probably won't see you anymore, Harlem."

My heart stopped beating. "You're not transferring out are you?"

"When I get home, I'm going to kill my husband. I'll kill him, or he'll kill me. One of us has to die."

"Daph—"

She fingered her eye and cringed. "I told myself if a man ever hit me like that, I'd kill him. He's been beating me off and on for over a year. He slapped me real hard in front of my friends, and now they won't call or come around anymore. My family won't help. I've let him get away with too much, too long."

"Just leave him."

"Where would I go?"

I couldn't answer. My heart wanted to say go with me, then I remembered where I was.

Daphane walked to the door and looked back. "Our secret."

I shook my head. "Don't. It ain't worth it. Do like Cassie did and go to one of those shelter things for women."

She walked over and kneeled by me. "When you killed that man, the one on the film. The Seven-Eleven man. When you shot him, it didn't look so hard. Was it?"

"That was different. That was me."

"What did you feel when you looked him in the eyes, when he begged you to just leave? Powerful? Free? What?"

"Nothing."

"Then I can do it to the man who brought me my pain and feel that same nothing."

"Don't."

"If I don't, then who will? Remember what you said your father did to you on the playground? Remember what you felt? The humiliation. The shame. The need for revenge."

"Don't. When I get out, I'll take care of it for you."

"You're here for at least another year. Maybe two. I can't wait for you that long. I could be dead by then."

"If I cooperated with Doc, made all the sessions real easy, played the game, I could be out in six months."

"That's a big if. And like I said"—she touched her face again—"I could be dead in six months."

"Help me get out."

"How would I do that?"

"Make it look like I escaped. I could do it late at night, when you're not on shift, when they got those whacked rent-a-cops watching the place. I could take them out real easy."

"No."

"If they catch me, I'm crazy. I'll just come back here, and you can read me the funny papers."

"That was nice of you." She smiled. "Thanks for the offer."

"I can't let you do that."

"You can't stop me."

"Well, what if I just told them what you're planning to do?"

"They won't believe you. Don't forget, they think you're crazy. You're the patient. I'm the nurse."

She kissed me on my lips, wiped away the lipstick, then walked out and locked the door behind her. From the other side, I heard her call back, "Take care of yourself, Harlem."

The sounds of her shoes screeching against the concrete quickly faded.

Twelve

Brewster and Phyllis finally came in for my afternoon session. Gila Face looked like she'd grown a foot of cheap hair. Either that, or she'd joined the Hair Club for Women.

"How're you doing, Weaverella? Waiting for that prince to come along and snatch that fake-ass horsehair out of your head? It probably looked better on Trigger. But then again, Trigger looks better."

She flipped me off with her eyes and continued scribbling nothing. Her hand shook, and a pulsating vein popped up in her neck every time I spoke. Today I decided to make my voice sound like the dark, cartoon Batman. Deep and sinister, shopping for a victim of the night.

"Where's Daphane?"

Brewster cleared his throat. "Gone for the day. She took ill. Phyllis is sitting in for her. Will you be polite to her? If you don't mind, Harlem."

"Phyllis, the woman of my dreams. Oh, how I think of thee, Phyllis—right before I puke. Quick! Douse me with thy overwhelming atrociousness, you hideous canker. Infect me with thine—"

"*Shutupshutupshutthehellup!*" Phyllis's eyes watered. She rubbed her forehead, then fidgeted with her ear. Jumped up and sat back down. "Why do you dislike me? What have I done to you? I'm trying to help your crazy—"

"I'm *Not* crazy. *Never* call me crazy. *Never.*"

"I'll call you what I like." She smirked under her tears. "Mr. Certifiable."

"Phyllis," Brewster said in a controlling voice. "Please."

"Let her go, Doc. I'm from the old school. I'll rank on her ass until she ends up in one of these beautiful suites. By the way, I've been meaning to talk to you about the room service. Can I get a room with a Jacuzzi?"

I decided to cooperate, because if they came back each day, I could get information on Daphane.

Today we talked about when I was in juvenile hall. Then about when I broke out and beat that old Asian man so I could get his car. Then about . . .

Thirteen

Daphane showed up four days later, just in time for my session with Brewster. After the pleasing session, they walked out. But Daphane doubled back a couple of minutes later. Before the door closed good, I asked, "Did you eighty-six your old man?"

"No." She looked at me for a minute, shifted side to side on the scarred heels of her nurse shoes as she pulled at her lips, then whispered a pissed, "I need your help."

"I'll do anything for you, Daphane. You know how much I love you."

Daphane needed a gun. I gave her the name of a friend, Teryl, who I did some time with. He could hook her up real cheap. Something untraceable. Daphane said her husband was too big and she wouldn't want the chance of him getting at her. Since she wasn't a big woman and definitely not that strong, I told her to get a .380 automatic. Small. Easy to hide. Easy to use. Especially from close range. It could hold six plus one in the chamber. I told her to go pick up some hollow points, because when they hit you, whatever they hit explodes. Pinhole going in; Grand Canyon hole going out. Left you hollow. Internal injuries like a muggerguggah. You could shoot somebody in the little toe, and they'd die from the pain. At least, they'd wish they were dead.

"Is that what you used at the Seven-Eleven?" Daphane asked.

"Yeah. That's how I know."

She smiled. "Good."

"Have you thought about it?"

"Yes."

She knew that after it was done, she didn't want to go to jail and she didn't want to die. Just to be free.

Daphane pulled some folded papers out of her pockets. "Look. Tell me what you think."

"What are these?"

"Maps. All the back roads are highlighted."

She wanted to run away to Canada or maybe try to make it to Mexico. As far as Los Cabos. Then she could start her life over.

She whispered, "I want you to go with me, Harlem. Would you?"

I didn't hesitate. "Yeah."

She told me how to get out, where the easy-out doors were, how to make it across the grassy hills unseen. The guards changed shifts at four, eight, and twelve. After midnight, only one guard patrolled inside. One old guy outside. The first five minutes of the shift were used to make rounds and check out the building, making sure everything was locked. They went from east to west on the patrol. If I let them go by, then went west to east, I'd be out in three minutes. They wouldn't know until sunrise.

"I'll be two miles down the road," she said. "Parked in my Mustang, with my lights off. How long would it take you to get there?"

"Dunno." My voice showed excitement from the possibility of my being free. "I haven't been any farther than this room. I'm stiff. Out of shape. Done put on a few pounds. Maybe twenty, twenty-five minutes."

"I'll wait until twelve thirty-five. Then I'm gone. With or without you."

"How am I supposed to get out of this door?"

"Don't worry about it. Just be ready."

This time Daphane kissed me like she was my woman. It was short, but deep and intense. She wiped the lipstick from my face, then swiped at her mouth, smiled and swayed to the door.

She winked. "See you on the outside."
I sat there, my heart beating fast, a man in love.

Fourteen

I walked around the room most of the evening. The babbling voices of other patients echoed in the halls. Screams. Curses. I think somebody got unruly and the orderlies had to subdue him or her. My joints were stiffer than I hoped. I stretched for twenty minutes. At eight o'clock, I used the bathroom to lighten my load, then took a nap.

Fifteen

Keys rattled, then my door clicked open at eleven fifty-eight. Lights from the hall cast a long shadow across my dark room. The ceiling light clicked on. The Hispanic-looking orderly, what's-his-face, came in with a cup of water and some pills. I pretended I was asleep until he called my name. I sat up and looked at him. He wasn't Hispanic. A light-skinned black man with sleepy, slanted eyes. Never even noticed that mutt before. Name tag read "Kevin."

He watched to make sure I took my pills, then headed back for the door. Right before he put his hand on the still-cracked door, it hit me. My last medication was at eight. Always at eight. This was how Daphane arranged it. Must've changed my charts.

Before he could get the door opened, I grabbed him from behind. I cupped the back of his head with the palm of my right hand and shoved his head deep into the wall. The wall wasn't hard enough to crack his cranium, but was sturdy enough to leave him KO'd. Kevin didn't even have time to scream. He looked so peaceful. Sweet dreams.

Sixteen

Two minutes past midnight. Keys jingled when the security guard whistled his way past my door.

Three minutes past midnight. I headed in the opposite direction of the whistles, and ducked into a closet when I heard an orderly squeaking down the hall. I walked by the nurses' station. The nurse on duty was so busy yacking and laughing on the phone that I just strolled by like I knew where I was going.

Four minutes past midnight. Concrete, waxed floors glistened in the moonlight as I crept through a side fire-escape door. One that had a freshly busted alarm. The one Daphane told me about. Down two flights of noisy, metal stairs in a musty, dusty stairwell. At the bottom, the exit door was already cracked open, held open by a thick stick.

The old security guard was right outside the door, about twenty yards away in my direct route to the fence I had to jump. His head bobbed. He was sleeping, with a Walkman on and a cup of java at his feet. I walked over to him and stood close enough to spit in his eyes. He didn't wake up. I could hear B. B. King crying from his headset. No cigarettes were in his pocket. Besides, he was old. Probably got a nice family at home waiting. I let him live. After I got over the fence, I looked back. He was still asleep. I waved good-bye to everybody and nobody.

Seventeen

I made it over the grassy hill and to the trees in two minutes. I was already tired. Sweating. Cicadas buzzed their songs in the trees. When I stumbled through a thick patch of mosquitoes, several stuck to my skin. I gagged on a couple that flew into my open mouth and took a tour down my throat. My stiff legs were starting to cramp up. I looked at the sky. The stars were so pretty. Big Dipper. Little Dipper. Star of freedom. Half moon. Planes passed by at different altitudes, going in different directions. My side stitched, but I kept moving. I started wheezing. Asthma was kicking in. It was damn humid tonight. I'd forgotten how humid it got on the outside. Felt like it was over ninety degrees tonight. Damn southern heat. I slowed down, splashed through a few pools of water that smelled like the Mississippi and muddied my bare feet, but I kept moving. My guess was it was about twelve twenty.

Eighteen

Twelve forty-five. Police sirens wailed past me, lighting up the streets. An ambulance followed. When I heard them approach, before they rolled up over the hilly road, I ducked back into the trees. When they faded, I took back to the streets and resumed my running-walking. From the woods echoed the love calls of crickets. My body was alive with pain. Sweat dripped into my eyes. Burned. Reminded me of my dreams. My armpits were soaked, shirt sweat-stuck to my back. Plus the medication wasn't helping. I stopped long enough to put my fingers down my throat and try to bring the poison back out. Didn't work. With my body temperature up so high, it made me jittery, anxious. I had to be almost three miles up the road and still didn't see Daphane.

Nineteen

Twelve fifty-one. The high beams of a slow-moving car came over the hill, heading the same way I was heading. I ducked back into the woods until I could see it was a faded red '66 Mustang. It passed by. Daphane. I whistled and waved her down.

She busted a U-turn without slowing, kicked up pebbles and a dirt cloud on her side before she whipped back to my side. I hopped into the back seat and slid down as deep as I could. No words.

She burned rubber before the door closed. A helicopter passed over with its spotlight directed into the woods closer to the asylum. Dumb bastards didn't know I was off the property. The gossiping nurse didn't see me. The narcoleptic guard probably lied and said he'd been awake the whole night and nobody came out his way.

Twenty

We traveled far enough down the road to get that safe, got-away feeling. When I sat up, I felt tiny, sharp objects on the backseat. Glass. I looked around and saw the passenger window was broken out. More glass was splattered across the front seat next to a brick. She handed me the brick, and I dropped it into the backseat.

"It took me longer because I locked my keys in the car. I tried using a clothes hanger, but it took too long. Guess I panicked. Plus, I didn't know if you were going to get out, and if you did, I didn't want to leave you hanging."

Daphane was dressed in Levi's, a black cotton T-shirt and driving gloves. She looked strange, different. Like Daphane, but not like Daphane. Then I realized it was because I'd never seen her in anything but a white uniform. Her hair was down. She looked funny. Maybe not funny, but just normal. Not the sterile way she looked at the crazy house. She looked beautiful. Like a woman.

My all-white uniform now was muddy, moist and musty. Swamp muck squished between my toes. After it filled itself with my blood, I killed a mosquito on my arm.

Daphane smiled.

I asked, "Did you do your husband?"

"No." She smirked. "But look."

She reached into her purse and handed me a .380 that had the serial numbers filed off it.

"Your friend said hello."

"Good."

She handed me the box of hollow points. I loaded the automatic. Six in the clip. One in the chamber.

"Where's your husband?"

"Home. I had sex with him before I snuck out, so he's sound asleep."

I didn't say anything.

"What's wrong, Harlem?"

"Did you enjoy it?"

"No." She frowned. "I just did what I had to do. I didn't want him suspicious."

"I understand."

"But I want to make love to you."

"For real?"

"Tonight. Can I? If you don't mind."

"I'd like that." I blushed. "Yeah."

"Lord knows, I can't wait. But, first we do this. Business before pleasure."

"How far to your house?"

"Ten minutes."

"Good. I'll do him."

"Make it quick. Like you did at Seven-Eleven."

"But I want to make a stop first."

Twenty-One

Brewster lived less than six miles up the road. A big, two-story, wooden house with no fence. Just a short, rocky driveway leading from the street to his house. Again, no streetlights. Darkness and solitude.

My trade-off with Daphane was this: I'd kill her husband, but not until she'd gone away long enough to establish an alibi. I wanted her to drive to a friend's house and call him. Make sure her friend picked up the phone and heard his voice. I showed her how to pull out the wires to her distributor cap so she'd have car problems. Get the friend to drive her back home. They'd both find the body. Then I'd lay low until she got the insurance money, and we'd meet a few days later.

But first, I wanted Brewster. Kill him, take a shower, get me some clothes. Money, if he had it lying around. Maybe wash myself down and make love to Daphane in his house.

Twenty-Two

I walked around outside the house and scouted, making sure he was alone. Brewster was in his study, in his pajamas, looking down over the tops of his wire-rimmed glasses, reading over my files. Ain't that a bitch. When I rang the doorbell, Daphane stuck her pretty face up to the peephole and smiled.

Before the door opened good, I was on him. It was funny, because he was so in shock to see me, to see us together, he didn't even move or make a sound while I put my dirty hands around his fat throat. As I wrung his neck, he fell, kicked and gargled, turned red, then faded. When he croaked, I got on my knees and closed his bugged-out eyes. I hated the way he looked at me. Now he would never look at me again.

"Harlem," Daphane said. She sounded disturbed, and that put me off for a moment. I hated for her to see me like this. But this was the plan. Our Bonnie and Clyde scheme. She was in too deep to turn back. I love her, but if she flipped out, I'd have to get rid of her. After we made love a couple of times, of course. I want to be free forever, and dead weight won't help.

When I looked up, Daphane was standing over me with the .380 pointed at my face. "So that's how you do it, eh, Harlem? That easy, huh?"

"Why you pointing the gun at me?"

"What did you feel when you killed him?"

"Daph—"

"What did you feel? Answer me!"

"Nothing. Don't trip. I love you, baby. I told you I was going to do him. You brought me here. I told you I'd kill your husband if you—"

"You already killed my husband."

"What are you talking about?" I asked. I wanted to make a move to her, but she had me trapped. Her finger was on the trigger. Point-blank range.

"You killed my husband."

I looked down at the man turning cold. "Brewster's your man?"

As she softly shook her head, tears rolled down her cheeks, but her face wasn't crying. She choked on her words, "Seven-Eleven. Cigarettes."

"Your husband? The white man?"

"Yes, my husband. He went to the store for me. That was my fault. This is for him."

"I thought your husband beat you?"

Her face told me the answer. She had set me up.

A car pulled into the driveway. Its high beams brightened the front room, shined right in my face. I felt relief, because I hoped it might be somebody coming to take me back to my room. The lights died. Seconds later, the doorknob turned and the front door creaked open. Phyllis walked in, dressed just like Daphane. Driving gloves. Nobody wore driving gloves in this kinda heat. They had them on so no fingerprints would be left behind.

I could hear the sounds of a car that needed a tune-up real bad— maybe some new fuel injectors—chugging out front. I slyly looked around and tried to find an out. Too far from a window. Nowhere to dive for cover. Nothing around me to pick up and throw. I glanced back down at blue-faced Brewster before I scowled up at the tag team. We'd both been had.

Daphane kept her distance, and her eyes on me, as she handed the gun to a grinning Phyllis. Daphane looked like she was in so much pain.

"I can't kill you, Harlem," Daphane said, and wiped her face. "If I shot you and I felt nothing, I'd be just like you. Nothing. But I can watch you die."

I grimaced at stone-faced Phyllis. She tilted the gun and held it sideways like the hoodlums did in the hood movies.

Phyllis said, "I guess you ain't got nothing to say now, huh? What's all that smack you said about me? Atrocious. Canker. C'mon, *Ronnie*, say something. *Ronnie Certifiable*."

"My name is Harlem!"

"Ronnieronnieronnieronnieronnieronnieronnie!"
"Harlem! H-A-R-L-E-M!"

My adrenaline rushed, clogged my head with memories of Ronnie, and before I knew it, I charged at Phyllis. Daphane screamed. Her legs collapsed, and she fell hard to the floor and shrieked, just as I got close enough to grab at the gun. Phyllis didn't even blink. Not the slightest jerk. She broadened her smile. Her finger tensed and pulled the trigger.

Twenty-Three

People used to call me Harlem.
    When they found my body, and the gun inside Brewster's hand, they couldn't figure out how, but they said we killed each other. Somehow, they figured, he'd emptied the clip, but I killed him before I died. They said it was possible, because I was crazy. Some sort of psycho strength and determination. I don't think they really cared.

Oh, the Mustang was Brewster's, too. Daphane stole it right before she picked me up. Easy. She had taken Brewster's keys out of his office and had them duplicated. She broke out the window and handed me the smutty brick to get my prints on it. She had planned to kill me in the car later. But since I had this passion for Brewster and insisted on a detour, I made it easier for her. Gila Face was trailing us the whole time with her lights off.

Cops figured I was going to use Brewster's car for a getaway. Said that maybe after I had broken out the window, Brewster heard the noise, grabbed the gun and came to the door. That was when I went after him and the struggle began. After they saw the gun was a throwaway, they figured that maybe Brewster took it from me while we fought.

I made the front page.

Fifteen more minutes of fame.

Good profile.

Should've been an actor.

Or model or something.

What was that? Where's Daphane at? Standing over her husband's grave, crying, smiling and laughing while she smoked a Kool down to the filter. If you asked me, I think she was already crazy. Because when Phyllis shot me, Daphane felt nothing. After all we shared, after all the love I had for her, she felt less than zero. Seven shots. Nothing. She didn't even twitch while I twitched. That shit hurt, both physically and psychologically.

Daphane built a shrine for her husband in her bedroom. Kept that door locked, and nobody went in there but her. Pictures were everywhere. Newspaper clippings from when he died. She wore his clothes, sometimes put on her wedding dress, played Nat King Cole, danced and talked to him and heard him answer. She was a New York minute from a total breakdown.

When Phyllis heard me die, when I wheezed out my last breath, she jumped up and down in joy and danced the butterfly over my bleeding chest.

Didn't matter; she was still ugly.

And she couldn't dance, either.

Breath of Life

Lawana Holland-Moore

1858, Futa Toro, Senegambia

*F**orward is the only way, and it is often without a clear path,* Oumar thought as he smoothed out a small piece of paper. He was focused as he wrote an inscription upon it, his script careful and deliberate. He carefully folded the paper before gently tucking it into a small brown leather pouch. After saying a prayer over the pouch, he handed it to the woman who sat across from him, her eyes downcast in a face that was worried and drawn.

"You have suffered so much already. This should help you," he said as she started to thank him profusely. "Allah be with you." The woman's dark brown hands were shaking as she quickly tied the pouch around her waist and hurried out.

He could hear the sound of women outside pounding millet with large wooden pestles, the rhythmic thumps complemented by their singing. *Perhaps things are finally returning to normal*, he thought. Picking up his reed pen, Oumar dipped it into the ink and started to write again. He looked up as one of the students from his Qu'ranic school came to the doorway.

"Excuse me, Teacher," the small boy said, swatting away a pesky fly that had landed on his face. "The *almami* and the council of elders want to see you."

"Thank you," said Oumar. The boy ran off to join his friends as Oumar carefully set aside the prayer sheets and papers he had been creating, their white surfaces covered with the black ink of his precise writing and geomantic drawings filled with graphs and symbols. After he rolled up the reed mat he had been sitting on, Oumar looked around his simple dwelling, with its thatched roof and mudbrick walls. A bowl of millet couscous with groundnut-leaf sauce sat waiting, as did a calabash of milk left for him by the woman for whom he'd made the gris-gris talisman earlier. Small wooden boards with verses from the Qu'ran that he had prepared for his students were neatly stacked against a wall, and he thought about his lessons and how school had been interrupted lately. An ornately carved wooden chest in the corner caught his eye, and he sighed as he looked at it.

This was inevitable. He stood up and straightened his robes and the fabric that hung loosely about his shoulders.

I am the only one now.

"Oumar Ba, we are sure that you know why you are here," the *almami* said. A reed-thin Toucouleur noble whose Arab heritage was evident by his features and light red-brown skin, Dényanké was leader of their village. Although he was the foremost person to take action on behalf of it, the elders actually governed and were consulted on all major matters. They scrutinized Oumar as he entered the room and took a seat before them. They sat silently with folded arms, their embroidered robes neatly falling in deep folds around them. Many had been friends of his father and grandfather, and he could see that all of their eyes registered doubt.

They must have faith. They must.

"Do you believe that you can overcome it?" Dényanké asked.

"What are our options? What other hope do we have for ourselves? For *them*?" Oumar said as he waved his hands toward the people gathered outside the doorway, straining to hear. "This thing is an abomination. It is an upset to *baraka* and an affront to Allah. It is not intent on contributing to the breath of life if all it will bring is death. I suppose that is why I must go after it. Who else *can*?"

"You are right," one of the elders said sadly. "There is no one else left but you now."

Dényanké's face looked grim as Oumar got up to leave. "May Allah be with you—and all of us."

Oumar walked back to his home, followed by children and villagers shouting out to him in support. As he stepped inside, he found his apprentice, Bayo, sitting there writing. Startled by all of the noise, Bayo looked past him at the crowd of people as he quickly put his work aside.

"Teacher, I hope you do not mind my presence right now. I thought I'd take care of some things while I had the chance," he said. "I take it the Council made its decision."

"Yes, and I am asking you to come with me. I will need you, starting with your help in getting prepared for the journey."

Oumar and Bayo went around his home, gathering supplies for the trip. Oumar walked over to the wooden chest—its golden accents gleaming—and opened it, fingering the papers and contents inside. His fingers tingled as he touched the cover of a well-worn copy of the Qu'ran that had been handwritten by his grandfather.

This is it, my ancestors. All you have taught me has led to this. May Allah watch over us all.

As Oumar prepared to leave the village with Bayo, he looked ahead into the distance. He walked slowly, with his head held high, but his soul was heavy, with the weight of the entire village's expectations pinned on him and him alone. In hindsight, Oumar thought that perhaps his statement may have been too cocky, too bold, too presumptuous.

For hours and hours they walked through the countryside, stopping only to rest and eat a little dried mutton from their bags and ripe mangoes from the trees. He squinted as the sun started to lower in the sky, causing the baobabs, with their twisted, gnarled branches, to cast dark shadows across the ground. He thought of the griots—the keepers of oral history, legend and song—who were often entombed within the baobabs hollow cores. He could feel the essence of those old trees as they passed, each one strongly pulsing with the heartbeat of the land, reminding him of the millet-pounding of the women.

The only person who had been willing to go with him on this hunt for the rogue djinn was Bayo, whose tall, lanky frame looked as if it had been swallowed by his long white tunic and loose slacks. Only his eyes were visible beneath the white fabric wound around his head and face, and they nervously darted from side to side. As the men made their way through the dry savannah grasses and sand, Bayo's fear was almost palpable. The young man shifted the leather satchel on his shoulder before turning to look at his mentor.

"Are we really going to do what you said when we find it?" he asked, brushing against the billowing white fabric of Oumar's voluminous outer robes.

"Yes. We shall talk," Oumar said.

"Talk? What if it will not reason? *If* it is capable of that. Then what?"

"If there is no reason—no compromise—then we will resort to our original plan. As for right now, all we can do is continue to wait."

Bayo didn't look too convinced as he joined Oumar—who squatted in the thick, peach-colored sand—and prepared to begin his prayers. When they finished, Oumar sat with his hands folded in his lap. His calm demeanor was in sharp contrast to how he actually felt: a little anxious about coming face-to-face with the scourge of their small village.

Oumar thought more about his task as he walked. A djinn. Not an angel, yet not a demon. Moving with the whirlwinds and whims of the desert sands, they could be mischievous one moment and spiteful the next. Yet, this one was different. It was unusual for a djinn to create the kind of havoc that had been unleashed on Oumar's village.

Too many times now had screams awakened him during the night, everyone shrieking at once as they rushed out to find chaos in the aftermath. The other villagers ran around frantically as women whirled in place, howling with grief as they clutched their children close to them. Even grown men cried out in horror as the corpses and body parts of loved ones, friends and neighbors were found scattered across the ground like petals. Oumar knew this carnage meant only one thing: *It had returned.*

Oumar winced just thinking about it. In the light of morning, he would reflect upon how the attacks seemed to happen so fast that even he was unable to feel or predict their coming. That was something that had never happened before. Amid the grief-stricken cries and wails from bereaved relatives, the dead—who had been mutilated and torn into pieces during the night—were properly put to rest, leaving those left behind with a choice they did not want to have.

"What will we do?" they all asked him as one by one they came to him for some form of protection—anything to comfort them against this unknown. "What *can* we do?"

Oumar contemplated everything he knew, reflecting upon the fact that he had probably been in training for a time like this all of his life, although he had hoped it wouldn't come to something like this. For years he had studied the mysticism of his Tijaniyya Sufi sect at Qu'ranic school under the disciplined tutelage of his father and grandfather, both powerful marabouts and leaders in their faith. With them both now gone, it was up to him to help his people.

He knew he was only one in a long line of Toucouleur marabouts and female seers. His ancestors had been among the first to help spread Islam in their region, yet even so, some of the ancient mystical ways still remained as well. So far he had shown the village only a sampling of the special things that he could do, but this time would be the ultimate test.

Oumar had been told the stories of the Unseen One and had believed them to be just children's bogeyman tales until his grandfather brought him the scrolls. Oumar had gasped as he looked upon the ancient records, written in a fading hand, that documented how their village had been preyed upon for centuries. That which had once been, but a story he now knew to be very real. Oumar felt it was his duty to try to defend his village the best way he knew how.

He was now ready to negotiate with it—or to battle it once and for all.

"Bayo, while we still have some light, let us do as we planned." The apprentice opened the satchel and handed him the paper shirts, drawings and amulets from within.

"Teacher, are you wearing the amulet that I made for you as well?" Bayo asked eagerly, as Oumar reached up and fingered the small bone-and-leather pendant around his neck that he had been wearing lately. "I made it myself, and I was hoping you still had it on."

"I am, thank you. I'll take whatever extra protection I can get," Omar said as they both rushed to put everything on under their robes. The two of them worked quickly to prepare the area around them as well, arranging the papers under the sand in a circle. The two of them surveyed their work, pleased.

As he and Bayo sat in the center and waited, the sun finally dipped even lower, throwing a spectrum of color over the dry, yellow-tan brush that stretched as far as they could see. Oumar could see the gleaming silver ribbon of the river in the distance as they sat in expectation.

"How do you know it will come?" Bayo asked with a hint of resignation.

"It will come because it is tired. It will come because it is time."

"And you are *certain* of this?" Bayo asked again with a long sigh as the last orange glow of the sun started to dissipate along the horizon.

"It will. Quiet now."

In the silence that followed, Oumar closed his eyes and relaxed, allowing himself to meditate and to concentrate on everything around him. With a flash of white, he felt his mind open up. He felt weightless in the void as it filtered all of the stimuli. He allowed himself to be open to the universe—including to its more unsavory occupants. A faint, thin smell came to him. The rank scent was growing stronger and stronger.

It is coming.

It was immense, and almost stifling in its anger and animosity, as it came rushing toward them with startling speed. Oumar could feel it—ancient, unstable, unsure of its intent. Almost as soon as he picked up on these impressions, the presence was before them.

Its voice, a low and guttural growl, came to him within his head before he actually saw it. He opened his eyes to see Bayo still sitting beside him. The djinn's attention shifted.

"You have no quarrel with him, Old One," Oumar politely told it in a calm, even voice. Bayo looked up, fear filling his face, but did as instructed beforehand by trying to remain calm.

Oumar could now see the djinn clearly with the disappearance of the sun. Tall, yet thin of build, the Old One was appearing to him as a man. Gaunt, with long, razor-sharp fingernails, it turned its milky, luminescent eyes upon them. The dust had started to settle around the djinn as it stopped moving, but its bloodied gray robes flowed around it in undulating tattered rags, as if still propelled by the whirlwind. Its forearms were covered with blood and thick, crusting gore. Oumar watched in barely contained disgust as the djinn licked blood away from its ashen lips, exposing sharp, fanged teeth.

"I see you are not surprised by my appearance," the Old One said, its voice now a series of rumbles like that of a storm passing.

"With all due respect, I am not here to comment on your looks. I am here to discuss, to negotiate with you."

"You? Negotiate with *me*? That is laughable," the Old One said in contempt as its milky eyes looked at Oumar. "It will not happen. I am owed as much for what was done to me so long ago."

"So long ago that it has faded into memory? Old One, let it blow away like this dust we now stand upon. You must let go of your past and your need for revenge. Be absolved. Move forward, and contribute to the universal energy once more. There is no need to continue down this wicked path."

"Never again. This is of my choosing."

"This is your wish?"

"It is," it said, taking a step towards them.

"Not one step more," Bayo said, pointing toward the ground for emphasis. "Not one step."

"Oh, he speaks, I see?"

"Bayo? You can see it?" Oumar said, his pride in his apprentice's awareness swelling just as the djinn moved swiftly, creating a strong breeze that shifted the dirt around it, exposing a paper mat with inscriptions. Angered, it turned and stood before Oumar. Oumar blanched at the djinn's discovery of his ruse.

It whirled around, its teeth bared. "How *dare* you try to trick me and bind me!"

Oumar stepped back, shocked that it did not work. *How could that be?* The djinn used this surprise to its advantage, advancing upon him with one hand raised, its claws menacing.

"Now my teacher! *Now!*" Bayo shouted, distracting the djinn for a moment, just long enough for Oumar to get his bearings and start to recite supplications to Allah. At that moment, the djinn paused on another of the geomantic papers that had been hidden under the sand.

The djinn screeched—a deafening, piercing howl—and its body lurched forward, before jerking backwards again, as if pulled by marionette strings. Despite its convulsions, Oumar's body started to chill and prickle all over as he felt the djinn building up the strength to combat all of their work by draining energy from the space around it. It looked at Oumar one more time before sneering and moving toward Bayo.

"*No!*" Oumar yelled as the djinn rapidly closed in on his apprentice. Bayo screamed, his eyes closed, as the djinn approached. It took one swipe at the young man, who cried out in pain as the djinn's talons cut into his flesh, tearing through his clothes and paper shirt, before it abruptly disappeared. Oumar turned around, looking for what he sensed was still there.

Where did it go? I can feel its essence, but where could it have gone?

Oumar caught his breath and turned to look at Bayo. He was surprised to see his apprentice standing before him with a large rock in his hands. Confusion spread across Oumar's face. "Bayo! What are you *doing*?"

Bayo's face was contorted with a delirious, feverish pleasure.

Oh, no.

Oumar's eyes widened with comprehension, and his hands flew to the amulet around his neck. The amulet! He had been deceived. Bayo had learned from him a little *too* well—including how to block Oumar's abilities when it came to this djinn. His mind raced as he thought of the village and its people . . . how they would be picked off one by one . . .

Everything around him blurred in his panic as Bayo suddenly brought the stone down upon him. He felt blood streaming from the side of his head, and once again he started to recite the supplications, repeating them over and over again, hoping the effect of the powerful words would help him. Oumar's voice sounded slurred and thick to himself as he began to lose consciousness. As his eyes started to close, he could see the djinn reappear beside Bayo, its sharp teeth curving into a smile as it raised one of its clawlike hands again. Oumar felt searing pain as it started to rip into him.

"I knew you would come," Bayo said to it, smiling as Oumar's body crumpled forward to the ground.

"I knew my master would come for me."

The Share

Terence Taylor

Kenny had been in the apartment for almost a week before he noticed the sounds. Running water from the kitchen when there was no one there. Soft, feminine humming in the next room. Music from a distance, faint as a whisper, yet intimately close—traces of Nina Simone and Toni Braxton, jazz classics and soulful R&B, with occasional flashes of percussive Third World rhythms. Whiffs of perfume every now and then, or a brush of warm air, soft as a breath, on the back of his neck. Nothing tangible, just dim echoes of a phantom female presence.

He dismissed it all as new apartment jitters. The acoustics were different here, that's all. So was the airflow. Thin walls made noises from other apartments sound closer than they really were. Air shafts outside the bathroom windows carried strange smells from floor to floor.

Wishful thinking played a part in it as well. Losing his live-in girlfriend, Nadine, after two years together had left Kenny hungry for the constant company of a woman, for her civilizing influence over his space and time. He missed the signs of femininity around his apartment, from scented potpourri sachets to stockings found in odd places, from potions to treat any ailment in the medicine chest to a refrigerator stocked with fresh food. Nadine had been more than his girlfriend; she'd been his anchor, his connection to the real world, the only thing that kept him from being an introverted, porn-addicted computer geek living on take-out food, like most of the programmers on his staff.

The last night Nadine made them dinner, she'd told Kenny it was over, and he couldn't believe it. How could she not have been happy with him when he was so completely satisfied with her? But, of course, his inability to see past his own needs was one of the reasons she had claimed to be leaving him.

Except that he was the one who had to leave.

This apartment in Brooklyn was the first he'd found that he could afford, larger than he'd expected to find, a one bedroom with enough space for a makeshift home office, and rent-controlled to boot. It was a corner apartment in an elevator building, with windows on two sides that poured in bright light during the day and offered good cross-ventilation when there was a breeze. North of Flatbush Avenue, it wasn't in trendy Park Slope, but in Prospect Heights, an up-and-coming neighborhood on the other side of the avenue. Still black enough for him to feel comfortable, it was just gentrified enough to have all the Manhattan comforts he'd grown used to uptown at Nadine's.

His only problem: the odd sounds and smells of the phantom woman that reminded him of Nadine when he tried to sleep at night, naked and sweating in record summer heat, unrelieved by electric fans and open windows. Kenny lay on a queen-size mattress on the bare floor in the dark, played blues on the stereo to block out the sounds of traffic and shouted conversation from the street below while he tried to masturbate himself to dreamland with memories of his lost love and DVD porn. Kenny was alone, on his own, for the first time in years.

He hated it.

The next week Kenny spent long hours at the office with no time to meet anyone new, finished up a major Web project for a big client. At home he'd discovered that the building was filled mostly with tenants who'd been there since their youth, holding onto rent-controlled leases well past retirement. Kenny finally spotted a neighbor around his age that weekend as he wheeled his bike down the hall for a ride in Prospect Park. She came off the elevator with a bag of groceries, smiled and nodded as they passed.

She was a petite young woman, gray-eyed with a cocoa-dark complexion and long cornrow braids. As she disappeared around the corner, Kenny caught a breath of her perfume, the same scent he'd smelled in his apartment. He'd finally found the source. She had to live in one of the two other apartments at his end of the hall.

Kenny thought about his neighbor that night instead of Nadine while he tried to sleep—what her skin would taste like, salty or sweet; how her braids would feel against his bare shoulders; whether she slept in a T-shirt, in the raw or in a silky negligee. He could almost feel her presence in the bed beside him as he slept that night, warm, close, her soft breaths matching his.

A few days later he saw her again on his way home. They met just as he turned the bend in the hall. She smiled and said, "Hi!" as she passed. Kenny nodded back, kept going to his door, as she vanished around the corner. She'd come from the far end of the hall, so she had to live in the apartment across from him. He considered knocking on her door later to find out if she was single by inviting her over for a drink, if he had the balls.

Rejection would be lethal, but friends had encouraged him to be daring and try new approaches after the breakup. He'd been off the market for two years; they said he had nothing to lose. Nothing, except that he liked this girl, what little he'd seen of her, and didn't want to blow his only chance of getting to know her better.

Kenny cleaned up the living room when he got inside, just in case; threw dirty laundry from his bedroom floor into the bathroom hamper. He did a little work on his computer and watched TV until later that evening, when he heard the door across the hall open and close as someone went inside. Kenny got up, pulled a bottle of Chardonnay from the refrigerator and two glasses from a cabinet, hoped that she liked wine, that she wasn't either AA or overly religious.

Kenny stopped himself from obsessing, juggled the wineglasses and bottle in one hand, used his other to open his door and crossed the hall to knock on hers.

There was the sound of movement inside, and Kenny felt his heart pound faster; a slight flush of flop-sweat bloomed on his back and cheeks. The door opened, and a skinny, old white woman in a worn, plaid housedress blinked at him from behind thick bifocals.

"Yeah?"

"I'm . . ." Kenny didn't know what to say. She was the last thing he'd expected to see when the door opened. Could his dark-skinned dream girl be this woman's daughter? Granddaughter? Caregiver? "I just moved in."

The old woman eyed the glasses and wine, warily. "Yeah?"

"I'm sorry. I thought someone else lived here. A young woman I saw in the hall."

"She lives there."

The old woman waved toward Kenny's door. He sighed. She wasn't just old; she was senile.

"Thanks. I, uh . . ." There was no use explaining further. Kenny floundered, backed away. "Nice meeting you."

"Okay." The old woman shrugged and shut the door after one last, longing look at the wine bottle. Kenny stood alone in the empty hall, closed his eyes and let his heart slow. Stupid. This was stupid. The girl must be in the other apartment, closer to the elevator. Then why was she coming from back here?

"Hi again," said a familiar voice, and Kenny opened his eyes to see her standing there, smelled her sweet scent catch up to them as she stopped at his door.

"Hi," he answered, and thought to offer her a glass while he fished for something to say. She took it with a smile. "I was coming over to introduce myself but got the wrong apartment. Kenny Gaines. I just moved in."

"Yeah? Me, too. Yolanda Morgan," she said, and clinked her empty glass against his. "You want to come in for a minute? Pour me some of that wine?"

She had keys in her hand, and before he could answer she slipped one into his lock and turned it. Kenny opened his mouth to protest, but when the door opened, words failed him. He walked forward in disbelief for a better look.

Nothing in the room belonged to him.

It was as if he had accidentally gotten off on the wrong floor and stepped into someone else's apartment. He knew his apartment was still almost empty, with only a few lonely pieces of scattered furniture bought at Pottery Barn after leaving Nadine's. She'd owned most of what was at their place before he had moved in. What little he'd taken with him barely filled a room, much less his apartment.

Instead, he stared at a fully furnished living room decorated with a woman's touch, a smart, well-traveled woman with great design sense and enough income to indulge it. There were African and Polynesian masks on the wall—good ones, not cheap knockoffs, but the sort of things you'd find on your own while on the road. A modern but comfortable sofa and chairs with clean, simple lines were positioned to let the art in the room catch your eye and interest, invited relaxed conversation over drinks. Big pillows covered in African mud cloth and Japanese textiles lay piled on Moroccan carpets between the fireplace and a low wooden coffee table, which was littered with architectural digests and art magazines.

Kenny stared up at a massive, framed, brightly colored photograph over the mantle signed by Lyle Ashton Harris, a popular black artist whose work he could never afford. At home Kenny had a five-dollar Jacob Lawrence poster he'd bought at a street fair taped up on this wall. He looked at the photo more closely.

It was Yolanda in an abandoned warehouse, eyes closed, face ecstatic, belly bare, feet naked, wearing large gold hoop earrings, a white tied-off blouse and floor-length skirt, hair bound up in a white cloth. The transparent spirit of a voluptuous black woman, scantily clad in yellow and gold, floated slightly above Yolanda's writhing body, the two figures captured at the moment of blending into one. The title under the signature read, "Oshun enters the Acolyte." Yolanda poured them more wine.

"Do you like it?" She stood beside him, looked up at the photo, talked about the art as if nothing was wrong. "It's a gift from the artist. I met Lyle at a gallery opening a few years ago, and he talked me into posing." Her relaxed at-home air only made the situation more bizarre. It was all so damned casual and ordinary. Kenny marveled at the weird beauty of the moment. If this weren't some kind of hallucination or psychotic break, it would be the smoothest pickup he'd ever made. "I love it too much not to show it, even though having a huge portrait of myself over the mantle makes me look vain."

"No. It's great." He turned away from the picture and blurted out, "I live here."

"What?" Yolanda looked sure she hadn't heard him correctly, a flash of confusion flickered across her eyes as she stepped back. "You what?"

"I don't know how to explain. It's crazy, but . . . I have to see something." He pulled her toward the door. She tried to break free, as if suddenly worried he was insane. "Just come outside for a second. Bring your keys."

He got her to the door and out, pulled it shut. "Lock it."

She shook her head and sucked her teeth, but did it. Kenny put his key in the lock before she could stop him. When she saw that it fit, she stared at the key, then at him, and waited. Kenny turned the key and unlocked the door. When he opened it, his apartment, the one he knew, was on the other side.

This time it was Yolanda's turn to be stunned. She stepped inside, walked slowly to the center of the room, shocked into silence. When she turned back to face Kenny, tears streamed down her cheeks.

"This is impossible. So God damned impossible."

She looked about to collapse. He grabbed her arms, supported her. "Tell me about it."

"Damn, Kenny! How . . . how did you stand there for so long without saying anything?"

"I couldn't believe it. I still can't."

They compared their keys, which were completely different, even though they both opened the same lock. To be sure they weren't imagining it, Kenny and Yolanda tried the trick a few more times, locked and unlocked the door with one key, then the other, to see the two apartments, then fled.

They went to a new jazz club down the street, declined the trendy ambience of the restaurant, sat at the bar and ordered doubles. Other young couples milled around them, laughed and joked their way through pickups and first dates, while Kenny and Yolanda drank in silence, listened to the music and tried to reclaim their hold on reality. Yolanda finally looked Kenny in the eyes when she was halfway through her second Hennessey.

He did his best to smile.

"So. Since we're sharing an apartment, I guess we should get to know each other," said Kenny. It was the only clever opening line he'd ever had. The tension broke, and they laughed until they cried, drifted close to hysteria and back, until words poured out as they tried to explain what the hell was happening. Dimensional warp? Quantum flux? Was it a time or space loop, black magic or mad science, a blessing or a curse? Kenny's nerdy high school years spent watching hours of *Star Trek* reruns and reading science fiction gave him an endless supply of possibilities to offer Yolanda.

For once, he was relaxed on a first date, if you could call it that. He entertained and soothed her by spinning out wilder and wilder theories, his hands carved out spatial explanations in the air of how two apartments could occupy the same space at the same time yet be completely separate.

"They couldn't be completely separate, though, could they?" Yolanda stared out the front window of the bar as the conversation slowed, looked through their candlelit reflections in the glass to the street as they finished their fourth drinks and ordered another round. The sun had set while they talked; car headlights flashed past, lit the street outside in lightning-quick bursts, like strobes. "I mean, the dynamic tension of trying to stay apart, it seems like there'd be some kind of leakage every now and then."

"Like osmosis. Things slipping through the membrane to whichever apartment has the least, trying to find balance."

"You just better leave my CDs and DVDs alone," she warned, and giggled at the absurdity of it all. For a moment, Kenny could see the girl the woman had been, sleepily curled around the stool beside him, guileless, trusting. A door in his broken heart opened and invited her in. He stood, put down money for the bill and tip, extended a hand.

"May I walk you home?" For some reason, that set them off on another round of laughter as he helped her to her feet and guided her out of the bar to the street.

At the apartment door, they both hesitated, unsure which key to use. Kenny waved Yolanda forward, and she opened the door. He shuddered. While the shock of their discovery had faded over drinks, conversation and flirtation, seeing her belongings behind what he had always known as his door gave him a chill again. She felt it, too, and paused before she went inside alone.

"I guess it's good night." She turned back to face him. "Thanks for everything. I know this is all pretty weird, but I still enjoyed meeting you."

"Yeah. Me, too. And, yeah, pretty damn weird." All he could see were her lips, full, moist, parted, tilted up at an almost ideal angle for him to lean forward and steal a kiss. So he did.

He didn't really steal it. Kenny could tell immediately that she gave it to him freely, and then some, a kiss that answered any lingering question about her availability. They pulled apart, startled by the intensity, but Kenny understood. He'd seen this exact moment in too many grade-B horror movies, when the hero and heroine fell passionately into each other's arms just when they most needed to run.

"I'm sorry, it's . . ." She glanced inside and actually trembled. "I think I'm just a little afraid to stay here alone tonight."

"If you want company . . ." he said, and winced. Any other time, it was a cheap line that would have gotten him an icy stare, but Yolanda looked relieved by his offer.

"Your place or mine?"

"As long as we're here . . ."

She laughed, stepped inside and pulled the door open wider for him to follow as she turned on the lights and low music, then went to the bar to pour them a nightcap.

They didn't have sex that night. Kenny curled up under the sheet spoon-style behind Yolanda, in his boxer shorts and T-shirt, gently cupped her warm, soft breasts in moist palms. As he fell asleep, he could smell coconut oil in her hair, gently kissed the back of her neck and tasted her when he licked his lips with the tip of his tongue.

She was both salty and sweet.

The next morning, Kenny and Yolanda tried to understand their unique living arrangement by conducting experiments. They addressed notes to each other and slipped them under the door to see which side they'd appear on, separated and shouted to see how much sound traveled between the two spaces, burned incense to see if smells crossed over, like demented high school science projects out of *The X-Files*.

Hours later, they still knew only what was happening, not how or why. The two keys opened the front door onto two identical copies of the same space, no matter who used the keys, and neither key had any markings to indicate where it had been made, except for an ironic "Do not duplicate," which was stamped on both. The rooms inside were the same down to the cracks in the walls and the leaky faucets, only the contents, including the cable and phone lines, were different, depending on which key was used.

After hours of investigation and experimentation, all they were sure of was that neither of them wanted to lose his or her lease. Even if they'd somehow stumbled onto the Bermuda Triangle of shares, like true New Yorkers neither of them wanted to move out of a great rent-controlled apartment in a rising neighborhood. The only question was how to pull it off without anyone else figuring it out.

"We can't pay two rents again at the end of the month. They're bound to realize something is wrong," Kenny said over lunch at a local bistro. "I'm surprised they haven't already, since they got two leases for the same apartment." He felt more like his father in daylight, examined the practical aspects of a surreal situation, when last night he'd explored the fantasy.

"So what do we do? Tell them we're sharing the apartment and split the rent?"

"Sure. It's not like we'll really be living together," said Kenny. "And we'll never find another deal this good. Believe me, I looked."

"Don't I know it."

They decided to work it out with the Russian super, but that evening, their frenzied torrent of words as they tried to explain without really explaining completely lost the recent immigrant. He finally silenced them. If his wife had given Yolanda a lease after he'd given one to Kenny, a mistake had been made. If they wanted to share the apartment, they had to pay one rent, but more for two tenants.

They gladly arranged to get back Yolanda's rent and deposit, gave the super a new check for the next month's increased rent. Yolanda then wrote Kenny a check to cover her half while she waited for her refund. Back upstairs, they opened the door to Kenny's apartment with his key to celebrate in his place with champagne, then stepped out into the hall and into Yolanda's apartment with her key to have dinner.

They fell into dating without thought, drawn into a relationship like coconspirators bound by a shared secret, went to movies and shows at the Brooklyn Academy of Music, free concerts in Prospect Park, jazz clubs in Fort Green, combed the neighborhood for fresh entertainment to enjoy together. Kenny started to feel whole again; Yolanda filled the void left in his life by losing Nadine.

It was more than just the strangeness of their meeting or the intimacy of their living arrangement that made him feel close to her. They shared a taste for the same music and films, got along with each other's friends and even looked right together when he caught glimpses of their reflection in store windows and restaurant mirrors. They fit. Kenny was falling in love, and each day he was sure he saw signs in Yolanda that the feeling was mutual.

When they finally had sex it was tender, prolonged, multiorgasmic for them both. They ended lovemaking wet with sweat and tears of laughter, held each other all night, amazed to be so lucky to have found each other.

They spent the weekend bouncing between their beds, cooked together in her kitchen, then scampered into the hall to go back to his place for DVD movies on his new flat-panel plasma TV. They talked about their childhoods, their first jobs, where they'd been and where they wanted to go. By the end of the weekend they talked about where they might go together.

Weeks went by as they continued to live jointly but separately in the same apartment, lives entwined but with enough distance to enhance the time spent together. Kenny felt a satisfaction he'd never known before, a sense of oneness that made him realize what he had been missing from other relationships.

Kenny had found more than a new partner in Yolanda; she completed him. He wanted to tell her that without it sounding pedestrian, when what he wanted was so much more than anything he had ever had, more than he'd ever believed possible.

That night, Kenny watched Yolanda all through dinner at a local restaurant, admired and desired her, as if she were a rare work of art. He listened to every word she said, but his attention was on the voice inside, which told him to tell her how he felt, to share what he wanted with her, for them.

"I love you, you know." He said it suddenly, before he chickened out, as if it were something he wanted to make sure got said before it was forgotten. Yolanda stopped talking, looked surprised and a little embarrassed, like he'd just squeezed her thigh in church.

"What's gotten into you?"

It should have been a warning, would have been to anyone else.

Not, "I love you, too," or "Thank you," but "What's gotten into you?" He pushed ahead, oblivious, Custer charging Little Big Horn.

"My time with you, it's all been so right, so perfect. You're more than my girlfriend. You're like a part of me. I don't ever want this to end."

Yolanda leaned back, stared at him with a smile on her lips but not in her eyes.

"Kenny, are you proposing to me?"

He hesitated, not sure if that was what he meant, but, poised at the cliff's edge, took the plunge. "Sure," he said, "Why not? That's a good place to start."

"A good place to . . ." She shook her head and laughed, but didn't sound amused. "Kenny, it's been a month."

"Over a month and a half."

"Too soon to talk about forever. I care for you, I do, but . . ." She stopped, her hands fluttered in front of her, helpless to shape the thought in words or gesture.

Kenny started to reply, then sense finally kicked in and he stopped himself from saying more. "No. I'm sorry." He waved to the waiter for the check. "It's the wine. It makes me overly romantic."

She took his hand loosely, with her fingertips, not a full-handed clasp. "It's a lovely thought. I just think we need to take our time."

"Of course, we do." He smiled and slipped his hand over hers, covered it completely. "I understand."

But he didn't.

They left the restaurant in silence, slept apart that night for the first time in weeks. Yolanda began to cool, even though she denied it, and the more she withdrew, the more Kenny wanted her. On dates she seemed distracted, distant. More and more often, when they got home to bed, they went to sleep without sex. Yolanda said she was busy with work and on a tight deadline, but Kenny's antennae were up. He'd been down this road before and kept an eye out for further signs.

It didn't take long.

Yolanda was at his place for dinner, already making excuses that she had to leave early to finish work on a presentation for a new architectural client. While he pulled dinner out of the oven, she wandered around the room with her wine, and stopped by the fireplace.

"What's this doing here?"

Yolanda picked up a small china dog, paws raised as if begging, a tacky souvenir of her dead aunt that was usually on the mantle on her side. She held it in her hand, stood near the hearth, puzzled. "I thought you hated it."

"I do," said Kenny. "As much as I could hate anything of yours." He went to Yolanda, kissed her hand as he took the dog from her and examined it like an artifact of some alien culture. "Did you bring it over?"

"No. Of course not. Why would I do that?"

She took it back with an impatient frown and left his apartment, her key in hand, and closed his door behind her. A moment later he could hear the ghost of the front door open on the other side, sense her step across the room as she blew through him like mist, and replaced the dog where it belonged.

She didn't speak of it again that night, but over the next few days, more items switched sides from her space to his and from his to hers.

"It's like we're moving in together," Yolanda said one night in bed on her side, after they'd found some of Kenny's socks in her drawer. "Like the two apartments are merging the longer we're together."

Kenny laughed. "Osmosis. That saves us some trouble. I hate moving, even if it is to live with you." He leaned over to kiss her, but she rolled away, sat up on the edge of the bed, her back to him, face averted.

"That's just it, Kenny. This came up before. I don't know if I am ready to move in with you."

Kenny felt an old familiar feeling constrict his gut. Her words had the same "We have to talk" tone of the conversation he'd had his last night with Nadine. He had seen it coming, but now that it was here, he wanted to put his hands over his ears and hum. Maybe little kids were right. Maybe if you couldn't hear or see something bad, you really could stop it from happening.

Yolanda didn't give him time to try.

"I need more time than you're giving me. You're still moving too far, too fast. I can see it in your eyes and . . . I don't feel the same way about you."

"I can slow down . . ."

"No. You can't. You know you can't. I'm sorry, Kenny. I should have said something sooner." She was on her feet before he could reach out to her, put on her robe, bound it tightly closed and moved to the door, still looking away. "Do you mind if I sleep alone tonight?"

Kenny's cheeks burned. "No." He picked up his robe, felt for his keys in the pocket. His slippers felt heavy on his feet as he made his way out to the living room to leave for what felt like the last time. "Can we talk tomorrow?"

She took too long to answer as she moved to shut the door behind him. "We can talk. Maybe not tomorrow."

The door closed, and the lock thudded into place. Kenny pulled out his key, unlocked the door and walked back into his dark, empty apartment and a dark, empty life.

Kenny flopped down on his mattress on the floor, lights out, no music, ignored the noises from the outside world; tears trickled from the corners of his eyes despite himself. It was because he was too stable, he thought, too quiet and reliable, that's why he kept getting dumped, because he wasn't some slack-jawed, low-life Neanderthal niggah who pumped them full of bastards and abandoned them. That's what black women wanted no matter what they said, he told himself, some macho, seventies-exploitation-movie, secret-garden rape fantasy. Not an upright, reliable, stay-at-home black man like him who knew how to take care of a woman, how to nurture and protect her, someone who wanted a real union, a bond.

A lasting bond.

He fell asleep as the sun rose, twisted and sweaty in his sheets as he dreamed he was being devoured by a burning bush with a multitude of hungry carnivorous buds that bloomed into the faces of all the women who had ever dated and dumped him. As his flesh was dissolved from his bones by acid nectar that poured from their mouths, he heard them sing to each other, competing with tales of who had hurt him the most.

When he woke that afternoon, Kenny resolved not to let this setback put him back into a depression. He was better than that. It was a dark, rainy Saturday, a good day to stay in and catch up on work. He sat in front of the TV, watched CNN and used his laptop to sign onto the Web sites his company had launched for clients that weekend, went through them page by page, made sure they were all up and running. He sent e-mail notes to subordinates as he found last-minute flaws to fix, and by the end of the afternoon, his work was done.

The weather was worse than ever. Kenny rummaged through refrigerated leftovers for lunch, nuked them in the microwave while he switched stations to see what was on the Sci Fi Channel. He dropped into his beanbag chair and waited for the timer on the microwave to go off when he felt something odd.

He felt Yolanda.

She was somewhere near. Very near.

The slight traces of her presence in the apartment that he'd felt when he first moved in had grown stronger since their relationship began. They'd spent so much time together, he hadn't noticed it, but separated, Kenny realized he could tell where Yolanda was on the other side, could even make little sensory connections between them as he followed her trail.

He forgot about the microwave when it called him with a chime, tracked Yolanda instead and picked up thin scents of what she smelled, faint snatches of what she heard. Rough terrycloth texture tickled his fingertips; his feet ignored his carpet to feel Yolanda's floor under her bare soles. Kenny sighed, content, breathed in and out at the same time she did and for a moment felt as one with her, as he had when they'd slept together curled up in bed at night.

Kenny could tell Yolanda was on the couch, reading. There was a warm spot where she must be; electric light reflected off her hair, shimmered like faint heat waves in the air. Kenny pulled his beanbag chair to the spot and fell asleep in her unseen lap while the afternoon storm raged outside the window for them both, the same raindrops striking the same glass.

For the rest of the weekend, Kenny trailed Yolanda around the apartment, got better at following her traces, learned to read the subtle signs that told him where she was and what she was doing on the other side. If she sat on her couch to watch TV, he changed to the same channel, sat in the same spot on his side and slowly matched his breathing to hers. A bath? He climbed into his tub, filled it and adjusted the water until he was sure the temperature was the same, until he felt like he was in the tub with her. They shared meals at different tables in the same space, he moved his mattress to her side of the bedroom and slept the same hours in the same positions she did, whispered her name in his dreams.

There was nothing she did he didn't echo, no move he couldn't shadow. As weeks went by, Kenny still had Yolanda with him in real and tangible form, despite the breakup. Even though he knew there was something wrong in what he was doing, he reveled in their ghostly reunion, at being able to keep her in his life in some way, no matter how small. He willed a deeper connection across the space between them, tried to pull her closer each day.

Items from her apartment began to appear in his again, the odd vase, a slipper, silverware, her comb. Either she didn't notice their absence or refused to talk to him long enough to ask for them back. Things came through more often and more of them, ever more personal, as if Kenny had broken through a dam, created a hairline crack between the two spaces that was spreading, crumbling, about to burst.

All he had to do was keep pushing.

Kenny woke in his beanbag chair, where he'd shared a long afternoon with Yolanda before he nodded out, and heard something slide under his door. He stood, stumbled over to see what it was, still half asleep. It was a sheet of recycled blue paper, a note from Yolanda on her stationery.

Kenny didn't even read it. If she had just left the note, she couldn't have gotten far. He opened the door, saw her slip around the corner and ran out to join her.

"Yolanda!" He slowed when he saw that the elevator hadn't arrived yet. She looked away, nervous, pushed the down button again. Kenny stopped between her and the door to the stairs, held up the note.

"What's this?"

"I need my half of the deposit back."

He opened the note, skimmed it. "You're moving? When?"

Her eyes looked past him to the elevator door for an out. One foot tapped the floor like a jackhammer.

"Tomorrow. I'm packing tonight."

"Why?" He squeezed the word through clenched teeth as his eyes watered.

"Baby, I've lived near ex-boyfriends before, even stayed with a few until I found a place of my own, but this, this is . . ."

She raised her hands, dropped them again, as if there was no way to describe what they had here. Kenny reached out, but she backed away, paused as if what she had to say was hard to get out. She spoke in a quiet voice, almost inaudible, couldn't meet his eyes as she said it.

"I feel you, Kenny. When I'm home. One breath away from me, all the time." She looked up, her eyes wet, anguished. "Things disappear. It's too much. It's like you're feeding on me. I need more than space. I need distance."

Before he could respond, the elevator door opened. She rushed inside, pushed the button to close it and get away from him. Kenny let the door slide shut without trying to stop her, felt his stomach and hopes fall to earth with the elevator.

She was really leaving him this time.

Kenny drank that night.

There wasn't enough booze in the house to do the job, so he had more delivered, more than enough to blot out the horror that lay ahead. He was so used to having Yolanda near that he wasn't sure if he could survive losing her cold turkey. It would be a terrifying life of real isolation, living alone with no one but himself, and he wasn't that fond of himself right now. When he thought about it, maybe he never had been; maybe that explained the continuous stream of live-in girlfriends he'd had since he left home. He'd never lived alone. As soon as one left or threw him out he'd always found another. Were they just buffers between him and himself? The thought depressed him even more.

He poured another drink, dropped the glass and, instead of looking for it, downed his next shot from the bottle as he enjoyed his last night with Yolanda. Kenny could hear the music she played while she finished packing—a vintage recording of Yoruba music she'd picked up on a trip to Havana. They'd made love on the floor of her living room to it one night, percussion pounding, rich vocals invoking Oshun, the goddess of love and beauty, who rules over the sweet rivers and streams of the Earth, fills them with her fertility.

The drums rose, thumped louder in his ears, as Kenny connected to Yolanda's ears and skin instead of his own, heard and felt the rhythms of She who blesses the river and is the river invoked by the recorded voices and rhythms of long-dead singers and musicians. Tears blurred Kenny's vision as he strained to see through Yolanda's eyes, tried to glimpse the portrait of the goddess floating on the other wall like a beacon, prayed for aid, called with her music for help, pleaded for her to reunite him with his lost love.

Almost as if in response to his drunken prayer, he felt Yolanda's presence near him. He drew her to him, could tell she sensed him, felt her pull away, but raw need poured from him in waves like a magnetic field, unseen but powerful, attracted like matter irresistibly closer. The music raced faster as wild laughter rang through the room from the speakers, the mocking titter of the goddess Oshun.

Kenny felt energy fill him, felt whatever force it was that shaped these two worlds and held them apart, felt boundaries dissolve as the two rooms blurred and merged, overlapped, until he could see Yolanda and her space clearly, cleanly double-exposed over his.

She was more visible as her fear grew; her will to resist him faded as the drums grew louder. Whatever power brought them together was Kenny's now, to push in any direction, to mold in any fashion. It was driven by his need, his desire, and his only wish was to have Yolanda again, to never be apart again. Whether the ability had always been waiting in the apartment, or had been summoned by some need of his so deep that it could twist reality to be filled, it was now Kenny's to do with as he pleased.

His physical body dispersed like gas as he melted into a fog that blew over Yolanda, enveloped her in a cloud. She inhaled him like smoke, like the breath of life; Kenny felt himself enter Yolanda's body, as Oshun had entered her in the portrait. He filled her lungs, her body, and without thinking took her apart, separated her cells like his and whirled them into a wet cloud of organic mist that was neither Kenny nor Yolanda, but a vortex of living matter that spun like a new nebula until it was both, united.

It was more than a physical merging; Yolanda's entire life was revealed to Kenny in all its intricacy, every moment, every wish, every thought opened one by one and consumed, made part of his life, his memory, his identity. Their identity.

There was a scream; Kenny couldn't tell if it was his cry or Yolanda's, a cry of pain, pleasure or both. A hot burst of bliss filled them like a perfect, prolonged orgasm, and they sank into deep sleep, the restful, healing hibernation of a caterpillar in its chrysalis. The cloud coalesced as the storm subsided, cooled and slowly took form like the surface of a new planet; bone gelled, hardened, gave root to muscle, which bloomed with the skin and hair of a new being. Drums played the fresh life to sleep as the goddess smiled and danced in dream into the dawn.

Afternoon sunlight crept across the floor, gently woke the solitary figure that lay asleep on the living room carpet. Kenny lay facedown on the floor at the front door, fists clenched in front of him as if he had gripped Yolanda's ankles and been dragged there as she walked out.

He was alone. She was finally and completely gone. He could feel it. Their merging had been a drunken fantasy, like the hungry, singing flowers on the burning bush he'd dreamed about after Yolanda had broken up with him. He'd wanted her so badly, his shattered heart had found a way to salve him to sleep while she left, gave him a vision of total union, a vision that was gone now, leaving him with an even greater feeling of emptiness.

Kenny wept as if at his own funeral; tears blurred his vision as his fingers felt something on the floor not noticed before. He wiped his eyes dry, picked up the pale blue envelope that had been slid halfway under the door: Yolanda's stationery, still scented with her perfume, Kenny's name scrawled in her distinctive cursive across the front. There was no note inside, no final parting message, just a single object made of stamped brass on a plain metal ring.

The key to Yolanda's apartment.

Kenny dressed, left and locked his apartment, then used the key to open Yolanda's. It was empty inside, broom clean, even the marks of where her furniture had been erased from the floors. He walked from the living room through the bedroom, the bathroom and the kitchen, all devoid of even the slightest trace that she had ever been there, air still sharp with the scent of cleansers.

When he walked back to the front of the apartment, Kenny saw that he'd been too hasty when coming in. The apartment wasn't completely empty. He had overlooked the obvious. There on the mantle was the little ceramic dog that had belonged to Yolanda's aunt, the first thing Yolanda had noticed crossing between their spaces, the beginning of their end.

Kenny didn't know if she'd forgotten it, if it was too frightening a reminder of what she'd nearly escaped, a warning to him not to be so needy or merely a memento, a good-bye gift. He picked it up, almost put it back down to leave when he had an idea, a spark that fired the flame in his heart again. He pocketed the statue of the little dog and rushed out into the hall to consider his options.

Kenny had the key, if not to Yolanda's love, then to her apartment and his future. Yolanda was gone, but with her key, she'd given him a way to fill the hole left by her departure.

He stood at a crossroads outside the two apartments, both keys in hand; he could dispose of the second one, forget it had ever existed and leave his love life to fate. Or he could use it to find a more suitable mate this time, a woman who understood the innumerable possibilities of their unique living arrangement, someone who understood him and could share his apartment, his heart and his life. It could take a while, but he would take the warning of the ceramic begging dog at face value and slow down long enough to make the right selection.

Two keys. Two roads. Kenny stood at the door and stared at them, one in each hand, and contemplated the consequences of each: happiness or madness, fulfillment or obsession, an answer to his prayers or a path to his damnation.

The only question left was which was which.

Sucker

B. Gordon Doyle

Talbot *liked* hotel bars.

Airport hotel bars, in particular, possessed a certain uniformity, familiar and virtually homogeneous, that soothed him and put him at ease. Certainly, there were other, less conspicuous places to hunt, but this was an environment he knew, and this was why he would return, again and again, a creature of habit in spite of himself. In spite of the risks of establishing a pattern, a predictable set of behaviors that could lead to discovery, he returned. Over the years, Talbot had found that these oases, these watering holes set on the edges of cities, suited his needs precisely. His need for familiarity and, not coincidentally, control.

Control was essential to the hunt.

Talbot smiled as he plunged his fork into the plate of sausage and peppers on the table, speared a gobbet of warm meat and popped it into his mouth. It had occurred to him that he could determine what city he was in by the condiments that accompanied his appetizers. Marinara, salsa or honey-mustard. Day-old mayonnaise going yellow around the edges. A different city, a different sauce.

Familiarity and control.

And need.

All these things Talbot knew fully. As he knew the stink of cigarette smoke and spilled beer, and the unceasing cacophony of ESPN on multiple televisions or vacuous light rock pouring from ceiling-mounted speakers.

No matter where he went, hotel bars were all the same. Mirrors and bar stools and pretzels in baskets. Cubs and Rangers and Saints and Lakers.

The liquor behind the bar and the people in the seats were all the same; the liquor was strong, and the people were . . . the people had their needs.

And Talbot had his. He was watching her, from his table across the restaurant.

All the same.

She was sitting at the bar, chain-smoking Marlboro Lights and wishing she were ten years younger. She wasn't unattractive, merely unremarkable, though the fullness of her breasts commanded attention far out of proportion to her slight beauty. Attention she could have done without.

Talbot closed his eyes and thought about her breasts. Pendulous. Bottom heavy. Wide nippled, with salty perspiration in the crease of flesh beneath. Her breasts, swinging, shuddering . . .

The woman at the bar shivered, and folded her arms defensively across her chest. She didn't turn around.

Strong, Talbot noted with approval. But then, you'd have to be strong.

Talbot smiled, consciously changing the color of his thoughts, easing into character.

I bet it happened quickly. All the fellas comin' around. Caught you unprepared. Daddy's little girl, his precious angel, suddenly a woman. Without warning, a woman. I bet they said things, filthy, hurtful things. Tried to put their hands on you. And worse.

Did they whisper when you walked into the dining room for Thanksgiving dinner? Did they stare at you in the showers after gym class? Did your momma try to explain why it wasn't such a good idea to hug Daddy anymore?

Did they call you Jugs or Elsie or Sheena as you walked home from the bus stop, your head down, tears streaming from your eyes?

No. Not Sheena. Irish McCalla was before your time. Just as you became a woman, before your time . . .

Tell me. I know about pain. All about pain.

She was drinking rum and Diet Coke, and Talbot thought that funny. He assumed that everyone knew that the bulk of the calories in a mixed drink were in the liquor. A small concession, the Diet

Coke; a reminder, perhaps, of some unkept promise or resolution. But it was no more than a gesture. Certainly, she knew that her skirt was too short for her heavy thighs, her face too round for the bright smears of rouge.

She simply didn't care.

Talbot had been watching her for nearly two weeks. He'd spoken with her twice, just small talk, *bar* talk. He'd even bought her a drink on the pretext of some celebration, a lottery win or contract award, and sat with her briefly, gathering information and personal history.

Familiarity. Because he knew, in the end, she would not be able to describe him.

Her name was Arlene.

She was twice divorced, had no children and worked as a consultant for a business association in Washington, D.C. She was on a ninety-day assignment to the Chicago office, installing a new accounting system, and had rented a small place nearby for the duration. She didn't much like the Second City; it was too intimidating, so every day she drove in and out, from home to work to home, door to door, without stopping.

But she liked this bar. It was close.

Talbot watched as she waved to the bartender for another drink. Her third.

Sometimes, when she didn't want to talk, she would bring a paperback to the bar, some potboiler by Clancy or Le Carré. On those rare occasions, she would arrive early and leave early; more often, the book would wind up facedown on the bar, and the drinks would come and she would stay until nearly closing. And when she stayed, she never left the bar alone.

Because the fellas still came around. They liked her then, and they liked her now. They liked her mousy brown hair and her sulky brown eyes and her chunky body. They liked her short, tight skirts and her tits. Especially her tits.

And she liked the fellas, after enough drinks. In her own bitter fashion, she liked them, too.

Talbot watched her as the moon moved to fullness. He watched her joke and flirt; he watched whom she encouraged and whom she rebuffed. His furtive pursuit was precise and uneventful, but wary; he was certain that the bartender was also watching her. Rather, watching out for her. He kept her hammered and happy, beneath his weathered eyes.

Because sometimes *things*, like people, have needs. And every bar needed a woman like her . . .

Now. It was time.

Talbot pushed away the plate of congealed meat, waved and dropped a handful of bills on the table. The restaurant was growing crowded as the surrounding office buildings emptied and workers stampeded to the nearest Happy Hours. It was barely evening, but Talbot knew he would have to move now, before one of Arlene's favorites appeared and swept her up for the night.

He slipped into a seat three bar stools down from her and ordered an Old Style draft. The bartender, young, with longish, blond hair and tired eyes, grinned and poured. He'd seen that Talbot was a good tipper; the smile wasn't free.

Talbot was ready to approach her when she placed her book on the bar and looked up and through him. Her eyes slid over him with no hint of recognition, no sign of interest.

No. This is all wrong, Talbot thought. *I was so sure . . .*

He could feel the tug of the moon in his blood; anxiety crept into his mind, muddling his thinking, giving him pause.

No! This is the face. I've watched her for too long, worked too hard. She should be *drawn* to me. There is no choice . . .

He heard a cluster of voices behind him, barroom *hellos*! And was suddenly afraid.

I *can't* lose her, he thought, his mind racing. Not tonight, so close. No time to find another. Too dangerous. It must be her!

Decide now. *Now!*

He left a ten and his untouched beer on the bar and hurried away. The bartender would remember the money but not his face. Talbot pushed through the door and ran into the lobby, bouncing off bodies, looking, looking . . .

Back upstairs to his room to change? No. No time. Some other male might poach his Arlene, get her scent, and his plans, so precise, so meticulous . . .

For naught.

Desperate. Looking. Looking.

And finding.

A place to change.

Talbot moved across the lobby to the souvenir shop and quickly bought a gray, hooded Bears sweatshirt. Tucking the garment under his arm, he stormed past the reception desk to the lobby men's room, his head swarming with a catalogue of Arlene's particulars. Whom she liked. What she'd said. He'd been overconfident; he'd mistaken her presence at the bar for *availability*. He'd have to rethink everything, change everything, to drive her to ground.

But he'd remembered the men's room. He hadn't panicked totally. Familiarity had its advantages.

Talbot reached the men's room door and swung it open. His luck held; it was a single, a courtesy, with a toilet, a small sink and mirror, and a hot-air hand dryer. And most importantly, a door that locked from the inside . . .

Shaking, he locked the door behind him and filled the sink with cold water. He pulled a fresh roll of toilet paper from the dispenser, nearly tearing the dispenser out of the wall in his haste.

He hoped there wouldn't be too much blood.

Talbot stripped, setting his shoes and socks on the toilet tank, hanging his clothes on a hook behind the door. He stood naked before the mirror, gathering himself. He'd never had to do this before, so quickly. But there was no time. Even now, someone might be sitting down next to Arlene, smiling at her . . .

No!

Talbot focused, and willed the change.

Athletes. She likes athletes.

Focus.

A college football player, ten years away from the gridiron.

Focus. See him in the mirror. Be him. Be him. Be . . .

A wave of nausea came over him; sweating, he gasped for air—as his bones began to move.

He plunged his hands into the basin, splashed cold water on his face.

Be him.

Talbot choked back bile, tasting the sausage again, as his frame began to flow and thicken. His joints cracked like pistol shots as the bones stretched, tearing at ligaments and muscle.

Bigger.

The skin on his arms and chest pulled taut, split and bled, until he stood in a puddle of his own blood. The pain drove him to his knees; he moaned softly as he mopped at the red rivulets that seeped from his rent flesh. But even as that bloody flesh tore itself, new skin, pink and smooth, pushed up through the wounds.

Face.

His jaw popped, dislocated. Spittle ran from his slack mouth. Talbot seized the jawbone and rammed it back into place. Gasping, he turned to inspect his profile and noted with excruciating irony that he now possessed the lantern jaw of some comic-book hero. And still the blood came; the basin was choked with red-stained tissue.

Eyes. Hair.

Talbot felt his cheekbones surge beneath new flesh, and red tears ran from the corners of his eyes. Gingerly, he reached up to his hairline, peeling away his scalp, tearing at the tufts of thick, dark hair that came away in his hands.

The unmarked flesh beneath showed fine, blond hair, like down, that grew longer as he watched. A mustache covered his upper lip, wild, unkempt. He bit at it, trimming it with his teeth.

There was a knock at the door.

"Inna minute!" Talbot barked. He opened the drain, let the reddened water run out. He dabbed at the closing wounds, slowly inspecting himself as he did. Gathering up the detritus of who he had been, he carried the hair and clotted blood and flesh and tissue to the toilet and flushed. It went down in a slow spiral of red water, down and away, as he zipped up his pants.

He wiped the last of the blood from the floor with his shirt, balled it up and shoved it into the toilet tank. He pulled on the Bears sweatshirt, tugged it into place and put on his socks and shoes.

The change complete, Talbot inspected the bathroom, turned and inspected himself. He looked one final time into the mirror, and it wasn't him looking back.

Arlene slid her tongue into his mouth as they rode the elevator upstairs to his room. His hands found the warm curves of her ample buttocks, lingered . . .

"Don' know why I don't remember you," she whispered, feeling his shoulders, "I'da remembered a big man like you . . ."

"It was a while ago. And you'd had a couple . . . what, rum and Cokes?"

"Diet Coke! You can't 'member anything either." She giggled. "What's my name?"

"Arlene. I remember you. Like it was yesterday."

"An' we're glad you did." She reached down and squeezed his cock, singing, "I be-lieve in yes-terday!"

They staggered out of the elevator, down the carpeted hall and into Talbot's room. His hands were shaking as he locked the door.

"Oops! Gotta tinkle. Make me a drink?"

Talbot poured her something from the minibar and left the lights off. He liked it dark.

Arlene was naked when she came out of the bathroom; for a moment, she was a lush silhouette, then she flicked out the bathroom light and lay down beside him.

High above, the full moon screamed his name. Talbot answered, slipping from the bed to open the curtains, so that a patch of moonlight fell across the bed.

He reached out and pulled her to him, kissed her roughly, playfully. He'd had only two drinks at the bar, and had nursed the second. She had had five. Or six.

"Umm. That feels . . . good."

Talbot bit her lips, her neck, her breasts, taking his time. She wiggled beneath him, eager to have him inside her, finally grasping the base of his thickened cock and guiding it into her wetness.

"Yeah . . . like that. Ooh, yeah . . ."

He reached under her, lifted her to him, digging his fingers into her fleshy bottom, rocking her slowly, letting her feel him.

"Ooh, yeah," she cooed. "That's it. Give it to me. That's . . . like that! Yeah! Fuck me like *that*! Yeah. *Ooh*. Like that fuck me like that . . ."

Talbot lifted her leg and buried his cock in her, his teeth at her throat, driving his hardness into her so deep, so deep . . .

"Yeah, baby . . . yeah, baby, fuckmefuckmefuckmmm . . . Oh! Oh, GodOhGod . . . *Yesssss!*"

So deep, so deep, until she came, heaving and hissing like an animal in a trap.

He pushed himself off her. Her eyes were as bright as new silver, and perspiration glistened on the curves of her body like dew.

"*Fuck*, baby," she said breathlessly. "Fast and furious. *God* damn . . ."

Talbot was silent. Arlene rubbed gently between her legs.

"Didn't you . . . ?"

"No," he answered. "I mean, not yet."

Silence. In the moonlit room, a silence complete.

And then, "Didn't you like it? I mean, it *felt* like you liked it?"

"I liked it fine," Talbot whispered. "I like . . . different things."

She reached for her drink, and drank off half.

"Different how?" she asked, and Talbot could hear a tired apprehension in her voice. "I don't *do* butt stuff. You guys always wanna . . ."

"No. No Greek. French. With you on top."

"French? You mean oral? Like sixty-nine?"

"Yes."

"Yeah." She curled up next to him, running her fingers along his still-erect cock, "Yeah. I like that, too."

Talbot smiled wolfishly as she turned and straddled him. He grabbed her hips and raised his head, burying his tongue between her legs.

The moon hung above him, beckoning . . .

Arlene lowered her head and grasped his cock, set her mouth to it. As she licked at the burnished tip, it grew even larger. She barely noticed; she'd seen lots of cocks, and his tongue was so good . . . so good.

She wanted him to come. She sucked his hard cock hungrily, eager to taste him, rocking her hips against his mouth.

She was ready to come again. Swept up, carried away by his agile tongue and the great thickness in her mouth so big, so *luscious* . . .

"Um. Ummm . . ." She moaned, widening her mouth until her jaws ached, taking him deeper, wanting it, wanting it . . .

And getting it.

Talbot growled; his legs curled up and seized her head, holding her immobile. And she came.

"More. Suck it more."

Arlene tried to pull away, but he held her fast, his huge cock thrust to the hilt in her mouth. She twisted frantically, making wet, unintelligible noises, guttural cries that couldn't be heard . . .

Too big too big can't breath can't . . . Ooh!

She came again. And then, the fear came.

She opened her eyes wide; in the darkened room, in the moonlight, she opened her eyes and dug her nails into his thighs and pushed with all her strength. Grabbed at his scrotum, his balls, and tore at them, choking, choking . . .

Tearing . . .

His scrotum writhed in her hands and, horribly, split, with the sound of wet flesh. White tendrils, wire-thin, crawled out of the bloody sac, seeking, undulating with a life of their own. Locked in his preternatural grip, choking on his swollen meat, she could not even scream as the pulpy fibers reached out and touched her face, caressing . . .

"Give it all," Talbot snarled, "to me!"

They plunged into the corners of her eyes, her ears and nose, curling upwards, crawling into her head, deeper, burrowing deeper into her very skull.

And behind the terror, behind the revulsion, in the place behind her eyes . . .

They were *feeding*.

Arlene on a green tricycle . . . gone.

Arlene crying over Barbie's lost shoe . . . gone.

Arlene on the porch in her prom dress . . . gone.

Arlene standing at the altar, two months late. . . . Arlene at the clinic, her heels in the stirrups . . . Arlene driving to the ocean . . . Arlene at home in a bar at work in class alone together, happy and sad and afraid and angry and all the things that made Arlene gone, gone, gone . . . consumed.

Sucked away. Sucked dry.

Gone.

A sickening heat filled her like black fire as the thing called Talbot arched against her and splattered his juices down her throat. She struggled and heaved and swallowed, delirious with terror and arousal, as the heat reached the bottom of her spine and she came again, bursting, gagging, and again and again, until all that was left of her was the devouring darkness and the shudder of her own febrile flesh.

His legs still locked around her head, his muscular arms tight as a vice around her hips, Talbot plunged his tongue into her, tasting every bit of her, savoring her . . .

There was no escape.

He curled around her like some great pale spider, and fed.

The two men stood at the foot of the bed.

"Christ! Can't you cover her up or something?"

Piazzo, the hotel manager, a gray-templed company man, was anxious. Marcus, his chief of security and younger by a score of years, was baffled. And amazed.

The woman who had been Arlene sat cross-legged on the bed, still naked, laughing softly at the shadows that fell across her body when she thrust her hands into the sunlight. There in the emptied room, there was no clue as to who she was or how she'd come to be there. She had no clothing, no money, no identification . . .

And no memory.

Marcus had already been over this once.

"And no, I can't cover her up," he added. "She don't like clothes. I tried to give her my jacket, but she just tossed it back at me."

Piazzo was at his wits' end. He had no idea what to do. Things like this weren't supposed to happen at his hotel, certainly not during his shift.

"So, run this by me again."

"What, you tryin' *not* to get a hard-on? I told you . . ."

"Tell me again!"

Marcus shook his head and reached for his notebook. Nine years in uniform as a Chicago beat cop had taught him to always take notes. He flipped to the page, licked his lips and began to read.

"Housekeeping found her around eleven–twenty. Therese, the new girl. She called down at . . . eleven twenty-eight, requested Security and . . ."

"I got all that. The room. Who rented the *room?*"

"Wait. Okay, here. The room was registered to one 'Ingemar Johansson' ten days ago. He gave us a valid Iowa driver's license and paid up front, in cash. White male, forty-two . . ."

"*Ingemar Johansson? The boxer?*" The manager groaned, incredulous. "*God damnit!* Who was on the front desk?"

"Goddamnit!" the naked woman on the bed repeated.

"Y'see that? That's what I'm talkin' about." Marcus looked up from his notes, nodded toward her. "When I first get up here, she was *out*, limp like a wet shirt. Thought she was an OD, ready for a bag. Now, she's laughin' and talkin'. An' look at her, she knows we're talkin' about her. She's like a sponge, soakin' it all in."

"A sponge. She . . ." the woman echoed, then knitted her brow, concentrating, "I . . . am like . . . a sponge."

"That's right, gorgeous." The ex-cop eyed her, noting her fit, muscular body and flawless, unblemished skin. This chick was hot. He figured she couldn't be more than twenty-two, twenty-five at the most. "A big, fucking, beautiful sponge."

"Beautiful," she repeated, and her smile reached her eyes.

His stomach gurgled softly.

As he dropped his bags on the bed, in a hotel room a thousand miles away, Talbot thought about hunger. He would have another week's respite, ten days perhaps, before the hunt would begin again. The moon would fill and call his nature, and the hunger would rise within him. Again.

Locate. Isolate. Predate.

He moved to the window and looked into the distance. The light of the waning moon filled the city streets.

There was consolation in knowing he was more than a mere predator. He left his prey alive; changed irrevocably, but alive. His kiss brought not death, but transformation. And that was consolation enough.

Soon. Soon, it would begin. The hunt would begin again. And he would find himself once more in the darkness, locked in that cruel embrace that left nothing behind, that swallowed whole all memory and vicissitudes and pain.

Yes, pain. He knew all about pain.

It was *sweet*.

Wilson's Pawn & Loan

L. R. Giles

Eddie dug through a dark cabinet filled with dust bunnies and things that scuttle. He found a shoe box of long-forsaken knickknacks and brought it to the scratched-and-scarred counter-top so the woman could see that he *was* looking.

"Oh, is it in there?" She dabbed tears from her eyes with a mangled Kleenex.

"I hope so. Maybe." It was the truth and a lie. He did hope he found her locket. But, judging from past experience, it was likely—damn near certain—that this woman's property was sitting in some second-rate jewelry shop on the other side of the world, if not around the neck of a new owner.

He continued sifting through broken children's toys, cheap gold-plated bracelets, a rusty tin police badge and other odd things he never imagined his father would pay for.

Then again, he never imagined his father would do a lot of things.

Like die so young.

Or leave Ma with no life insurance or savings.

Or, by being so irresponsible, condemn his only son to this hell he had liked to call—with affection—"the family hustle."

"It has to be here," she said with weak conviction. "Mr. Wilson said I had ninety days to claim it." She tapped the handwritten claim ticket with his father's signature on it for the fifth time. "See? I'm only a week late."

For the fifth time, he read it:

Item 10329754-A
Gold, heart-shaped locket and chain
Qty: 1

His father's girlishly neat signature verified the ticket's authenticity. And, like she said, she was a week past the agreed-upon claim date. Still, he felt no better.

Eddie had been in charge of the shop for the last three weeks, and *he* hadn't sold the woman's locket. Which meant . . .

It meant his father had broken the agreement.

No surprise there.

"Eddie," Pop had told him on more than one occasion, "sometimes you can look at 'em and tell they ain't coming back. It's like instinct. If you got a buyer in the door looking to pay top dollar, you got to look out for the shop."

Yeah, Eddie thought, *try telling* her *that*.

The woman let out a series of hitching sobs that scared Eddie into thinking she might go into a seizure. "I shouldn't have . . . done this. Things were tight, but I . . . shouldn't . . . have . . . done this."

"I could just be looking in the wrong place." Another lie. He knew where Pop kept the good shit.

More sobs.

"How about I keep looking? It might turn up in a day or so." He didn't know why he said it, but hope glistened in her watery eyes.

She blinked away her tears. "Really? You'd do that?"

Eddie swallowed hard. "Sure."

"Thank you so much." She flipped over her claim ticket and scribbled her name and number. "Please call me here as soon as you find it."

The woman turned toward the exit. Eddie couldn't help but notice the thin patches at the elbows of her sweater and the budding lint balls on the back of her stretched, too-small skirt. A nylon rag tied her hair, and the sole of one shoe flapped like a jawbone when she walked. All that going on, and she still managed to scrape up the required ninety dollars to buy back her locket. He wondered whose picture he'd find in it, if it were possible to find it at all.

Chimes sang when she opened the door. Halfway out, she gushed, "Your father would be proud of you, Little Eddie."

Then the pneumatic arm swung the door shut behind her.

He sighed. "You must not have known my dad very well."

He was alone again in a prison of other people's things.

Thanks a lot, Pop. Then, as an afterthought: *Bastard.*

The blanket of night had been draped over the birdcage called Portside, Virginia. Eddie sat under yellow light bars in the empty store while his mother detailed the minifeast she'd prepared just because.

"Ma, you don't have to . . . Why are you slaving over a stove on a Wednesday? I told you . . . Fine, fine. I'm about to close anyway . . . Okay, I'll lock up and come straight home . . . Love you, too. Bye." Eddie sat the phone in its cradle and checked the five alarm clocks—priced from ten to thirty dollars—next to it. Six forty-five, fifteen minutes until closing.

He spun on his stool toward the register. His plan: to eject the tape and do the day's accounting at home. He nearly wet himself when he saw the man leaning over the knife display.

"Shit," he shrieked, stumbling off his perch. "When did you come in?" He hadn't heard the door chimes.

"Only a moment ago," the stranger said. His voice was a mix of Barry White and Darkness from that old Tom Cruise movie, *Legend.* "I wanted you to finish your conversation with your mother before we concluded our business." He stood—more like unfolded—to his full height.

Easily six-foot-six, he could dent the plaster ceiling panels with his head if he suddenly stood on his tiptoes. He wore a dark fedora, and a pale jawline was the only part of his face visible beneath the brim's shadow. His trench coat was black, its sash double-knotted and cinched so tightly around his narrow waist that the bottom portion flared like a ball gown. Eddie couldn't see his feet beneath the hem.

Somewhere in the back of his mind, something screamed, *That's Death, man!* Irrational fear knotted his insides. "What business do you and I have, mister?"

"None." The stranger glided to Eddie's counter. "My dealings are with your father."

Are. Not *were.* Are. Present tense. This guy didn't know Pop was dead. If he was Death, or an agent of, he hadn't been reading his memos.

Eddie relaxed and cursed his silliness. "I'm sorry to tell you this, but my dad passed almost a month ago."

Usually, folks offered their condolences when given the news. This man reached into the inner flap of his coat and brought out a folded, yellow slip of paper. He placed it on the counter. "I have a claim ticket."

Eddie retrieved it. The slip was warm with the stranger's body heat. He was instantly disgusted, but it passed. Unfolding the slip, he saw the shop name—Wilson's Pawn & Loan first—and instantly recognized the wrongness. It was the ampersand. The "&."

The place was called Wilson's Pawn *and* Loan. It used to be the other way, when Eddie was still a kid, but he remembered when Pop changed it. An S & K Menswear had opened on the same street as the shop. Shortly after, a billboard went up for the country/western radio show *Donkey & Kim in the Mornings*. Eddie came to the shop from school one day and overheard his father ordering a new neon sign and stationery; he suddenly felt the store's name was "too much like the white folk."

Still, though unusual, it wasn't impossible for the guy to have a ticket from back in the day. Whatever he'd come to claim was surely long gone, but the ticket could be authentic. It was the next bit—the item number below the old letterhead—that proved the guy was trying to run some kind of game.

It read: *1.*

"Okay, man. What's the deal? What are you trying to prove with this?"

"I've come to claim what's mine."

"With a fake ticket?"

The man showed no emotion, no signal that he was busted or embarrassed or offended. "The ticket is genuine. Please collect my merchandise."

It was time to school this joker. "Pay attention, okay? I'm going to show you why this ticket can't be real." He walked to a slip of paper under spotless glass on the wall behind him. "See this? This is a carbon of the first claim ticket my pop ever filled out."

The fedora brim tilted in the direction of the frame.

"The item number on this ticket is two. The reason it's not number one is because my dad messed up on the first ticket and had to throw it away. He told me when I was six years old. So, your ticket can't be genuine. The item-number-one ticket was gone before I was even born."

"And your father isn't above lying, of course." There was no inflection, no indication that the words were a question or a statement. But Eddie's mind created its own implications.

Defensive now, he said, "Fine. You want to play games. Since you've got the very first claim ticket to ever come out of here, let's see what it's for." He read the description. "An umbra stone? What's that supposed to be?"

"It is about this size." With hands as ghostly pale as the exposed portion of his face, he indicated something roughly the size of a Ping-Pong ball. "An oval-cut ruby."

"It looks like a ruby?"

"It *is* a ruby."

Yeah, right. Eddie pointed to the jewelry display to the stranger's left. "As you can see, we carry a wide array of all the finest stones, from quartz to precision-crafted cubic zirconia. Unfortunately, rubies are currently out of stock. Jay-Z and Beyonce wiped me out like an hour ago."

No smile, scowl or anything from the stranger. "It would be in the safe. The one in the floor beneath the filing cabinet."

Sweat beaded on Eddie's chest and back, pasting his undershirt to him. That safe was his father's most closely guarded secret. He hadn't known about it until the old man had revealed the combination on his deathbed. When he had passed the knowledge on to his mother, she had been as shocked as he.

Of course, he'd checked the safe since his dad's death—nothing there but two hundred dollars in cash and some pictures from old titty magazines—but, this guy even knowing about it was . . . unsettling.

"What did you say your name was, man?"

Still expressionless. "Check the safe, please."

Without another word, Eddie went to the back and into the office. He slid the file cabinet aside, pried up the floor tile with his house key and spun the dial left-right-left. The door swung outward, and for a moment, he saw what he'd left in the safe the last time he'd opened it: legal documents regarding the store and a family of dust bunnies.

Then he blinked.

When he looked into the safe again, the air wavered like gas fumes on asphalt in summer.

He blinked again.

There was a small bundle in the corner of the safe now.

"What the hell?"

He reached for it, hesitated, then grabbed it. Something rigid was inside the dirty cloth. He tugged at the folds of the rag and revealed an angular, red corner.

Eddie glanced toward the front of the store. From here, he couldn't see the stranger and the stranger couldn't see him. Yet, he had a feeling that the stranger would know he'd found the stone.

Fuck it, he thought. He tried his hardest not to think about how he couldn't have overlooked this item in the tiny safe. *Just give it to him. Whatever gets him out of here.*

He swung the safe door closed and returned to the front of the store. "It's weird, but I guess you were right, mister."—*Please take it and go.* "I'll get a bag for you."

The bags were under the counter. He knelt to retrieve one, scanning the cubbyholes beneath the register while he unwrapped the jewel. His fingers tingled.

He looked at the stone, the apparent source of the pins and needles.

Oh, God.

Oxygen lodged in his throat like a chicken bone; his heart raced like a rabbit in a snake pit.

The flat face of the ruby was a translucent red window, the window to a cell. In that cell, he saw a small, naked man pressing his face to the glass. His little fists pounded silently. His screams went unheard—at least in this world.

Eddie didn't mean to speak. His body remembered how to breathe, though, forcing him to suck down a lungful of air and immediately vomit it back up in the form of a single word.

"Dad?"

He stood quickly and backed into the worktable behind the counter. His feet scrabbled at the floor; he was going nowhere fast.

The stranger extended one hand palm up and said, "Hand over my property, please."

He was smiling now.

At the age of five, Eddie had been introduced to his first can of

SpaghettiOs by Chef Boyardee. He had been instantly hooked on the mushy noodle rings and synthetic tomato paste. So much so that when he dreamed, the one constant was always a goofy man in cooking whites with a handlebar mustache. Good dream, wet dream or nightmare, it didn't matter. Nine out of ten times, the chef himself, Mr. Boyardee, made a guest appearance in his fantasy world.

It was weird. He knew that.

He never shared this oddity with anyone and had wished on more than one occasion that the chef never showed up in his dreams again.

Now, behind the counter, with the stranger demanding his merchandise, it was the opposite. He wanted the chef, prayed for him to come through the door, dancing, with a can of SpaghettiOs in each hand. That would mean he was dreaming. He needed to be dreaming.

"That's my property you're holding," the stranger said. "Give it to me."

"What is this?" Eddie held up the ruby. "What's going on?"

That chalky grin widened. "I don't think I really have to tell you. I believe you're smart despite the things your father told me. You can figure it out."

Maybe. In the back of his mind, there was a theory, a twitching, scurrying thing that wanted to come into the light. Eddie shut the hatch on it, refusing to go there. Yet.

"Who are you? I can't figure that out on my own."

"At one time, I was a silent partner in this"—he sneered, his fedora brim moving like a turret as he surveyed his surroundings—"establishment. It's all yours now. As soon as I collect my dividends, that is."

"My father didn't have any partners. He opened his shop with his own blood, sweat and tears." He realized he sounded like a human recorder, spitting out his father's tired spiel verbatim.

"Again, if Big Eddie said it, then it must be true."

This guy was crazy. That's all it was. Simple solution for that, though. "Look, I don't know you, and I don't buy your BS. You've got to go. I'm calling the cops."

Not taking his eyes off the Man in Black, he scooped up the receiver. The screams from the phone could be heard before it even reached his ear.

"Don't give me to him, son. If you ever loved me, don't give him the stone. Please!"

Eddie slammed the receiver back on its cradle hard enough to crack the plastic casing. The stranger chuckled. It was a low, slow-paced grumbling, like gears ticking in a huge clock.

There was no fighting it. No more denying that something wasn't right here. This was beyond the scope of an off-his-rocker customer. This was supernatural. Evil.

Eddie snatched the pump-action shotgun from the catch beneath the counter. "You've got five seconds to get out of here."

The fedora cocked to the side; the expression beneath the brim was nonplussed. "You're throwing me out? I thought you wanted to know my name."

"It's going to be Victim if you don't roll up out of here."

The stranger held up his clenched fist, knuckles down. The fingers uncoiled, and two red shells the size of C batteries bounced onto and then rolled off the counter. "You may wish to load it first."

Eddie worked the pump. No shells ejected. The gun was empty.

He dropped it and ran for the back of the store, slipping the stone in his pocket. At the exit door, he twisted the thumb latch and lunged into the alley. Only . . . it wasn't the alley.

His hips collided with the countertop, bruising them. The stranger's open hand was inches from his face. Somehow, some way, he was back where he had started, at the front of the store.

"My name is R. S. Skinner." The stranger lowered his hand. "I met your father long before you were born, helped him accomplish select goals. He, in turn, made a promise. I imagine you can guess what the promise was, and you understand what it is you hold in your hand."

"It's a rock. That's all."

"Let's stop this game, Little Eddie. You *know* what it is."

He looked at it, really looked at it. It wasn't the bright, shimmering red of Dorothy's slippers. The ruby was murky, the color of large scabs. Yet, clear enough for him to see his father inside.

It wasn't his father, though. Not exactly. Men of flesh and blood don't shrink and fit inside jewels. Men of flesh and blood die and rot in pine boxes. But, what of their spirits?

Like the stranger—Skinner—had said, he *knew* what it was.

It was his father's soul.

"Are you"—he took a deep breath and forced the question that had to be asked—"are you the devil?"

"Hardly. But we do deal in similar goods." He huffed. "The devil. Maybe you are as dense as Big Eddie claimed."

Eddie felt an indignant stab in the pit of his stomach. "Well, whatever you are and whatever your game is, you ought to know that if you met my dad before I was born, then there's no way he could've said that about me."

"If? I have no reason to sully your father's name. He did that well enough on his own, wouldn't you agree?"

Eddie said nothing.

"I met him before you were born, and we spent much time together since. Often, it was in Atlantic City where our paths crossed. Blackjack was his game. Whenever he went on a losing streak, he'd bring you up. Funny, he always equated you with bad luck."

Nice try, buddy. "You've got the wrong guy. My dad never gambled. He said it was just another way for fools to part with their money."

"Poor Little Eddie, still clinging to your father's word like a buoy in a storm. Tell me this: What kind of business trips does a sleazy pawn-shop owner like Big Eddie Wilson need to take? Since you've taken his post, have you been invited to a Pawnbrokers of America convention?"

Eddie opened his mouth to utter some other feeble defense for his dad, another lie. But, almost involuntarily, his jaw snapped shut. He could not force another untruth past his lips.

"Another question for you, Little Eddie. If your father was so great with finances, where's the money now?"

Eddie lowered his eyes, not out of fear of R. S. Skinner—though he *was* afraid—but because he thought the man was reading his mind. He'd asked himself the same questions dozens of times in the last few weeks.

"I'm making you uncomfortable, aren't I? Let's talk about something else."

Skinner turned to his right and glided to a display case full of a hodgepodge of items. Everything from Walkmans to old smoking pipes. He passed his pasty fingers over the glass with a whisper.

"What a gorgeous pistol. Your father planned on selling it to a man named Lance Dartin. Lance works for a criminal group known as the Organization. Kills people, in fact. He can't buy a gun in most places because of his lengthy criminal record, but your father didn't judge a man by his colored past." Skinner's fedora rose. "It was all green to him.

"Dartin used to pay Big Eddie double for the . . . convenient shopping. Unfortunately, your father died before he could put this baby in Lance's hands."

"You can't know that." His voice sounded small.

"Oh, but I can. Just like I know you don't doubt what I'm telling you."

"Why are you doing this?"

"Doing what? I just want my stone."

Eddie was tempted to toss the stone into the black shadow beneath his hat. He wanted Skinner gone. Forever. But, something still gnawed at him. As wrong as this whole conversation was, there was something else *not right* tugging at him.

"Now that I've met you, I think you would've done all right at Commonwealth University."

"What? What's that supposed to mean?" Eddie noticed Skinner's grin had returned.

"Big Eddie used to tell me over the roulette wheel about your desire to teach, that's all."

A low heat burned in Eddie's chest. When he was in his junior year of high school and he brought college up to his old man, the response was always a grunt followed by, "Waste of time and money."

Never mind that he always made the honor roll and his guidance counselor pushed him in that direction. Dad didn't want to hear it. All he saw in his son's future was pawnbroking.

After a while, his college dream had faded like every other dream he had had outside of this damned shop.

"My dad talked to you about my schooling?"

"Only that you wanted to go," Skinner said. "Personally, I thought it was a good idea."

"Yeah. Well, I already know what he thought about it. So don't bother with the mudslinging."

"You're right. No need to open up old wounds. It's a shame,

though." He turned his back to Eddie to examine an electric guitar slung up on the far wall. "You'd think if he was willing to pay Terri's tuition, he would've paid yours."

Eddie was in motion before he knew he was. He rounded the counter, crossed the floor and yanked Skinner around by his coat sleeve. From this close, he thought his initial estimation of six-foot-six might have been conservative; Skinner seemed closer to Shaq's height. And the air surrounding him was *cold*.

It did nothing to cool Eddie's anger. "Who the fuck is Terri?"

"Merely your father's friend. A female."

"He had a mistress?"

"I wouldn't go that far, Little Eddie. Your father's tastes weren't like those of a young man's. He enjoyed being a spectator more than a participant. From what I understood, the young lady was an excellent entertainer."

"So, you're telling me he paid some stripper's way through school?"

"Little Eddie, don't sound so put out. It's not like anyone was going to leave *her* a claim on the family business. I believe she's a teacher now. Isn't that what you wanted to be?"

"That mother"—he stopped, snatched the stone from his pocket and directed his anger toward it—"you mother fucker. How . . . how could you? I'm your son."

"Don't take my word for it," Skinner said, breathing icy breath on him. "I'm a stranger, remember. You don't know me from Adam. I could be making all of this up."

He wasn't, though. That was the thing. Eddie's father was capable of everything Skinner had just said—the lying and the cheating. He had a black heart and bottomless soul, and didn't care about anyone but himself.

But, a slithery voice in the back of his head hissed, *who's got his soul now?*

The little man inside the ruby continued to pound on the walls of his prison.

"Are you going to give me my merchandise now, Eddie?"

Something flared in Eddie's mind. Something small and bright enough to be visible through the angry fog that clouded his mind. His mental recorder—the same one that had sucked up so much of his father's bullshit propaganda over the years—played back what Skinner had just said.

Are you going to give me my merchandise now, Eddie?

It rewound further, to when he'd attempted to call the cops and heard his father's shrieking, fearful voice through the receiver.

Don't give me to him, son. If you ever loved me, don't give him the stone.

That word. Give.

"Mister Skinner, I have another question for you."

"You want to know something else about daddy dearest?"

"No. My question's about you," Eddie said, shaking his head. "Why haven't you just taken the stone from me?"

Silence.

"You're not a man, I know that now. Why try to outsmart one? That is what you're trying to do, isn't it?"

Skinner spoke then, his voice shaky and tense. "I wanted to open your eyes, Eddie. Your father's been cruel to you in ways you couldn't even see. I just wanted you to know the truth."

"I thought you just wanted your stone."

The air changed. It was still cold, colder than before. Now, it crackled with unseen electricity. The hairs on Eddie's neck and arms rose like quills on a porcupine.

Mister Skinner's coat suddenly seemed too small for his frame. Where he was slim before, he now appeared stockier, with protruding areas beneath his coat's fabric that didn't seem quite natural. The fabric flexed and bulged like a bag of snakes.

"I'm going to give you one more chance to hand it over."

He stood his ground. "If it were that simple, you would've done it at first. You can't take it from me, can you?"

"Be done with my stone, boy," he spat. "You owe your father nothing. He's trapped you in a meaningless existence and erased your future. Give him to me, and he'll pay for what he's done to you and your mother. If anyone deserves the torment I have in store, it's him."

The guitar fell from the wall. Two display cases exploded. The shotgun shells on the floor went off, spraying a wall with stray buckshot. Through the display window, Eddie saw a car veer off the road onto the sidewalk and back onto the road, barely missing a telephone pole.

Still, he did not budge. "I'm not giving you this stone."

Skinner's chest heaved for a few scary moments, then his breathing steadied. He shrank back into his previous form and tugged on the lapels of his coat as if to signify that he was back to normal. "Even after all I've told you and all you already knew, you won't hand him over to me?"

"I don't know what you are, Skinner. But I'm not giving him to you. He's a messed-up guy, but he's still my dad."

The brim of the hat shook side to side. Skinner lowered his head and spoke to the floor. "You're still a cheat, Big Eddie. Even in death."

Little Eddie didn't know what that meant, but when the fedora brim rose again, he saw Skinner's eyes for the very first time.

They were two rubies like the one in Eddie's hand. Umbra stones. In each, he saw his father shrieking and pounding, trying to fight his way out.

Skinner raised one hand and flicked the fingers. The stone in Eddie's hand became so hot so fast that it caused a second-degree burn on Eddie's palm before his brain could send a signal to drop it. Eddie let the umbra stone fall to the floor, where it shattered into a thousand clear pieces. It had turned to glass.

The Man in Black turned for the exit.

"No, wait." Eddie ran to grab him, but he spun, spotlighting Eddie in those blood-red eyes. Eddie backed away. It felt like he was shriveling under that gaze. "You can't take him. I didn't give him to you."

"I already have your father, Little Eddie. From the moment his final breath left his worthless carcass, he was mine."

"That's not true. Why'd you come here then?"

"You stupid little man. You don't get it. A man like your father doesn't have the power to trade his soul for the meaningless things he desired. His willingness to barter on that level already guaranteed that someone like me would lay claim on his essence when he died."

Skinner, apparently done with the conversation, turned to leave once more.

Eddie pounded on his back with his good hand. "No. You came here for me to give him to you. You can't just take him."

Skinner didn't look back when he spoke. "I came here hoping you would be willing to give him up. I'd been counting on it. When I met Big Eddie, he was single, with his life in the toilet. He told me he wanted a business, money and women. In return, I needed something that he was capable of coming up with on his own. The ingrate couldn't even get that right."

An invisible rubber band drew taut and snatched Eddie off his feet. He was slung backwards and collided with a wall. A rainstorm of merchandise followed, showering him, causing bruises, nicks and cuts. From his position beneath all the junk, he could see Skinner step onto the sidewalk. He watched Skinner's black elbows piston as he undid the sash at the front of his coat. The thing that was Skinner shook off the garment, revealing no body, no true arms or legs. There was only a swirling mass of shadow and blood. An inky tendril yanked off the hat and tossed it. The shadow split into blotchy winged shapes and flew away.

The wind from their wings sounded like his father screaming.

What had just happened?

He couldn't honestly say. The event was rising and fading from the surface of his mind, like cigarette smoke from an ashtray. He pulled himself up, his eyes watery, and went to the glass shards on the floor. Before he could kneel and examine them more closely, a snatch of yellow caught his eye.

On the counter, Skinner's claim ticket spun like a top in the draft from the open door.

Eddie snatched it up and read the print. It was different from before.

Wilson's Pawn & Loan
Item 1
Wilson's corrupted soul
Qty: 2

Quantity: two?

With that, Eddie understood. His father hadn't sold his soul to R. S. Skinner. He'd offered it as a down payment. The balance was a soul that had yet to be corrupted.

A soul that didn't even exist at the time of the deal.

A soul that wasn't supposed to care—let alone fight—for a loved one.

You're still a cheat, Big Eddie. Even in death.

Eddie understood Skinner's words now. He crumpled the yellow slip in his seared palm and mumbled the most horrible truth of the evening: "Dad sold me."

The Light of Cree

Chesya Burke

Cree had become a woman exactly five days ago. Twelve years old and already a woman—who knew? She didn't feel like a woman; didn't particularly look like one, with the front of her blouse clinging to her chest like a flat piece of paper. But she *was* a woman. At least, that's what Momma said. And Momma was never wrong.

"You've come on your period, baby."

That's what Momma called it. Period. Which meant that Cree would leak every month like a broken water main. And that was how she felt—broken. Like something was wrong with her. Momma had explained to her that every girl has to go through this, but that didn't matter. She still felt . . . different. Like something was off. As if she had become a completely different person overnight. But of course, she had . . .

You're a woman now, she told herself to no avail.

Now, that feeling of change could have less to do with the fact that she had come on her period and more to do with the man she had seen the other day—the strange one.

She had been walking back from the cemetery with her grandmother when she had first seen him. She and her grandmother would go there every so often, clean the stones and pick the weeds. *"We've a lot of people buried here,"* her grandmother would say. *"We gotta take care of 'em. You'll do the same for me, I hope."*

"Yes, ma'am," she'd say.

That's when they saw him. A man, perched with both feet on a single fence post, staring at them. A big, wide-brim hat covering his face, a long black coat, draped over the post that he crouched on, flapping in the wind. Though she couldn't see his face, she saw his eyes. They were bright, like a shining sun, staring at them from under that hat.

She'd grabbed and squeezed her grandmother's hand, scared, and the old woman had pulled her onward. She'd wanted to stop, to turn and walk the other way, but the woman wouldn't let her.

The man hadn't moved, his coat swaying, cracking in the wind, his hat shadowing his dark face, his eyes fixed on Cree and her grandmother.

"Keep walking. Don't even look at him," her grandmother had said.

"But, what . . ." Cree had started to ask.

"Don't. Don't," her grandmother had warned her.

Cree didn't try to talk again. As they reached the man, his head turned slightly toward them. She tried not to notice, but from the corner of her eye, she kept seeing that hat move, almost as if the hat itself were watching them. Once they had walked past, Cree sighed a bit. Behind her, she saw the man's coat flare up as he jumped from his spot on the fence.

Her heart jumped in her chest; she knew he was chasing them. She squeezed the old woman's hand so hard, she thought she'd break it, and her grandmother squeezed back, reassuring her. Behind her, Cree could still hear the man's coat flapping as he chased behind them.

She couldn't help it; she had to look. She jerked away from her grandmother and turned to face the man. She wasn't going to let him attack her from the back, and she wanted to see his face. Needed to see that dark space there, where the light didn't shine. Wanted to know who he was and to let him *see* her face. She didn't know why, but she had to . . . to show him . . .

But he was gone.

She scanned the woods from side to side, but could see no trace of him. The wind had died down a bit and she tried to listen for his footfalls in the woods, but she could hear nothing.

He was gone.

Now she couldn't get that image out of her mind—him standing there on the fence, staring at them through no eyes at all. It scared her, even now.

"What was he?" she had asked the old woman.

"A Dark Man," the old woman had said. "A memory."

"A memory of what?"

"Of that man. His own memory of himself."

"You mean he was dead?"

"Yes, baby, he was dead. He's lost, like . . . like in those woods there." She had pointed to where the man had come from, her finger shaking. "Remember when you was little and you got lost in Cavanaugh Woods? Remember how scared you were, and you thought you'd never get home? Remember?" Cree nodded. "And your brothers found you in the barn, crying. You weren't very far from home, but to you it might as well have been a million miles away. That's how it is for him. He's right there, but cain't find it home."

"To heaven?" she asked.

"To heaven, baby." Her grandmother had bent down, her knees creaking from the weight of old age, and looked into Cree's eyes. "Sometimes, sometimes, they need a guiding light.

"You're special, Cree. I've always known it, since the day you were born with that caul covering your face. The veil of sight and knowledge. That's why you can see him. That's why he can see you. You must come of your own soon, and find your own way."

Now that Cree thought about it, perhaps they did relate to each other—seeing this dead man and becoming a woman. After all, she had seen him for the first time the day she'd come on her period, hadn't she?

"You know what this means, don't 'cha?" Cree's friend Karen asked her.

"What?"

"You're a woman now."

"I wish people would stop sayin' that. I ain't no woman."

The girl laughed, her round face lost in her dimples. "Now you gonna go and get fat. Start eatin' up everythang. Get all moody, and mad at everybody for no reason at all."

"Why would I do that?" Cree stared at her reflection in the pond, her dark skin smooth and youthful in the crystal color of the waters. She thought maybe she'd see something, any hint of her woman-hood. Nothin'.

"I don't know. That's what happened to my sister—at least, that's what my brother said. He said she was painted."

"You mean tainted?"

"No, he said painted. Thought he was being funny. You know, like ... red." The girl looked at her, serious. "They say this thing can change you. That it hurts sometimes. Makes ya do strange things—*see* things."

Cree nodded, not saying anything. She *had* seen things, after all. Strange things.

"You ready for tomorrow? The water's cold this time of year. When he throws you in that water, it's gonna seem like you're down there forever. That's what Joe Ann said."

"He's my daddy. He won't leave me down there long."

"I hope not." The girl put her arm around Cree's shoulders. Cree shuddered; she couldn't help it.

Today she would be baptized. Brought to the Lord. At least, that's how Daddy had put it. *And he won't leave me down too long.* She was sure of it.

Not only had she become a woman only a few days ago, but now she would become a Christian, too. Boy, how time flew. Now was the period—poor choice of words—of cleansing. That wasn't what Daddy said, but that was how she felt. Like they were washing away sins that she had yet to commit.

Not long ago, the pains had started. They began as throbbing sensations in her belly and raced up her back to her spine. "Birthin' pains" was what Momma called them. "Crawl-into-your-bed-and-never-get-out-again-pains" was what she called them.

Would this ever stop? She had asked her momma how long this period thing would last, and the old woman had said that it would be her close friend for the next fifty years.

Fifty years! Would she even live that long? Cree wasn't sure, but with a friend like that, who even wanted to?

The pain moved from her stomach and raced up her back and kept pounding that sin into her somewhere in between. She just wanted to lie there and die. She waited in her room, in her white gown, her hair combed and braided into four tight plaits on her head, with white bows tied at the ends. She sat on the bed, staring out the window.

Toochie walked into the room, wearing her Sunday dress, and sat on the bed beside her. "Nervous?"

Cree kicked her short legs back and forth, and didn't answer her sister.

"Don't be. It's not that bad. Daddy just says a few words, dunks you and that's it. Everyone'll be watchin', but that ain't no big deal."

"He doesn't hold you down there long, does he?"

"No. A few seconds. Just long enough to wash all that sin away." She laughed.

"You sure?"

"Yep. I wouldn't lie to ya, now would I?"

The sun was shining and coming up nicely, the orange and red light spilling into the room, bleeding onto Cree's toes. Toochie had polished Cree's toenails just for this occasion: auburn.

They wouldn't be having regular Sunday services today. No, instead everyone would be meeting at Muller's Creek, so as to see her baptized. They had done it for her sisters and all of her brothers. In fact, they did it whenever the time came for a child in the church to come of the Lord.

Her father stood in the lake, the water up to his knees. He didn't bother to roll up his pants either. He never did; just stood there in his Sunday's best, wading in the water.

The rest of the congregation stood off to the side. Wide-brim hats for as far as she could see, dark faces staring at her, smiles adorning the faces, as if they were so proud to be bringing another soul to Him.

Daddy reached out his hand to her. She walked over to him, the icy water making goose bumps appear on her skin. She couldn't believe how bitter the sensation was between her toes, of all places. The sun had yet to reach its peak and the pond was still hidden in shade, and when the water reached her ankles, she almost cried out from the cold.

Then Daddy grabbed her hand and all other thoughts faded away. It was so soft, so soothing. He had a way of making everything seem okay, as if nothing were allowed to hurt her when he was around.

He pulled her close to him, smiling. He looked so proud, his long face not showing a hint of his age. He whispered to her, "Don't be afraid. I'll hold on tight."

And she knew he would, too. He would hold on to her for dear life and never let go. Her pulse, which had begun to race a mile a minute, slowed to a simple crawl, and she smiled back at him, trusting him with all her heart. All her mind, her soul.

He spoke, more to her than to the gathering crowd. "We've all come here to witness your rebirth. Now shrouded in darkness, a symbol of the life of darkness you're leaving behind, you shall come into the light . . ." The words were drowned out, not by the water, but by her mind. They went into her ears and got all mixed up in her head. It wasn't that she couldn't understand him. It was just that she was too nervous and excited—all at the same time—to focus on the words. They were foreign to her.

Suddenly he dunked her. Water enclosed her face as she fell backward into the pool. Her eyes, nose and mouth became surrounded by water, and her ears drummed from the rushing coldness. Underneath, she felt a sense of wellness, almost as if what they said were true: all of her sins were washing away in that water. Everything was great. All was well. She felt happy, good.

For a split second, she opened her eyes. A bright light loomed around her, and she saw her daddy's face staring down at her. She was surprised that the sun had risen so high and that it now shined down on her. The water around her heated, and she relished the warmth.

She continued to stare into her father's eyes, as his smile suddenly turned to a look of concern. The light grew brighter, and she realized that the glow was not coming from the sun, as she had previously thought, but from her.

That's when her grandmother's words rang back into her ears. *Sometimes, sometimes, they need a guiding light.*

A guiding light . . .

She *was* the light.

The light was within her.

You're special, Cree, the old woman had said. *I've always known it, since the day you were born with that caul covering your face.*

That's why you can see him. That's why he can see you. You must come of your own soon, and find your way.

Slowly she rose as she felt her father's hands guiding her back to the surface. Her feet reached the ground, her hands still at her sides. She felt great; she never wanted this feeling to end.

She stood on her own two feet as the water ran down her face and the air reached her nose again. She breathed.

Cree looked over to her father and realized for the first time, that he was not holding her. In fact, he was standing far away from her, toward the edge of Muller's Creek. She had been holding her own—she was coming of her own.

Everyone was staring at her, strange looks on their faces. And *he* was among them.

The Dark Man. The one she had seen with her grandmother when they were walking from the cemetery. He was staring at her, too. His eyeless sockets fixed on her, as she came to a realization . .
.

She was the light.

The Guiding Light. Those words sprang to her mind as the revelation dawned upon her. She knew now what she must do. Just as the sun rises, brightening a new day, so too must the Light of Cree.

Deadwoods

Brandon Massey

"**D**ad, can you come outside for a sec? I want you to look at something."

Paul raised his head and looked at his son. He'd been poring over the "Jobs" section in the Memphis newspaper, *The Commercial Appeal*, red pen in hand, the mug of Maxwell House at his elbow forgotten and cold. He might as well have enjoyed the coffee while it had been hot. All of the jobs listed either paid insufficient salaries or were outside his field of expertise.

Fifteen years old, tall and lanky, Akili stood in the kitchen doorway, a puzzled look on his face. He scratched his upper lip, which boasted a smear of a youthful mustache.

"What's wrong?" Paul said. "The lawn mower die on you? Please don't tell me that, 'cuz we don't have the money to get it fixed."

"Uh, no, Dad, it's nothing like that," Akili said. "Will you just come check it out? Please?"

Perhaps his son had stumbled across an unfamiliar species of insect, Paul thought. Either that or something that would otherwise engage Paul's scholarly nature. Because if it were a real problem . . . well, it was an unspoken rule that Akili's mother was the go-to person for that kind of thing.

Paul followed Akili into the backyard. It was a beautiful, warm summer morning. Mornings like this sometimes made Paul glad that they had moved back to the old family home in Hernando, Mississippi. There was a purity in the air here that just didn't exist in Memphis.

Country living is better for our health, Paul thought. He would
tell that to his wife, Christine, when she and his daughter returned
home from getting their hair done at her sister's house. Paul believed that when you were handed lemons in life, you should learn
how to make lemonade—and his brother had handed him a lemon
the size of a boulder three months ago, when he'd forced Paul out of
the family business and given him a pitifully meager severance
package. They'd sold their home in Memphis and moved here,
where the cost of living was lower and they could stretch their limited dollars further. Although it was a comfortable house that sat on
four acres of gorgeous land, no amount of "look on the bright side,
guys" comments had been able to sway Christine and the kids. They
hated living there. Predictably, Paul felt responsible for their misery.

Akili stopped in the middle of the yard, where he had left the
John Deere riding mower. He pointed toward the back of their
property.

"See it, Dad?"

Paul looked. And gasped.

"Where in the world did that come from?" Paul said.

Akili shrugged. "I was kinda hoping that you'd know."

A tree had appeared on the perimeter of the yard. It was not an
ordinary tree: it was colossal, with a trunk boasting a circumfer-
ence of over ten feet, countless leafy branches, and a crown that
peaked, Paul estimated, at over two hundred feet in the air.

Paul's mouth grew dry. He could not be seeing this.

A cool wind blew, rippling the leaves, which cast a net of shade
that covered half of the lawn.

"That wasn't there yesterday," Paul said. "Good Lord, it would
take decades—hundreds of years—for a tree to grow that big!"

Nodding, Akili said, "It looks kinda like one of those redwood
trees they have out in California. I remember hearing about them
in a science class. Those redwoods live for over a thousand years or
something, right, Dad?"

"Yeah. But this doesn't look like a redwood to me."

Paul walked closer. The tree did not resemble a redwood. He
wasn't a professional botanist, but it did not resemble any species of
tree that he had ever seen. The bark was ash gray and spotted with
green-black blotches that looked like cancerous tumors. The leaves,

each one the size of his hand, were a strange bluish green, and they were formed in an unusual shape: thin, leggy blades sprouted from the leaf stalk, giving the leaf the look of a tarantula.

Then there was the smell.

A rancid stench oozed from the tree, as if the trunk were a hollow tube chock-full of the corpses of putrefying dead animals. Paul covered his mouth and stopped about ten feet away from the tree. If he walked any closer, the smell would knock him on his butt.

Akili came beside him. He protected his nose with his Memphis Grizzlies T-shirt.

"Deadwood," his son said, his voice muffled.

Paul coughed. "What?"

"I just made up the name. The tree's tall like a redwood, but smells like something dead. So I called it a deadwood."

Akili fancied himself a rapper, always composing lyrics, which he carried around in a leather-bound journal. Paul wasn't surprised that he'd come up with his own name for the strange tree.

"Makes sense," Paul said, but his thoughts continued to circle around the fact that did *not* make sense: how in the hell had this thing turned up in their backyard?

No answers popped into his mind. But he found himself thinking of something that had happened a couple of nights ago.

A light sleeper, Paul had been awakened by a boom in the backyard. It had sounded as though someone had detonated a cherry bomb. It was a few days after the Fourth of July, and his neighbor had two rambunctious teenagers who loved fireworks, so Paul dismissed the noise as the work of the kids depleting their remaining bottle rockets and whatnot—until a greenish glow flared through the venetian blinds.

Curious, he reached the bedroom window and peered outside in time to see the odd light at the farthest reaches of their lawn. Then the glimmer sputtered out, like a dying ember.

Probably a rocket or something those kids launched onto our property, Paul had thought. But he had never seen a light quite like that one, and he did not see or hear his neighbor's children, either. Those kids were so noisy that it would have been obvious if they were outdoors playing.

He thought of going outside to investigate and decided against it. It had grown quiet and dark out there again. It was nothing worth checking out, he figured. He might have even imagined it all. Since he'd lost his job, he spent so much time daydreaming that he would not be surprised if he had hallucinated the spectacle.

Now, however, Paul wondered if there was a connection between the mysterious light he'd seen and this tree. The deadwood, as his son had labeled it.

The wind blew, and the rattling branches sounded like dry bones. As they quivered, he thought he caught a glimpse of something hidden high up in the tree's dense leaves, something blue-black and large. But when he blinked, the visual impression was gone, and he was again left wondering if his acuity was slipping away.

"Did you hear me, Dad?" Akili said.

"I'm sorry, son. What did you say?"

"I said, what are we gonna do about this thing?"

Paul scratched his head. But his answer was automatic. "Let's see what your mother thinks. She'll be home soon."

"I knew you'd say that," Akili muttered.

Christine was horrified.

"Where in God's name did this come from?" she said. Like Paul, she stood at a distance from the tree. She gagged. "And it stinks!"

"I don't know, honey," Paul said. "It showed up here this morning."

"That's impossible," Christine said. She turned on him, her gaze sharp, her demeanor every bit that of the high school calculus teacher known for not tolerating any foolishness. "Trees this big do not magically appear, Paul. It's impossible."

He shrugged. What did she expect him to say? He didn't have the answer. Did he ever?

"What species is it?" she asked, squinting at the tree. "I've never seen anything like it, and I've been gardening for years."

Paul stuck his hands in his pockets and looked at the ground.

Christine sighed, clearly exasperated. "Do I have to solve all the problems in this family? I'm already the sole breadwinner, for God's sake."

Paul winced.

"I'm sorry, I didn't mean that." She touched his arm. "We've all been stressed lately, what with the move and adjusting to living here. Something bizarre like this tree showing up only makes things worse."

"What should we do?" Paul asked. "I think we can probably leave it out here. It's weird, but it's only a tree. I know it stinks, but we don't spend much time out here anyway."

"Are you serious? We're *not* allowing this filthy thing to stand on our property. We're going to get it chopped down. I'll call around this afternoon to get some quotes."

"Quotes? You're talking about spending money to handle this?"

"Of course, I am. We don't have the tools or the skills to do it ourselves."

"But we don't have the money to pay some folks to cut down a tree," Paul said. "The truck needs new brakes. Then we've got to pay for Jamila's braces next week—"

"I'll take care of it somehow," Christine said. She massaged the back of her neck. "Don't I always?"

Her words, though delivered with weariness, not malice, stabbed at his heart. But she was right. She always took care of it, whatever "it" happened to be at any given time. They had first met in college twenty years ago, and Paul had wanted to ask her on a date but had been terrified of rejection—and Christine, sharing a mutual interest in him, took the lead and asked him on a date. When they married, Paul had been reluctant to move out of his parents' house, preferring to stay there indefinitely and not risk living on their own until they were ready—but Christine found a cheap apartment for them and arranged the move. Paul's father had run a successful construction business, and Paul had been content to keep a low-profile management position and let his younger brother assume the role as his dad's right-hand man—but Christine had relentlessly pushed Paul to work for more responsibility and respect, and when his father died, six months ago, Paul had risen to a leadership role nearly equal to his brother's.

He loved Christine, but sometimes he despised himself for being incapable of accomplishing anything without her guiding hand. His woman was his crutch. She deserved a stronger, more decisive man. So did his kids.

But he was forty-one years old. Stuck in his ways. Surely, God had sent him Christine because He knew Paul needed someone like her in his life.

Christine returned to the house, leaving him alone outside.

Paul looked at the deadwood.

He wondered, if God had sent him Christine, who had sent him the tree?

Disturbed by the question, he quickly went inside the house.

That night, Paul had a nightmare. In the dream, his younger brother, Glen, aimed a shotgun at Paul and his family and forced them to board a flimsy sailboat. Soon after they climbed on the boat and pushed away from the shore, they found themselves caught in a storm, lightning cracking on the dark horizon, the turbulent waters heaving their vessel into the air, and then a wave reached overboard like a giant hand and grabbed Christine . . .

Paul woke covered with icy sweat.

Only a dream, he told himself. Relax.

He reached toward the nightstand to get the bottle of water that he kept there. His mouth was sandpaper-dry.

When he took the first sip, he heard a sound that caused a fresh coating of sweat to break out on his forehead: a piercing, animal-like cry. It came from somewhere outside.

They didn't have any pets, but his neighbor had a horse he kept in a stable, and the shriek sounded as though it could have come from there.

Whatever it was, the creature was in agony. It bleated once, then fell silent.

Paul got up and shuffled to the window. He didn't see anything out of the ordinary—except for the deadwood. It hulked in the darkness like an evil skyscraper.

Fear nibbled at his guts.

Whatever happened, it's none of my business, he thought. Go back to bed.

Instead of returning to bed, he slipped on his robe and slippers. He grabbed a flashlight, too.

Outdoors, the warm night was silent and still. Normally, crickets and other creatures were abuzz. Tonight, they were eerily quiet.

He switched on the flashlight and walked across the lawn. He moved toward the wooden fence that separated his property from his neighbor's. His neighbor's stable was near the back of the yard. Paul shone the light beam over there.

A horse lay on the ground. Slaughtered.

The flashlight trembled in his hand.

What had happened? Who had done this?

Suddenly, a large, shadowy figure darted from behind the stables. It leaped over the fence, landed on Paul's property and scrambled through the darkness, headed toward the giant tree.

Paul tried to capture it in the light, but it moved too fast. In seconds, it had scurried up the trunk and vanished in the concealing leaves.

I didn't just see that. I imagined it. In fact, I'm dreaming right now. In reality, I'm curled up underneath the covers, snoring.

His heart boomed.

No one else had come outside. His neighbors, hard drinkers that they were, were probably in a drunken stupor. His wife and kids were hard sleepers, too.

The night belonged to him . . . and the thing that had crawled up into the tree.

Common sense cautioned him to go back inside the house. Curiosity and a sense of duty compelled him to move forward across the yard. If everyone else was asleep, then it was up to him to check this out.

Besides, if he were really dreaming, no harm could come to him. You couldn't get hurt in a dream. Right?

As he neared the tree, the stench made his nostrils dilate.

This is no dream, and you know it, he thought. A dream could not possibly be this vivid.

When he accepted that he was, in fact, awake, a powerful compulsion to run seized him. He wanted to drop the flashlight and run like hell back inside.

But he didn't. He was so close. He only wanted to peek. One quick look.

He only wished he'd brought the shotgun. A lifelong hunter, his father had kept a collection of firearms in the gun cabinet in the den.

Too late to worry about that.

He edged underneath the leafy boughs. He slowly raised the flashlight.

Something wet and fleshy plopped onto his face.

He shouted, backed away. He tore the thing off his face and flung it to the ground.

It looked like a strand of steaming, bloody intestines.

From the slain horse . . .

He stumbled away, dropped to his knees and vomited.

The thing in the tree, it had killed the horse. It had chewed on the horse's guts and spat them on him, a gesture of utter contempt and arrogance.

The creature wasn't stupid. It was smart enough to mock him. And it was intelligent enough to use the cover of the night to hide its murderous activities.

Paul wiped his lips and backpedaled across the yard, keeping his gaze on the tree, ready to bolt if something rushed him.

Inside the house, he locked the door. He bolted the windows, too.

He stared at the deadwood, out there in the darkness.

Be honest, Paul. It's not an ordinary animal hiding up in those branches. Both the tree and the thing living up in it are not of this world.

It was an incredible explanation, but the only one that made some sort of sense to him. He was not the kind of man who spent time wondering about the existence of extraterrestrials, but he never discounted the possibility of alien life. There were billions of worlds in the universe. Why couldn't aliens exist? Why couldn't they visit Earth? It seemed flatly impossible that every supposed UFO sighting and every single alien abduction throughout history could be dismissed as figments of human imagination.

He could not debunk what he had seen with his own eyes. There was an otherworldly creature in his backyard, and it was a killer. It had all begun with the explosion and the flare of green light that he had witnessed a few nights ago; that was when it had landed on Earth. How considerate of it to make its new home in his yard.

But what was he going to do about it?

He thought of Christine and realized, with a rush of anxiety, that this was one problem that his wife would be unable to solve for him.

The next morning, Christine awoke Paul. Her eyes were troubled.

"Eddie stopped by," she said. "Someone killed his horse."

Paul had barely slept at all last night and was instantly alert. "Really? That's terrible. Did he call the police?"

"He did, but he wanted to know if we heard anything last night.

You know I sleep like the dead, but you're a light sleeper. Did you hear anything?"

"No," Paul said quickly. "Nothing."

Christine sighed. "It's such a shame. Who would do something like that to a harmless animal? Eddie said the horse was literally disemboweled. That's so sick. Jesus, whoever did it is sick."

Paul's stomach roiled at the memory of the animal's innards slapping against his face. "Could it have been a wolf? Something like that?"

"Eddie doesn't think so. The stable doors were locked. A wolf couldn't unlock the stable and drag a horse outside. It's the work of something a lot smarter than a wolf. It had to be a man. Someone psychotic."

"You're right," he said. "I'm sure they'll catch whoever's responsible."

"I hope so." She shivered.

He didn't enjoy lying to her, but he didn't see any alternative. What could he tell her? The truth? *Honey, last night I saw an alien climb that ugly tree, and it spat the horse's guts in my face.* Sure. Christine already thought—correctly so—that losing his job had worn down his nerves. If he told her the truth, she might decide he'd suffered a nervous breakdown. Lying was his only recourse.

"When are those folks going to come chop down that tree?" Paul said. "Didn't you say tomorrow?"

"Tomorrow, yes," she said. "No one could come any earlier to handle such a big tree."

"No one can come today?" he said.

She shook her head. "I already asked, Paul. Tomorrow is the earliest they can do it. You know I want that eyesore cleared out of here, wherever it came from. That damn thing makes me uncomfortable."

With good reason, Paul thought. You don't know the half of it.

"Why are you so interested in the tree being cut today?" she said. "The last time I brought up the subject, you tried to talk me out of getting it removed at all."

"I guess I've accepted that you know what's best."

"Okay, Paul." She smiled, but it was a sad expression. He knew what she was thinking. *My poor, sweet husband always relies on me so much, and I wish he wouldn't, just once.*

This time, he was going to surprise her. As soon as she and the kids left (they were going to spend the day in Memphis, as usual), he was going to handle that tree himself.

Paul gripped the old but sharp ax in his hands. He faced the tree, like a warrior confronting a mortal enemy.

Sunlight glinted off the shiny, blue-green leaves. Spotlighted in the golden rays, the unusual tree exuded a bizarre sort of beauty. But Paul was not fooled. The alien predator, probably slumbering, was hidden in the branches, waiting for night to arrive.

Paul wore a disposable mask, which he'd found among Christine's pottery tools, over his mouth and nose to protect him from the tree's nauseating odor. As he approached, he glanced upward to make sure that nothing dropped down on him. He didn't see anything.

He focused on a section of the trunk that was about waist-high. He swung the ax toward it with all his might.

It was like whipping a plastic bat against a concrete wall. The blade bounced away from the tree with a loud ringing noise, and the recoil flung the ax out of Paul's hands.

He stepped away, his hands trembling. He saw that he hadn't so much as chipped the bark.

It had to be superstrong wood or something. Cutting down the tree wasn't going to be that easy.

Time for plan B.

He went to the garage and returned with a can full of gasoline. He saturated the trunk with the fuel, splashing it across the bark in great arcs.

Then, standing several feet away, he lit a match and tossed it at the tree.

There was a loud *whump* and a burst of flames that baked the sweat on his face.

"Gonna burn you down, sucker," Paul said.

But incredibly, as quickly as the flames blazed to life, they began to die. As if the tree were made of fire-retardant material. It actually looked like the alien wood *absorbed* the flames, as absurd as it seemed.

Within a minute, the fire sputtered out. The trunk was not even smoking, not even singed.

"This isn't possible," Paul said.

He didn't have a plan C. He'd tried to take matters into his own hands, and he had failed. This problem, like most of life's important problems, was beyond him.

Head lowered, he grabbed the gasoline can and the ax, and shuffled back to the garage.

A sparkling, black BMW X5 roared down the gravel driveway. Paul had to jump out of the way to keep from getting run over by the vehicle.

This is the last thing I need right now. Damn.

Glen got out of the BMW. Casually dressed in a golf shirt, slacks and Kangol cap, he'd likely spent all morning on the links and left the work of running the company to one of his yes-men, Paul thought.

"Hey, big bro, what's happening?" Glen said. "Doing yard work?"

"Something like that," Paul said.

"More power to you. My landscaping crew takes care of that work for me. I make too much money to waste time with manual labor."

"Why are you here?" Paul said. "Since you're such a rich-and-important man?"

"Watch the sarcasm. It doesn't suit you. And you know better than to talk to me like that."

Paul had a shamefully wicked notion: he could tie Glen to the tree trunk, and the carnivorous creature would find a hearty meal waiting for it this evening.

The thought made him laugh.

"What's the matter with you?" Glen said. "Did I make a joke?"

"Never mind, I've had a long night," Paul said.

"Whatever. I'm beginning to think that living out here in the boonies is doing something to you, man."

"Why are you visiting, Glen? I know it's not because you're concerned about my mental health. Get to the point."

Paul rarely was so direct with his brother, or with anyone, for that matter. The words sounded strange coming out of him. But it felt good to speak his mind. It felt real good.

Glen blinked. "Well, damn. Someone ate his Wheaties this morning, didn't he?" Leaning against the SUV, he looked taken aback. "Anyway, I'll be brief. I'm selling the business."

"You're what?"

Glen smiled, once again in control, wearing his arrogance like a favorite suit. "You heard it right, big bro. I'm putting Simmons Construction up for sale. I'm in discussions with several interested buyers. I'm gonna make a killing on this deal."

"You . . . you can't do that. You don't have full ownership."

"You're right, I don't. We own it jointly, fifty-fifty—even though I sent you packing a few months ago." Glen grinned at the memory of that coup. Paul still wondered what had been wrong with him when he'd allowed himself to be fired from a family business that he'd helped develop with their father. Well, no, he didn't wonder what had been wrong with him; he understood very well what had happened and was loathe to admit it. Glen had bullied him, and he couldn't handle the pressure. Plain and simple. Glen had strong-armed him right out the door, and he'd planned it so masterfully that not even Christine and their attorney had been able to get Paul back inside.

"So I dropped by today," Glen said, "to tell you to sign over your share of the company to me. Then I can wrap up the sale."

"You planned this all along," Paul said. "Fire me, lean on me to give up my ownership, then sell the company. I bet you couldn't wait until Pops died, could you? You selfish bastard."

"Who do you think you're talking to?" Glen said. He hitched up his belt. "I'll kick your ass all over this place, Paul. Don't push me."

He glared at Paul. Paul returned the stony stare without blinking.

God help me, I want to bust him in the mouth. I really, really do.

He'd never hit Glen in his life. Glen, only a year younger, had always been taller, stronger, meaner. Avoiding scuffles with him had been a matter of survival.

But there was a dangerous creature in his backyard, and that was a hell of a lot more frightening than his greedy, self-centered brother.

Finally, Glen took a step backward.

"I don't have time to fool around with you," Glen said. He flung an envelope at Paul's feet. "Those are the terms of what you'll get once the sales transaction is complete. Read it over, whatever. I expect to see you at my office tomorrow morning at nine o'clock sharp to complete the transfer of ownership. Understood?"

Paul didn't bother to pick up the document. "It's time for you to leave, Glen."

Glen shook his head sadly. "Man, you need to get your shit together, get back into the city and be around folks. Living out here's driving you outta your mind." Glen opened the door of the SUV. "Tell Christine and the kids I said hello. Remember, tomorrow at nine sharp."

The BMW rumbled down the driveway.

Paul drew a breath, raised his face to the sky.

Why is this happening to me? What did I do to deserve this?

He turned to look at the deadwood.

He would go inside, and he would think of something. The onus had fallen on him; Christine's plan to have tree cutters take care of the deadwood would never work. He was the only one who really understood what was going on. He would come up with a plan to handle this, and he would do it before night came. He was afraid to spend another night with that tree looming like a dark tower in his yard.

But evening came, and in spite of Paul spending several hours on the Internet researching extraterrestrials and a plethora of other topics, he did not have a single usable idea about what he could do to conquer the deadwood and its bloodthirsty occupant.

His family took dinner in the dining room, as was their habit. Fried chicken, spaghetti, green beans and rolls. Christine and the kids were hungry from a full day of spending time with friends and family in Memphis, while Paul picked at his food and continually looked out the window, at the tree.

A thunderstorm was predicted to strike that night. Already, purple-black clouds were stacked up in the heavens. Flickers of lightning danced on the horizon.

If we're lucky, lightning will hit that damn tree, Paul thought. Certainly, a lightning bolt would hurt it. Or maybe it wouldn't. Maybe it could withstand that, too.

"What's wrong, Daddy?" his daughter, Jamila, said. "Why ain't you eating?"

" 'Aren't,' not 'ain't,' " Christine said. "Good question, though. Why aren't you eating, Paul?"

"I betcha it's that tree," Akili said. He gestured to the window behind him. "The deadwood. Dad can't keep his eyes off it."

Christine looked at Paul, an inquiry in her eyes. "Well?"

Thunder grumbled through the night, like massive stones grinding together in the sky. The ceiling light wavered.

Paul drummed his fingers on the table. He had not told her about Glen's visit, and he hadn't told her anything about his adventures with the tree. It was not like him to keep secrets from her. He shared almost everything with Christine, because she invariably guided him through his troubles. But she wouldn't have any answers for this one.

Nevertheless, withholding the truth could place them in danger.

"Okay, I'll tell you. It's about the tree," he said. He looked at Jamila, hesitated. She was only ten years old and scared easily. Once she had watched a horror movie at her cousin's house, without their knowledge, and had suffered bad dreams for a week. "I don't know if Jamila should hear this."

"Tell us, Daddy!" Jamila pleaded. "I won't be scared!"

"Paul, please," Christine said, in her I'll-handle-the-kids-later tone.

"All right. I know what got Eddie's horse last night," Paul said. "It wasn't a man . . ."

He told them everything, concluding his narrative with his opinion of what they were up against.

"An alien?" Christine said. She tapped her lip. "Wow, Paul. Coming from you, that's something else."

"I believe it," Akili said. "I mean, seriously, what else could it be? That tree came out of nowhere, Mom."

"I believe it, too," Jamila said, eyes bright. She appeared to be more excited at being included in the discussion than afraid.

"It's my honest opinion, the only thing I can think of, as crazy as it sounds," Paul said.

Thunder banged, clinking the dishes in the china cabinet.

"We'll continue this discussion in a minute," Christine said. "I'm going to get some candles."

Paul had a horrible sensation of dread that lay against the back of his neck like a cold towel. They should have left the house tonight—that was the move he should've made. They should've stayed in a hotel in Memphis and called the FBI. Let the experts deal with it. Like in the *X-Files*. He needed Mulder and Scully to solve this. He was stupid and reckless for staying here and jeopardizing his family.

Christine probably would've thought of that, if he'd told her the story earlier and hadn't been so intent on handling this himself.

Another rumble of thunder shook the house. Lightning licked the sky.

Then the lights sputtered out. Darkness enfolded the room.

Jamila let out a gleeful scream.

"Be quiet, girl, Mom's coming back with candles," Akili said.

Paul pushed away from the table. He suddenly realized he would feel a lot more comfortable with a shotgun in easy reach. His father's gun cabinet was in the den. He'd wait for his wife to come back and would then go get it.

Christine returned. "Never fear, candles are here." She struck a match and lit the wick of a tall white candle.

That was when they saw the creature watching them through the window.

Jamila screamed, for real this time, and Christine was so startled that she almost dropped the candle. Akili shouted, too.

Paul got his first good look at the thing. It resembled a man-size spider. Covered in thick, blue-black fur, it had three beady, greenish eyes set in a round head and large, deadly pincers.

The creature screeched, a sound like chalk being dragged across a blackboard. It vanished from the window.

"Jesus, Jesus, Jesus," Christine said. She put her hand against her chest. Quickly, Paul went to her.

"Honey, I want you to take the kids to the basement," he said. "You'll be safe down there."

"What?" She shook her head, dazed. "Paul . . . no . . . what about you? You can't handle this by yourself."

Her lack of confidence in his ability hit him like a blow to the stomach. But he recovered.

"Maybe I can't, but I'm sure as hell going to try," he said. "Now, let's go. We have to hurry!"

More than anything, he worried that the creature would get inside the house. It possessed a frightening intelligence, the cunning mind of a predator. He was certain that it was attempting to find its way in. Every second was precious.

He ushered his family into the hallway. Blackness had swallowed the entire house. The only light came from Christine's flickering candle.

The door to the cellar was at the back of the kitchen. But to reach the kitchen, they had to go past the breakfast nook, and there were glass patio doors over there—large portals that the creature could easily crash through. Darkness crowded against the glass, concealing whatever might be lurking outside.

"Hurry, don't stop for anything," Paul said.

They hustled past the breakfast area and into the kitchen. Akili ripped open the basement door.

Behind them, glass shattered: the patio doors.

Paul pressed his family toward the cellar. "Don't look back. Just get down there! Stay until I say it's clear."

The kids rushed down the stairs. Christine started down the steps, found something on the wooden shelf beside the staircase, pressed it into Paul's hands. A yellow utility flashlight.

"Be careful," she said. "Do what you've got to do."

Nodding grimly, he closed the door and engaged the deadbolt.

He switched on the flashlight and swung the beam around the kitchen.

He was alone.

A knife block stood on the counter. He pulled out a butcher's knife. It wasn't a shotgun, but it was better than fighting empty-handed. The blade gleamed in the light.

He stood, listened.

The house was graveyard-silent. The only sounds came from the storm: rain pounding against the roof and rumbling thunder.

Holding the knife in one hand and the light in the other, he crept across the kitchen. He peered around the corner, toward the patio doors.

A big, ragged hole had been smashed through the doors. Shards of glass covered the carpet. But the alien arachnid was gone.

It had to be somewhere in the house. The damn thing was hunting him.

Perspiration seeped from his palm and saturated the wooden knife handle.

He had to get to the gun cabinet. Battling an extraterrestrial beast with an ordinary butcher's knife was the epitome of foolishness.

Stealthily, he moved past the breakfast nook and into the hallway. He checked both ways. Clear.

Where had the creature gone? Had it run back outdoors, perhaps injured by the breaking glass? It could not have simply disappeared.

The den was at the end of the hall, on the left. He tiptoed to the doorway.

The creature was hunkered in front of the oak gun cabinet. Its eyes glowed with what appeared to be malevolent joy.

Oh, shit. This thing's outsmarted me.

It squirted a jet of yellow fluid at him. Paul ducked. The sticky substance hit the wall with a wet splat. It was like a thick rope of taffy, and if it had captured him, he would've been like a fly trapped in a black widow's web.

Panting, Paul dashed down the hallway.

The alien screeched. Its hairy feet pattered across the hardwood floor.

It was coming after him.

Not wanting a stream of that icky mess to hit him in the back, Paul raced into another room, and slammed the door behind him. He was in the guest bedroom. There was absolutely nothing of use to him in there, but it was a safe refuge—for the moment.

The arachnid monster clattered down the hall. It did not so much as pause at the door to the guest room. As though it were not really interested in him . . .

"No," Paul said. "That sneaky bastard."

He tore open the door. He swung the flashlight toward the kitchen.

The beast was in front of the basement door. One of its furry tentacles tapped at the lock.

Paul remembered that the alien had been clever and agile enough to unlock the door to his neighbor's stable to get at the horse. A simple deadbolt lock was the only mechanism that separated this abominable thing from his entire family.

"Stay away from them!" Paul shouted.

With the deadly swiftness of a quick-draw gunslinger, the spider-thing shot a stream of fluid at Paul, and this time, he didn't move fast enough. The slimy stuff hit his arm.

He dropped the flashlight. It smacked the floor and rolled, creating wriggling shadows.

Paul tried to wrestle out of the web, but couldn't. It was like superglue.

Worse, trying to get it off only tangled him in it more. Within seconds, his arm was wrapped behind his back. He lost his balance and fell to the floor, and then his legs became ensnared, too.

But he still had one free hand. In it, he clutched the butcher knife. He didn't dare lose it.

The arachnid-thing emitted a wail of murderous delight. It scrambled toward him through the shadows, wicked pincers flexing.

Above the creature's trio of glowing eyes, a raw, pinkish pad of flesh pulsated, like an exposed heart. Paul understood nothing about this alien's anatomy, but he recognized an Achilles' heel when he saw one.

So when the alien spider pattered up to him, reeking of death and uttering a strange hum, Paul raised his free arm and rammed the knife in the center of that throbbing hunk of flesh in the thing's head.

The blade plunged in, deep, all the way to the hilt, with the ease of sinking a spoon into a bowl of warm jelly.

The creature shrieked. Blind with agony, it teetered away, smacked repeatedly against the wall. Greenish blood leaked from its head wound, dribbled onto the floor.

Repulsed, Paul rolled away from the injured beast.

The alien continued to bounce against the walls, wailing, steadily losing strength. At last, it hammered the wall one final time and then fell against the floor on its side. Still. Silent. Dead.

Paul released an explosive breath of air.

The web loosened its hold on him; the substance had lost its strength. He brushed off the slimy ropes, lips curled in revulsion.

The lights came back on. Paul unlocked the basement door and invited his family to come out.

"Is it over?" Christine said cautiously. Her eyes were red.

"It's done," Paul said. He took her hand. "I did what I had to do. Finally."

"Look!" Jamila shouted. She pointed outside the kitchen window, jumping. "Fireworks!"

Puzzled, Paul looked.

The deadwood was on fire, but it was not like any kind of fire that Paul had ever seen. Luminescent green flames lapped hungrily at the trunk, traveling quickly from the base all the way up to the crown. Paul worried that the conflagration would spread across the property, but strangely, the fire seemed to be confined to the unearthly tree.

"They were joined together biologically," Akili said matter-of-factly, as if he had studied the phenomenon in a science textbook. "The deadwood and that spider thing. When one dies, so does the other."

"How do you know?" Christine said.

Akili shrugged. "Just makes sense to me, Mom."

And the craziest thing, Paul thought, was that his son proved to be correct. From the patio, they watched the deadwood burn itself up, until all that remained was a heap of stinking ashes.

"Now all we've gotta do is get that monster's dead body out of the house," Akili said. He looked at Paul.

Paul smiled at Christine.

"Let's see what your mother thinks about that," he said.

A week later, Paul was driving his Chevy Blazer on I-55 South, returning from Memphis.

"The meeting with Glen went well," Paul said to Christine, on his cell phone. "He's agreed to sell his stake in the company to me, and he accepted less than what I thought he'd ask for. I honestly think he only wanted to get out of the business altogether."

"I'm so proud of you, honey," Christine said. He could hear the smile in her voice. "The kids will be so excited to hear that we'll be moving back home."

"I don't know, I kind of like staying in my dad's place," Paul said. He chuckled.

"Then you can stay here by yourself," Christine said, and then she laughed, too.

They kept chatting while Paul pulled off the highway and into the parking lot of a BP gas station. He parked beside a fuel pump.

A knot of people stood off to the side, talking and looking around.

Paul climbed out of the Blazer. Frowning, he looked to see what held these people's attention.

The cell phone dropped out of his hand.

He saw them. They towered like giant soldiers in formation across the countryside, all the way to the rim of the horizon.

Deadwoods. Everywhere.

Smoked Butt

Brian Egeston

First time I saw it, he was howlin', hollerin' to the dark like screamin' was gonna heal him. Through the night shine, I could see sweat runnin' over big shoulders and arms.

Just across from the barn, near a rickety outhouse, a barrel was steamin'. Smoke curled out and rose into the night. Looked like ghosts runnin'.

I figured he was evil. Anything make ghosts run, gotta have some devil in him.

Wasn't thick white smoke like I saw when leaves burned or charcoals flamed in a pit. But it was faint and gray. Made it seem like ancestors was comin' back inside of thin clouds.

Behind a tree, I crunched dead leaves where I walked. Didn't figure I'd bother nobody, 'cause he was howlin' so.

Smoke from the barrel danced soft and slow like a party was endin' and people was growin' tired of jiggin'.

He quit howlin' and tugged at his feet. Had one of them club shoes people wear if God ain't finish making one of they legs. Boy in my school had one of them legs. We called him Pogo.

The man flapped down his suspenders, yanked at his shirt like it was filled with chigger bugs.

Moon lit up the ground, and I saw him, naked as a jaybird. Closed my eyes for a minute, but couldn't help lookin' to see what else was gonna happen. He howled again, then hopped his naked self on top that steamin' barrel. Started bouncin' on it. He started breathin' heavy. Smoke blew out from under him, then it seeped out whatever cracks it could find. Smoke puffed like they say them Indians used to do with smoke signals. I thought maybe that's what he was, some kinda Indian or witch-doctor man. Read about them kinda folks in some books my cousin brought me from the city.

I watched him for a good long while. Seem like somebody let the air out of him or the ghosts inside that smoke had done left. Clouds rolled by, stars moved on about they way and the man lumped over like he was just about dead. I went in the woods, crunchin' leaves and sticks fast as I could run, 'cause I was supposed to be at Auntie's house 'fore the sun quit workin'.

"Parthenia Phillips, you lost yo' mind, girl? Where you been?" Auntie screamed at me time I come through the door.

"Been where I been, I guess."

Auntie gave me that look. Same look I got 'fore I woke up on my back when I sassed her about eatin' pecans out her icebox.

"Got lost in the woods tryin' to find Ms. Jessie 'nem place."

"Next time I send you out and you get lost, don't come back. You messin' wit' my money."

Auntie cooked for the sick and shut-in. Church paid her to make plates and deliver them to folks who couldn't do for theyself. Trouble was, she had so many plates to make, she ain't have time to deliver 'em. So she had me walkin' all over tarnation to take them folks they food. I ain't care for it too much, until I saw that man on the barrel. Then I had reason to wander out and get lost.

Second time I saw him, he was runnin' in the field. Well, man with a pogo leg can't really run, but he was makin' a go at it. He'd skip and hop and skip and hop, then do a little jump. I had took a plate of greens and dumplins to Ms. Hatchie Lee. It was some biscuits in there, too, but they ain't make it.

The barrel was smoking somethin' awful this time. I mean, look like one of them volcano things was coming up. And the man had a whole lotta evil in him that night. He was pogo-runnin' all over the place. Just a runnin' and skippin' and hoppin' and tryin' to jump with that club shoe. It was a cold-water well a little ways inside the field, so I ran to it and ducked down behind it to get a better look.

He had strong muscles and was stripped down plumb naked again. Seem like muscles was tryin' to break through his skin.

He jumped on the barrel. Plopped his hind part inside the top. Soon as he got on that thing, he jumped back off. It burned him, and I knew it. Smoke was flyin' out somethin' heavy. Smoke that big gotta be makin' some strong heat, I figure. It's a wonder that whole barrel ain't catch on fire. He started runnin' again, and howlin'. He moaned, so I figured he was a witch doctor, 'cause Indians ain't moan like that and I ain't never seen no Indian wit' no pogo leg.

Smoke kept risin', and the man kept runnin'. He howled some more and slapped his behind. I mean a smack somethin' awful, too. Like he was givin' hisself a beatin'. He beat his own hind, then holla. Same kinda holla I made when Auntie gave me whippins. I knew that hurt, and I ain't know why a man wanna make hisself feel that way. He hit hisself one more time and stopped. Stopped howlin', hollerin', skippin', runnin'. He stopped like the ghost had left him, or a different ghost had come to take over his body. He stood in the middle of the field, then turned to the water well.

The man started that old crazy limp right toward me.

I was gonna take off runnin', but I ain't know how fast a ghost could fly or how strong witch doctors could put a spell on somebody.

I wished I hadn't ate them biscuits. That's why he was comin' for me, I figure. 'Cause I had done ate food for the sick and shut-in. God had sent this witch-doctor man to get me. And he was gonna stomp me to death with that club foot 'cause I had called that boy at my school Pogo. I ain't wanna move. I was too scared. That man sat on fire, so I knowed I couldn't hurt him.

I could hear him comin' closer. I heard his good foot step and the clubfoot drag. Step-drag. Step-drag. I know he was close, 'cause in my mind, I could see him walkin'.

I heard him breathin' and moanin'. His breath made loud grunts. Sound like Auntie's friend when he come over and stay all night in her room wit' the door closed.

The man kept comin' at me, and I was thinkin' how long it take somebody to die when they gettin' kilt. Figure God wouldn't make me hurt too long for three little ol' biscuits.

That ground was cool. Figured that'd be the last thing I felt—cool grass right 'fore my hot blood spilt on it. I wanted to run, but I couldn't feel nothin' in my legs 'cept for hot piss runnin' down my pants. Figure it didn't matter much if I had wet myself. Ain't gon' be wearin' no mo' pants no how.

Step-drag. Step-drag.

I could hear the pogo leg tearin' through the grass. That moanin' and gruntin' was 'bout as loud as I ever heard. Sounded like he was hungry to kill somebody and . . . he was gon' put me in that barrel.

That's what it was. He kilt people and burned them in that barrel. Think I read a story like that.

That's why he howled so, 'cause people's souls was inside that barrel, and smoke was dead souls comin' back to get folks.

I hope he wasn't gonna set me on fire 'fore killin' me. That's too much to suffer for some biscuits. God ain't hate me that much, I know.

He started howlin' again.

I heard the bucket unwind. It was droppin'. The well echoed when the bucket bumped the sides. The rope kept unwinding until it splashed.

He was gonna drown me, gonna throw me in that well! I hoped I'd be dead before I hit the bottom. I ain't care about breakin' my neck, but I ain't wanna die drownin'. I put my hands together and prayed for God to forgive me for callin' that boy Pogo and for eatin' the sick and shut-ins' biscuits. Prayed that I'd die 'fore I hit the water. The bucket started windin' back up. The man was right on the other side of the well. I could smell him. Smelled like work. Smelled like steel on hands and sweat on a back. Smelled like bein' outdoors all day. He hollered as loud as he did the whole night. He hollered with some words I couldn't say.

My eyes started to close like I was sleepy.

That man was puttin' a spell on me. I read that, too. Witch-doctor men could make you turn into stuff. That's why I ain't wanna run, 'cause I figure soon as I made it to the woods, he'd turn me into some kinda animal everybody wanna kill.

The bucket hit the top of the well, and my eyes was tryin' real hard to close. I was just waitin' now. Waitin' for his spell to work, and waitin' to see if God had done heard me. He started howlin'. I closed my eyes. He hollered. I bowed my head. He moaned. I prayed. He moved. I listened.

Step-drag. Step-drag.

The sound got softer. Step-drag. Step-drag. He was movin' away from the well, holdin' that bucket of water. I stood up—slow. Peeked my head up over the well and watched him step-drag to the barrel, where he poured water inside. The smoke jumped up in his face, and he threw that barrel on the ground, then jumped on top of the barrel, looked up to the sky and went limp like the ghosts had left him again.

I jumped up and ran into the woods, thanking God, but still prayin' that Auntie wouldn't be mad when she saw my pants.

"Get that basket right there. Hurry up, girl. I ain't got time to fool wit'chu."

Auntie stayed mad for two days after I came back late wit' piss in my pants. She thought I had delivered the plates like that and said people wasn't gonna eat her food if I smelled when I came to they door.

"You gon' learn them routes and learn 'em good. You messin' wit' my money, girl. You gon' deliver these plates wit' me, and if you get lost again, you gon' lose some skin off yo' 'hind."

We had been walkin' a while when I saw a open field. Through the trees I could see a cold-water well. I ain't know if it was the same one, 'cause it looked so different in the daytime and we was up on a high road. We kept walkin' up, and Auntie was mumblin' every step. Somethin' about gettin' lost and beatin' my tail and messin' with her money. She kept mumblin' until we came up on this clearing that led to a path that ended at a house.

"Whew, I don't know why these folks live all the way up on this hill," Auntie said.

The front porch was filled with broken pieces of wood and a few rockin' chairs look like somebody had made by hand. It was a hole right in front of the door. Look like somebody had dropped a big ol' boulder right through it.

"Watch where you steppin', girl. Don't fall in that hole. I'll have to carry you all the way back home, and I'll never have enough time to make my pies for tomorrow."

Auntie knocked on the door real quick and hard.

The door jerked. Auntie looked at me. The door jerked again. Auntie shook her head and hollered to the door.

"Loodie! It's me, Virginia. You gon' let me in? Brought y'all somethin' to eat."

The door jerked again, and then somethin' started makin' a noise inside. Sounded kinda like a animal laughin'. One of them hyenas. It was real high, like the lady that sing them solos on Sunday and make people on the front pew close they ears.

"'Ginia! Heeyyy, child. This do' givin' me fits! Aahh-kah-kah-kah-kah!" Whatever was inside started laughin'.

The door started jerkin' real bad, and then it opened up.

"I got it open! Aaah-kah-kah-kah-kah!"

Auntie jumped over the hole in front of the door, and I followed her. I saw a long piece of old rope tied to the doorknob. I looked at the knob and tried to see where the rope ended. It was droopin' on the floor, wrapped around a book, draped across a ironin' board, tied up to a washboard, looped through one of them animal traps, hooked up to the bottom leg of a stove, tied on the handle of a fryin' pan and wrapped around the biggest wrist I had ever seen in my life.

"That's some way to open a door, ain't it? Ahhh-kah-kah-kah-kah!"

This was Loodie sittin' on the bed, I figured. I do believe she was the biggest living thing I had ever seen. She was bigger than some of the animals I had seen in books. Only thing I figured bigger than this woman sittin' on this bed was that whale Ahab was ridin' on. She had ponytail balls done up on the sides of her head. Made it look like she had horns. She had the brightest lipstick I had ever seen wiped all across her mouth.

"Loodie, this here's my niece, Parthenia."

"Hey, Parthenia, wit' yo' pretty self. Just as pretty as a Bessie bug. Ahh-kah-kah-kah-kah."

She made that laugh, and I saw inside her mouth. Look like God was in a hurry and just threw some leftover teeth in her mouth and didn't care which way they was sittin'.

"Come on over, Parthenia," Loodie said.

I asked Loodie, "Is you sick, or is you shut-in?"

"Parthenia!" Auntie hollered at me. I don't know why. I was just askin'.

"This one's a kicker here, 'Ginia! Aah-kah-kah-kah-kah!"

Every time she laughed, she got to shakin' and jigglin' and wobblin'.

I looked around the house. I saw some books on a shelf. I walked over to see which ones they was, but none of 'em had titles.

It was a window over by her bed, but it had bottles stacked up, so you couldn't really see out, but the sunlight could still come in.

She had a sink full of dirty forks. Wasn't no plates I could see, just forks.

"Loodie. Brought some roast beef, mac and cheese, fried chicken, dumplins, and biscuits."

"Oooh, that's my favorite, 'Ginia."

"Which one?" I asked.

"Food! Aah-kah-kah-kah-kah!"

"Well, we bes' get goin', cause—"

"Sit for a while, y'all. I hear Clem comin' up the way now."

The whale lady looked out the window. I don't why. She couldn't see nothin' for the bottles no way.

"How you see somebody out that window?" I asked her.

"Child, I can't see nobody. I can hear. Listen."

She was quiet, and the house got loud. I heard acorns bombing down on the roof. Floorboards was creaking. Probably mad 'cause she walked on 'em. A long tree branch was brushin' up against the side of the house. Then I heard . . .

"Hear him? Comin' up the way now," Loodie said.

Step-drag. Step-drag. Step-drag.

I looked at Auntie. "It's time to go, ain't it, Auntie?"

I grabbed her hand and took her to the door.

"Girl, let go my arm. We gon' leave in a minute."

"Gettin' dark, Auntie. Better leave now."

"You been comin' home in the dark from my deliveries. Ain't seem to bother you then, did it?"

Step-drag. Step-drag.

Maybe he was gonna fall through that hole in the porch. Or maybe that pogo leg would fall on the broken pieces outside. He could hit his head and get knocked out. Step-drag. Step-drag. Stop.

He was outside the door. I guess he ain't howl in the daytime. Maybe he was a witch-doctor vampire, and only time he got possessed was at night.

The front door creaked. He opened it. I closed my eyes.

"Clem, sugar baby! Come on over here and make it sweet! Aaah-kah-kah-kah-kah!"

"Jelly-roll. Jelly-roll!" the man said. He had a deep old voice, like a nice grandpaw. It ain't sound like no witch doctor.

I opened my eyes and looked at his clubfoot. It was just like I remembered it.

He was dark as the night. Surprised I could even see him at all when I was out there. Had big ol' eyes, almost like a fish.

"I'm hungry like a wolf, woman," he said to Loodie, and then turned to Auntie. "How you doin', ma'am?"

"This is 'Ginia from the church. She brought me some food, Clem."

"Brought *you* some food?"

"Brought it for everybody. Bless all of y'all," Auntie said.

"Clem don't need none of this," Loodie said.

"Go on now, Loodie. Hush. I can eat it," Clem said.

All he ate was blood, I bet. Dead people and dogs, I figured.

"Clem, you know what's gonna happen if you eat all this meat and cheese," Loodie said.

"Hush up now, Loodie. I'm hungry, and I'm gonna eat."

The man went inside the basket and tore into that food like he was possessed.

"Clem, don't do it!"

"Shush, Loodie. Let me eat."

"You know what's gonna happen!"

My stomach started to shake. He was gonna turn into that monster, and Auntie had more prayers than me. She was gonna be okay, and I was gonna be kilt for sure.

"Clem, if you don't stop—"

"Loodie, be quiet!"

"Stop, Clem!"

"Loodie, shut up!"

"Clem, don't do that! You gon' be back down there in the field howlin' and screamin' and—"

"Loodie!"

"—sittin' on that barrel tryin to steam off yo' hemorrhoids."

Our Kind of People

Michael Boatman

"**D**on't you want to come in?" Ms. Wrong Number Who Gives A Fuck purred. "I do one hell of a good Screaming Orgasm."

Marc Craft stared at the beautiful young woman with whom he'd just wasted four hours, and stifled the urge to smash her perfect nose.

"I'd better not," he said.

"Why?" the waste said.

Because if I come inside, I'll cut your head off.

Instead of throttling her, he smiled.

"I have to go," he said, injecting just the right note of sincerity, along with a hint of frustrated lust. "I have a deposition in the morning."

The blind date smiled, her full lips curving upward in a predatory sneer that was supposed to be sexy. She opened the door to her apartment.

"Just one drink," she pouted. "You know, I've wanted to get with you from the moment we met."

She stepped in to him, into his space, and Marc kissed her. He poured himself into his performance. It was easy: the warmth of her lips, the taste of her tongue—merlot and fresh berries for dessert—made the kiss tolerable enough that he had to remind himself not to wring her neck.

The blind date had been set up by his father and Miss Wrong's father, an old family friend who also happened to be a prominent black judge. She was a former Miss Black New York, an accomplished young physician only recently arrived in Manhattan. She hailed from one of the better black families in her upper Westchester County town.

The right kind of people, Marcellus, his mother had said on his voice mail. *Our kind of people.*

And she couldn't disappear.

Miss Wrong's hands fluttered against his chest, pushing at him. When he finally released her, she staggered and almost fell, dropping her keys and the single red rose he'd brought her.

"What's wrong?"

Miss Wrong shook her head. She was staring at him the way a dog stares at a television program *about* dogs, attracted by the sights and sounds of something familiar, confused by the play of light and shadow.

"I'm . . . I'm sorry," she said. "I . . . I don't feel well."

"Are you sure?" he said. "Can I help you?"

"No," she said. "Some . . . some other time maybe."

He stooped, grabbed her keys and the rose. She took the keys from him and stepped quickly into the darkness of her apartment.

"Are you sure I can't help—"

She slammed the door in his face.

Marc smiled. He turned and tossed the rose into the trash can on his way out. He hit the sidewalk and headed south, barely able to keep from sprinting. If he hurried, he just might make the twelve-thirty train back to Brooklyn.

The love of his life was waiting for him there.

He caught a cab back to Times Square and headed down into the subway station at 42nd Street. He had to wait for half an hour on the nearly deserted platform before the F train creaked into the station.

The only other riders on the platform were a pair of young lovers, too high to care about the lateness of the hour, and a New York City Transit employee, a driver or maintenance man, Marc couldn't tell.

As the F train lurched to a halt, Marc reached under his jacket and touched the hilt of the hunting knife he carried with him every Date Night. Reassured by its comforting bulk, he got on the train.

Marc, the transit employee and the young couple were the only people in their car. It always amazed him how, in a city as busy as

New York, the subway seemed to clear out after midnight. At least, on the weekends.

He chose a seat close to the front of the car, hoping to surprise his love when she arrived. He chuckled at the flutter of nervousness in his gut: He was always wrong when it came to anticipating her comings and goings. He never surprised her, and he never outguessed her.

The doors hissed shut, and the F train slid into the dark tunnel, bound for Brooklyn. Marc settled in, failing miserably to suppress his excitement at the thought of meeting his One True Love.

Tonight, he thought. *It's got to be tonight.*

Love is for fools and dreamers, Marcellus, his mother's voice reminded him. *People like us are bound by a greater responsibility.*

Over in the corner, the young lovers were having some difficulty. The boy was apparently ill, convulsing from whatever he'd ingested earlier. He lay moaning with his head in the girl's lap, while she whispered into his ear. As Marc watched them, the boy fell forward and vomited on the floor.

"You folks alright?" the Transit employee said.

"Fuck off," the girl snarled.

The Transit employee shrugged and went back to his newspaper. Marc studied the big man for a moment, the thick forearms, the narrow waist just beginning to expand over his belt, the broad shoulders and heavily knuckled fists.

The Transit employee would be difficult in a hand-to-hand encounter: Marc would have to use stealth and cunning, sneak up on the bigger man and slice his throat before he could react.

Marc turned his focus toward the young couple.

The boy was tall enough, nearly as tall as Marc, who stood six feet one inch in height. But he was thin, too slight, with nothing like enough bulk for Marc's needs.

And there was the problem of what to do with the girl.

She was staring at him, plainly interested. He knew he was a catch, kept himself fit through proper diet and intensive exercise. He never stepped out of his apartment unless he looked his best.

Especially on Date Night.

His father, however, had beaten him unconscious the one time he'd dared to bring a white girl home from college.

You are here to elevate the race, fool, the Admiral had said. *Your mother and I sacrificed to make sure you got exposed to the right kind of people.*

"Our kind of people," Marc said to no one.

The train pulled into the 34th Street station. The doors slid open. Marc leaned forward, his breath catching in his throat.

We've given you opportunities we never had, Marcellus. It's a parent's duty to make sure his children grow up ready to conquer the world.

A group of young black men burst in through the doors. They shoved and jostled each other, noisily mock-fighting for seats on the empty car.

"Stupid-ass faggots on this train," one of them said loudly. The others laughed. Marc knew they were talking about him, but he didn't care. He was different from them, *better* than them. He had to be.

I don't hit you because I hate you, boy, his father's rage whispered. *I hit you to make you strong. You're to be a credit to the race, Marcellus.*

As the train rolled on into the darkness, Marc considered exactly how much of a credit he'd become: The child of upper-middle-class African-American professionals, he'd grown up in a respectable neighborhood in Hartford, miles distant from the urban nightmares of places like Stamford and New York.

He'd graduated from Yale Law, landed a lucrative position as a young associate at a prominent Manhattan law firm. A year later, he'd bought a spacious apartment in Park Slope. Everything had gone according to his parents' plan. Their sole disappointment was his inability to settle down and find the perfect girl to become Mrs. Marcellus Craft.

The race must be perpetuated, elevated, the Admiral would say. *But not just with any kind of girl. She needs to be the right kind of people.*

One of the young men was coming toward him, chin jutting, head tilted at an angle meant to intimidate. He was big, ebony-skinned and broad-shouldered, with a scraggly beard and the eyes of a corpse. Behind him, the other young men cackled and egged him on.

Marc banished the voices, instinctively switched his perceptions to assess the threat presented by the bearded man. The hunting knife at his side dug into his rib cage, and he shifted to ease the pressure.

"Yo, man," the bearded man said. "Why you wearin' them clothes like that? You some kind of entrepreneur or somethin'?"

Marc smiled. He was keenly aware of exactly how many of his teeth he was exposing, aware of his every verbal nuance, facial twitch and eyelid flutter. He'd mastered the art of subtle intimidation at the negotiating table, facing adversaries who counted their worth in the billions.

He had murdered men more desperate than this one and sung along at a Broadway musical twenty minutes later.

"I'm talkin' to you, man," the bearded man snapped.

"I'm an attorney," Marc said.

"What kind?" the bearded man replied.

Marc made it a point to look the bearded man directly in the eye. It was a lesson he'd learned at the ends of the Admiral's fists. It was a lesson Marc had passed on to his victims before they died.

Look me in my eye when I speak to you, boy.

"Who wants to know?" he said to the bearded man.

The bearded man looked back over his shoulder at his friends. Something in his aggressive stance wavered; some reservoir of bravado ran dry. His tongue flicked out and licked at his upper lip.

"Do you read?"

The bearded man's brow furrowed. "What?"

"I'm going to kill someone tonight," Marc said. "You look just about the right size."

He reached into his jacket, produced the big hunting knife and showed it to the bearded man.

The train bumped over a rough spot on the track and slowed down, easing toward the 23rd Street stop. Then the doors slid open, and Marc's One True Love walked through the far entrance into the subway car.

"Oh, shit!" one of the young black men snarled.

Marc stifled the urge to gut the bearded thug where he stood, staring at him like the idiot he obviously was. His Lady came on, pushing her cart through the gauntlet of gaping thugs. As she approached, the young men cursed and leaped out of their seats. They scrambled through the open doors and out onto the deserted platform.

The bearded man swore as Lady Love squeaked closer.

Yes, Marc agreed. *She is beautiful.*

Her skin was the color of a cadaver's sclera, her hair the color of ravens' wings, encrusted with filth. Dirty black spikes leaped out from her head like a shout of exaltation.

Her eyes were the color of summer skies, piercing in a face nearly black with blood and dirt. Her jaw had been paralyzed on one side by a stroke or birth defect. Her mouth hung open, her face fixed in a silent shriek.

She had covered herself in a one-piece jumper or snowsuit, stuffed at the sleeves and ankles with newspaper to keep warm down in the tunnels at night. The snowsuit was torn in too many places to count, the holes overflowing either with flesh or gray wads of newspaper.

Her feet, swollen from years of walking and neglect, had burst, black with gangrene, from the thick-soled cotton boots he'd stolen for her on their last date. Now, she plodded forward on bare, festering stumps. Things were moving beneath the rumpled skin of the snowsuit: Parts of it seemed to shift and shudder, as if the flesh beneath played host to multitudes of vermin. Behind her, a brown stream of liquid leaked down the backs of her legs and trickled out of the snowsuit, leaving twin trails of fetor in her wake.

Lady Love was pushing a grocery cart up the long aisle toward them. Something moved inside the cart. Marc stood to get a closer look at the gift she'd brought him.

It was a dog. A golden retriever.

Someone had broken the retriever's back. A loop of intestine hung between its jaws. It lay, twisted and shivering, atop Lady Love's ubiquitous wads of newspaper. Marc thought he saw tire marks across the dog's midsection, but he couldn't be certain.

The retriever's eyes rolled heavenward, bright with suffering, and focused on Marc. It whined and snapped at the loop of gut dangling from its mouth.

Marc didn't hear the doors open, didn't hear the bearded thug and the other people scramble out of the car. His focus never wavered from Lady Love's face. Tonight, he knew, she would favor him.

Confident, he extended his hand.

She accepted.

* * *

They found a spot on the tracks, well away from the glaring lights from the 14th Street stop. He hurried her along as quickly as she was able to move. They only had fourteen minutes before the next train.

If I died in her arms, it would be worth it, Marc thought.

They lay down in filth, his heart racing as she reached for him, undid him and tugged down his pants. He fumbled at the zipper of her snowsuit, his fingers clumsy with his excitement, and pulled it down, freeing her.

He stopped. The heat and smell that enveloped him were almost more than even he could bear. Parts of her body were moving in the darkness, sliding over his thighs, his groin, stroking, teasing him.

From somewhere far behind them, he heard the golden retriever whimpering in the shopping cart where they'd left it at the entrance to the tunnel.

What have you done this time, boy?

Then his Lady grabbed him with hands and mouth and things he couldn't see, *wouldn't* see, things that caressed him wetly, pierced him, sank talons into his flesh and hooked him to her.

He lost himself in blood and heat.

He lost himself in her.

Afterward, he lured a junkie down into the tunnel, ordered him to strip naked and slit his throat. He dressed in the junkie's clothing while his Lady fed.

Then Lady Love screamed.

Marc ran to her, fell to his knees at her side. Her shrieks echoed up and down the tunnel, a dark cacophony of barks and growls that accompanied the suffering of the crippled golden retriever.

She squirmed there, a dark, toxic wonder, naked and vulnerable, her skin shining in the dim illumination. The parts of her that Marc would not let himself see hissed at him and tore her flesh like hate-starved lovers.

Lady Love lifted her head and shrieked. At the far end of the tunnel, the golden retriever howled.

Then something wriggled out from the dark thatch between her thighs. In the half-light from the platform, Marc could make out only a vague outline of the thing, which twisted on the floor between his lover's knees. It mewled, and uttered a tiny, gurgling whine.

Then it slithered onto the Lady's stomach.

It was the deep red color of heart's blood, about twelve inches long, a squirming tuber of bio-matter. It twisted and writhed like a snake trying to shed its skin.

The red thing lifted its front end and chattered at Marc, revealing a circular row of needle-sharp teeth. Then it opened its eyes, and Marc Craft's tenuous grip on sanity blew away, like trash in the wake of a speeding juggernaut.

A second tuber pulled itself up onto the Lady's stomach, then a third and a fourth. In moments, her lower half was crawling with more than a dozen squirming, crimson larvae.

As if cued by an inaudible signal, the first larva, the one with the Admiral's eyes, began to crawl toward Marc. He tried to crawl away, but something like a tentacle extended out of the Lady's torso, wrapped itself around his neck and pulled him down, held his face close to her belly, close enough for the first larva to bite his cheek.

The bite sent a shock of agony through his nervous system, and he screamed. Another larva tore his right ear off. Marc grabbed the tentacle that held him fast, tried to tear himself free. Lady Love barked and pulled him closer, groping at his face. Nails like black claws reached for the soft meat inside his mouth and tore it free.

We raised you up to produce something new, Marcellus. Your children will conquer the world. But they'll have to be the right kind of people. Our kind of people.

As his crimson offspring consumed his flesh, Marc Craft remembered his parents' advice. And as Lady Love tore his eyes from his head, two words occurred to him:

Mission accomplished.

Natural Instinct

L. A. Banks

Before the sisters in Philly cast aspersion on my character, let me be clear—I ain't no dog, not even a coyote. So, believe what you want if a lot of females start telling you a buncha mess about how Mike Adams is just wrong and is a natural dawg. But at least let me explain my lupine ways.

Fact: Wolves do mate for life, once we settle down. It's the finding-the-right-female-along-the-way part that gives us our bad reputation. However, as a friend, we're loyal, and you can't have a better brother watching your back.

Now, true, around this time of the month, I confess, I have a little problem. I get edgy, gotta eat right and definitely gotta get laid. But, hey, that don't make me a monster. Being held hostage to a twenty-eight-day lunar cycle is a real bitch. The day before the full moon and the day after, I got issues. Also on the night it rises. What can I say? All right, so for three days a month, I trip and trip hard. The rest of the time, I'm a regular kinda guy. I ain't as bad as most; don't do nothin' really foul. Curbed that side of me a long time ago, like most of us have.

But, see, here's my problem: Women can't leave sleeping dogs lie. I've tried to get the women in my life to understand that monogamy with a human, literally, just ain't in my DNA. No matter how diplomatically I put it, they seem to hear only what they wanna hear. It's beyond a man thing that they wouldn't understand. Then, when they don't get what they want—a total commitment— come the tears and drama, and accusations the day after I roll . . .

but, hey, like I said, a brother has to do what a brother has to do. Plus, I'm always straight with them from the jump, and I always tell 'em the deal going in—but somehow, it always gets convoluted after we do the wild thing. This, I frankly don't understand.

The way I see it, if they were really honest with themselves, they'd admit that they love the dawg in me. Every man has a little bit of that in him, right? Maybe I just got more than my fair share, but that isn't my fault—that was fate. Accident of time, place and birth. I'm not the marrying kinda brother. Besides, it's not like I haven't tried to go straight over the years. I really have, but Lord have mercy . . . when the moon is full . . . what can I say? It is what it is.

So, tonight, I'm gonna take my ass home solo before it gets dark. A brother is trying real hard to break a love 'em and leave 'em cycle, feel me? I'm calling in to the captain, telling him I'm sick—which is the truth—and can't do the night shift working vice detail. Aw, hell no. That's an accident waiting to happen. Thirty-two is way too old in canine years to be actin' the way I know I'ma act. I already got wood just thinking about the fine tail in the clubs, and it ain't even sundown. Plus, if some dumb bastard pisses me off tonight, I ain't responsible. Why even go there? See, I know my limits.

Rational thought continued to battle within his mind as he pulled his squad car in front of the Sixth District, East Side Precinct. All he had to do was cough, rub his stomach and put on a show for the captain well before his shift was over.

"Hey, Michael," the station's dispatcher murmured. "How you doin' today, baby?"

See, the shit was already starting. Neecy needed to stop. *Now.*

Against his better judgment, he leaned on her desk and offered her a dashing smile. That woman seemed to know his cycle better than he did; could always mysteriously tell when his resistance was low. The girl had to be psychic. "I'm all right, sis. How you livin'?" He glanced at his vibrating waistband, ignoring five calls. His cell phone was already blowing up, and the moon wasn't out yet.

"Aw'ight," she said with a well-timed, feminine sigh. "Can't complain. Ain't no use in that any ole way." She gave him a sexy wink. "Didn't expect to see you in here during your shift. Must be my lucky day." She giggled, glanced at his cell phone for a second and smiled wider, allowing her gaze to sweep the full length of his six-foot-four frame.

His gaze lingered on her pretty brown face for a moment, then trailed down the front of her uniform to her cleavage and held the line. "Yeah . . . me neither." Shit, this woman wasn't superfine, but she was all female. However, Neecy was good people. Cute as could be, actually. He liked what she'd done new to her hair. The ponytail was working, even if it was acrylic. He pushed himself away from her desk as her eyelids lowered and her lips parted.

"When do you get off?" she whispered.

He stared at her for a moment too long. "Four."

"So do I."

He backed up. "But Cap says I gotta work a double tonight, and I ain't feelin' so good."

"Then maybe you should go home and get some rest."

He watched her breathe out the statement.

"Yeah, maybe I do need to go home and lie down."

She swallowed hard and licked her full, gloss-shined lips as though her mouth had suddenly gone dry. "You need to go to bed, baby."

"I know," he murmured, but wanted to kick himself. Not tonight. He was going cold turkey. "So, you get off at four, huh?"

"Yo, man, whassup?" Derrick said, walking up and breaking their trance.

Michael bristled, backed farther away from Denise James's desk and looked at the guy from his squad hard.

"You all right, man?" Derrick's gaze shot between Michael and Denise. "You ain't having another episode, are you?"

"No, he's not all right," Neecy said, annoyed at the intrusion and folding her arms over her chest. "He's sick, ain't feeling good, but Cap says he has to pull a double tonight. You should see if you can work his shift to give the man a break—dang."

Derrick nodded and relaxed, but offered Mike a sly smile. "I feel you, man. But if you don't want the overtime, I'll work a double-bubble for you. Cool?" Derrick sighed and gave Neecy a wistful glance. "Shit, unlike you, I'm married, got kids to feed and my woman is always bitching about money."

" 'Preciate it, man," Michael said, feeling relief waft through him. Yeah, it was definitely time to go home. The sun dropped early in the winter. His boy was about to get a bone snatched out of his ass for interrupting a hunt. Might not have been so bad if Derrick wasn't like him—a big, burly mother—but the brother had just a little bit too much testosterone to be rolling up on him like that without warning.

More steady now, Michael remembered his motive for coming into the station. "It's flu season, my stomach is all jacked up and I need to go home."

"Whatever, man," Derrick said, beginning to walk away. "Tell Cap I'll cover your shift, and then you can take your evil ass home and drink some Thera Flu." Derrick stopped and gave him a wink. "Or do whatever else you need to do to chill out. I gotchure back."

Michael nodded, glanced at Neecy once and began walking toward the captain's office. No drama. Not today. He could feel every female's eyes on him as he passed secretaries and desk cops. It was like they were turning and staring at him in slow motion. Their bodies gave off more heat than usual, left an infrared glow that fused with their scents. Damn, they all smelled so good . . . By the time he got to Captain Thomas's office, he had a headache and was hungry as hell.

"Don't even ask me, Adams," the captain said without looking up. "You take off once a month like you've got a fucking period, and you're out of sick time, so save the story—you're working tonight."

He looked at the top of the captain's gleaming bald scalp, wondering which fist could more quickly smash the man's brown-melon head. "I have a condition, and you know my doctor said—"

"Look, I don't care about being politically correct or whateva." The captain glanced up. "All I know is, you're jacking up my schedule. So, whether or not you've completed your anger-management classes, have a group therapy meeting or a fancy note from your female doctor, who you've probably slept with to get a hall pass, tonight coverage is mandatory—"

"D said he would work my shift," Michael argued. He could feel his voice come out close to a snarl, and glimpsed the setting sun.

The captain narrowed his glare. "Derrick Montague would clone himself and work three shifts at the same time if he could. That's not the point, Mr. Hotshot. Been promoted too many times too early for your own arrogant damned good. There's already a short-age, and some nutcase is out there butchering women on the stroll in the high-rent district. We need to bring this shit to a conclusion before the media jumps on it and the mayor and city council start bringing additional pressure we don't need. You're the best I've got for night detail, sad to say, so this is a skills matter. I just don't want a body filling a suit; I want somebody who can bring this perp in. If you take off tonight, don't say another word, just hand me your shield."

Michael felt fury ripple through him. As long as that foul shit was going on in Baltimore, it wasn't exactly his business. But now something was hunting in his territory? Most times, his own kind would quietly take care of rogues to keep their clans on the DL. Humans were off limits; there was plenty of livestock on the hoof already butchered. This didn't make no sense.

He leaned down to stare at Captain Thomas, bracing his hands on the desk. "When did the body come in?"

"About an hour ago," the captain said, shaking his head. "Homicide is on it, but I want someone from vice on this, too. You know the politics."

"Yeah, I do," Michael muttered. "You got photos?"

The captain cast a manila folder across the desk and waited while Michael reviewed what was left of the body. From what he could tell, the redheaded female looked to be nineteen or twenty, but something had torn out her throat and opened up her midsec-tion, leaving entrails everywhere, and then ripped flesh from her once-shapely thighs. No, it didn't make sense, not when there were fully stocked meat-processing plants and butcher shops every-where these days. Raw beef was available in high supply down on 9th Street at the Italian Market and by the waterfront. Disgusted, Michael closed the folder and shoved it back toward the captain. That was not what the female body was for. Such a waste.

"Did the crazy SOB leave DNA evidence?"

The captain nodded. "All over the place." He pushed his pudgy frame up from his chair. "Hair, nails. Looked like he practically shaved in bed, and splattered everything in the room like he was pissing a border around it. Left enough sperm all over the bath-room to—"

"Now the shit is *personal*," Mike said, beginning to pace back and forth. He was mad enough to howl, but checked himself. "Not in my yard!"

The captain stared at him for a moment. "Glad you're suddenly feeling better and are ready to sniff out this case."

"Damn, baby," Neecy said, panting, and dropped her head forward to rest on the pillows for a moment. Her arms trembled and finally gave out under her, leaving only her behind risen for him. "You gonna kill me if you don't stop. I thought you weren't feeling good."

Michael cocked his head to the side as the dark thought slid through his mind, exited, and the sensation passed. He studied her high, wet ass as he pulled out, holding the rim of the condom. His daddy didn't raise no fool; it wasn't about leaving a bunch of pups up and down the eastern seaboard, no matter how good the tail was.

He kissed one of Neecy's plump butt cheeks, slapped it just for the hell of it as he rolled away and allowed his hand to trail down the slit between them, the scent of raw female sex making him temporarily shut his eyes. "I'm still on duty and gotta get back to work. Whatchu got to eat in here?"

"I can fry you up some chicken, or—"

"Whatchu got already thawed out? I only do chicken as a last resort. You know that."

"Nothing really," she admitted, and flopped down on the rumpled sheets. "I didn't know you'd be stopping by, since you never give me any—"

"Girl, don't start sweatin' me about a commitment or my schedule. You know how I roll and what this is. All I asked you was—"

She held up her hand to stop his argument, and sucked her teeth and rolled her eyes at him. "All right. Fine. We can order in, if—"

"I ain't got time," he snapped, practically barking at her. He closed his eyes, stood and tried to mellow his next response. It wasn't her fault, and Neecy had been very, *very* sweet this afternoon. She was a much better option than the other, high-maintenance women he could have gone to see. Michael took a deep breath and let it out slowly. "It ain't you; it's the case. Look, don't get all salty on me, my bad. You got a microwave?"

"Yeah, baby, sure." Her smile returned, and the hurt look on her face slowly faded.

"You got anything in the freezer worth defrosting?"

She hesitated. "I don't do a lot of red meat, but might have—"

He held up his hand and found his clothes, too done for words. What was wrong in America? People didn't do the basic food groups any more! "Next time I fall through, I'll bring you some real groceries."

Oh, yeah, it was time to go. Every man knew you didn't feed 'em if you was gonna leave 'em. The statement was a lapse. He'd almost messed up by promising groceries, and this was *not* permanent.

"I'm sorry," she said, gathering up the sheets close to her body. "Baby, if you want a steak, or lamb chops, pork chops . . . sheeit, after what you just laid down, brother, say the word. I ain't mad at you." Neecy sighed, and snuggled back against the pillows. "Six-foot-four, two hundred and forty pounds worth of chocolate thunder—hell yeah, I shoulda figured you didn't do yard bird or bird food."

"Do I ever?" He chuckled, discarding the used latex in her wastebasket. Now, that was more like it. His way or the highway.

"Half the time, you don't stay long enough to eat, and never really take me out, so how would I know?" She gave him a sheepish glance that made him smile wider as her eyes trailed down his body and lingered on his exposed, still-hard groin. "But your ass is so fine, I put up with the nonsense. That ain't right."

While she spoke the truth and the compliment was nice, her food descriptions had almost made him drool. Tonight a cheese steak wouldn't cut it; she was beginning to look more delectable than necessary, so he was out. "Next time," he muttered, knowing there wouldn't be a next time this month. But the gracious sister had taken the edge off, so he needed to chill.

"You coming back tonight?"

"Yeah, probably," he lied, then again, maybe. He glanced at her as he pulled on his pants and put on his shoes. Neecy was built for the punishment, even though no human female had ever been able to take his full length. But, as human females went, she did have plenty of nice assets: short corkscrew curls that didn't get in a man's way, narrow waist perfect for the grip, thick in the hips, fat thighs that touched when she stood up, an *unbelievable* ass and small, cone-shaped breasts that perked high, plus the girl sounded like she could cook. "I don't like my meat overdone, though," he said, hedging, fighting against the instinct to return to where known primal pleasure resided.

"Okay," she whispered, drifting off to sleep. "I'll put a half a side of beef in the fridge if you promise to come back through here like this again later."

All right, see, now it was on. Everybody with this lupine condition knew that a man's territory was a man's territory. You didn't piss in another man's yard—it wasn't done. There were basic rules of clan conduct, unless it was time to square off. Mating season wasn't till the spring, and last he'd checked, there wasn't an available female with his same problem in the state. So, there was no reason for some stray bastard to cross Pennsylvania lines.

Matter of fact, the few in the region within his pack were all cool and had spread out through Amish country, the Poconos and up near Penn State, where his daddy had been made. He'd won the badlands in Philly fair and square in the last pack standoff. His brothers had all gone down to North Carolina and down toward Florida, and this wasn't their style anyway. The moon wasn't up yet, hadn't crested full, but he was gonna howl at that sucker tonight!

He pulled his Crown Victoria over on 6th and Spring Garden, shut off the engine and locked the car. On foot was the only way to pick up a scent. Technology was simply bullshit that got in the way—but, damn, he was hungry.

Cap said the murder took place in a quiet little bed-and-breakfast in the historic district, around 3rd. Nobody had heard a sound, so this had to have been a lightning-fast, frontal attack while the perp was still in human form. Instinct told him that the rest of the gruesome carnage was from a post-mortem feeding.

The lid was on the case at the moment so the media wouldn't scare off tourists or cause patron alarm. The department had used the ruse to claim that they needed a few hours of quiet air to track the hot lead to the felon. That wouldn't last long, though. Money was always the first consideration, so time was of the essence. He knew that was the way things went down in the town, where you had to pay to play. Whatever. All he knew was that he hated the winter, but still loved being outside, especially at night.

Heavy cloud cover shielded the moon as he walked, his black leather bomber taking the brunt of the elements. It was almost dark. He had to resist the urge to rip his jacket, pants and cable-knit sweater off. He was burning up underneath the fabric; it felt like he was wearing two coats, even in the nineteen-degree temp with a wind chill of minus two. His feet demanded freedom from his shoes. He was designed for the raw elements. The call of the wild was in his bones.

Scents slammed into his consciousness as he continued toward 3rd Street, making his nostrils flare, and he inhaled deeply. The overhead fluorescent streetlights sputtered on and shattered his nerves. Artificial light was nothing like the stars and was a distraction. The darker the better. He could see better then. But the urban jungle had been his choice. Hell, he'd been the one to choose the city as his territory. Maybe later he'd just go for broke in Fairmount Park, but for now, he was working and had to remember that. Cap just didn't understand what this force of nature was like.

As soon as he got to the curb in the Betsy Ross Historic District, he stopped abruptly and stared up at the bed-and-breakfast building. "Oh . . . shit . . ."

Michael tilted his head, closed his eyes and almost howled. He could smell it—*everywhere*. Didn't need to go in, didn't need to pass the crime-scene tape barrier that would be on the fourth-floor hotel-room door. The trail was still hot, and it led down the street to a pub.

He shoved his clenched fists into his pockets and quickened his pace, his attention focused. When he arrived at the tavern steps, the hair on his neck and arms stood up. He pushed through the door with his head and nose held high. His eyesight sharpened, and he almost felt his ears go back against his skull as he entered the dimly lit establishment.

With the grace of a skilled predator, he moved through the after-work crowd, separating out scents, voices from the music, kitchen clatter and general din. He didn't need the Glock 9, which weighed heavily under his bulging arm in its leather holster. The straps holding the man-made iron weapon constricted his chest, felt like a leash, and he could feel his shoulders thicken, the muscles beneath his skin knitting and churning, as he moved toward the source of the scent.

When he saw her, for a moment, he couldn't move or speak. She turned around slowly on a bar stool and glanced up at him from her martini, her smoky eyes holding him where he stood.

"Took your ass long enough to track me," she murmured, and hailed the bartender. "What are you having?"

"You . . . or scotch, whichever comes first." *Damn*, she was *fine*.

She returned a sexy smile without showing any teeth, her lush, red mouth poised over canines that momentarily rose within it and then vanished. It blew him away. He hoped she was alone, or he'd have to fight the sonofabitch that had bedded and fed her in his yard . . . but he could understand how that mighta happened. This woman was definitely worth a body or two.

"Please bring this man a twelve-year-old Dewar's," she said to the bartender, appraising Michael thoroughly while she ordered his drink. She then glanced over her shoulder and issued the poor human male on the stool beside her a sultry look. "You won't mind giving him a seat, will you?"

The businessman stared at her, seeming nearly hypnotized but still conflicted, as though half-indignant and half-ready to oblige her request. But he obviously made his mind up quickly, as he glanced over his shoulder, saw Michael, hesitated for a second, his expression stunned, and slid off his stool.

Michael waited a beat, needing to gather calm before sitting. If the fool challenged him, or accidentally bumped him in passing, in this condition, it was on. Then how would that seem? He glanced around the tavern for evidence of another male of their kind. Seeing none, he temporarily relaxed, lolled his shoulders and approached her.

Finally he sat beside her, picking up the tantalizing scent of her raw animal femaleness, along with blood, flesh and sperm. Now it made perfect sense.

"You turned on him while he was coming and ate the guy, right?" he murmured under his breath.

"Yeah," she said with a shrug. "He was her john. Wasn't very good in bed. Didn't have a lot of respect for women. What can I say?"

"Where's the body?"

She sipped her martini carefully and chuckled low in her throat. "Wasn't much left. I was really hungry. Hadn't eaten since Baltimore."

"Where's the body?" Michael repeated low in his throat.

She seemed nonplussed by the threat of his tone, which momentarily disarmed him.

"Oh, okay . . . I dragged it up to the roof and buried it in the tennis-court hedges." She offered him a sexy smile, allowing the martini to wet her mouth. "Satisfied?"

"We're not supposed to do humans anymore. Remember the oath? That bull got a lot of us hunted to near extinction. Very uncool."

"It was my time of the month, and he was into child-porn and all sorts of dirty deeds anyway, sooo . . ."

"You got a man?"

He stared at her. She smiled.

"Are you asking, did a male lup help me do the takedown to feed me this afternoon?"

He smiled and allowed his gaze to eat her up as it traveled across her voluptuous body. "I could understand it, if that's what went down."

"I'm an independent woman and do my own takedowns. I'm not currently mated, if that's what you really want to know."

He let his breath out hard, accepted his drink and stared down into the short rocks glass. He wasn't sure if it was relief or sheer awe that had made him sigh. All he knew was that it was getting hard to breathe sitting next to her. But, girlfriend was still way out of order.

"I hear you, baby," he finally coaxed his voice to say, "but the chick . . . that was really over the top—"

"An accident," she whispered, gazing up at him with a dazzling, innocent look in her eyes. She placed her hand over his arm and stroked it in a meaningful way, causing him to briefly stare down at it. "She came into the bathroom and got in the way. I was going to pay her and just see her out of the room, first, and then finish eating. But she barged in to do the three-way he'd paid her for, so I had to take her down before she even screamed. You know how humans are; she would have freaked when she saw him dead on the floor. I had to do her. Her scream would have started a wolf hunt. You know how things happen in a split second on a hunt. My natural survival instincts kicked in, and before I knew it, her throat was gone."

She patted his arm and looked up, then covered his hand with her own and squeezed it, her big brown eyes searching his face for understanding. "It was fast and painless. Then I had to make it look like a crazed human male did it to keep the authorities off my trail." She smiled. "Then, again, I was hoping you'd show up."

Her smooth, warm hand was melting his, just like her deep brown eyes were liquefying him on the bar stool. "I am a cop, and the authority in this—"

"I know. My bad," she murmured, cutting him off. "I figured if I marked the perimeter, it might make *you* investigate. It was his bladder, not mine. Relax. But, listen, can we get out of here?"

What could he say as he stared at her gorgeous, almond-shaped eyes, which were the color of midnight, allowing his gaze to rake her high cheekbones and deep mahogany complexion, which didn't have a mark on it? He owed Captain Thomas a steak dinner for sure, even though part of him knew he'd been set up by this sister. He knew it like he knew his name; she was hunting him.

He had a decision to make. Her silver fox coat was leisurely draped over her shoulders, and her thick, dark brown, velvety hair nearly fused with it. But the coat couldn't hide her body. This woman was the definition of "fine." *This* was what he'd been talking about. Tall, leggy, doing a little black dress to death, with cleavage to make even a human male howl at the moon.

Oh, yeah. They could definitely get out of there. He tossed down his drink without a word and stood, just so he could see her walk out of the joint in front of him. She picked up her small, black-beaded clutch bag and glimpsed at him as she slid off her stool, uncrossing her long silky legs with purpose. Mesmerizing.

As she strode ahead of him, his imagination didn't disappoint. This sister was gonna make the hair grow on his knuckles before it was all over. Baby *had back* . . . shit.

"You wanna go to the park . . . to talk about this in private?" she said in a low rumble that came up from her chest.

"Yeah, we can do that," he said, bending to nuzzle her neck for a moment as they loped away from the tavern. "Damn, you're fine. Where'd you come from again? Baltimore?"

"Out West. Baltimore was a pit stop." She threaded her arm around his waist. "Where's your car?"

He smiled. "You need one?"

She laughed, leaving his side. "I told you, I'm not from around here. How far is it?"

"Maybe five miles tops." He could feel a sly smile ease along his mouth. Oh, man, to run with *her* under the moon. But he'd gained a healthy respect for traffic, ever since one of his brothers had tangled with an eighteen-wheeler and lost on the Jersey Turnpike, chasing tail.

She waved him away and glanced at an alley, then looked down at her strappy, black stiletto heels. "That's not far without these."

This woman was lethal. An alley could work right about now, but a sister like that deserved better. He already loved the sound of her voice, and almost passed out when she took off her shoes. She did it one at a time, real slow and sexy, then stood on tiptoes on the cold ground and raised one foot up like it was injured. Once she transformed under the moon, he knew she'd be stunning. The car would be faster, but a flat-out run would be awesome. Conflicted, he hesitated, something he rarely did.

"You hungry?" He couldn't stop looking at her or at the way her fur coat whipped about her legs in the wind. A sister like this needed prime rib, hot off the bone, dripping. He could feel his jaw beginning to pack tight, and he rubbed it as he continued to look at her, trying to figure out what gifts to lay at her feet—all the while knowing she was becoming the beginning of his many problems. Uhmm, uhmm, buddy, his daddy ain't lie—a woman like this would open your nose and make you hunt bear.

"I've already eaten, thank you," she said coolly. But there was a sense of merriment in her eyes, a bit of naughty intrigue as she shifted her weight from foot to naked foot.

"Right, I forgot," he said, chuckling low in his throat. "And now you're gonna make me work OT to have it look like a mob hit or something. I hope you dumped what was left in the Delaware River, if you didn't bury all the bones up in the tennis pavilion?"

"Of course, silly." She smiled, but allowed her voice to dip to a dangerous octave. "I'm sorry about the poor girl. I've never done anything like that in my life. She was hooked on drugs, had a whole lot of problems, and maybe this put her out of her misery?"

It still wasn't right, and that disturbed him deeply. That reality tempered his libido. The john, yeah—he could see offing a twisted bastard like that. A child-porn freak, whatever, the world was better off. Now he'd have to find a mob pimp, pin this whole shit on him and locate some poor pit bull to say the bodies had been fed to the dog to settle an outstanding debt. Which would mean some helpless animal would be put down by Animal Control to clean up this sister's mess. The only saving grace in any of this was that she'd help him bust a ring that targeted children. Still . . .

"Was the chick helping with the kiddie-porn operation?" He needed something to cling to.

"Yes, if that's what you wanna hear?" Her answer was breathy, sultry, causing a desire shudder.

Again, he could only stare at her. All his life he'd been telling women what they'd wanted to hear, just so they'd do what he needed at the moment. Her story sounded weak, even as his mind processed it, but it was so hard not to allow the probable lie to justify what he really wanted to do right now. "You sure?"

"Do I look like the kind of woman who doesn't have a heart?"

Oh, shit, she was awesome. Working his ass to the marrow, and he knew it. Was her coat silver or dark like her hair, he wondered. One could never tell with women. Especially lupine women. And one *like this* had never strayed over his borders and into his yard before. She was fine enough to make a confirmed bachelor settle down for life. He'd had one of his own kind only a couple of times, back when he was young and foolish, and almost lost his life for the trouble. He'd learned by experience not to mess with one of the big dawgs' women. But now that he was a big dog himself, and she'd wandered onto his porch . . .

"Are we gonna stand out here all night, or go play?" She gave him a pout. "I'll help you clean up and put your nose on the evidence trail, if it'll make you feel better."

His mouth was going dry. Maybe she was telling the truth. Please, Lawd, let her be telling the truth. Still, there was this problem of how two bodies dropped on his watch at a historic B&B. He could feel her hesitate, growing unsure, while at the same time the anticipation around her was thick enough to gnaw through.

"Let's go by car," he finally said, hating that her smile had slightly melted away while he was deciding. "It's not like out West on the plains, baby, or in the Sierras. Out here you can find yourself road pizza. Beautiful as you are, I'd hate for that to spoil the night."

She sighed and put on her shoes, and waited. "Never mind. You don't seem in the mood for a run. Maybe I'll just go back home and—"

"Naw, baby . . . uhm . . . see, I just needed to be sure, because it's my job and all . . . and, uh, you don't have to leave just yet, do you? I'm not accusing you, just asking questions."

His heart was pounding hard enough to make his ears ring. You slow, you blow, and he didn't want this fine thing to go anywhere, especially *not tonight*. Now, true, he still had his pride, wasn't gonna let no woman just work him like that, but as she turned to walk away, pride was breaking him down hard.

"Look, for real, let's just talk." He held up his hands, forcing the tremor out of his voice, and tried to hold his ground. "We do things a little different in Philly, that's all."

"I know. It's so different out here. Not a lot of room to just privately get your run out." She sighed, cast her gaze up to the still hiding moon and closed her eyes.

That's the moment he knew he was done. Her head back, lupine profile lit by streetlamps, coat flowing in the wind . . . oh, shit, he *had* to get with her tonight.

"Do you ever feel like your natural instinct is making you crazy?" she whispered with her eyes still closed.

He swallowed hard. She shivered, wrapped her arms around herself and looked at him like she could eat him alive.

"Yeah. All the time." He knew exactly what she meant, and he draped his arm over her shoulders, enjoying how she snuggled up against him. "But you can't just drop a body real obviously either. In fact, you have to be smooth, do the meat houses and leave live kill for deer country—understand?" It was a compromise.

He laughed when she snarled and nipped at him but didn't answer. "Yeah, yeah, yeah, but nowadays, there's shit like forensics, okay? You have to be cool."

"I don't even know why I bothered to come out here then?" She gathered her coat closer and broke his hold on her as she quickened her pace toward his car.

"Well, if you don't like how we roll in Philly, then why'd you come out here?"

"Because where I'm from, our kind, well, they're all getting old, are already mated, and a lot of the good ones have been hunted to death." There was a hint of desperation in her eyes. "The human males are all dawgs—*they cheat*. They don't pair and mate for life. Once they marry, they *still* cheat. Can you believe it?"

"Girl, you know how they are," he said with a shrug. But as he kept staring at her, he realized that the sound of her voice was a little more strident than necessary, if not bordering on hysteria. "You can't be more than twenty-five or so, and settling down is—"

"Is what we all want in the long run." Sudden moisture filled her eyes and made them prettier. "I'm the only sister of twelve brothers, and I don't want to be . . ." Her voice was filled with emotion as it trailed off. "I had to leave home at my first heat, and I've been on my own since ranchers shot my mom. I can't go home unmated. Not till my last brother is gone. The scent makes them overly aggressive, and I don't want them to go to jail or worse. Other females won't let me near their perimeters until I'm mated. Human males aren't . . . I just can't tolerate . . . why are you making me explain?"

He nodded with appreciation. *Twelve brothers*, and she was the only female in the house? Aw, man . . . No wonder girlfriend was on the run. And what fool would be stupid enough to show up on her daddy's porch to go through old battle rights to claim her?

"Where, exactly, out West are you from?"

"Kansas," she murmured. "Cattle country."

Why did he even ask? Yeah, it was a bitch being out there by yourself as a lup, dealing without a pack, no real den, living a double life, but he wasn't making no commitments—not tonight. He was not going to Kansas. Not.

"Your pop, uh, is he old school? Still believes in asking for a sister's hand the old way?"

"Yeah," she admitted sadly. "He's from the last of the old clans, stands about six-nine, weighs about three hundred and twenty pounds and is *very* old fashioned. I couldn't even date till I finished high school, and he used to lock me in the cellar when the moon turned full. They broke the mold." She looked up at him with hope shimmering in her hypnotic eyes.

Oh, man, this was not good. See, he wasn't down for this—her pop was no joke. Michael massaged his neck and just listened. True, if he had a daughter as fine as her, he'd be the same way—all lup males were. But still. Being on the other side of that equation wasn't the place to be. *The old brother was six-nine?*

"He was gonna ship me to the Caribbean, where's there's still a lot of us, or to Africa—but the men there are thinning out," she said, her beautiful eyes capturing and haunting him. "A lot of them are sick. He said maybe Canada, over where the arctic hunts are still really good. Before I came here, I was in Alaska for a while. Beautiful country. Last resort is Europe, to the Black Forest. I don't want to go, though. All my girlfriends are here." She looked him up and down, her tone becoming more urgent, yet gentler. "But, you're six-four, I don't know, what—like two-fifty? And you're young. You could take him, couldn't you?"

Him? Right. Take a six-foot-nine male lup weighing three-twenty or thereabouts, one that was fired up under the moon, ready to kill, had righteous fury in his eyes for his daughter's honor? Oh, no. This wasn't the Dark Ages anymore. That's why he'd come to the urban environment, was trying to blend into human life, and he wasn't even trying to go out like that.

"Baby, you don't even know me. I mean, for us to get all tight so fast, and be meeting each other's people, it's—"

"I know you better than you think I do," she said softly. "I've been watching you for a long time. You're a lone lup, like me. Plus, you're a cop—"

"See, that's just it. I'm supposed to uphold the law, and girl, you've broken so many of them, I can't begin to—"

"Which means you were drawn to the profession because you have some integrity. You've made detective and are still young, which also means you have to know how to hunt, can fight, can drop a body and have a work ethic."

Her smile felt like it was licking a shiver down his spine. She was turning him on so hard with the truth, he almost winced. Her voice was making him cock his head to the side and stare up at the sky. Heaven help him.

"I was just looking for a decent, honorable man to date. One who might want a relationship, if compatibility presents itself. What more does a woman need in a mate? You've got a built-in serve-and-protect instinct, can feed a family both ways—by human cash and by our way, meat. We can find out the little details later, like what music you like, conversation, sports, whatever. As long as the basics are covered, the rest is manageable for most females. Is that wrong?"

He said nothing. He had to regain his composure, not blow his cool. Her quest was insane. Just because she was the marrying kind didn't mean he was. Sure, he wanted to get with her tonight, but wasn't down with all the rest of the drama. Right now, all he could do was look at her hard as he thought up a way to extricate himself from a sure trap.

Anyway, realistically speaking, even if her old man was fifty or sixty years old, he'd get his ass kicked for sure! Naw. Women didn't take realities like that into account. Mortal combat? Uh, uh. This wasn't even a conversation that he'd heard. He was a free agent, a lone wolf. It wasn't about getting tied down, feeding an entire pack of hungry mouths, taking out the trash, having his male freedom revoked or anything crazy like that. No choker chain for him, nosiree. He didn't even know how this discussion came up. But, damn, she was fine . . .

"You're young, plus it's not even spring yet. That's why I can't figure out why the rush—"

"I should have gone to the old countries, like Haiti, or somewhere our ancient ways are still appreciated!" She began to walk away, shaking her head and waving her arms.

He'd taken too long to respond. He knew it, and knew what came next. Michael let his breath out in a weary sigh and leaned against his car, distancing his emotions as he listened to her rant, trying to remain cool and dispassionate. Yeah, he wouldn't arrest her—she was too awesome for that. Her kill had been pretty. And no matter what lies he told himself, he knew he couldn't drag her into the station in cuffs. He didn't have it in him to battle with her in the streets; they'd end up screwing in the middle of traffic, possibly stuck together, the way he was feeling tonight. So, the best bet was to let her take her wild ass back to wherever she came from. And true, the more pissed off and snarly she got, the sexier she became, but he wasn't dealing with this off-the-hook female either.

"Lupine men aren't what they used to be," she said, continuing to rail. Her voice was nearly strangled as she sputtered her complaint. "Nobody will come to your door, court you like they're supposed to and bring a pound of flesh to your clan as a good faith offering, or face your family with honor—but I thought *you'd* be different. Silly me."

"Girl, please," he said with bravado. "This is the *new* millennium. *None* of us do that anymore." He opened his arms to the sky. "Be serious. Meeting people's fathers, facing off in duels. That shit went out with high-buttoned shoes." He dropped his arms in frustration and sent his gaze out into the darkness. Obviously, he wasn't getting any tonight. Just his luck to run up on a superfine but old-fashioned lup. The situation was so ludicrous, he almost laughed through the brimming tears. The sister was wasting time. Damn, the moon was *righteous*, baby. Please, have a heart.

"And to think I tracked *you* halfway across the country, and for what? To be humiliated in the street, just totally turned away on a full moon?" She opened her arms and looked up at the sky. "I'm done. I've never been with a lup male in my life, and I'm *done*. I'll settle for a mere human, raise my children the best I can, alone, and curb my nature. Fine." She looked at him, rage making her glittering tears a beacon. "But I would have loved, just once, to let my hair down and get a full run out with a male like you. My. Bad."

Her impassioned confession was his undoing. It was unraveling the rational part of his mind. When she turned away, glanced over her shoulder and then murmured the next statement, he almost transformed to full wolf on the spot.

"Do you know what it's like to go into a lup heat and not be able to be with one of your own? Just once . . . I wanted it like that. I'll lose my mind if another spring passes without a mate."

That was it. All common sense shredded. He grabbed her arm, turned her around hard, holding her shoulders, and pressed her against his car. Before he could stop himself, he'd lowered his mouth to hers. He could feel her teeth thicken within her jaw as their tongues dueled. "Just tell me where they made you, and I'll go there with you, girl . . . no lie."

The moment he said it, he knew he'd live to regret it, because she fused to his body like a handmade sheath. Oh, yeah, just once— an available female without boundaries. Right about then, the clouds began to part, and the moonlight hit her first; she was poetry in motion. Her shape-shift was so fucking sexy as she slid out of her clothes to land on all fours, there was nothing left to do but drop his gear and follow her in a flat-out run. What murder case? What job? Screw traffic and her daddy, he was on her.

Her trail was like a magnet as she dashed headlong toward the park. Screeching SEPTA buses, mass transit, SUVs, four-by-fours, stricken nighttime pedestrians, trucks, whatever—yeah, he'd be road pizza for her, if it came to that. Fight her father and twelve brothers? Okay, this was love. She was right; they could work on the details later. But tonight, shit, he just needed to work on her. He couldn't stop running behind this woman to save his life. She homed to the woods, right off Kelly Drive, near the water . . . in the dark. Just call my name, princess, and I'm there!

She was silver in the moonlight, eyes the color of glowing bronze, and when she threw her head back and howled, her voice ran all through him from two miles away. She was dodging him, leading him in circles, refusing to come out of hiding, each call driving him crazy.

It was beyond instinct. Her lonely cry was a pleasure-coated stab to his groin. The forlorn wail traveled up his shaft and ravaged his senses. She had awakened the beast inside him, the procreation imperative. Anything that came between him and her tonight he'd slaughter. He needed her so hard, he was going blind—anything not giving off infrared heat, he couldn't see. Anything that wasn't her sound, he blocked out and wasn't trying to hear. Anything except that wondrous fragrance she sent into the air with her call, he couldn't smell. If another male had locked in on her and was crazy enough to go for her, mortal combat would result. He took a high position on a ridge, threw his head back and rent the night. *Sweet Jesus, where you at, baby? I'll make it all right, I promise.*

Her reply went under his coat, got all into his skin, sent ecstasy prisms through his loins, made him holla and chase her even harder. *Oh, shit, just once with this one.* He was panting. He'd transformed many a night, *but never like this.* Yeah, this fine lupine he could marry. This one would keep him honest, penned in. Aw, Lawd, let her be willing and not run home to her daddy!

Panting, frantic, his howl echoed after hers, creating a fervent call and response that made dogs from distant alleys join in. Freedom be damned, he knew the moment he found her, the moment he slid against her and she fit him like a glove. Her whimper told him all he'd needed to know: She hadn't lied. If so, it didn't matter, he'd lie to himself for the both of them. She'd never had a heat with another lup. Tight, slick, wanton, wet female. Her first full belly needed to be loaded with his seed. He'd take care of whatever he made, *just don't stop moving under the moon.*

He came so hard the first time that he almost bit his own tongue. Then she was gone, had slipped from beneath him while he was semidazed and had set him on her trail again.

Nose to the ground, he was on it. Once was not enough. She couldn't go home, not yet—not now. He could not lose this woman; she was the one. That was no lie. And, naw, his daddy hadn't lied either. There was a fragile breaking point when a lupine male just lost his nat'chel mind. Tonight he'd left his somewhere out in Fairmount Park; it had to be floating down the Schuylkill River—'cause he couldn't get up off this woman if they put a crossbow to his head. The old man told him there'd be one out there, one day, or night, that would bring him to his knees and tame the wild in him. One woman, one howl that he'd answer to any time he heard it. It would put him on all fours, make him stupid nuts. Make him promise her the moon, and anything else she wanted to go with it. Yeah, no lie.

It was the deepest truth of his kind, 'cause, like his daddy had warned, that's where he ultimately wound up. On his knees on his bedroom floor, stuttering, slobbering on himself, his face pressed against her supple back, no condom, sweating like a dog, getting it so serious and so hard that he thought he'd have a seizure.

Never had a woman smelled so good, felt so good, or ever been able to hang like this—take him all the way to the hilt, matching him lunge for lunge, panting and hollering, till he could barely breathe.

When she made him stop for a minute so she could get some water, panic claimed him. There was no such word as "stop." Stop? Was she crazy? Now? He almost followed her into the bathroom, even though he knew that's how the guy before him had died. But it was an animal thing not to let her out of his sight while hoping for just one more shot, hoping to coax her to stay in his townhouse, having left a stack of raw meat at her feet.

He watched her graceful strides as she crossed the floor—her shapely legs moving in a slow lope, her full breasts swaying while she stooped to eat—and then shape-shifted again back into wolfen form. And the way she did it was so awesome that it made his erection throb harder. She was beyond comparison. "Magnificent" was the only way to describe her as she ate, delicately licked her paw and then casually changed back into human form right before his eyes.

"You made me rob half a meat warehouse for you, baby, just to coax you back to my den," he rumbled, stalking toward her, not sure which form of her he enjoyed most.

She shrugged, and picked at an uncooked piece of filet mignon with two dainty fingers. "Aren't I worth it?"

He shifted his shape, coming to her on his hands and knees as a man, nuzzling her waist. Her taut, cinnamon-colored nipples drew his attention. "Yeah. Definitely." His hands skimmed the surface of her damp, dark skin, reveling in the silken texture of it. Everything about her was like velvet, just like her silvery lupine coat. He stroked her hair and let it fall between his fingers, just staring at it. "You are so beautiful."

"Where is this going, though, Michael?" She looked at him, her eyes searching his face. "I don't want to be used. In the long run, I want a real relationship."

He blinked twice. Trouble. "Uh, baby, why don't we just—"

"No," she said, her upper lip beginning to curl into a snarl. "I'm different, not like those hoochies you can just tell any ole shit to and it's okay. My girlfriend's cousin in Vegas said you were out there one summer, and messed with her *married cousin*, and—"

"I know, I know. See, what had happened was, I went out there with my brothers, she was in heat, her husband was old and—"

"That don't make it right!" She folded her arms over her chest and glared at him.

He looked out the window. Damn . . . the moon was still full, his dick was still hard . . . true, he'd acted a pure fool out in Vegas, but he couldn't think about anything like that right now. Not while the moon was still full anyway. "C'mon, baby, that was a long time ago, and—don't be like that."

"They warned me about you. All of them did," she said, her voice quiet and laced with attitude. Tears of disappointment glittered in her eyes. "You can't even give me half a commitment, can you? I let you be the first lup because . . . well, when you changed, had that deep, sexy voice, could hunt, had a good job . . . jet black coat," she looked at his feet and chuckled sadly. "Huge paws . . ." She looked up from the floor, her voice faltering. "You stand fucking three and a half feet at the shoulders! What was I supposed to do? And to think, I wanted to have your children! We're both from the same clans!"

She was on her feet in an instant and headed for the door, naked, tears streaming down her lovely face. He didn't even know her name! How did he find himself in this predicament? That was the fifty-million-dollar question. He had two bodies to pin on a pimp mobster, a very fine lupine female in tears about to go into her first heat and a slew of human females blowing up his cell phone most likely—wherever it had landed when the moonlight hit him—not to mention, Neecy was gonna pitch a bitch in the station and be salty forever because he never came back to her place tonight.

"Wait, wait, wait, wait, wait," he said, blocking her exit with his body and opening his arms wide in self-defense. "You hunted me down, stalked *me*, left a trap filled with human remains, remember—on a full moon, girl, in the winter, when a brother can't hardly get none from experienced females in the territory without getting his chest ripped open." His hands found her shoulders, but she flinched away. "I didn't know it was like that, that you were feeling some type of way, and Lawd knows, you're fine and everything, but . . . I mean, we sorta talked about it earlier, but—"

"You couldn't spend the rest of your life with me," she said flatly.

"Baby, we just met," he said, trying to bring reason into the standoff.

"With our kind, is there much more?" She looked at him hard. "We meet, sniff each other out, sync up age-wise, test each other's hunting skills and, if there's chemistry, then we mate under the moon, and it's permanent. You know lups don't play games with each other, especially with spring in the offing—so?"

"Aw'ight, true, but see . . . what I'm trying to say is, uh . . ."

"Fine. It's over. I'll just shape-shift back, go get my clothes, and I'm going home."

"Just like that? Tonight?"

"Yes. Tonight."

He stared at her. The woman's body could stop traffic on Broad Street. Her threat of leaving now was definitely stopping his heart and his argument.

"Look, baby, let's eat, calm down and talk about it."

She folded her arms, her eyes blazing. "You are not *ever* mounting me again, hear? So, there's nothing to talk about. And, when I go into heat this spring, don't call me, understand? I ain't answering no howls, don't want to hear jack shit, okay? You call those human bitches of yours, and see if they can do for you what I just did, all right? Because all I know is, I came to you, found you, gave you my all, but you wanted—"

"No, no, no, you got it all wrong, baby." He stood, arms opened wide, in front of the door, still body blocking her. Her threat was real, and it was giving him a nervous tick. The long, lonely, howling days of spring stabbed at his mind. Summer would be even worse. Last year he'd almost lost a limb messin' with a chick from Georgia who already had a big dog on her porch. "Don't you know I love you, girl? C'mon, now, why you wanna act like this?"

"You love me?" Her voice dipped to a calmer octave, a throaty pitch that stroked his groin.

"Yeah, you know that." He nodded toward the carnage of beef on the floor. "I don't do that for everybody."

"For real?"

He shook his head no. "Never did, before you."

Her hot body neared his, making a slight shudder run through him. "You ain't lying?"

"No," he murmured. "It just sorta went down kinda fast."

"You gonna marry me?"

He raked his fingers through his close-cropped hair and hung his head. He could feel her bristle and begin to turn away. But he opened his arms before she could. "Yeah, boo, I mean, I was gonna . . . do it right, and uh," he glanced at the sky through the window. "Baby, stop playing while the moon is still high, okay? You're compromising my shit, girl."

"Promise, or my daddy will rip your throat out."

He closed his eyes and leaned his head against the door. "That's not right." Say what she would, he still wanted her so badly that his shaft was dripping. "I'm not marrying you because I'm scared of him. I'm agreeing to this because . . ." He looked at her, the moonlight reflecting in her eyes, "because you're one of a kind. Until you rolled up on me, I didn't know it could be like this, didn't know they even made one like you that was available. One that could hunt like

a male, negotiate like one, too . . . and—" Her hand against his
stomach stopped his words. "You want the rock, I'll give you the
rock—but don't threaten me, or rush me, hear?"

"All right. I'm sorry."

"Just tell me your name, girl."

A warm murmur coated his ear. A hot body fused to his. The
moon was his enemy, his tormentor, because this was not at all what
he'd planned tonight. But the woman was fine, the night was a
drug, and what was a brother to do? He couldn't send a woman like
this back out to the streets, or send her out west for some human
bastards to mess over. She was everything he'd always wanted, had
dreamed of, and she was scaring him to death. He was lying to himself when he thought he could make this casual. That became
clearer as she wrapped her legs around his waist and backed him up
against his own door, then blew his mind again till he howled.

"You look like shit," Captain Thomas said with a chuckle. "Rough
night?"

"In a manner of speaking," Michael muttered, and threw a stack
of new evidence on his desk. "I'm in no mood, Cap. Didn't get much
sleep." It didn't help that Neecy wasn't speaking and had simply
rolled her eyes at him as he'd passed her desk. All these females
could take a hike. In the cold light of day, with his head on straight,
he could think clearer, and that new chick wasn't making him do
jack before he was ready. But, if she had only stayed till morning,
hadn't left him all messed around and in an empty bed. His body
still ached for her, and he'd never be able to forget her voice. Shit!
"I'm out, Cap."

"Seems like you were working hard last night, man," Captain
Thomas said, sounding impressed as he looked over the evidence
and not at Michael.

"You have no idea." Michael massaged the tension in his neck.
Sunlight made him squint. Stubble was still on his face. He hadn't
even had time to shave, and was wearing the same clothes he'd left
the station in.

"You wanna make the media statement when we go get this bastard?"

"Naw. But a few days off to rest could work."

* * *

A few days didn't help. Nor did he have any interest in Veronica, Neecy, Angela, Shantae, Melanie or Kim. He simply got a new cell phone, changed his number and worked. That was all there was to do.

The problem was, there was this distant scent still in his nose. Every now and then, it sent a shudder through him. He'd even been so crazy as to hang onto his old sheets, from time to time looking across the bedroom toward the overflowing hamper and inhaling her long-lost scent with a whimper. If she never came back, he'd never wash them. They were a shrine. How could she do him like this?

But he was a man, all-male lup, and wasn't gonna be held hostage by the one who got away. He could tough this out. He wasn't going to no damned Kansas, no matter how horny he got. He wasn't ready to settle down yet. No female was gonna steal his pride and back him into a corner. Uh, uh. Damn, where was she?

Days turned into weeks, and weeks soon became almost a month, and his willpower began to erode with the coming moon. Sleep was impossible, wet dreams for her the norm. He couldn't eat. Didn't shower. Just moped.

Her voice was an old razor, cutting dull and slow and painful in his memory. It got so bad one night that he found himself on his fire escape howling. *Shit, baby, I'm sorry. Call me.* If he wasn't a cop, the neighbors woulda called the police. The day before the new cycle, he was rocking on the edge of his bed, his head in his hands, near tears. Damn, he missed that woman! That night he was so jacked up, he would have mounted anything walking. But that was the problem. He didn't want any ole tail; he wanted hers.

Plus it was almost spring, too. The month of April was gonna kick his ass for sure. She hadn't answered his calls, obviously meant what she'd said. No meant no. Why were women like that—so cold?

The next thing he knew, he was at Philadelphia International Airport with a ticket in hand. How he got there, he wasn't quite certain. All he was clear about was the fact that the moment he touched down in Kansas City and the doors to the plane were opened, he smelled her.

Never in his life had anything so intense rippled through him. It set his teeth on edge, sharpened his senses like a new blade and made him very impatient as he waited his turn for a rental car. By the time he got his keys, he was snapping and barking at everybody. All he had was a first name, a scent and a desire that wouldn't quit.

Now, you have to understand, Kansas is a huge, flat state. One can drive for hours and still be in the same county. But this afternoon, distance wasn't an issue. He didn't need a map, just the windows rolled down to find her.

And, of course, she was way out in no-man's-land. The farmhouse she grew up in was on a lonely section of road that had no markers. He brought his car to a stop in the dust, and breathed in. Her people kept pigs and goats and sheep and cows. Cool.

Although instinct made him want to jump out of the vehicle and rush her door, he had to chill. She'd warned him. Her daddy was old school, and he had no idea how many brothers still remained home on the farm. So he did what any reasonable man would do. He got out slowly, picked up the freshly cut steaks he'd couriered all the way from Philly and advanced with caution.

Instantly, two burly males appeared from the side yard and snarled.

"You here for our sister?" one growled low in his throat.

Michael quickly appraised the smaller of the two males, who stood six-six, wore tattered overalls covering a thick, ebony body and had him by weight and reach. The younger one had a crazy look in his eyes, and his wild, lopsided Afro made him truly appear insane. His biceps bulged under his sleeveless T-shirt, making the wolf tattoo on his swing arm move with a warning. The other male, wearing a blue mechanic's one-piece, whom he hoped was just her brother, was even thicker, taller and darker. He didn't look as crazy, just meaner—scary cool. Sunlight glinted off the grease between each cornrow on his head. Shit. It was now or never, a time when a man had to stand his ground or die trying.

"Yeah," Michael said, adding bass to his voice. He might be dead meat, but at least they'd have to respect him. "I brought something for your pop. She home? My name's Mike."

"She home," the bigger one said. The elder brother glanced at his sibling. "You the guy she met in Philly?"

"Yeah, I'm from Philly." True, he wasn't no punk, but he was wise enough to adopt a semisubmissive tone of voice this time. He watched her brothers sniff out his package from where they stood, their glares almost withering. The taller of the two nodded and, after a while, seemed to relax.

"I'm Bo, dis is James," the elder brother finally said.

"You the one that made our sister cry, and sent her home from back east?" the younger one asked, bristling. "You know that's our boo."

"I came to apologize," Michael said quickly, backing up a bit to give himself lunge range, if it came to that.

"All y'all young pups is all alike," a low, thunderous voice said from behind the screen door, making the three men in the front yard look up toward the porch.

Michael's voice halted in his throat. Pure darkness had filled the doorway to the wood-frame farmhouse. The biggest, burliest, meanest looking dog he'd ever seen slammed open the door, brandishing a pump shotgun. Without being told, he knew it was her father. The scent of silver also told him that the shells in his double-aught were meant to put a lup down, and put him down hard. A golden-eyed gaze narrowed on Michael until he lowered his head.

"Y'all come sniffin' around here in the spring every year, looking for my baby girl. But she ain't like the others, to be messed over and played with. State your intentions, and state 'em clear, boy. I'm old school, and you don't want me to come down offa dis here porch fer yer ass."

"No, sir, you're right. I don't," Michael heard himself say. Survival instinct eclipsed all pride. "I'm not playing with her, sir, or with you. I brought this to make amends. We had a little misunderstanding back in Philly, but I'm not like that. She's—"

"The marrying kind," the old man said through his teeth, glancing up at the waning sun.

"No doubt, and, uh, that's why I'm here."

Quiet filled the yard. All eyes were on Michael. He swallowed hard as the sun dipped behind the trees.

The old man smiled and calmly leaned his shotgun against the porch rail. "You know how this was done in the old days."

Michael nodded and closed his eyes, hoping his bladder would hold. "Yes, sir. I came here with honor, and can take whatever you dish out. She's worth it."

When he heard deep, resounding laughter coming from the old man, he peeped open his eyes, surprised to still be standing and alive.

"So you brought me meat from Philly?"

Michael nodded, and tossed his package forward.

Her father caught it with one hand, sniffed it and turned up his nose. "Boy, we from cattle country. You crazy? This ain't real beef—not like we used to out here. Corn-fed, free-range, c'mon now. I'ma hafta show you how we do out here. Git you some real barbeque."

"I'm sorry. Uh, listen, if you want me to go hunting tonight and bring you back something righteous, I can do that, sir."

Their eyes met. The old man smiled wide, and threw back his head and howled. "Whoooowee! *This one got it bad.* Must be the real McCoy. All right, son. I'ma give you a pass on the old ways, since we are in the new millennium. Won't whup your ass like I oughta for laying your hands on my girl child and making her cry. Only reason I'm not is on account of she so soft on you. Begged me not to pull out a hair on your head, if you did come callin'. Umph, umph, umph. That's still my little girl; can't deny her anything she wants." He whistled through his huge, yellowed teeth. "Lee Lee! Come on out here, girl, and stop making this young fool act simple on my steps!"

Michael held his breath as a shapely female form filled the door. He held back the shudder that ran through him when he saw her. She had on a pair of cut-off jeans shorts that were gonna get him killed. He couldn't look at the white tank top she wore without a bra—not in front of her pop. It felt like the whole yard was closing in on him, and her scent filled the spring air.

"Hi," she said softly. "You meet my brothers and my daddy?"

He nodded, but kept his eyes lowered. "Yeah, and I just came to say, uh—"

"Just spit it out," her father ordered. "Say what you've gotta say before the moon comes up and I have to fucking kill you."

Somehow instinct had put him on his knees in the yard. He wasn't sure how that happened, but he was looking up, she was so pretty standing on the steps behind her dad . . . and the next thing he knew, he was babbling.

"Girl, listen, I can't live without you. I wanna marry you, for real. Just say yes, and come back to Philly with me. I'll take care of you and any kids we have. I got a good job. I work hard. Girl, I'm serious. Come on back, and we'll pick out your ring."

He was expecting a flat-out frontal assault from three huge males, but instead they smiled, howled and went back into the house. Her daddy stayed at the door for a moment, his eyes glowing gold, but he could see a mist forming over them that brought him to his feet.

"She reminds me so much of her mother," the old man said in a slow, calm rumble. "That's all I wanted to hear. Now I can go on and rest." He glanced down at the package in his huge hand. "This Philly meat ain't so bad, I reckon. Just different. You two younguns git." But he looked up from the package slowly, his eyes holding Michael's for a steady, threatening moment. "No, I ain't lying when I tell you, if you hurt her, I'll hunt you down. If I'm long gone and you don't treat her right, know she got twelve brothers who will track you to the ends of the earth to hurt'cha bad. But you treat my baby right, the youngest of mine, and I'm family for life. Will help ya anyway that I can. That's a promise. Word as my bond, old school."

With that, the front door closed, the moon came out of hiding, she sauntered down the steps and slipped into a form that by design would drive him wild. And he found himself running too far too fast into the nearby bushes about a mile away. She'd gone into heat, and he'd temporarily gone insane.

I'ma tell you the truth. It can happen that fast. Snap your fingers, and your glory days are gone.

See how I'm up here, in the suburbs, taking out the trash, right next to average-Joe humans, and driving a minivan? It don't make sense, this thing the female kind got over us. Five kids. Can you believe it? When did that happen? Not that I don't love 'em all, every single one. But *five* kids? Stair steps. All born the same time every year; every spring we swear we're gonna be careful. But, hey, that woman is something else.

And I don't know what you heard, but I don't miss a day at work—like my boy, I can't. I'm begging Cap for overtime any chance I can make it, and I haven't slept with another woman since my wife. Me. Me? I ask you, is there something wrong in the universe?

Not that I would, don't need to go there, my life is complicated enough. And Lawd knows, my wife is beyond compare. And no sister better be off the chain enough to mess with her either. What, and be calling the house for me? Never happen. Y'all know my wife is crazy, right? Leisa is deep. They seem to know not to fool with her, even the baddest of sisters. Shoot, I don't even trip with her like that. She gets a look, and even the kids back off her. She was raised by twelve brothers, can fight like a she-demon, and Daddy Williams don't play. Girlfriend has told my sons more than once that she might eat her young. We don't mess with her. But, if I ever have a girl, that's when you gonna see *me* act ridiculous. Good thing boys run hard in both our families.

All I wanna know is, *when* did I become like my father? Chained to the fence? The brother used to be a playa. He was the one, *da man*. Then, he got married. Now here I am, on a short choker chain like he was. It ain't right.

But, for all the daily drama . . . on those rare nights when the moon is full . . . Aw, man, I love my wife. Natural instinct. That's my boo.

Lord of All That Glitters

Anthony Beal

Tahseen finds the loft-style studio's only windowsill sooty yet cool beneath her backside. That anyone was leasing any part of this warehouse-district four-story was news to her. Local legendry that still surrounds the place and its past as a crematorium had hurt its market desirability as well as that of neighboring addresses, and had kept it largely untenanted for years. Tahseen stretches, arching her bare, sticky back, supposing that perhaps some truth lies in the adage about time healing all wounds. God knows she needs it to be true, after her unexpected performance here tonight.

The night steals a taste of moist skin, its humid breezes lapping reverently at her tender nipples and still-tingling sex. Across the room, the door to the refrigerator where Myles chills beer for visitors hangs open, and Myles, a sinewy masterpiece of angled cinnamon, stands relishing the coolness therein. "A five-minute break," he'd promised her hours ago; then they'd continue the photo shoot. Five orgasms later, the camera lies as forgotten as the clothes she wore here. Phantoms of her photographer's hands frolic over her arcs. Myles licks Tahseen's payment from his lips.

"Delight Your Man With Nude, Sensual You," read the classified ad that lured her here. Tahseen lounges ravaged and sticky, imagining her lover's eyes as he peruses the personalized erotic pictorial that will be her gift to him, every page featuring her Burmese mystique, each picture's thousand words speaking of unabashed lust. On those weekends when his band tours out of town, these photos taken tonight will remind her Andrew that one-night stands make poor substitutes for what exotica awaits his return. They'll testify to Tahseen's devotion to a fiancé she didn't think of once while Myles was inside her.

"Whore," the night whispers to Tahseen, demanding explanation for the taste spicing her tongue, the flavor of the naked man standing halfway inside the refrigerator. Clutching her cardamom-colored shoulders, Tahseen laments her indiscretions tonight. She thinks of Andrew and wants to die. She watches Myles stalk toward her and wants to live.

Accustomed by the benefits of trim ankles, taut buttocks and shimmering black hair to propositions from the lusting populace both male and female alike, she wonders what has compelled her to forego typical casual flirtation for infidelity with *this* man after rejecting countless others. She wonders what makes her already want him inside her again.

More than twenty minutes have passed without a word between them. Myles sweeps cottony, cocoa-colored dreadlocks away from his ruggedly hewn face, stepping over emptied Trojan packages and spent condoms, to hand Tahseen an opened bottle of lager. He holds the bottle just below his waist, near the glossy, espresso column of his cock. Tahseen's hand brushes the taut muscle, lingering as she receives his offering. Draining their bottles in silence, they stare down the accusing night sky as if watching for the arrival of angels come to Hell's Kitchen to punish their abandon.

Tahseen finds herself sweating despite the cooling night. Restless hunger licks her between the thighs, leaving her feverish, starving to fuck again. Squeezed between Myles, her hard-muscled Adonis, and thoughts of Andrew, she contemplates the loaded glare of the moon as Myles's fingers thread through her hair. If there be angels seeking to punish her indiscretions this night, then let them come. Let them arrive to find her every orifice anointed with Myles's seed.

Enough rest, declares her full-body shiver. Tahseen's knees kiss the floorboards. Her molestations claim his firmness. Myles groans, and stiffens as she swallows him.

Her mouth is a womb. Her mouth is an awesome cherry-peel machine reverently wringing forth the sacrament from her lord of licentiousness. His fingers winding her hair into handles, the growing urgency in his thrusts, his furtive oaths wafting away like blue bubbles into the night set Tahseen's skin burning. Bathed in pheromone-laced fucksweat, her brow glistens, feeling scorched with her efforts.

Tahseen's vision swims as Myles' pearlescent tide swells. Washed beyond coherence by his frothing eruption, Tahseen can only grunt her assent as Myles sinks to his knees behind her, presses his chest against her back and impales her anew.

Myles is speaking to her, firing incomprehensible words, the understanding of which her senses insist on deflecting. A strange kind of vertigo has reduced him to a caramel-colored blob. He feels heavy, a slick and burning weight forcing air from her lungs, further bathing her in the pheromone of his sweat and saliva. She smiles through the searing pain assailing her skin as his softening penis withdraws from her anus. Strangely, her unsated feeling lingers. Her thoughts and memories of Andrew do not.

"Thanks, sugar," she would hear, were she capable of understanding. "You're the first meal I've had in weeks. And you were absolutely delicious, without a doubt. You saved my life." Could she see straight, Tahseen would notice something different and discomfiting about his teeth. Inebriated by the bioelectrical emissions he's spent all evening drinking from her orgasms, Myles stands, lifting her along. It is time he finished immortalizing her as his advertisement promised.

The affronted scream of aged gears summoned to action splits the evening's calm as Myles leads her to the elevator cage that carried her to his fourth-floor studio. Tahseen is contented enough to follow wherever he may take her. She doesn't even realize that neither she nor Myles have dressed. It feels too good to be nude right now. His arms around her as the elevator descends to a destination he has not yet shared with her, his lips creeping along her neck feel too good, too right for her to concern herself with asking questions to which answers are surely forthcoming.

"The time has come for a little confession on my part, baby. I confess that I tend to fall in love with all my subjects," the creature wearing Myles' skin says, leading Tahseen nude into the larger of two rooms leading from that black-painted brick one that has served as their fucknest all evening. He says it smiling, that bashful, indicted smile from whence all Tahseen's infidelities sprang; the one that makes him look so unspeakably fuckable. If only she could see it now. She might find herself galvanized by a different set of inclinations, could she view the explosion of crescent-shaped needles currently replacing the pearly whites of which she'd been so enamored upon first meeting him.

"I love my work. Positioning each subject for my cameras, lining up the shots, choosing the props, the backdrops. And please, believe me when I tell you that I sincerely love each lady. Each lady is my passion when she's here, just as you are my passion tonight," he goes on. "When I have them here on their knees, on their backs, in my mouth, I make them glow, and for those few moments, they're mine. *You* are mine. The hard part is having to smile graciously and give you all back to your boyfriends and husbands once a shoot is done."

The brick-walled room they enter is low ceilinged and cozy. Its hardwood flooring is lacquered to a bloodlike hue. Three rows of ivory shelves deck all but one of its four walls, and luxurious blue velvet drapes each of these. Spaced along these velvet-festooned shelves, diamonds of varying shapes and sizes wink at Myles and Tahseen in the meager lighting, not that her eyes are obeying her demands that they focus enough to discern her surroundings. A miniature inscribed gold plate is set before each gem, not that the plates are visible to Tahseen's severely dilated pupils. An expansive and aged-looking iron door is the only adornment reserved for the room's fourth wall, which is composed entirely of firebricks.

The steel sliding tray behind the iron door opening unassisted by anything except Myles' telekinetic direction is human-sized, reinforced to support up to four hundred eighty pounds. Myles hefts Tahseen in his arms and places her upon it. Even as the notion of some wrongness unfolding here breaks upon her, Tahseen's limbs feel too heavy to lift. Even if she could grasp the danger of her situation as more than a fleeting flash skirting the periphery of her mind, she could offer no resistance. The sedative contained in the sweat and saliva of the creature she knows only as "Myles" has anesthetized her too efficiently for her to object to being entombed in bricks.

"You'll glow, too, precious," Myles tells Tahseen, smiling reassuringly with his newer, sharper teeth as he slides her into the gravelike enclosure built into his wall and bolts the iron door closed.

Nourished by Tahseen's energies, Myles is strong once again. Strong enough to ably wield the gifts granted to his species centuries ago. Myles concentrates, murmurs in that dead language that has served him for over a century. Tahseen's scream is a scarring thing that rouses tears to his eyes as spontaneous flames that burn hotter than the most efficient crematorium engulf her.

It occurs to Myles hours later as his mental energies clean out the tomblike space that even her ashes are beautiful. The dead language he speaks as he works extracts carbon from those ashes. No matter how often he commands it, the sight of human detritus shifting and parting and rearranging itself unassisted by his hands always offers him an impressive spectacle. The ageless creature in his skin spends more than an hour working to compress the roiling globule of carbon that forms between his splayed fingertips, crushing, shaping it beyond human capability, visiting hundreds of pounds of telekinetic pressure per square centimeter upon it. Though exhausted, though washed in sweat, the creature soon draws Myles' cheeks wide with its sated grin.

He will not keep the photos he took of Tahseen tonight for keepsakes. They will burn, as do those of all his subjects, as do the subjects themselves. What remembrance could ever compare with the diamond that embodies each woman's feminine essence, the jewel created by the sheer force of his will and sorcery? The gemstone created this night from what precious carbon existed in his latest love is no mere memento of Tahseen. The gemstone upon which the creature known to so many women only as "Myles" places a longing kiss *is* Tahseen—what greater tribute than this could ever honor the woman?

Myles places Tahseen upon the highest shelf at his back. She will rest there, between diamonds bearing the respective nameplates of "Lisa" and "Angelique." Tomorrow, he will fashion a nameplate bearing the name of his collection's most recent acquisition. Tonight however, exhaustion has left him capable of little except sleep.

"Giving my ladies back to lovers who underappreciate them has always been the most difficult, most loathsome part of what I do," Myles ruminates, as if explaining himself to his newest acquisition. "So you see, I've simply stopped giving them back. But here, you'll glow. Here, you, Tahseen, are immortal. Just like me."

Sparse light winks across the surface of the diamond that had been Tahseen. Myles, accepting this as all the affirmation he should ever need, winks back.

Leviathan

Christopher Chambers

LEVIATHAN, n. 1. An enormous aquatic animal described by Job in the Bible (see BEHEMOTH, KRAKKEN). 2. A demon spawned in a man's own mind and fed by his own misdeeds and failings, thusly allowing him to wax blameless for his own torment.
—Ambrose Bierce, *The Devil's Dictionary*

The Portuguese brig *Maria Gômes* was Yankee-built and brand spanking new, having slid down the ways at Baltimore Towne in March 1754. At full canvass, she could slice the water like a razor through supple flesh. But not on this night, so black and moonless. The wind was dead. Weeds enmeshed the ship's keel from bow to rudder, there atop a floating mat of vegetation in the Atlantic Ocean three hundred miles wide, six hundred miles long. The Sargasso Sea.

Not a man wanted to be on deck in that murk, in the stillness, in the unnerving quiet. Yet not a man wanted to be below decks either, as a wicked stench permeated every beam. And below decks it was *never* quiet; each crewman slept with wax plugged in his ears as a buffer against the wails, coughs, whimpers and curses oozing from the cargo hold.

A loud splash off the starboard side and accompanying swell broke the moribund calm. The starboard lookout couldn't discern a damn thing. Another whale perhaps? Cows and calves swam near the sargassum weed, but never into it. Only humans made that blunder, and the mistake was compounded over the past few years as more Portuguese, British, Dutch and Spanish ships tacked the westerly trade winds from Africa's Gulf of Guinea to Braŝil, then north to the Caribbean. The Sargasso Sea swallowed two schooners and another fast brig that year of 1754 alone. But the appetite for the cargo those ships and the *Maria Gômes* carried was voracious in Bahía, Havana, Port Royal, Barbados and the British Carolina and Virginia colonies. Greed trumped common sense. Just before the wind abandoned them, the *Maria Gômes'* crew spotted a whale carcass floating belly-up in the weeds. Hunks of meat had been ripped out of its head and tail. Purplish, circular wounds pocked what was left; each was the diameter of a grog cup. Tiger sharks or orca did it, the sailing master reckoned. Yes, tiger sharks or orca— but didn't they chase only calves? This was a full-grown cow, a thirty-footer.

When a second great splash and heave rocked the *Maria Gômes*, its master ordered muskets and cutlasses passed from the armory. Sailors sent a lime buoy over the side. The fizzling green glow from this floating lamp illuminated only a small radius. It was better than scanning blind. But soon the weed-choked sea quieted once more, save for the thumping of beating hearts on deck.

Several dark fathoms under the keel, a creature's skin tasted the filth leaching from the foundering ship's bilge. This sip was confirmation that there was soft, wriggling food inside that hard wooden shell. And so two eyes, each as wide across as a man's arm, peered upward. A huge, muscular siphon sucked in a hundred gallons of seawater and then expelled it in a jet propelling three tons of horror to the surface.

Muskets had no time to lock, fire. Shouts on deck turned to screams, and then the screams ceased. Masts snapped like twigs, and the hull cracked amidships before sinking toward a rasping maw. And finally, the muffled wails from the cargo hold could be heard in the open air. A few voices sang a prayer. *Ay-Koja, Witch of the Western Sea. Deliver your stolen children from oblivion, quickly and painlessly.*

Yes, death would come swiftly. But it would be painful. Ay-Koja fed well. Exceedingly well.

* * *

Kiriqui Sifua Kiriqui, only nine years old and thus four seasons shy of circumcision, beamed his eye-toothless smile at his father. What an accomplishment for such a little fellow with lanky arms and legs and a protruding belly—presenting his journal as if a true man of science! He had recorded observations over the past two moons: Monkeys on the north bank of the Goma River learned to shake heavy bushia fruit from the high branches and eat it on the ground once the pods landed and split open. On the south shore, the monkeys ate the bushia blossoms rather than the pods, hence they remained arboreal and almost never set foot below.

"And these monkeys are of the same species of crested macaques?" Owuda Sifua Owuda quizzed his son, who nodded intently in reply. "Yet the south monkeys are indolent and stupid, mindful only of the eagles. But what of the north monkeys?"

"Their legs are stout like a man's," the boy chirped. "And they pop up on them to see if there's trouble coming, like a boar or a farm dog, even a leopard. They look smarter, Father, and their tails do not seem to be as big now."

"Uh-huh. Because they are adapting?"

Kiriqui nodded again. "Becoming something better!" Then he smiled once more. "And, Father, the bushia trees on the north shore have a better way of spreading their seeds in the monkey poop. It's not good when the south monkeys eat the blossoms. Now the north trees cannot live without the monkeys. But the south's wish them ill."

Owuda handed his son a piece of sugar cake as a reward. The cake was still warm, having been baked that morning in Mother Barinda Sifua's clay oven. Barinda, who was Kiriqui's grandmother, lived on a houseboat like Owuda's, but closer to the harbor town of Goma-ifo. She'd delivered some fat sea bass as well as cake. Barinda was the brashest, most foul-mouthed fishwife in Goma-ifo and had been admonished by the Fulani imams and the town's constables for her lack of deference to men and married women. The Fulani Muslims were probably more offended by her lack of cover for her head and ample hanging bosom than by her bawdy hawking. But how was she to get noticed in the market's crowd, sell her fish? Timidity meant no profit, and she needed all the money she could garner in order to help her son pay down his debts, with a little left over to fund his research. Owuda couldn't buy food and raise a son alone on the meager wages the Fulani chieftains paid him as physician and surgeon.

Kiriqui wolfed down a bite of cake, then spoke with his mouth full of another. "Father, may I show my notes to the imam at my school? I've written them in Fulani, too, so he can read it. I practice Fulani just like it's written in their Holy Quran."

Owuda sighed heavily, shook his head. Kiriqui's excitement deflated like a lamb's bladder bag. In his zeal and pride, he'd asked an importune question. Owuda was now staring emptily at a bleached porpoise skull hanging from a post. "I'm sorry," Kiriqui whispered as he battled back tears. Owuda didn't answer him, and the child shrank onto his little straw cot, clutching a piece of cake.

Despite the volumes of books and scrolls on anatomy, physiology, pharmacology archived by the Fulani, and the natural science tomes brought by caravan from the Arab lands, imams decreed that all living things were as Allah made them on the day the Earth began. Just three moons prior, Owuda sold a paper to Jojof scholars in Benin, explaining how the porpoises of the Goma estuary once walked the shores as otters long ago and evolved to fishlike form after eons of adaptation. Their nostrils moved to the tops of their heads and became blowholes. Their paws turned to fins. But the imams ordered the honorarium disgorged. The money was escheated to the Fulani viceroy, of course.

Owuda had dedicated that paper to Efia, his wife and Kiriqui's mother. She'd died of tumors in the womb close to five seasons ago. Owuda had gone into debt procuring medicine for her. As succor for his despair and failure, Owuda indulged in beer, lettuce milk opium and dice. The vices sucked him deeper into poverty. His creditors were all vassals of the viceroy, and by law the viceroy could call due Owuda's debt at any time, for any reason. Barinda knew this well, and she labored to help her son regain his dignity and livelihood. And Owuda vowed to train his son, despite mandatory schooling of all Goma children by Muslim clergy, and then move the family to Benin, where men of science were respected, not hounded as heretics. Maybe the *tuabo*—whose asses the viceroy kissed in return for rum, muskets and musical clocks—would allow the family passage to one of their universities far to the north in the cold and snow? With their tall ships, brass instruments, great looms and foundries, these white men surely appreciated science, even if they did dress in smocks that reeked of sweat and their tobacco, and pantaloons were stained with dried piss. He spoke a little *tuabo*: Portuguese and even some English, learned from a bearded shaman in dirty homespun robes who came to Goma-ifo to spread the word of the prophet Christ to the fishermen and boat builders. The Fulani, who rode horses and camels and cared nothing for things nautical, heard only the word of the Quran's prophet and messenger of Allah, named Mohammed.

Now, Kiriqui resolved not to act like a baby for making his father sad. He blotted his eyes dry enough to see that Owuda was no longer in a fugue. Rather, Owuda was on his knees, eye-level with his worktable and staring at his specimen jars of live, soft and shelled creatures from the deep sea and tidal mangroves. The boy joined his father on the plank floor. There was a puddle of water down there, and the table itself was wet. Kiriqui finally noticed why. The two largest glass jars had been uncorked. Kiriqui had sworn both containers were sealed tight when he awoke that morning; the roiling mass of arms in the bigger jar made his neck tingle. It was an octopus. But what scared the child the most was how this little beast's mottled skin seemed to spike or flatten and tint pink to brown, as if that was how the animal showed joy or hate or hunger or fear. In the open jar adjacent to the octopus's container was a slurry of tissue, shell fragments and severed claws that was once a reef crab.

Kiriqui sputtered, "I-I didn't touch them, Father. I swear . . ."

Owuda tapped the octopus's jar. "I know, son. This is . . . extraordinary . . ."

Then the child spoke the unthinkable, and his words made him quake. "Father, he opened his own jar . . . and the crab's? He ate it and went home?"

"She, not he," Owuda whispered as he studied his specimen. The creature's eye widened, then narrowed, as if confessing to this stealthy escape and murder.

"She could have come out and got on my face . . . wh-while I was asleep?"

"No, of course not." Owuda then motioned for Kiriqui to fetch a skewer from the hanging iron stewpan. Owuda opened another jar containing live prawns and speared one with the skewer. He brought it to the top of the octopus's jar, holding the morsel just above the rim. Two thin tentacles, brown and wrinkled like wet paper, uncoiled and tasted the air. Once they felt the wriggling shrimp, the skin suddenly fired bright orange, like a mango's flesh. Kiriqui gaped when he heard the tiny round suckers adhere, and gasped when his father's wrist bent from the octopus's tug as the doomed prawn disappeared from the skewer. Owuda related how the octopus is an ambush killer, stalking unsuspecting prey, while its cousin the squid chases down fast swimmers like fish. Both had beaks like a parrot's made out of the same material as a man's fingernails. Both had spiny, rasping tongues for scraping meat.

Meal consumed, the octopus resumed its serene pose and pallor. But its flesh blazed again when Owuda shot to his feet. Barinda was shrieking from the riverbank.

Two men flanked her, gripping her thick arms. They were the viceroy's Goma constables. A third man showed Fulani cheek and chin scars, though he wore *tuabo* pantaloons and buckled shoes. He leveled a musket as he stepped to the houseboat's mooring. "Physician Owuda Sifua Owuda!" the man shouted. "You and your whelp are hereby commanded to appear before the court of the viceroy, Djenu the Magnificent. Put on your sandals and come with us! No questions!"

Though the armed man made no attempt to muscle his way onto the boat, Owuda nodded and slipped on his sandals. He'd seen the fear in his son's and mother's eyes.

"Bring your medicine bag and instruments!" snapped this musketeer. Owuda complied again, slinging his kits. He ushered little Kiriqui off the boat onto the shore.

"Now release my mother," Owuda calmly asked the musketeer after swallowing a throat full of terror. "You made your point."

The musketeer grunted, and then motioned with his head. The Goma men let Barinda go, and immediately she rushed to Owuda. The musketeer shoved his weapon in her path, but she crushed it to her breasts and enveloped her son and grandson as completely and tightly as the sinewy tentacles of that octopus.

"Djenu is a pig-fuck who would sell his own mother to the *tuabo* for snuff," she hissed in Owuda's ear. Kiriqui clung fretfully to her mighty thigh.

Owuda kissed his mother's wet cheek. Pulling away, he forced a reassuring smile that hardly reassured little Kiriqui. He peeled the boy off Barinda's leg. Owuda's complicity likely saved a beating from the knotted cat-o-nine tails hanging from the constables' belts.

With the sun starting its slow dip to the sea, Owuda and Kiriqui clambered into a dugout for the trip into Goma-ifo and Djenu's villa. Weeping, Barinda waved at Kiriqui, even though Owuda kept the boy's eyes facing front. Many river folk had gone to Djenu's villa, never to return. Many *hundreds* of river folk. Thus a curse passed Barinda's lips. *Ay-Koja, Witch of the Western Sea. Destroy all who thieve my blood toward the setting sun.*

The Fulani were a big, slender people seemingly ill-suited for the small ponies on which they swept from the dry plains of Mali. Djenu stood shoulders above most Goma, Ashanti and Uwethi folk, and his scarlet turban made him look even taller. He always looked as if he was posing for a *tuabo* artist—hands on his hips, head cocked. As Owuda entered the hall of teak and mahogany inlaid with mosaic tile, he saw two *tuabo* seated at the viceroy's table and a Fulani maid filling the men's cups with pungent spiced beer. The men kept their swords in their scabbards and pistols shoved in their bandoliers. No one was allowed arms or blades within twenty paces of the viceroy. No one but the *tuabo* apparently. Owuda bowed to the man called the Magnificent and made sure Kiriqui did also; Kiriqui whispered he had to pee.

To Owuda's surprise, it was a *tuabo* with long, stringy black hair who spoke first, and it was in agitated Portuguese. The viceroy just nodded, shrugged uncomfortably. Owuda wished he could smirk. The *tuabo* called himself Captain Anselmo Gonçalves, and then he finally allowed the Magnificent One a chance to posture.

"Physician," Djenu bellowed, "you must know why I've summoned you."

Owuda acknowledged that he had debts, but inquired nonetheless if Djenu or his courtiers were ill. Perhaps a boil had to be lanced, penile chancres treated with tincture? Djenu didn't take the facetious bait. Rather, he called to his guards, who disappeared and then returned with a litter bearing a *tuabo* swaddled in bandages brown with dried blood. The man's chest still moved, and that was the only indication he was alive. The two other *tuabos* winced. Owuda watched with a doctor's eye, though Kiriqui cowered behind his father. He took some peeks nevertheless.

The viceroy couldn't mask his own queasiness as the guards gingerly removed the bandages to reveal huge red, circular wounds that oozed pus. The poor devil's left leg was severed, and the stump still bore a tourniquet.

Duty to healing rather than to Fulani overlords pulled Owuda to the man's side. "I could apply a poultice," he thought aloud, "and feed him arrowroot fungus for the infection." Owuda looked up. "But, *how long has he been this way?*"

Captain Gonçalves answered in fractured Goma that his crew fished the man from the weed sea one moon ago. Three weeks. The amputation was butchery; the *tuabo*, for all their wondrous machines and mastery of land and water, were barbarians when it came to caring for their own.

Owuda examined the circular wounds. The skin was abraded from extreme suction. Owuda suddenly pushed back from the litter to chase an insane thought from his brain. Captain Gonçalves must have read Owuda's face, and he spoke in Portuguese this time, slowly so Owuda could understand.

"You—witch doctor. Your head man, Djenu, says you know sea beasts, too?"

"I am *not* a witch doctor. Please, keep this man drinking plenty of clean water or tea, and diluted fruit juices . . ."

"We give him rum, nigger." This white man drew closer, and his breath stank of gum rot. "Listen. This is Rodriego. No others survived the sinking. Not crew or"—his head dipped slightly—"cargo. Our patrons want the losses to stop, and they will, by God—even if it means listening to what you lot have to say."

The other *tuabo*, visibly shaken by his cohort's suffering, pleaded with the captain to allow the man his death rites from a Christian shaman. The captain growled back no, then pressed Owuda further. "The marks on him. Tell me, nigger—what does this?"

Owuda shook his head. "I know only what can be empirically tested . . ."

"*Huh?*" the Captain intoned. "You're a cheeky one, eh? Don't *test* me."

Djenu the Magnificent barked to his guards, who were happy to return to their trained vocation as thugs. One yanked little Kiriqui away from his father. The other brute drew his scimitar and brandished it at Owuda. Djenu said, "This boy is too young for circumcision, thus he remains your property . . ."

"Lordship," Owuda answered, "I have given you loyal and expert service, and I must protest your—"

"And since *you* belong to *me*, then this boy is my property, too!"

"Belong . . . *what*? I am a physician and surgeon of Goma, and I—"

"You are a dog who owes sums now declared due, with interest! Can you pay them? Ah, I think not. Like the other dogs who cannot pay rent or taxes to me, you're no more than a thief. A *criminal* . . ."

It felt like the guard's sword had already cleaved Owuda's skull or ripped into his viscera. Mind howling, Owuda wanted to tear this Fulani garbage to pieces. But they had his son. His precious little man of science. His living fragment of Efia. And so Owuda closed his eyes, absorbed a vision of his mother, Barinda, and his own father, long dead, then muttered, "What is your pleasure . . . Lordship?"

Djenu pronounced that Owuda Sifua Owuda and his son were now his chattel, but he hereby deeded them to the Royal Lisbõa Sugar Company. The guard released Kiriqui, who hadn't a clue what the viceroy meant. He ran to his father, kissed him and said, "So now we go home to Gran-ma?"

Owuda hugged him so tightly. He thought of a lie, but Anselmo Gonçalves beat him with words in pidgin Goma.

"No, boy, you go with your father on a boat. You go find what hurt our boats. Then you go to Braśil or Virginia—and work."

Before Owuda and Kiriqui could weep together, the *tuabo* in the litter loosed his own cry. "*Olho gigante*," he wheezed in Portuguese. Big eye. "*Muite olho*." Many eyes? "*Serpente* . . ."

Sunrise brought this man's death. Sunrise brought father and son to a raft paddled slowly to a huge *tuabo* ship anchored off Goma-ifo.

This was the fodder for cane and tobacco, gold mines and brick pits: including Owuda, twenty-two men, ten women—one pregnant and one older than Barinda. Two young girls who belonged with the old woman, and a little boy around Kiriqui's age who seemingly belonged to no one. This child was the only soul not sobbing or spitting at the *tuabo* sailors, and he called to Kiriqui to ask sweetly and blithely why Owuda wasn't yoked with iron or bound with hemp rope like the other adults. Kiriqui was too sick with fear to answer, but Owuda took the child to his side. The sailors didn't rebuke him for this instant adoption. Thus two boys and a grown man would occupy a cubby under the quarterdeck four feet wide, five feet long, two feet deep. Nevertheless, uncaulked seams around a small hatch offered a bit of airflow. Sailors stuffed everyone else in the hold, stacked like fish on a drying rack, with one glass-enclosed tallow candle for light. Shrieks and moans very quickly replaced the echo of rat squeaks down there; the odor of vomit displaced that of must and seawater.

Gonçalves himself made an appearance in this hatch above Owuda's head before shutting it to all light. The passage would bring the ship south of the Sargasso Sea, he said in Portuguese. But they would stop, sail a zigzag like whalers—in the event they spotted something "extraordinary." He didn't elaborate on what he defined as extraordinary. "Witch doctor," the captain said, "my ship's surgeon has your sharp knives and tongs from your bag, lest you get any funny ideas. Keep the rest of your spells to treat the sick. I've lost enough money this year."

Something extraordinary occurred on the morning of the fourth day at sea.

Gonçalves ordered all Negroes other than Owuda and the boys to be rinsed with lard-soap suds and cold seawater. The crew didn't mind herding almost forty people onto a now heaving deck, given the smells in the cargo hold. Indeed, sailors flushed the hold as well. The filth settled into the bilge, seasoning the ocean as the pumps evacuated it. Owuda boiled bushia-bark extract into a tea to stanch diarrhea and vomiting. He brewed only enough for each person to take one sip. All but one responded in Goma or their native language, "Thank you, doctor" or "Bless you, brother." The one who didn't was the old woman, who growled, "Why can't you just poison us all?" Owuda had thought of it. But he was a healer, not a killer. Once Owuda dispensed the tea, Kiriqui and the little boy who called himself Ademe acted as nurses, assisting him in tweezing maggots and salving sores. The boys halted when a crewman called to them in English. "*Kevin, Adam!* Come. Port bow!"

He was a Yankee named John Brewster who was too lazy to pronounce either boy's name correctly. Owuda despaired that his son and Ademe responded to these ugly *tuabo* names, but at least Brewster was kind to the little fellows, sneaking fruit or a carved ivory toy to them. Kiriqui quickly hollered for his father, and Owuda joined them to see a sea turtle—an adult Owuda reckoned to weigh at least two hundred pounds—bobbing atop the mountainous waves off the port side. It floated upright, not upside down, as anyone would expect a dead turtle to float. The top of its thick green shell had been ripped open, and all of its organs and meat had looked as if it had been sucked or scraped clean. Brewster fetched a billhook and snagged the carcass, yanking it to the port gunwale as spray from the heavy seas drenched the rail. Captain Gonçalves arrived with the master's mate, both cursing at Brewster in English. They ceased when they saw the turtle's shell.

"Help stow the niggers below," the captain snapped at Brewster. "Batten them in. Storm looks to be on us soon." He turned to Owuda and spoke in Portuguese. "But you, *doctor*"—as he now called Owuda, rather than "witch doctor" or "nigger"—"stay."

The boys returned to their hole below the quarterdeck, just as the two nameless young girls who were loaded in Goma-ifo were separated from the others being slid back into the hold. Ademe related with a giggle that the girls—who both looked maybe thirteen or fourteen—received an extra cleaning and some sassafras to chew on, presumably to drive the puke smell from their mouths. Kiriqui frowned. He'd spied on his father while he had worked on both the girls the previous night, before the wind had gotten fierce. The *tuabo* made him do something between their legs. Stretch them wider, John Brewster had said, so they wouldn't cry when the *tuabo* men lay down with them. Kiriqui told John Brewster about Fulani girls who'd get cut, and then they felt nothing when they lay down. John Brewster answered that the crew only wanted these girls cut a little bit. They wanted the girls to feel good between their legs, as he said that Negro girls liked to "crow and buck." "Listen," Kiriqui whispered sternly to Ademe as they were shut into their own dank space, "we'll hear them scream soon, when the men start kissing them."

With most of the ship's second watch thusly occupied with the girls, Captain Gonçalves had to help hoist the turtle carcass on deck. He kicked at the dead beast, but never peeled his glare from

Owuda. A squall's rains finally hit, driving the rest of the men up the rigging to trim the canvas.

"So now you'll be truthful with me?" Gonçalves asked. "I have seen this before . . . before Rodriego was pulled from the weed sea. No shark, no orca. No men could do this, even ones starved for meat. *Empirically.*"

Owuda was kneeling close to the gaping hole in the shell, and he squinted against the biting wind and stinging raindrops. He discerned the smell of ammonia. It was a by-product of digestion, found in human urine. But in this concentration? No, only large birds on land excreted this much—or soft creatures in the sea. Squid. Octopus. Big ones. He turned slowly, peered up at the captain. "No shark, no man."

Gonçalves beckoned him to get up. He pointed Owuda to the roiling gray clouds above. The wind was now blasting the ship broadside. "Nor' by nor'west," the captain muttered. "The winds are pushing us into the weed sea."

The blow died the following morning. And by the afternoon of the ninth day out from Goma-ifo, this ship was mired in the vast Sargasso Sea.

The sun was high and hot, and it cooked the floating sargassum into a foul salad. In the hold, the cargo was silent. The *tuabo* thought they were asleep, but there were murmurs. Fretful murmurs. The Goma among them knew where the ship was. They translated to the others, and the others were frozen silent with fear. The crew wasn't speaking much either, save for John Brewster. He stood above the small open quarterdeck hatch, passing the last of his molasses candy to the two little boys.

"Your papa . . . he with the captain," he assured the boys, combining English, Portuguese and a little Goma. "Captain like papa. Talk to him more than the master's mate. Master's mate don't like that. Nobody like master's mate anyhow!"

"Father . . . he be come here . . . soon?" Kiriqui asked in broken English.

John Brewster nodded. He didn't tax the child's newly minted vocabulary. "Captain just wants your papa to keep niggers healthy, is all," he answered in Portuguese. "That'll help once you all are sold. Sell you all as family. Him keep niggers right as rain and working hard, like prize stallions and mares, eh?"

* * *

Captain Gonçalves poured more wine for himself. Owuda hadn't touched alcohol in six months. The head *tuabo* toasted him anyway.

"Here's ... to *Doctor Owuda*," Gonçalves stammered. "Not a single nigger has been lost to sickness, not one has even jumped overboard. And that is good, as not all were bound for Braśil." When Owuda shrugged, the captain explained, "We were going to sell all the women and five men in Bahía to cover costs. Then we refit, revictual. You and the rest, along with nutmeg and mace, are going to Barbados, thence with raw molasses and what few of you remain, we go to Charles Towne, then Boston. Then I go back to that buffoon Djenu and start all over again."

"So we are to be sold in Barbados."

"Hmm ... perhaps" Gonçalves said, slicing off some sausage for himself and his guest. "Two hundred slaves a day die there in the cane fields. That's worse than in Bahía. Owuda, your services would be valued. We could change the bill of lading and sell you in Carolina. Niggers treat ailments with spells and dances there, too."

"Seaman Brewster told me of Boston. I would like to go there with my boys."

The captain chuckled as he chewed, swilled wine. "First we make it out of here. And now that I'm no longer sober, explain this to me again. The sea beasts?"

Owuda saved the sausage piece for the boys, then said, "Certain animals can grow to immense size in the deep ocean. Our fishermen, your sailors, all have seen whales bearing the scars of giant squid. Scars as on your man. The arms could easily be mistaken for a large eel, even an aquatic serpent. But these squid surface only to die. And they cannot destroy a ship."

"Then an octopus. You ... you spoke of an octopus ..."

Owuda shook his head. As a child, he learned about the Witch. How God, whom the Goma called Otumere, cursed her, posted her at the edge of the world to guard against arrogant men sailing into the Sea of Heaven. She was an octopus. She was a silly myth designed to scare children and ignorant fishermen. "In the deep water," this physician and man of science began, "there are nutrients to feed the animals that a huge animal could then prey upon. It is cold down there. Yes, tolerable for a squid. But other soft creatures, no. The octopus craves warm water. Reefs, rocks, so it may den or use as a blind from which to pounce on slow creatures that do not live in cold, deep water."

"Doctor, the water isn't cold in the weed sea, even at soundings a hundred fathoms down. There isn't even a current. This I know."

"Perhaps there are caverns . . . plateaus under us. If there was an apparatus for a man to view the sea bottom, I myself would love to be the first man to go."

The captain stood and relieved himself in the porcelain pot under the table. "The size, Owuda—could such a beast live despite all you say?"

Owuda told him of his outings in the clay hills a two-day walk from the river. There, he found the stony skeletons and imprints of plants and creatures both odd and terrifying. He surmised that the hill was once under a shallow, warm sea.

Gonçalves sat back down, chuckling once more. That shallow sea was from Noah's flood, he affirmed. How else could what was once underwater now be dry land? Owuda was acting less an educated semihuman and more a silly nigger! But Owuda ignored him and described a bizarre imprint in the hillside: that of a tentacled animal with a conelike shell that was as long as two oxen and just as thick. Including arms and head, the beast would have been the length of the ship's mainmast. The captain ceased laughing. "Again," Owuda concluded, "I need more empirical facts, observations. Will you give me some paper, a pen?"

Now sullen, Gonçalves motioned with his head toward his cabin door. "Time to stow you," he mumbled. "No hard feelings." When Owuda arose and went to the door, the captain called, "Say nothing of our conversation to crew, the niggers."

"You mean the *other* niggers . . . sir. By your leave."

Gonçalves jerked a nod. "We carry more than niggers, Owuda," he suddenly added. "Under where we keep you. That other hold is copper-lined. Know why? Can't have a spark, can we, eh? Djenu and some of our client Tuareg, Hausa, Gozo . . . they defaulted on a payment for eight very big casks of powder, lock-fused in case buccaneers or the French try to seize us. Enough to blow us up to God and then back down to the Odd Place beneath the waves, and all resting under *your* ass, Owuda."

"Why are you telling me this, sir?"

"All of us share risk in this passage. All of us are niggers of somebody."

On the evening of the twelfth day—four adrift in the weeds, awaiting a southwest wind on which to tack—all aboard were praying. Some canticles were for Jesus. Some, to she who swam below. Jesus wasn't listening this night.

A crewman named Lopes should have been on watch but instead had a girl pinned to the bow windlass. He shoved his fingers between her legs, his other hand cupping her breast. She was stonefaced as he nuzzled her throat, cooing only for effect. He backed off to loosen his pantaloons and dirty draws. The girl's eyes widened as big as the moon above, and Lopes snickered. He figured he must've scared this negress—he always said he laid this angry cock against any nigger's, and his was a hard fit for a quim or a mouth. But the girl was sinking to the deck, chest heaving. She was no longer a virgin, so Lopes cursed her fear. But then he saw a shadow move cross her face. Big, like a passing cloud would cast if it were day. He heard a whine, a splash of water. He turned.

With a whoosh, the great arm smacked him to the pine deck as a hand would swat an insect. The suckers ground into his skin, lifted him skyward. Mercifully, the blow knocked Lopes unconscious. Unmercifully, he would awaken when he hit the water, just long enough to see the unblinking eye, then a chomping beak, then bubbles and his own blood.

The girl's hoarse screams shook the rest of the crew from its languor. In an instant, five other huge, suckered arms flailed at the bow. Glum laziness turned to utter horror. Amid the shouts and crack of wood and cordage came a loud hiss as water and air rocketed from the beast's siphon. The ship lurched upward at the stern, jamming Owuda, Kiriqui and Ademe into one end of their cramped cubby. The boys cried as Owuda kicked at the hatch. After another violent heave, he heard the blast of muskets, more shouts. And then Gonçalves' voice: "Bring the doctor *now!*"

The hatch opened. The boys smiled because it was John Brewster's face in the lantern light. But the boys just as quickly recoiled when a piece of the jib boom flew by the sailor's head like a javelin. John Brewster tugged Owuda out. Owuda ordered the boys to stay in the cubby, no matter what. But keep the hatch open, he said.

Owuda tumbled forward, as now the stern was dry out of the water. When he caught himself against the rail, he saw what was down at the other end of the ship, and his stomach plummeted to his knees.

Two eyes. Arms grasping, crushing, breaking, squeezing. A snapping beak the size of the archway into Djenu's villa. And within that maw, a great barbed tongue, dripping with poison and digestive juice, hanging with torn flesh and clothing. Owuda the physician and surgeon, the man of science, was silent. Owuda, son of Barinda and Kwame, circumcised and baptized to serve Otumere, whispered, "*Ay-Koja . . .*"

And two gigantic eyes focused on him. Saw the black face. Stretched an arm. Tasted. Slapped Owuda down. Wriggling under the broken oars of the captain's wrecked skiff—the only means of escape—Owuda avoided being taken. A crewman popping up to aim his musket wasn't so lucky; the force of the grabbing tentacle severed his arm as the gun fired.

Gonçalves was in the thick of the menace, waving his cutlass. Exhorting his men. Hollering for Owuda. But Owuda would not come to him. He scampered to the main hold's cover. He could hear the wails and shouts below. That old woman could see him through the iron grillwork and called, "Do not save us, Brother Doctor!" And a man's voice, also in Goma, shouted, "Let us die with dignity in her belly. Better than to serve the *tuabo* . . . like you, traitor, up there!"

It was then that the master's mate caught Owuda, pushed him to the captain's side. The hull heaved up again, then twisted as if the monster was a mammoth dog ripping a lamb shank. Gonçalves yelled, "You, Doctor, where can we hit it to kill it? One spot! Maybe a harpoon?" When Owuda shook his head, backed away, Gonçalves struck him with his fist. "You owe me! You owe me! We'll all die here!"

Better than to serve the *tuabo*, Owuda muttered inwardly. But the timbers around the forward hold were cracking. The bottom decks were flooding, and the cries were louder in the night than the gunfire or the hiss of this creature. Tentacles were finding bodies therein, and bodies were going willingly, limply, into the wet and rasping mouth, as if sacrifices. Owuda could bear no more. He ducked the next swing from Gonçalves—this one from a cutlass— then landed a punch to the captain's ribs. The cutlass dropped. Owuda scooped it up and tore back to the quarterdeck, which by now was rising higher as the monster dragged the bow into the sea.

Owuda heard the boys whimpering for him, and there stood a quivering John Brewster, trying to ram a ball into his pistol barrel. Owuda seized the *tuabo's* arm and sputtered in English: "Boys are Kevin and Adam now. Not animals. You save them!"

Then Owuda released him. He didn't understand what this Negro meant. Or what this Negro was doing with a cutlass. Or why this Negro didn't run him through and jump with the boys himself. But when he watched Owuda smash away the latch to the powder hold with the blade, he knew. John Brewster genuflected, then leapt up to the hatch to pull the boys out and huddle them at the stern rail.

With another cutlass blow, Owuda freed two of the kegs, each waist-high and as big around as the monster's thickest tentacle. Attached to each like a spigot was a lock-and-flint hammer not un- like those on a musket. These contraptions were covered in greased cloth to prevent sparks; Owuda ripped off the covers and toppled the first cask onto its side. He hadn't a clue from where came the strength to do so. His thighs, shoulders and back burned as if on fire.

The first cask rolled and bounced down the inclined deck like one of Kiriqui's toys, wedging at the sunken bow between a felled yardarm and the monster's maw. Owuda tipped the second cask, this time controlling the fall with one of the severed restraining ropes.

Owuda could not hear the captain's curses or the prayers of drowning Brothers and Sisters from the hold. He could not hear the wail of his son or Ademe as John Brewster held both close, shield- ing them from what was to come.

Two yellow eyes peered down on Owuda, and the flailing arms stilled for a moment. Owuda looped his fingers around the now- cocked hammer of the cask he'd rolled.

Owuda spoke this in the few seconds before he died: "*Ay-Koja, if that is what you are. Forgive me. But you can't destroy one evil . . . with more evil.*"

The blast shot fire into the other cask, and it, too, detonated. After the shower of singed timber and flesh, only three souls remained to see the dawn.

H.M.S. Achilles, on station against the French at the western edge of the Sargasso Sea, came upon the wreckage on the seventeenth day out from Goma-ifo. The warship's captain would log that he'd found three survivors lying on a capsized skiff and other flotsam: John Brewster, age nineteen, of Boston, Massachusetts Bay Colony, in service to the Portuguese. A Negro boy named Kevin, age nine. A Negro boy named Adam, age eight. As the children had no marks or brands, and no documents survived the sinking, the captain recorded his concurrence with Brewster that the children were *not* bound Africans. The Yankee seaman said only that the powder hold went up when the crew, grim and indolent from heat and foundering in the sargassum, smoked pipes carelessly. The captain noted that it was a shame that almost forty Africans worth of profit went to the bottom.

But the joint stock owners and bankers who were the tentacles of the behemoth named the Royal Lisbõa Sugar Company had paid generous insurance premiums, as did all companies whose ships tracked the Middle Passage. This disaster would be forgotten, and the trade in flesh would begin anew. Feeding the monster of greed in the Americas and Europe. Feeding the monster of pettiness in Africa. Ever hungry.

The Arrangements

Patricia E. Canterbury

Agrimonia Eupatoria—October

I opened the mail that was delivered addressed to Grandfather. I had no way of informing Mrs. Lily Parks of his passing a month earlier. None of his correspondence to her was addressed to other than the house on Thorne Island, and she lived on the Island only during the late-spring and summer months. I absently tapped the letter on the side of my computer, then opened it to read:

Mr. Harrison Snyder III
Attorney-at-Law
Thorne Island, Vermont

Dear Mr. Snyder:
   I hope that your family is well. It is time once again for my daughters and me to return to our summer home. Will you ensure that the house is aired out and that Simon has the garden ready for our arrival, as I would be most pleased?
                    Your humble friend,
                    Mrs. Lily Parks

The letter was written on old-fashioned stationery with embossed exotic birds in the upper-right-hand corner. The handwriting was weak and spidery, as one would expect from a woman of advanced age. Mrs. Lily Parks would have to be in her late eighties or early nineties. She and Grandfather were close in age. Grandfather had been taking care of Mrs. Lily Parks's legal affairs for over sixty

years. I smiled remembering that after all these years, Grandfather
was still Mr. Snyder and she, Mrs. Lily Parks, so unlike today's instant familiarity with strangers. I looked at the letter, at everything
about it: the halting handwriting, the scent similar to a spring bouquet. The sentence structure screamed elderly grandmother. It
was addressed to Grandfather, and I had been expecting it since
late March. Grandfather left specific instructions that I was to follow the information received from Mrs. Lily Parks, and to expect a
letter no later than April 1.

Mrs. Parks and her four daughters were a legend on the Island.
Only I had never seen them. I usually spent my summers in New
Orleans, Paris or New York—any place but Vermont. The old
women spent theirs on Thorne Island. Every year for as long as I
could remember, Grandfather spoke about how the women would
board up the house in September and return the last week in April.
It was as if they brought spring with them.

Grandfather and others who call Thorne Island their home all
year state that the Parks Family has some of the most beautiful
women seen in the northeast. I couldn't imagine that anyone
would find sixty-, seventy- or eighty-year old women beautiful,
but I indulged the old-timers as I cleared out my grandfather's
business.

"To bad that you're not takin' your grandfather's practice," old-
timers would tell me when I'd see them in the bank or grocery
store.

"Thanks. I have plans that don't include Island practice. Perhaps
when I'm a little older and more settled," I replied with a smile, so
as not to hurt the natives' feelings. To tell the truth, the only reason
I was even *on* Thorne Island was because I was Grandfather's only
living relative who was also a lawyer.

"Paolo, you should think about living up here on Thorne Island.
You could make a lot of money. The folks in Vermont are real nice,
and you would start with my dear friends Mrs. Lily Parks and her
lovely daughters," Grandfather said just last fall, after he'd called
me to come up to see his practice for myself.

"Gramps, I didn't go to the university to settle on a tiny island on
Lake Champlain. Perhaps when I'm much older, settled, married,
the kids in college, maybe then I could get acquainted with the

Island folk." I didn't mean it, of course. I had no plans to settle on an island, but it made Grandfather happy, and I knew that he'd be gone long before I would be ready to settle for small-town America. Of course, I had no way of knowing that he would be dead so soon after that visit.

"Tell me about Mrs. Lily Parks and her daughters," I said the last day of last year's visit. The women had just left for their winter home. I should have noticed then that Grandfather was fading, but I was preoccupied with getting on with my life. I wish I had paid attention and asked more questions.

"There's not much to say. They're quiet and keep to themselves. If they need my help to get the house ready, I hear from them in late March or early April. As you know, I'm responsible for their winter mortgage. I make sure that it's paid monthly. They may send their handyman and gardener, Simon, to get you. He's been with the women forever. He seems almost as immortal as the women. But you should go and see them. They live in one of the most beautiful homes on the Island."

I was always too busy to follow up. Besides, with Grandfather alive, there wasn't a reason for me to spend any time with a bunch of sixty-year-old spinsters and their aged mother. Nor did I question their equally old gardener. And I didn't question why after sixty years, Mrs. Lily Parks was still paying a mortgage.

Another week passed since the arrival of the letter before Simon, the Parks's gardener, came to the office and informed me that Mrs. Lily Parks had some urgent business with me.

"Mrs. Lily Parks requests the honor of your presence for tea at three o'clock," Simon whispered. He was nearly as old and withered as I assumed Mrs. Lily Parks to be. His lean, ebony body was rock hard from years of backbreaking work. Yet, his voice was as soft and smooth as if he were speaking in a cathedral. He had an odd gracefulness about him, a sense of authority, as if he were used to giving orders rather than following them.

"Simon, tell Mrs. Parks that I will be pleased to meet with her this afternoon." Simon nodded, and walked out of the office.

I was not calling Grandfather's place mine even for a short time. I have played and replayed that conversation over and over in my mind. Why didn't I ask Simon more questions? Why didn't I ask Grandfather more about the women when we talked? Why didn't

Grandfather feel free to warn me? Did he know about them? At the time, none of these questions was anywhere near my consciousness.

Lily — April

I drove to the Parks's estate, which had a magnificent view of Lake Champlain from three of the four sides of the wraparound porch. An eight-foot-tall rustic gate was right in front of the circular driveway and seemed to keep strangers from wandering through the beautiful wildflower garden that greeted visitors from the main road and the fourth side of the porch. The gate appeared locked, so I got out of my car and looked for a bell to announce my arrival.

Simon appeared seemingly out of nowhere and opened the gate. "Welcome, Mr. Snyder," he said in a low voice that I had to strain to hear. "You can leave your car here and follow me onto the grounds. Mrs. Lily Parks will see you on the east porch."

I thought it strange to leave my car on the street when there was an empty circular driveway large enough for ten cars just inside the gate, but I didn't say anything. I grabbed the bouquet of cut flowers I had purchased for Mrs. Lily Parks.

I also didn't notice how Simon opened the gate, but seconds later he and I stepped past the gate and onto a rough, small-pebbled walkway that led to the house. The yard was filled to overflowing with plants. Butterflies and ladybugs seemed everywhere. It was as if every flower had its own personal butterfly.

Something slithered through the tall grass to my right.

"Are there snakes here?" I asked. Snakes and I were not on nodding terms.

"Snakes? Why yes, sir, there are harmless garden snakes. You don't have to be afraid of them." Simon smiled, shook his head and continued walking. I watched my step as we approached the house.

"Have a seat. Mrs. Parks will be with you shortly. Let me take the flowers, and I will take care of them," Simon said as he gestured to a high-backed rattan chair near a round table that held a silver teapot and two pale blue china cups and matching saucers. He then walked through a door that opened into what looked like a formal dining room from what I could see through the lace curtains.

"Mr. Snyder, I'm sorry to keep you waiting. Simon told me about your grandfather. You have my deepest sympathies. I should have sent a condolence card earlier," a short woman the hue of café au lait who appeared to be about forty-five years of age and had premature gray hair said, as she reached out and shook my hand. Her skin was petal-soft and the smoothest that I'd seen on anyone older than sixteen. She was dressed in a milk-white silk suit with a pale yellow silk blouse beneath the jacket.

I noticed women's clothing. It was a gift that came naturally, one that I cultivated to a fine art in college. It helped me to size up professors, mates, best friends and one-night stands. Clothes say a lot about women.

Her tiny tan feet were clad in snow-white sandals, and her silver hair was cut short and smooth, close to her head. She wore a thin, dark yellow silk scarf around her neck. Her eyes were clear and the darkest black I'd ever seen. She wore the most alluring perfume, which seemed to shift strength in the breeze.

"Hello . . . I-I'm waiting for your grandmother? Uh . . . Mrs. Lily Parks?" I managed to stammer. I thought Grandfather said that none of the Parks daughters were married. Well, things happen. No one needed to be married for there to be a granddaughter. And this woman was one of the most beautiful I'd ever seen; she had to be a Parks relative. Her skin, hair, eyes, all were flawless. She looked fresh, as if she'd just stepped from a shower. She exuded warmth.

She laughed. The sound was like glass wind chimes in the distance. Her laughter reminded me of a sound I'd heard at a temple in a village in Africa.

"How sweet. But I'm Lily Parks." There was something so formal about her that I immediately realized why Grandfather always referred to her as Mrs. Lily Parks, as did I from that day forward.

"But . . . I-I was told that Mrs. Parks . . . uh . . ." I let the words fade in the air as an equally gorgeous but much younger woman opened the door and said, "Mama, do you want more tea?"

I was still standing somehow unable to find my voice. I felt as if I were fourteen and trapped in a room full of college-age women and that whatever I said would sound childish.

"Mr. Snyder, please have a seat." Mrs. Lily Parks gestured toward the rattan chair. "Rose, we haven't drunk this pot yet. Mr. Snyder, I'd like you to meet my eldest daughter, Rose," Mrs. Lily Parks continued.

While Lily was dressed in white and her skin was golden, the color of winter wheat, Rose was dark brown like fresh mud, and she wore a pale green sleeveless summer dress that hugged her tiny figure and accented her round hips, even teeth and bright green eyes. I'd never seen a person as dark as Rose with eyes as green as hers. She smiled, and the air seemed to grow visibly warmer.

If I'd been a betting man, I would have bet that Rose was no older than thirty. Who were these women who looked at least thirty to forty years younger than their true ages? What had my grandfather been doing for them over the past sixty years? What was their secret?

"Call us if you need us. We're going down to the lake," Rose said, her voice a whisper even softer than her mother's. "Nice to meet you, Mr. Snyder." I shook her outstretched hand. It was smooth, soft and velvety.

I'm sure that I responded, but I have no idea what I said. I sat down and watched as Rose and two other young-looking women ran out of the house, across the porch and down the hill to the water. A third woman, dressed similar to Mrs. Lily Parks, glared at me, then kneeled over a mound that I swear looked like a tiny grave, where she buried the flowers I'd just purchased. I was too stunned to say anything. Instead, I looked over to the lake side of the Parks's property, which was steep, rough and extremely dangerous looking. I had no idea how the women climbed down to the sand. I couldn't see steps or a gate in the rusting iron fence. None of the women looked at their mother and me as they left.

Mrs. Lily Parks poured a cup of green tea. She lifted her cup to her lips. I stared at her as if I'd never seen a woman drink before.

"Uh . . . your daughters?" I asked, gesturing in the direction of the disappearing women.

"You've met Rose. The next are the twins, Violet and Daisy, then my youngest, Daphne. You'll meet all of them in due time. Right now, I need to follow up on the instructions that your family has followed regarding the care of the house during the winter months. I noticed that one of the tower windows was broken and not repaired before our arrival. I cannot have that. Your grandfather was a very exacting man, and my family trusted him completely. There were never any problems."

Even though I was being scolded, I seemed to be locked in a time warp and was helpless to do anything but agree that I was not fit to fill my grandfather's shoes. I, who had no intention of following in Grandfather's business, felt ashamed that I was not going to be working for the beautiful Parks Family.

I didn't say anything about not taking over from Grandfather, yet the disappointment in Mrs. Lily Parks's eyes was almost more than I could bear. Somehow she knew that I would be leaving as soon as I completed the last of Grandfather's duties and found someone else to pay the winter mortgage. I found myself trembling, and apologizing for not meeting her standards. Grandfather's papers indicated that he had begun his practice with the newcomers to the Island, folks who would take a chance on a black man during the forties. It didn't occur to me to question Mrs. Lily Parks, as it seemed natural that the longtime African-American inhabitants on the Island would turn to Grandfather for his legal expertise.

My body sat on the porch and listened to her lecture and to her history as I drank her tea and ate the cinnamon cookies that I had failed to notice when I first sat down. All the while, my mind wandered to where her daughters played. They laughed and giggled like teenagers. Their laughter rang through the trees and seemed to surround the house. I wanted to join them. I wanted to listen to their laughter. I, a worldly man of thirty, found myself lusting over women more than double my age. I looked over at Mrs. Lily Parks. She smiled as if she could read my thoughts, and I felt the familiar swelling between my legs. I blinked. How could this be? What was in the tea? That's it. There had to be something in the tea that made me think that the women were as beautiful, young and firm as my eyes told me.

After what seemed like an eternity, I got up slowly from the rattan chair. "Thank you for your afternoon, Mrs. Parks. I will make sure that someone repairs your broken window immediately. I have to get back to the office." I had been daydreaming about how Mrs. Lily Parks's skin would feel under my fingertips. I wanted to know if she tasted as nice as she smelled. I wanted to . . . I dared not think of what I wanted to do to her for fear that I would rip her clothes off and ravish her within the sound of her daughters' laughter. I had to get away. I needed to think.

"Oh, you're leaving so soon? The girls will be disappointed that you're not staying for supper." With those words, Mrs. Lily Parks got up and extended her hand.

I felt that I should kiss it instead of shake it. It took all of my willpower to shake her hand and then to walk down the four stairs to the walkway. I'm sure that she noticed my erection. How could she not? But she turned away from me just as Simon walked around from the side of the house. He accompanied me to the gate.

"Simon, how long have the Parks lived on Thorne Island?" I asked, my voice and body returning to their natural state.

"The Parks have been here since before the Island was named."

"I mean, how long has Mrs. Lily Parks and her daughters lived on the Island?"

"I believe that I answered your question, sir." We were at the gate, and I stepped outside and got into my car. I needed to find out who had worked with Mrs. Lily Parks prior to Grandfather. And I needed to find out what was in the tea I'd drunk and the cookies I'd eaten all afternoon.

What was left of the afternoon I spent in exhaustive research of my grandfather's papers. Nothing in the office told me anything further about his relationship with Mrs. Lily Parks or her daughters.

When it grew too dark to read by natural light, rather than turn on the lights and encourage curious neighbors, I decided to walk home. The house, my grandfather's house, was small, comfortable and highlighted by large windows that looked over the main street and the lake beyond. I would soon be selling the house along with the practice. The house—I had forgotten to search the house for clues about the Parks.

I hadn't eaten anything except the cinnamon cookies Mrs. Lily Parks served with tea, and my stomach growled, reminding me that nourishment and a clear head went hand in hand.

"Did you attend school with any of the Parks daughters?" I asked the waitress in the local mom-and-pop diner. She looked every bit of the sixty years of age that I assumed her to be. She wore her lined face and pursed lips proudly, much like a badge of survival. Her eyes were clear and gray, the shade of gray that changes color with whatever the person is wearing. The waitress, Dottie, according to what her name badge said, was stooped from years of standing on her feet, carrying trays and working long hours. She still had a flirty, if tired, smile. Her silver hair was pulled back in a neat bun at the nape of her neck. She wore serious walking shoes and white socks. The clean, washed-out, blue-pinstriped uniform showed that once she had had a decent figure.

"The Parks women keep to themselves. I've seen them shopping in town, and they've never come in here for eats. None of them grew up here, so we didn't go to school together. They return every spring. They always look so fresh and new. Wherever they spend their winters sure agrees with them. I wish I had skin like theirs. It's so soft, petal-soft. Me, I look like a dried prune." Dottie smiled, removed the pencil she'd placed behind her ear and waited for my order, having exhausted her knowledge and appreciation of the Parks women.

"I'll try your steak, rare, baked potato with sour cream and butter, and a piece of raspberry pie."

"No vegetable?"

"No vegetable. I'll have a bottle of local beer."

"I hear that you're Harrison Snyder's grandson."

"Yep. Just here to clear out his business affairs and sell the house. Do you know of anyone looking for a nice sturdy old home?"

"Nope, but some summer folks—a couple—will probably buy it. We can't seem to keep young men on the island. Seems like just when a nice-looking young man starts getting interested in property or a business, he changes his mind and takes off in the middle of the night. Not your grandfather, though. He stayed a long time. I miss him. He'd come in at least once a week for either lunch or an early supper. Not many black folks on Thorne Island. I think there's a family or two up on the eastern side of the island. Some said your grandfather was an excellent lawyer for them that needed one. Me, I never needed an attorney. You're not going to take over the business?"

"No. Actually, there's not much of a business to take over. Grandfather had sent most of his clients to friends off the island. He represented only the Parks women for the past few years. I guess

I'll have to find someone to take care of them." Dottie didn't recommend anyone. A little later, she brought my supper, which I ate with an appetite I thought I had lost. Everything tasted new, delicious and nourishing. By the time I walked home, I was too tired to look for any papers Grandfather might have stashed in the house. After a long, hot shower, I fell into bed. And dreamed.

I dreamed the most erotic dreams, which involved Mrs. Lily Parks. We made love like wild cats, clawing and nibbling one another. I ran my hands over her muscular, smooth body, and she answered each of my strokes with a cry like something out of the jungle of Kenya. Hers was not the body of a woman older than twenty-five. The wonderful creature of my dreams resembled Mrs. Parks but could not be her. I awoke more spent than I had been in years. I inhaled. Mrs. Parks's perfume saturated my bedroom; a pale yellow, gauzy nightgown was bunched at the foot of my bed. The woman in my dreams had briefly worn a nightgown similar to the one that lay at my feet. I got up slowly and rubbed my face, feeling a small scratch on my neck that my dream woman had left.

I showered, dressed, made coffee and began searching Grandfather's home for clues about the Parks women.

Rose—May

I spent the next four days going through every book, ledger and bank statement that I could find of Grandfather's. I flipped through all the books in his library; I went through the glove compartments and trunks of both cars. I called my father, my sister, my distant cousin—anyone who had spent any time on Thorne Island—for help in finding out anything about the Parks Family. No one knew anything about their business with Grandfather. It was as Simon had said: The natives couldn't remember when they had not been on the Island, and no one knew where their winter home was.

The Parks women had always been just the same: mysteriously beautiful creatures who kept to themselves and who arrived in late April and left in early September. They were rarely seen in town.

Simon purchased their groceries. They didn't receive mail, except the usual junk mail that every summer visitor received.

On the fifth day of May, when the Island folks decided to celebrate *Cinco de Mayo*, I was once again summoned to the Parks's estate. I was delirious to see the women in the flesh again, and terrified that they would somehow know that I dreamed of their mother every night. Every morning, I awoke exhausted, confused and spent.

The nightgown was missing when I returned home after that first morning, and since then, nothing remained of Lily Parks's night visits to my bed but her scent. Also, after that first night, I apparently began sleepwalking, or to be more accurate, sleep-driving, because my car would be in a different spot from the previous evening and ten miles would be added to the mileage. It was exactly ten miles to and from the Parks's estate. But why would I drive there and not remember? Were my dreams real? Was I actually sleeping with Lily Parks? No, I couldn't be. Besides, I remembered nothing of where I'd been during my night outings. I only remembered the sex.

"Good morning, Simon," I said as I pulled my car to the massive iron gate. "I believe that Mrs. Lily Parks is expecting me."

"Yes, sir," he whispered, and opened the gate. I again followed him to the spot where I had first met Mrs. Lily Parks.

"Miss Rose will be with you shortly," Simon said as he disappeared into the house. I heard a screen door bang shut and turned, but no one was on the porch with me. I got up, opened the door and entered the dining room. The room was large and airy, with sturdy oak furniture and elaborate runners on the dining room table and buffet. Both pieces of furniture held enormous bouquets of artificial flowers. Odd. I would have to remember to ask about the flowers, since so many beautiful wild ones grew in the garden.

Then I saw her coming down the stairs toward me. Rose. She was even lovelier that day than on the first day I'd met her. She wore a sleeveless orange gauze dress that complemented her dark skin. Her curly black hair was pulled on top of her head and fastened with a string of orange beads that were a shade lighter than her dress. She was barefooted. Her dress flowed around her knees, and blew and billowed when she walked, so every once in a while I saw a glimpse of her thigh. She had very long legs.

"Mr. Snyder," she whispered. I'd nearly forgotten the breathless manner in which she spoke.

"Call me Paolo."

"Paolo," she replied, and I wanted her then and there, in her mother's house, on her mother's dining room table. I forgot her age. I forgot that just that morning, I had awakened lusting for her mother. No woman had ever said my name the way she had, not even the Mrs. Lily Parks of my dreams.

She smiled and walked outside to the porch. She sat down in one of the rattan chairs, crossed her legs, smoothed her dress and poured a cup of tea.

"Uh . . ." I had worn a light, open-necked cotton shirt. I pulled at the throat, gasping for air. "No tea for me," I managed to strangle out.

"You look uncomfortable, Paolo. Have some water or lemonade. It has been extremely warm today." She took out a small wooden fan and waved it in front of her face. The fan gave off the scent of cedar. Then she poured a tall glass of lemonade. She took a sip of it, then handed it to me. Her pale orange lipstick left a faint mark on the glass. I drank from the same spot.

"I asked you here because it is time for me to make out my will. I'm not getting any younger." Rose laughed, then she leaned forward and I smelled the perfume in her hair.

"I'm sure . . . I'm sure that we have plenty of time for a will," I managed to say, and then I poured myself a glass of water. I could still taste her lipstick on my mouth. It had the same seductive properties as the tea that I'd drunk with her mother.

"This was the year that all of us were going to write out our wills for your grandfather. He was such a dear man. We loved him immensely. He will be missed." Rose sat back in her chair as a droplet of sweat, which reminded me of fresh dew, rolled down her chin and into the hollow of her throat. This time, she did not wave her fan, but let the droplet pool. I watched as her pulse beat pumped the droplet. I wish I could take that next second back, but I couldn't help myself, and before I knew what was happening, I had leaned over and licked the drop from her throat.

"Mr. Snyder," she yelled in what would normally have been an average tone. But it was a shout from her. "I thought you were here for Mama. Isn't she the one in your dreams?"

I was stunned that she mentioned my dreams. Was I that obvious?

"You will have to choose which of us you want. I do not compete with Mama. Here, have something to drink. You will feel better." She handed me a glass of lemonade and watched as I drank all of it. I should have known that the Parks women were not ordinary women, but I was blinded by lust.

I hadn't been with a real woman since the February prior to coming to Thorne Island. I was somehow satisfied with my dreams of Lily.

"Perhaps you can stay for supper. I hear that you eat meat. We also are carnivores. We will prepare something for supper. It is *Cinco de Mayo*, so we will have tacos and beer. Then you can tell me what to put in my will. You will see Mama. I think she likes you, and you can choose which of us you want to stay with tonight."

"We also are carnivores" was an odd way of stating that they ate meat. But I didn't ask the question that formed in my mind. What I asked instead was, "No salad?"

"We don't *eat* plant life," Rose replied, and shuddered as if the idea of eating fruit and vegetables was the most disgusting thing imaginable. I thought about Rose, whom I wanted desperately right then, but found myself sipping lemonade and listening to her make plans for supper. How could I awake in lust for the mother and not five hours later want the daughter? It took every ounce of my willpower not to rip her clothes off and take her on the porch in much the same manner I had thought about with the mother during our first meeting. There had to be something in the lemonade. I had to excuse myself and return to the village, where I could think. Here at the Parks's, my mind was too clouded to think things through clearly.

"Thank you for the dinner offer, but I need to get back to town. I have to have time to complete your requests." I got up and raced to the gate.

Simon stood by the open gate.

"Have a good afternoon," he whispered. A praying mantis walked between the gate's rails and disappeared into the hedge. It was one of the few insects that I'd noticed in the garden. I looked more carefully. Ladybugs and tiny translucent snails hid among the fresh fern and healthy loam near the gate. The garden was in balance.

"Simon, your garden looks very healthy," I said as I stepped onto the street.

"Thank you. I talk to the flowers *and* the weeds. It makes them happy to know that someone cares for them." He smiled as if thinking of something I would never understand.

Violet — June

Rose invited me back to the house to sign some final papers. We were, as always, seated on the porch, drinking lemonade. A tea service was on the table, although I had not drunk tea since my first day at the Parks's home.

"I'm Violet. We haven't met," were the first words she said to me as I finished a glass of lemonade. When I stood up, I accidentally knocked over a teacup, breaking it. Shards of glass bounced along the porch. Violet stopped and picked up the broken cup, cutting her index finger. She extended her right hand while licking blood off her left. For a second, it appeared that her blood was clear, then turned a dark, healthy red as the drop was sucked into her mouth. She smiled, watching me watching her.

"I'm sorry about the cup. I think I might have suffered from a momentary flash of heat stroke." The sun was in the west, high in the sky, and the table and chairs where Rose and I sat were bathed in sunlight. My shirt was drenched, and my linen slacks were wrinkled and bunched at the crotch.

"That happens to folks occasionally—heat stroke. Perhaps you two should move inside. The library is much cooler, and you can finish your business in there. No one will disturb you. Mama said that you remind her of your grandfather. I don't see the resemblance." Violet looked like a girl of seventeen or eighteen. She wore a muted-blue cotton blouse and a multicolored skirt that swayed around her midthigh. She was the first Park woman I'd met who wore jewelry somewhere other than in her hair. Her ears were pierced six, no seven, times and sported tiny golden hoops. She also wore golden bracelets on both wrists and an ornate golden symbol of the sun around her neck.

As always when I was at the Parks's estate, I found myself lusting for one of the daughters. Just before Violet arrived, I had been daydreaming about Rose.

"I need to apologize to your sister." All of my lust had evaporated when the cup fell. I felt like a stupid child caught trying to make out with my best friend's mother.

"Why? Rose is very—how should I say it—beautiful, in a fragile way, aren't you, sis?" She bent over and kissed Rose on her left cheek. I had now met three of the Parks women, and all were enchanting. Violet smiled again, then walked into the house. A butterfly followed her to the door. She let it land on her injured finger for a second and then shook it away. The red and angry cut looked instantly healed. Violet turned and went inside.

Daisy and Daphne often waved at me and whomever I was with on the porch as they rushed to the lake or ran into the house. Neither had much to say to me. All of the women seemed to crave water, and swam and danced in the lake during much of the day. Of course, my curiosity grew each time one of them was within sight.

My dreams about Lily and Rose continued. Time moved quickly. I sold Grandfather's home the first week of June. I remember sitting on the Parks's porch, which had become my unofficial office, during the second week of June. That particular afternoon, I was joined by Violet. I had not seen her in nearly a month.

"There's plenty of room here," she said during a lull in our conversation.

"What?"

"I said, there's plenty of room here. Your grandfather's home is sold, and you can stay in the guesthouse while we complete our paperwork for this summer."

"Guesthouse?" I had spent a lot of time at the Parks's yet I had seen very little of their grounds. Simon seemed to be weeding or cultivating a new patch of flowers whenever I was near, yet I never saw cut flowers in any of the vases on the porch.

Mostly, I worked at one of the tables on the porch. I had observed the iron fence in back of the house near the cliffs. It was old and rusty-looking, and didn't appear strong enough to keep out a determined intruder.

"Yes. See, it's right there." She pointed to a small log cabin that I had failed to notice previously. "Let's go look at it." I followed her, observing her long dark legs and the green, cotton sunsuit that resembled old-fashioned tennis shorts from the twenties. Her skin glowed, and her eyes sparkled as she clapped her hands together like a child opening a new present. Both Violet and Rose were taller than their mother, and the younger women had very long legs. Violet enjoyed wearing shorts that showed hers off.

She opened the door, and we entered a large room that contained a stone fireplace and a sofa. The room opened onto a small kitchen, bathroom and bedroom. I ran my fingers over the flower-print fabric of the sofa. The bedroom was just large enough for the iron double bed and a tiny wooden nightstand.

A handmade quilt covered the bed. "This is very beautiful. Wonderful workmanship," I said. It resembled some of the outsider art that I'd seen elderly women making in the Carolinas.

"Thank you. I made it. The design is the 'Wedding Rehearsal.' I'm pleased that you like it."

The bathroom had an old, white, claw-footed tub, a pedestal basin and a pull-chain toilet. The cabin looked very old and lived in, yet brand new and virginal at the same time.

"I'm sure that you would be happy here during your short stay," Violet said. There was a hint of something just behind her eyes. I felt a chill, but dismissed it, and we walked back outside. "I'll have Simon bring your things to the cabin while we have supper."

All of my dinners at the Parks's had consisted of elaborate meals with appropriate wine or beer and coffee. The women had healthy appetites and ate as if they tasted food for the first time. I loved watching them eat and drink. I had assumed that women that healthy would also eat healthy, but they ate only meat, fish and a few dried nuts. After supper, the four of us would retire to the library, where we would have a glass of brandy, then I would leave for Grandfather's home, where I would dream of one of the sisters. Daisy and Daphne always had plans and were never home for supper. Yet I yearned for them also.

Last June was Violet's turn to wind her way into my night thoughts. I wanted her in a manner different from her mother and Rose. She played the cello, and I dreamed of being the instrument on which she practiced. I wanted her lean, tan, compact body. I wanted to drink in her dark blue eyes and run my fingers through her blue-black hair, which she wore long and straight, like an Indian princess. This daughter was bolder and earthier than her mother or her sister Rose.

Violet was a tease. I knew that if I ever slept with her, I would not go back to her mother or Rose. Even in my dreams, she was aloof, her own person. I never got her to bed. I'd kiss her, and she'd laugh and find something to talk about that was so fascinating, I fell asleep on the sofa only to awake to an empty house. What would happen once I was living on the estate? Perhaps she was waiting for me in the guesthouse, on the iron bed, under the "Wedding Rehearsal" quilt.

Daisy—July

"She's just like Mama, only taller. They even dress alike. Isn't that silly? She's *my* twin." I looked up as Daisy walked out of the house and onto the porch. It was my first evening staying in the guesthouse. Daisy was Violet's identical twin. However, they were very easy to tell apart. While Violet wore clothing suited to her name—blues, blacks, greens—Daisy was fond of white. Both women wore yellow like no woman I'd ever noticed previously. I was completely under their spells.

"So we finally meet, Mr. Snyder," Daisy said, holding out her hand in the same manner that Violet had a month earlier.

"Call me Paolo. Your sisters do."

"Paolo? Odd name for a black man. Portuguese?"

"No. My mother loved to travel, and my sister, Chi-Na, and I have names that remind Mom of exotic places."

"I don't think that we need to discuss my will. I'll have the same thing as Violet and Daphne." I watched as Daisy walked away. I noticed her long legs. There was something wrong. I looked at her again. Yes, there was a greenish hue to them. Then just as quickly, as if she'd noticed me looking, her legs were tan, strong and healthy.

Why was Daisy so aloof? She seemed to resent my presence, yet I had just met her. It was she I saw burying the flowers I brought the first day. Surely, she couldn't have resented a gift of flowers. Perhaps it was that she suspected I'd mentally slept with her mother, older sister and, hopefully, twin?

"Daisy, Paolo is staying in the guesthouse until the end of summer," Violet said to her sister's retreating back.

"The guesthouse? I thought I saw Simon bringing in suitcases. Welcome."

Daisy's welcome was cold. Yes, there was a definite hostility toward me. She did not want me in the guesthouse, at supper or anywhere near her family, and she made no effort to hide her displeasure.

"Daisy has difficulty warming to folks. Sometimes she seems so rude, but she'll come around. I've sat you next to her for supper," Violet said.

The rest of July, including the fourth, went by in a blur. The Parks women had a million and one changes to make to their wills. I had to confer with attorneys on the main land and travel to Montpelier, the state capital, to go over land grants, of all things. Whenever I returned to the Parks's estate, I fell into bed and dreamed of the sisters.

Daphne—August

"We'll be shutting the house soon. It's too bad that you cannot come with us. We tried to bring your grandfather with us when we first met him, but he was too fragile," Daphne said one particularly hot August morning. She was the youngest and strangest of the Parks women. She made the most unusual statements. Her sisters often stopped her or corrected something she'd said. It was as if she were still extremely young or mentally challenged, and said whatever popped into her mind. Yet, she had to be in her early fifties.

Even with the outside temperature in the mid-nineties, she wore a sweater and a scarf. She loved wool clothing and could never get warm. Daphne was the only one whose hands looked like those of a very elderly woman. Hers were bony, blue-veined, with knurled knuckles that resembled withered branches. While her mother and sisters seemed to be smooth, with soft edges, she was sharp and harsh. She almost always wore gloves. I never dreamed about the youngest daughter.

Her voice, while quiet like her mother's and Rose's, seemed strained, as if she were not used to speaking. None of this warned me of my fate. I blindly went about the business of the Parks women, finalizing their affairs, as well as closing escrow on Grandfather's house and getting ready to move back to New York.

Paolo—September

"We have enjoyed this summer. It's time to leave. We will be back next year. I'm sure that we will be pleased with the attorney that you've found for us. Now, what's his name?" Mrs. Lily Parks asked on Labor Day. She and I were seated on the side of the porch overlooking the water. The wind had come up, and there was a slight chill in the air.

"Raymond Gonzales. He's new to the Island, but I've checked his credentials. He's single, thirty-five and plans on making Thorne Island his home. I'm sure that he will be an excellent representative for you and your daughters."

"We thank you for your time and *energy*. My daughters and I have *enjoyed* you immensely. I think that Daphne may like Mr. Gonzales." That's when I noticed it: The color of the grass seemed to have changed, and the cottage where I'd spent the last three months suddenly looked overgrown. It was as if fall had descended overnight.

Simon walked up the path and onto the porch.

"Is it time for the planting?" he asked. I noticed the spade and pick in his hand.

"Yes, we have to leave tomorrow, and we need to ensure that everything is in order for our departure," Mrs. Lily Parks replied. "Paolo, have a cup of tea." She poured the brown liquid into an earthen cup. It was the first cup I'd seen that wasn't fine bone china.

"I don't really feel like tea. I have to pack," I replied.

"Pack? Oh, dear. I'm afraid that you will have to remain here. It's much too late for you to leave now. Besides, Daphne needs you to introduce her to Mr. Gonzales."

"Daphne? She's barely spoken to me. If she has any additional information for Gonzales, she will have to send it to me, because I'm leaving in the morning."

"Simon?" Mrs. Lily Parks looked over at her handyman and nodded.

It happened so quickly that I was unable to react. I was slumped down in the wicker chair that I had claimed as mine. My back was to the lake. Simon swung the spade and hit me in the back of my head. I fell down to the porch floor. I hit with such force that I thought my neck was broken. I was unable to move my arms or legs.

"Here, Paolo, drink this tea. It will make you feel better." Mrs. Lily Parks kneeled over me. Her suddenly dry, rough hand brushed my face as she poured the tea into my mouth. She seemed to age before my eyes.

I didn't feel a thing, not even a headache. The next that I knew, I was here, in the ground, looking up at the sky as a ladybug crawled past, then a green garden snake. They were nearly at eye level. Simon was correct—I had nothing to fear from them. I tried to look around, but my feet and ankles were buried in the earth. I was *in* the garden. There was nothing left of the rose bush but thorns. The spring and summer flowers had disappeared just like the Parks women. Gone to seed. I tried to look around, but my thin body bent in the wind.

It rained, and I got soaked. I heard someone approaching. It was Simon.

"Good, you're taking root well. I told them that you were strong. I told them that you would replenish the garden. It is difficult to find someone who can give to all the flowers, but you were outstanding. Do you have any human memory left? I doubt it. You are now what is called *Agrimonia eupatoria*, a common weed. Most folks don't know that some of the flowers cannot renew and become beautiful without the common weed. Without you, some flowers would perish. The Parks needed you, and I made sure you were available, as have been others like you. You are the strongest. The other young men lasted only one winter, but you have your grandfather's genes and will last a very long time. He was too old to help in the garden, but he was invaluable during the summer. He never understood his contribution to the Parks Family. The cottage will protect you, and I will take care of you, see you and make sure that you are ready for spring. Remember, when we first met, I told you that I always talk to the plants and weeds in my very special garden." He smiled, and turned up the dirt near my roots.

Here I am, the keeper of the dreams of flowers, waiting for their return in the spring.

Good 'Nough to Eat

Rickey Windell George

"You know what they say about black men, about the size . . ."
Things people say that "we know" are *mostly* true

"You can never have too much of a good thing . . ."
Things people say that "we know" are *mostly* false

It was every man's dream, but it was Kelly's very real nightmare. It felt like sleepwalking, staggering onto the stage with the head on his shoulders light and spinning, while the other bulged in its too-small pouch, bouncing heavily upon his every stride. And then Kelly was washed in liquid-red luminescence. The spotlights found him, the heat like a thousand pinpricks making his pores bleed sweat.

He could feel the tremble in the pine flooring of the stage beneath his bare feet, and it wasn't the music. He could feel the charge in the air between the audience and himself, and he knew that their attention belonged to him.

Life had shown him that everyone had an appetite for his big dick; it made some eyes dance with mad circles of desire, while other eyes flipped somersaults of envy. It was always the topic of conversation:

"Is it true what they say . . . ?"

And for Kelly there was nothing truer.

"Man, you walk like you got a weight between your legs."

And he did walk funny—it was quite a load.

"I can see it right through your pants. I'll give you ten bucks to take it out."

And though he felt cheap doing it, when he needed the money he'd unzip his fly, and what waited on the other side was like the shit inside Pandora's box. You could never predict the reaction a person would have to it, just that there would be an intense one.

The female patrons of Silvia's were no exception.

At every angle, women were coming out of their seats, bumping and grinding and pushing and shoving to get the best view. The audience had been rowdy to begin with, jockeying for the attentions of the other members of the Male Review, but before Kelly they'd become a feeding-pool full of big-black-and-beautiful bad-mamma sharks. They were circling for Kelly now, scenting the enormous treat that was buoyed by his loincloth. And Kelly could feel their treat between his legs, like the anchor it had always been, dragging him down.

It was every man's dream, but all that adoration and worship had never felt like love—it was only appetite. And the reactions to that special something about Kelly were often self-destructive and violent.

Tonight, every pair of lips—facial or otherwise—was moist for a taste, and every pair of eyes met his stare full of hunger.

Tonight, in the front row, more than just one woman was running her tongue across the edges of the bared cutters of her teeth; and tonight, for the first time in a very long while, Kelly was afraid.

It had not been so much like dreaming awake a few hours earlier.

Kelly's balls had been aching again as he shoved through his creaking front door, slamming it so fiercely that dust-rain came down from the cracked ceiling. Asbestos dust powdered his face, while larger chunks of peeling paint—like heavy yellow snowflakes—tumbled, landing in the top of his 'fro.

The place was practically falling down around him, but none of that mattered.

What mattered was getting out of his pants—not his clothes, but just his pants. Swinging down the worn leather satchel that was riding his shoulder, he hit his belt buckle hard, unhitching it, tugging the leather, whipping it loose from the loops with a swish of cut air. Even before the discarded belt thumped the floor, he was ripping at his zipper feverishly, bringing it down and over the familiar bulge with a loud raspberry sound.

Then he was bunching his trousers down his thighs, into a wad around his ankles that already he was kicking to be free of; and while his still-boot-bound feet kicked for freedom, his hands were on a mission also, sliding down the elastic band of his underwear.

His boots came off in the knot of fabric around his feet.

His ragged Fruit of the Looms, moth-bitten and aged off-white, joined the tossed-about mess of would-be-worn-again things on the floor, but begged for the trash.

And there, bare-legged and sweater-topped, Kelly stood with the long, limp sausage of his penis resting across one palm, while the fingers of his free hand massaged his stinging yam sack. He was what some people referred to as "a shower," which was to say that he was big when flaccid, long and thick enough to show all his promise even when soft. "Growers," on the other hand, were small when soft, but might balloon a great deal more than their shower counterparts when it was time to stand at attention.

Kelly was a *shower*, better than a half-foot strong all day every day, and thick too; but Kelly was also a grower, as there was another half-foot of him still in hiding.

Let it hide, he thought as he felt the slight tingle rising from the working of his fingers in the nest surrounding his scrotum. *God, just let it hide, and let the ache stop.* And then his eyes fell hungrily upon the broken-down recliner in the far corner of the living room, and his weary legs began walking in the direction of the La-Z-Boy that he'd found on the side of the street, some rich person's garbage. The springs and gears that at one time closed it were ruined, but Kelly's thought today was the same as when he'd fetched two of his buddies to help him drag it back to his place: What was a recliner for, if not for layin' back?

And there, he flounced his two hundred and twenty pounds down.

Through the fabric he could feel a spring threatening to jab him in the ass, but that spring bluffed every day.

"Babe," he called into the depths of the apartment, his voice seeming to make the clouds of dust motes dance in the slices of light coming in through the small, grimy windows. "Babe, I need my . . ."

And then, before he could finish, Sheila slunk through the doorway that connected the living room to the kitchen. She was stark-naked sex, sweat-shined caramel flesh, gripping a glass of water in her left hand and a bottle of Bayer aspirin in the right, with what looked like a black shoelace wound around her wrist.

"You're home," she said. "I been thinkin' 'bout you all day."

"Don't get your hopes up," he grumbled, his eyes prying themselves away from the heavy globes of her breasts, the dark arrow-head nipples. Flipping his stare out the window, he gazed past the rusted iron railings of the fire escape and into the orange light of desolation. "They ain't hiring for shit."

"Oh, baby." It was her sweet voice then. "My hopes are up, but not for that."

Kelly's eyes were on Sheila again, on the way her stare was fixed upon his groin, the way her tongue kept wetting and rewetting her lips. "There's an eviction notice on the door," he said.

Her head shook. "Not anymore. I took it down this morning."

"Okay, so there's an eviction notice somewhere in this god-damned, overpriced roach motel."

"Yup," she agreed with a nod, and then sauntered toward him, revealing through the click-click of her steps that she was wearing heels—stilettos, more than three inches high—and nothing else. "I know you need your aspirin."

"Yeah, my nuts are killing me." Kelly's eyes rolled. "Been walkin' this good-for-nothing asphalt all day, just one step from begging, tryin' to keep my head up."

"Well, I got an hour before I gotta be at Roy's," Sheila said.

Kelly nodded, taking the pill bottle from her, throwing way more than the recommended dose down his gullet as he tossed back his head. And after draining the glass of water in three gulps, he was spreading his legs for Sheila to stand between his knees, he was holding her round, firm ass in the expansive grip of his hands, and he was growing.

She could not take her eyes away from the magic of it.

She could not help but smile at its beauty.

And then she was on her knees in front of him, winding the thick shoelace tight around the base of his penis and his scrotum.

One loop . . .

It took a lot of blood to fill the foot-long snake.

Two loops . . .

Left to its own devices, it could take a while to become fully ex-cited; and even once full and so very heavy and sweet, there was so much of it to manage that it might lose some of its rigidity.

Three loops, four . . .

The noose, however, would keep that beautiful dick tight, would keep it right. On the seventh loop, Sheila tied her cock-noose with a fancy Girl Scout knot, a reminder that where she'd grown up, there'd been parks and picnics, and grassy backyards, Girl Scouts and Cub Scouts, and even now *she* could go home to daddy.

"How'm I gonna get that loose?"

"You're not," she breathed through a grin. "You're all mine 'til I say otherwise." And then Sheila's head was descending, mouth gaped in preparation, in anticipation. It was, she had said more than once, the most unbelievably sexy penis she'd ever seen on a man; and when her lips sealed around it, jaws stretched to their limit, mouth absolutely full, there was no doubt in Kelly's mind that she meant those words. Feeling was believing.

The weight of him melted like chocolate under steam.

Expertly she traced the dome of his glans, tickling under the ridge of his very pronounced and bulbous helmet with her tongue, and his body came alive with the charge of her hunger for him. It felt so incredibly good that the ache in his sack grew dim, his brain forgetting how to process the pain in light of so much pleasure. The weight of three months of overdue rent dissolved as a sheen of sweat swept his body in a tide, and washed in all that heat, he began shrugging off his sweater and the T-shirt beneath it.

Only half of him could be consumed—there wasn't room enough inside Sheila's mouth, inside her head, for the rest. To reach those other blessed inches, she worked him like a harmonica, lapping his delicious flavor up and down the pole, tracing the great bulging arteries that stood out along his shaft all the way into the bush of his pubic nest, wherein she found warm eggs, also ripe for her mouth.

Throwing back his head, Kelly enjoyed the service.

He didn't buck his hips about, as instinct wanted him to; he'd learned not to over the years. When his organ was being serviced, it was best for him to be still. Though his eyes might be closed, a mental eye was always open—he was never fully relaxed. The measure of the tool made it impossible for him to have reckless sex.

If he were reckless, someone would damn near get choked.

If he was reckless, there might be blood.

If he was reckless, "hurts so good" could turn to "hurts so bad" very easily.

Kelly had been over at Josh's house having beers earlier in the week, trying to get his mind off his money problems. He'd been in his friend's bathroom relieving himself of the excess Heineken he'd drunk when the words "Jesus, man, you're fuckin' huge" had reached his ears.

The door had been cracked, and a hazel eye was pressed to the sliver—an ash-blonde eyebrow, a bit of a matching bang above that.

"Shit, can't a man piss?" Still holding himself, Kelly had angled toward the door, moving to bump it shut with a shoulder. But the spatter of his urine stream across the floor made him turn back to the toilet, and the action served only to present a momentary profile of his glorious endowment. The spying eye had bulged to fill the opening between door and jamb.

"You know me, K, I'm not a homo. It's just, shit, man, why didn't I get a dick like that?"

"'Cause you're a white boy."

"Some white guys got dick, K, just not me."

Kelly was throwing hostile looks over his shoulder at the sliver while he dribbled dry, when his friend—ever brazen—delivered the sixty-million-dollar question: "So, what's up? Can I just . . . look at it? Feels like forever I been tryin' to spy 'round urinal walls or peep you out in locker rooms, and the shit is stupid. I'm your boy; I just wanna look at it."

"Fine, get it out yo' fuckin' system then. But touch me, and it's a fight."

The bathroom door creaked on its hinges, and then Josh was flicking on the light above the medicine-cabinet mirror, in addition to the ceiling light that already burned. Kelly felt like a giant drumstick underneath the red-orange heat lamps in some Popeyes chicken hut. "That's amazing," Josh said, hovering up close, gazing down. "You're bigger soft than I am hard. Man, if I had that . . ."

"You'd be some kinda freak show, with a big black penis swingin' off yo' skinny white body."

"Nigga, please, I'm not skinny." Josh had been born and raised in this same black neighborhood, and he knew the talk, the vulgar music of it, as well as anyone else. "I'm in the gym every day." And lifting his shirt he revealed the pale rigid washboard that was his stomach. "Feel that," he insisted.

"Are you out yo' mind, motherfucker? I ain't feelin' shit on yo' body while I'm hangin' here in the wind."

"I'm just sayin', pudgy," and Josh punctuated by jabbing a finger into the flat but soft surface of Kelly's stomach. "I'm hard, m'man. I'm ready."

"Ready to what? Be in one of yo' uncle's movies?"

"Yeah, if I had what you got. The solution to your money trouble has been swingin' between your legs all along, and I'm sittin' right here with the hookup. Cheap Jew bastard says I'm not hung enough for his films. But you—you're like a horse. He'd love you."

"Yeah, okay. Well, my mama taught me not to peddle my ass for money."

"It's your dick, not your ass."

"It's my dick, and I'm puttin' it away now."

"Wait, man, wait. How big does it get?"

Kelly stared then at the other man's hawkeyed focus on the meat slung over the waistband of his sweats. There was a subtle note of desperation in Josh's tone, and a kind of hunger, too. His dream was right there in front of his eyes, attached to someone else's groin.

Kelly had taken himself in hand to retuck and reclaim his privacy when Josh interjected: "Shit, man, just play with it for a second, okay? I just want to see. When am I gonna see a real one like that again?" His tone trembled slightly, as if he might cry were the meat pocketed so soon.

"I'd give it to you if I could, Josh."

"You lie."

"Grass is always greener, m'man. You want to watch me jerk it, right? Guys always like that." Kelly began a deliberately pronounced stroke, snapping the meat like a whip, making the big head thrash about. "It might take a while—these big ones take a lot to fill."

Josh didn't care. The words were right there, but he didn't know how to fix them on his lips and make them sound right. *I could help you; I could touch it with you.* The words never surfaced, as there was no right way to say them, but in his eyes the language of it lingered plain as day.

"It's no fun, man," Kelly said, trying to convince him. "You can't fuck in the positions you want 'cause you end up hurtin' the ladies, your balls are always stinging like you been kicked in em' 'cause you got too much ridin' up front and no kinda underwear has the right support, and people are always staring 'cause you can't hide the . . ."

Kelly's stroke had continued all the while, and the meat was responding. And Josh, his bottom jaw hanging, was hypnotized by the cobra and completely unmoved by what his friend had to say.

I'm not gay, read the words in Josh's eyes now, *but I'll suck your dick if you'll let me, just to see it full-grown, just to live through it for a few vicarious minutes.*

"Go ahead," Kelly said, his temper at a boil, his eyes bloodshot from all the flared arteries clouding the whites. "Suck it," he said in a booming monotone.

For the first time in a while, Josh's eyes elevated to meet his friend's; he wanted to say something and Kelly knew what. "I know, Josh. I've heard it all before. You're not gay, but you *do* wanna suck it. Everybody does, so go ahead."

Josh nodded, and the next sound was the thump his knees made hitting the ground. In tandem, Kelly's heart seemed to slam the floor of his stomach. *They* were all the same; everyone, the same; everyone hungry.

Kelly shut his eyes as Josh's jaws opened.

Something inside him was screaming . . .

Something inside him was breaking . . .

All he knew was that he couldn't watch.

That night, in the cramped quarters of Josh's bathroom, the space behind Kelly's eyelids had been bottomless black. But the longer he drifted in the nothing of it, the more it changed, its sealing embrace tightening into a stranglehold. Obsidian dark turned storm-cloud gray, then ethereal white. And like thinning smoke, there were shapes whirring on the other side—ghosts, waiting as if behind a veil.

It was the veil of his mind.

It was a scene snatched from some raw spot in his cerebellum, a forgotten moment seeping from an old mental wound, now reopened, like blood from a poorly stitched gash.

Kelly's buddy Josh had made the wound bleed again—his hot mouth, his course tongue, the occasional panting utterance: "Oh . . .

Oh, god . . . it's huge!" All conspired to rip through the scar tissue time had woven into place.

Kelly was in the locker room during his freshman year of high school, in the shower, his bronze back bent like a question mark in the interest of hiding his penis, like a dog might hide its tail between its legs. His hands were down there as well, groping, trying to cover and conceal it. The shower spray was a relentless waterfall pounding his skull, his chest, every stinging bead an accusation.

"Check Kelly out. Fucker's hard again."

"What a homo."

The other boys, all naked and leering, barking and pointing, had formed a crude circle around him.

"Every time we come in these showers, Kelly's got wood. What's the matter with you, faggot? You got everybody scared to drop the soap."

"I ain't no fag." Kelly's eyes, had they been daggers, would have unseated the boy's newly grown Adam's apple from his throat.

It was like this every time he took his clothes off in the locker room. They thought he was hard because he was bigger soft, bigger all day, than any one of them with a full hard-on. They thought he got off looking at them, but as his hurt, angry eyes roved the circle, it was sadly obvious that the shoe was on the other foot.

They were the ones watching him, covetous and lusty, and covering up their own confusion with this nasty game of odd man out.

"Look how big that shit is," another voice called out of the circle.

"Yeah, this faggot's a big mutha. Gonna fix your ass, Dreaves. Fix it so you can't sit down for a week."

"I don't give two shits about Dreaves's ass!" Kelly straightened his backbone, and found his accuser's eyes. "I said, I ain't no faggot."

"Yeah, you are. Your boner's sayin' what your lips don't."

The pink-faced boy with all the mouth was pale and skinny, and had a flaccid penis like a button. All of them, pink and brown, a few dark chocolate, even the largest of them, were small by Kelly's measure. In years to come, he would find the words, but at fourteen, the lexicon had been far beyond him.

At fourteen, he'd wondered *why* he was different.

He'd wondered what was wrong with his penis, why it wouldn't just shrivel down and go away like everyone else's. Why did it want to make him out to be a fruit.

Someone threw a bar of soap, which connected with his left temple, popping him hard, ricocheting as it staggered him. Laughter moved through the circle like cancer metastasizing inside the frailest of bodies, and another bar was flung, and another after that. Like slippery stones, they stung Kelly's chest, bloodied his nose, and when one of those blocks of soap pounded his groin, striking his penis and his left testicle, he buckled over and groaned.

This was when they seized him.

"You gonna like this, faggot."

All their names were lost to him now, and even their faces were mostly blurs, but what they did with those bars of soap he would never forget. The way they forced him down to the wet tiles; the way the mildew looked overgrown in the grout line his right cheek had pressed into; the way all that angst and boy sweat and Ivory soap stunk to high heaven.

"I ain't no faggot," he had sobbed.

Two boys had sat on his back to keep him down.

"I ain't no faggot!" he had screamed. "I'm not! I'm not!"

His arms were held while two fellows made a wish with his legs, opening the gate for a third. By the time the coach intervened, screaming and cursing, and snatching naked youths off Kelly, slapping the one with his hand in the cookie jar, the damage had already been done.

It had taken two hours in the emergency room for the doctors to extract the three bars of soap Kelly's so-called teammates had wedged up his rectum. The entire junior varsity football team was suspended for the two weeks that followed, but that was a small price to pay for what they'd done. While they lounged at home, Kelly had been wearing sanitary pads to school. The way those bars of soap had reamed him, he'd bled for days after, and shitting had burned like there was a blowtorch stuck up his ass.

For months afterward, he'd wake in the small hours of the night washed in sweat, with the words "I ain't no faggot" still falling off his lips.

Those words found his trembling lips again in Josh's bathroom.

"I'm not . . . I'm not . . ." Kelly whispered with his eyes sealed, his voice painfully naked.

Josh nodded, his mouth full.

"I ain't no faggot," Kelly said as his eyelids sprang open like shades snapping to the call of their springs. The base in his voice was mounting in tune with the tremble in his balls. "I'm not . . ."

Josh's eyes gazed up to his wide-gored mouth. *Me either,* said those hazel eyes. *It's just so amazing that I had to see it in action.* His eyes said a lot, but his mouth said more. He was a cocksucker, and it was Kelly's cock. If they were not queer, then what were they? What would the boys from the shower room think?

"I'm not a faggot!" Kelly boomed as a stream of tear-water rolled off his left cheek.

Then grabbing Josh by the head, by two fistfuls of hair, he bellowed it again and again as he drove himself into the tight *O* of that little mouth.

The sounds turned suddenly into muzzled gags and Josh's telling looks turned to terrorized alerts as his hazel-emblazoned eyeballs threatened to pop from the sockets. Josh's arms and hands sprang up, striking Kelly's forearms, as if to throw loose his hold, but Kelly was fifty pounds the greater man, even if his stomach lacked the deep abdominal cuts Josh was so proud of. Kelly's arms were like immovable logs, and his clenched fingers were as certain as a death grip.

Scrambling, choking, unable to grasp anything else, Josh caught the slack at the seat of Kelly's sweatpants, dragging the cotton down the sprung-wound hemispheres of the other man's ass, leaving claw trails in the bronze skin as that relentless pelvis locked out and fired in with mechanical determination. And when Kelly at last shoved away from the smaller man's head, he was roaring, screaming from one mouth and spurting from the other. And Josh was also spurting—vomiting—as he toppled backward.

The first convulsive gush had fired not just from Josh's mouth, but also from both his flared nostrils. The second wave found Josh on his knees with his face in the bowl of the toilet. Kelly was snatching up his pants then, trembling, taking unsure stumbling steps toward the door.

"That . . . that was my fault," Josh sputtered between gasps, an arm jutting out, his fingers clutching after Kelly's leg, only to have the fabric wrenched from his grip as the other man moved through the door.

"C'mon, man, don't let this fuck up our friendship."

Kelly froze, head slowly rotating to cast his sight back the way he'd come, not knowing what to say. How could this idiot have thought this scene could do anything other than fuck up their friendship? Guys didn't suck their friend's dicks, even the really big ones.

"Did I hurt you?"

Josh stared, again with pleading eyes—sincere eyes. "It was my fault," he said.

"I'm goin'."

"Alright man, but don't be a stranger." The shame was like a shadow over Josh's entire person. "I-I'm sorry, I shouldn't have . . ."

Kelly was sorry, too, but the words never found his lips. His legs made long strides in which his gonads were, as ever, being painfully jumbled and gnashed.

"Wait!" Josh shouted after the man, stalling him at the front door. Turning on his heels, Kelly found the other man's silhouette hovering in the bathroom door, his shadow falling into the dark hall ahead of him. "I just wanted to say, I know you're not a faggot."

Sheila's wildly dilated eyes told the story of the hunger in her, the fire that could never be snuffed, born out of the need to consume all of Kelly. Her lips tensed, her bottom jaw trembled at the tremendous effort. She wanted the probe of him to journey so deep that the fat, round glans might somehow kiss her living, beating heart.

But this was only fantasy; she was no sword swallower. And when her jaws had taken all the strain they could and her tonsils could be lodged no farther back in her throat—the gag reaction kept at bay no longer—it was then time to explore another angle, another orifice.

Kelly's worries over the eviction notice were forgotten, along with the ache in his balls, and even the unwanted memories from the shower room of his youth and that recent raw night in Josh's bathroom, as Sheila's face came off the stake of him and the glistening hole of her mouth formed words hot as molten sex. "Fuck me," she said.

And then it was as though their movements were rehearsed. Fluidly Kelly came up out of his old La-Z-Boy as Sheila swiveled on her heels to present her upturned rear.

"Take my ass," she offered. "Take me hard."

His hands held the hemisphere of her buttocks like two basketballs pressed together, though these tawny globes were warm and malleable to his touch.

Eyeing the wonder of the whirl, he knew Sheila would do anything for him.

She would give any part of herself to what hung between his legs, what weighed on her now, like a supermarket-checkout separator, dividing the halves of her buttocks.

Directing the spear lower than where she'd asked, Kelly slid instead into the velvet tunnel of her sex. The action garnered a long rolling moan from the O of her mouth, and several ticks later came the familiar gasp as the enormous bauble head thumped her cervix.

It hurt a bit, the increasingly thunderous pounding by a loving battering ram bent on bringing down her walls.

It hurt so wonderfully that she had to scream, had to cry.

The music of their sex bore a note beyond the ordinary, beyond the raucous moaning Kelly sometimes heard through their too-thin bedroom walls and beyond the soundtrack that filled the halls of the whorehouse on Summer Street, where the sounds of animal sex were omnipresent.

Sheila's vocal gymnastics—the booming bellows all women made with Kelly—had an edge something like the sound a woman might make when being punched in the stomach.

He would be gentle with Sheila because he loved her. He wouldn't dip much more than half of himself in the well of her, a well in which his bucket was already scraping the bottom. He would never take her ass, as she'd implored, because the harpoon of him would, at the very least, have her feeling as though she was split in two.

He would go slow and easy, and only halfway, and still she would bleed.

They always bled at least a little bit.

* * *

There were times when Kelly didn't want to be gentle, though, when the urge to fuck came over him like a rage, and stirring only half his spoon inside the pot wasn't good enough. At these times, he liked to visit the whorehouse on Summer Street.

If he was paying, he didn't have to be gentle, and there he could order what he wanted—a bottomless pussy, though none were without bottoms for him.

The last time he'd been down to Summer Street, he'd come through the rusted iron door that hung on the face of the con-demned-looking building and entered into the many-shrouded receiving room to wait his turn.

Everywhere the eye fell, some length of fabric hung from the walls, covering the boarded windows, draping the room, such that it looked the way an Arab harem must. It always struck him how different the inside was from the out. The production was much more than one would expect from a ghetto whorehouse, and the woman responsible—immense and boisterous behind the receiving table (what part of her large body didn't blossom out around it)— was Big Mamma, a personality who also outstripped the expectation of the female pimp.

Kelly had strode up to the table. Tall behind the scrawny black scab of a man in front of him, he had overheard the smaller man's complaint: "What do you mean, Regina's still out?"

"I mean, she's sick, and she's got the night off." Big Mamma's eyes never even settled on the little man. Rather, they drifted Kelly's way, measuring his broad shoulders, traveling down, down until she was also measuring the pronounced bulge that began at his groin and journeyed like a snake down his right leg. That night he hadn't worn underwear.

"What about an Asian girl?" The scab was talking again.

"This ain't no Chinese restaurant," Big Mamma said.

"I need a tight girl, though."

"This ain't Burger King neither, motherfucker. You can't have it your way."

"But I need a really tight fit."

"Yeah, well, I got a needle you could thread."

The scab's face crumpled, and he'd already spun on his heels to storm away when the anger in Big Mamma's eyes turned to dollar signs. It was bad business being cruel to the clientele. "Wait a minute," she said, extending a hand, grasping the scab's knobby shoulder. "Big Mamma's just had a long day, baby. I know Regina is your regular girl and all, but I got another girl, a real pretty one. She's a hundred dollars 'cause she's done a few movies, you know. You might not have heard of her, but you will. She's a limited offer, you see. Up and coming. Calls herself Temptation, and I can promise you, she ain't gonna be whoring these streets for much longer." Big Mamma drew near then, her breath hot and scented with Tabasco. "Best part is, this girl's got a pussy so tight, you'll think yo' dick is in a hydraulic vice."

The scab's eyes lit. He had fifty dollars clenched in his right fist, ready to pay for his usual girl, but now he had to dig deeper, had to empty out his wallet and gather every nickel and dime in order to come up with the ninety-two fifteen that inevitably sealed the deal.

"What's your pleasure tonight, sweetie?" Big Mamma said then, her eyes filled with a smile. Kelly always got a smile from the ladies; there was something about him.

"I'm lookin' for a pussy ain't got no bottom."

"Hot damn," Big Mamma had boomed, her voice sonorous, large as she was and textured with a bit of a husky scratch. "I know that's right," she added. "Can see that much right through yo' pants."

Kelly had grinned. *It* was always the subject of admiration. No one knew that his balls were on fire any time he had to walk any distance. Big Mamma hadn't known his back was calling for a bed that very moment just to get off his feet, to get the weight strung from his groin supported by something other than his legs.

"I gotta tell you that's a sweet sight. And I hear you lookin' for a job."

"You offerin' to pimp me out too, Mamma?"

Big Mamma chuckled. "Better than that, baby. See, that crazy white boy you run with was in a couple days ago. He stays in this place, you know; got him a thing for brown sugar. I don't know how the talk got started, but he was goin' on and on 'bout you, 'bout how big you was. Now I don't know 'bout yo', boy. He might got a thing for black dick, too . . ."

"Big dick," Kelly interjected. "Don't matter if it's green, purple or blue, though as black goes, he'd charbroil himself to a crisp if it meant he'd grow bigger."

Big Mamma had smirked. "Well, anyway, a couple of my girls

you've been with corroborated the boast. Make a long story short, he was askin' 'bout my girlfriend's club; said you was perfect for the male review over there."

"Male review? I ain't no stripper."

At this point, Big Mamma presented him with a business card. "Maybe," she said, her eyes affixed to the bulge. "Maybe, baby, you should be. 'Cause right through yo' clothes, you lookin' good 'nough to eat, and Silvia's got an opening."

Kelly took the card.

"Savage Thugs Male Review," he read. His eyes rolled up to latch with Big Mamma's. "There's one hell of a hook."

"No, baby, the hook's in your pants, and ain't no shame in usin' our God-given gifts to make a little money."

Kelly stared at the card, his mind spinning, his need for a *job* expanding like a dark and threatening thundercloud filling up his mind.

Big Mamma's next words were very far away when he heard them. "Now, 'bout that girl with the endless pussy."

That night Kelly had pounded the whore, as if to break her back, as if to drive her through the foam-rubber mattress and the floor beneath it, as if to split her with the log of himself.

The whore was called Trix; Big Mamma had said it was because her pussy knew every trick. Indeed, she'd shown Kelly one such trick the moment he'd entered the dank, little room with the lone window, through which the purple-hot radiation off of a nearby neon sign was seeping. Maybe the sign spelled "Pussycat," but the part Kelly could see through the grimy glass was simply "Pussy," and he'd just finished reading it when Trix offered him a drink from a long-necked bottle of Heineken that she'd been warming in the tunnel of herself, that she extracted slow and easy, uncapping it then and bringing the drinking end to her lips.

Then Kelly had shown her a trick, undoing and bunching down his pants, unveiling his magic wand. It was enormous and growing still, longer than her beer bottle by far and easily as fat. Black and arterial, and swinging as he walked, slapping the left thigh only to bounce over and slap the right, only to bound back again. It wasn't until the trickle hit her breast that Trix realized she'd forgotten to swallow her beer and the gap of her mouth was spilling the stuff down her chin and chest.

Then Kelly was right there in front of her. He watched her eyes travel up and down the organ again and again, never seeming to fully discover it. In the effort to wrap her mind around it, her entire being became so fixed upon it that she seemed to stop breathing, and the only movement about her was the rapid up-and-down scanning of her eyes. One might have mistaken her state for that of a petite mal seizure. But Kelly's penis always provoked an intense reaction.

In those long, staring moments, it owned her.

She scarcely even realized Kelly was attached to it, or that he'd taken the beer from her and was drinking. Her eyes followed the meat when he sat, as he took a thick rubber band from around his wrist, where he'd been wearing it as a bracelet. Perhaps she saw his makeshift cock ring glide into place as he pulled himself through the loop. But the bulging arteries fattening by the second seemed to be her chief concern.

It was longer than she was thick.

It was deeper than the well of her by far.

And though the moments leading up to it were a blur, she knew for certain when Kelly put her on her back and put himself inside. It was the most delicious hurt she'd ever experienced, a genuine pain that brought tears to her eyes.

It was a battering ram pounding down the door of her cervix, making her feel more full than a stuffed Thanksgiving Day turkey. Every time Kelly pressed to his limit, her mind's eye filled up with a livid white, which spilled out to blind her physical eyes as well. Wild images danced in the blizzard of pain and ecstasy, and far away she could hear herself screaming, crying out, and she could hear the grunts and groans of a man in rut. He was booming curses and blasphemies and unintelligible things, and inside her uterus he was screaming as well, bucking and shifting and lighting every part of her up.

Trix imagined this was what it would feel like should her aborted children rise up from their graves, whole and fat and bloated, goring her in their effort to wedge themselves back into the only safe place they'd ever known. It was what she deserved, that pain; it was what all whoring, murdering mothers deserved.

But where was Kelly?

His organ was there, stabbing deep, so very deep.

His body, the anchor off of which the appendage hinged, was there also.

The man, however, was far, far away, so distant that he couldn't hear the slant in the whore's voice change, too deep inside himself to realize the woman's insides were tearing. Kelly was so vacant behind his staring edge-of-orgasm eyes—eyes still teary from the high school showers, eyes still shell-shocked at the sight of his best friend's pink lips stretched around the dark cherry of his bone—that he didn't feel the whore's claws raking down his back and across the ovals of his ass, drawing blood as her nails broke the skin and dug up the meat, as the long nails on several of her fingers broke.

Then, like with the breaking of a dam, it all flooded his ears: the woman's screaming, groaning, and his own, and the bruising smack his pelvis made crashing into hers, and the slosh of his reaming penetration. Flaring his lip and gritting his teeth, he bellowed out a booming grunt as he loosed a flood as well.

And then he could feel the ache in his own pelvis, the sting in his abused genitals. And he could feel the scratches, the places where her fingernails had broken off and were still stuck in his flesh. Unsheathing revealed the crimson color that coated his still-rigid meat. A shift revealed the space between himself and the prostitute, the dark color where the foam bed had been soaked, more a shade of brown-approaching-black than red.

Even as Kelly was falling, tumbling backward off the mattress, the prostitute was reaching for him with bloody fingertips, with nails broken down to the quick.

Her vagina yawned, made a raspberry sound as the swirl of his excess and her blood seeped, as her pursuit of him caused her to sit upright. "Don't go!" she shouted. The look in her eyes was full and famished all at once—full with the mad electric arcs of orgasmic pain, famished from never having been so completely fed before. "Oh God, give me more, I need more."

Kelly, however, was still tumbling, rolling off the mattress and over the mess of his discarded clothing. He collected the items as he encountered them. And then the whore was screaming, "Damn you, don't leave!"

And as she tried to stand, a red stream broke from her groin, zigzagging and splitting into wild tributaries down her thigh.

Pitching to one side, falling half on her face, she found that she couldn't walk, and so she crawled, still reaching, still screaming for more. "Please, please, damn you . . . make me feel good . . . make me feel . . . make me feel."

Kelly and Sheila's lovemaking was done, though Kelly still was playing the missionary, hoisted up on all fours, with Sheila beneath him on her back. The angle was good in that it hid the scars up and down his back. But neither Trix's nor Josh's scrapes were the first to mar Kelly's hide. Sheila's own digs were there, fresh trails and faded ones, and if she knew the difference between the marks she put on him and the ones she didn't, she never said so.

"Before you, I could never feel," was what she did say, speaking into the mic jutting from Kelly's groin, where she'd slithered down to undo the knot of the cock noose she'd tied. As she worked, she kissed and nibbled his choice parts.

"Are you alright?" He'd been as gentle as he could, but still he had to worry.

"Gonna be walkin' funny down at Roy's tonight. Hope I don't drop nobody's order."

"I'm sorry," he said as his brows knitted together and the skin of his forehead creased. He was indeed sorry—sorry for things that she knew, and sorry for so many she did not.

"I'm not," she said. "I'd rather stop walking than stop fucking you." The knot came loose at last, and she kissed the tender flesh where the loop had left its imprint.

"I don't understand you. It hurts, don't it?"

Kelly turned onto his side on that note, and Sheila, still playing the snake, slithered up his leg, coiling herself into his arms.

"It hurts," she said, with the sunset light soaking and saturating them, making the entire room the same orange as the glint that lit her eyes. "But before you, I never had an orgasm."

Kelly sighed.

"I wish it didn't have to hurt."

"I wish I didn't have to go to work, so we could do it again."

Kelly forced a smile, but it wouldn't sit right on his face and soon slid off and into the shadows between them. "Guess somebody's gotta work 'round here."

"I love you," Sheila said between the circuits her tongue made around one of Kelly's nipples. "You make me feel," she said. "When I'm with you, I feel everything." Her lips sealed upon the small, hardening nipple. "And you taste good," she said through a grin.

"I know," Kelly whispered, hauling her close, more breathing the words into her ear than speaking them. "I taste good 'nough to eat."

When Sheila was gone, Kelly loaded up on aspirin and began his trek to Silvia's club, down on Seventh Street. This was not his first trip to the nightspot. It was his fifth, and each visit had been like walking in a dream—and each time he told himself that soon he would wake.

His first meeting with the four-hundred-pound diva that was Silvia had instantly shown the truth in Big Mamma's assumption. Silvia's eyes had sparkled diamond light at the sight of the pronounced speed bump beneath his fly, at the whiskers the fabric formed straining to contain him.

"Show it to me, sugar," she'd said. "Show Silvia that beautiful thing she done heard so much about."

As his fly hissed open, Kelly had told himself that the whole scene was unreal. And when Silvia's fat, hook-nailed index finger traced his arterial length from stern to bow and her eyes—full of hunger and dollar signs and hungry dollar signs—lifted to reach for his glassy stare, the way her words found him was more like lip-reading than hearing.

"Sweetie pie," shaped the large, ruby red lips that hung on her face, "you got the job." But he hadn't wanted the job. And still he drifted, dreaming on his feet.

As Silvia read the arterial tracks of his penis like brail, the world spun into a blur, and only a lone fact emerged clear as crystal. Everything and everyone was indecent because of the meat God had strung between his legs, and Kelly hated every inch. All he wanted was a regular nine-to-five, but here again, his dick was towing him down a far darker and more perverse path. Kelly told himself it was a dream, but come daylight, in the real world, there were no decent jobs to be had, and indecency promised to keep the lights on and the roof over his and Sheila's heads. And no, he couldn't let her ask her father for money, because he was the man—her man—and besides, her father hated him.

So the next night found Kelly at the back of the club watching the strippers do their thing for the ladies. He watched from between panels of draped curtains, hidden so that the ladies would not see him. It was a lady's club, no men in the audience, and as for his soon-to-be-a-part-of-the-show status, that much was a surprise not yet ripe. Watching from behind the gyrating shadow of a sea of lecherous females, he observed how scorching hot the cycling spotlights (red and orange, yellow and blue) seemed to be, blazing down upon the oiled hard-bodies. He watched how the men sweated as they strutted, stripped and slung their moneymakers. He said to himself, "Not me. I'll find something else before it's my time to get on stage." But the truth was that he'd always been on stage, on display, beneath those burning-bright lights. Eyes were always on the meat.

He'd have taken anything. Dirty work would have been fine: hauling trash, cleaning toilets. Backbreaking work was okay by him, too. Anything was okay so long as it wasn't cock-shaking work. But sunup found no one hiring and the line at the unemployment office flowing out of the building.

Then it was time for sizing at Silvia's.

He stripped naked and let them all gawk at his measurements. He was going to be some kind of a jungle man, a black Tarzan, wearing a leopard-skin thong specially cut for his dimensions. And while the costumers did their thing, having to step back at times just to admire the meat they were dressing, the other Savage Thugs, his soon-to-be brothers-in-arms made comments about the new he-man. Big as they were—and these men were all handpicked for the fact that they were huge—he was the titan:

Hercules in a bathhouse with strong men . . .

Christ at the supper table with the saints . . .

Satan in the ninth circle of Hell, grinning mutely at all the sinners.

And at rehearsal, he showed them that he knew how to move his ass. Dancing wasn't his thing, but the Savage Thugs Male Review wasn't really a dance camp. Bass lines pounded, and the beats shook the club from its footers to its eaves, but it was the rolling pelvises, pumping hips and jumping, bucking, swinging penises that got these ladies' hearts to racing.

It was an everything-comes-off kind of club, and it was Kelly's night to go on stage. The leopard loin pouch with the floss-sized back had come in, and was in place, like a spotted fur sock in the front, with a string running the gauntlet of his crack in the back.

He'd been given a dirty magazine backstage to jerk off over, to get warmed up with, but Kelly was such a shower that he didn't need to get warm for his meat to turn heads. Inside the pouch, as in all the costumes at the club, a rubber C-ring was sewn in place. Silvia knew big men's bodies, knew what they needed to show best. Kelly could feel the rubber ring, a size too small perhaps, pinching his package, a hair uncomfortable, but a welcome distraction from the ache in his gonads and the rattling of his nerves.

Kelly had tossed back a few drinks and way more than his daily dosage of painkilling aspirin, and in his belly the soup of it was bubbling, making him light-headed.

And then hands shoved him through the curtain, pushed him out and onto the stage, where the spotlights were roving to find him. The lamps were hot, as he'd known they would be: like the neon lights that flipped their burning purple heat in the Summer Street whore's boarded window; like the burning yellow bulbs blazing above the sink in his best friend's bathroom: like the noonday sun that beat down on the desolation of the ghetto when Kelly was trekking around looking for a job. And not least of all, the heat on stage was like the white-hot fluorescents that had blazed above the shower spray all those years ago while he'd been pinned to the tiles screaming.

The stage was a three-ring circus, with Kelly sweating in the center. To his left, Randy—a coal-black South African import—was writhing on the floor beneath a vibrant cyan light, which made his ashen complexion appear deep purple. His ass shined, and his pelvis pumped with vigor; he was fucking the stage, but there was no hole. On the right, in the fallout of a yellow lamp, a young hip-hop type named Ty had his fat penis flayed over the top of his low-hanging jeans. Having stepped down off the stage (which was only a six-inch rise), he was mixing with the front row, allowing the ladies to help him show off the fact that it took two hands to fully grope the rope of him.

And there was Kelly, bathed in liquid-red luminescence, bulging in his animal-print loincloth, feeling the tremble in the floor and the electricity in the air as the audience's attention shifted, as lips were licked, and whoops and howls began to spread like the ripple a pebble makes when cast into still water. Kelly was that pebble, and the audience that lake, and the ripple would not stop now until every woman had been touched and transformed.

"Introducing the new king of the jungle! Let's all give a red-hot Silvia's kind of welcome to Kelly!" It was Silvia's voice rising above the thump of the music and the roar of the crowd to introduce him, and when the music returned to full volume, the midrange portion seemed to have dropped out the bottom, and all Kelly could hear was the bang of the bass like the pounding of some tribal drum, and he began to move, to gyrate his pelvis, which made the meat pouch jump. And even through the fur sling, all those hungry ladies could see the size and shape of Kelly's endowment, and it was driving them mad.

"Take it off, baby!"

"Bring it over here, big pappa!"

And the balled green bills were like breadcrumbs, being flipped onto the stage to entice him in the direction of the biggest spenders. Kelly strutted toward the most money, feeling the bills crumple under his bare feet, feeling the weight of his cock double as with a simple unsnap the pouch opened and the junk flopped out of the trunk. And then Kelly was stroking the growing serpent, and then he was pumping his hips to swing it, making it slap his sternum on the up and allowing it to fly back between his legs to spank his ass on the down.

And the ladies were up and out of their seats, reams of big bosoms jostling, pair after pair of juicy lips pursing. They tucked bills behind the elastic of his loincloth, which remained in place even while the pouch was open and his goodies out. Hands groped and grabbed, large hands mostly, attached to very big women like Silvia and Big Mamma. Upheaved bosoms offered glistening cleavage for the serpent's kiss, and Kelly obliged, grinding his hardness into the bosoms of the hungry, allowing three or four Janes to swing from Tarzan's vine at a time, sitting on laps while facing the females, as to make a sandwich of his meat between his body and theirs.

And all the red tongues were licking the red lips, and all the eyes bore the same insatiable hunger-light. And soon the women could

not contain themselves, could not restrain themselves to just rubbing and being rubbed by it. They wanted to sample the meat, to
taste its flavor.

As the first mouth sealed around the dome, Kelly hadn't realized
what was happening. All he'd known was that the velvet warmth
was further distraction from the pain in his balls.

"It's so fucking big," a rugged female-voice screamed over the
den, and then a head pushed its way up under his arm to get at his
chest, to get a long tongue to work at teasing his right nipple. Something was happening in the crowd. A chair fell over somewhere, and
then another and another. The howls of a boisterous good time
found a new threatening high, and it was no longer the whooping of
the fun loving, but the howling of several dozen hungry huntresses.

There was a woman between Kelly's legs on the floor then, her
mouth seeking out his scrotum, jaws stretching to engulf it. There
were hands on his ass, fingers in his ass and lips all over him, kissing and licking. Two meaty hands encircled the face of the woman
whose mouth had the pleasure of pleasuring him, and with vicious
fervor, that face was wrenched from its post of worship and dragged
backward into the crowd. In its place, three rotund faces leaped
into focus, mouths open, white teeth glistening.

The suddenness startled Kelly, and he tried to take a reverse
step, which caused him to trip over the women at his feet. He toppled backward on top of them, and like obese, seething snakes, they
wormed beneath him, all hands and hunger. The spear of his erection swayed where it aimed for the rafters, while Silvia's voice, now
panicked, flooded the loudspeakers again. Silvia instructed the
ladies to find their seats, but all ears were deaf, and all eyes were
blind to anything but the beauty of Kelly's organ.

His penis was like that—it provoked intense reaction.

A woman built like a sumo wrestler and not wearing any panties
tried to mount him. Knocking several others out of her path, she
squatted, took him into hand, aimed and inserted. She'd been ready
to drop the all of her considerable weight upon his spear when a
folded chair was leveled against her bulk and she was toppled to
one side. Kelly's heart leaped as a half dozen fresh pairs of lips
began to kiss and caress his length, more joining every moment,
knees in his chest, bodies pinning his hands and pinning other bodies, appetites engulfing him. He was pinned under too much lady-

flesh to measure, pinned just as he'd been pinned in the showers—pinned, as always, because of his big dick.

He cried out for help, but no one came.

The first bite was just a nip, an unusually sharp eyetooth catching the ridge of his pronounced helmet, scratching it. But then the sharks tasted the blood in the water, and each one, desiring nothing so much as to possess more of him than the next woman, bared her teeth.

It was an enormous, bloated face with teeth like pearl razors set behind a row of iron braces that took the head off, chewing rather than spitting even as the carmine spray flashed her and a half dozen others in the face.

After that, the mouths were indiscriminate, each gaping to consume a bigger chunk than the one before, while Kelly twitched. He was a short-circuited sex toy vibrating underneath them as they ate down the pole of him, snapping and biting at each other in the awful process.

Madness flooded their eyes.

Blood flooded their eyes.

And somewhere there were sirens, and everywhere there were screams, though the convulsive sputters coming up from Kelly's throat had turned to a tortured kind of chuckle. His scrotum came out from between his legs in a ragged tatter as the last of the cannibal females was pulled out of his lap by an officer's nightstick hooked under her chin. Kelly convulsed while it happened, but returned again to a chuckle bisected by desperate gasps.

The paramedics and the police seemed to be hovering very high above him, their voices ringing out of truth, their horror contorted faces telling the terror of his condition, all their eyes locked on the raw absence where genitalia had been. Josh was there sobbing like a baby. He'd snuck in to watch the show no doubt, and had seen much more than he'd hoped for. Kelly's teeth ground together as through a growing haze he watched the man's eyes. Josh was crying for the meat, Kelly knew.

The dark was creeping across his vision from the outer corners of both eyes like a curtain being closed as the paramedics began packing the wound with gauze, and laying very still now and feeling very warm even though his body temperature was dropping, Kelly could think no thought but one. He had a message for Josh and for

Sheila and for all the others—a message for the world. Reaching, touching Josh's hand, his eyes did the rest of the job in drawing Josh down onto his knees, near enough to hear.

Perhaps Kelly's larynx pushed the whisper out, and perhaps his lips could only shape the words. Maybe it was neither and the thought inside his skull never made itself known at all, but what ticked in his brain before the dark sealed around him was five simple words echoed again and again:

It don't hurt . . . no more.

It don't hurt . . .

no . . .

more.

Milez to Go

Linda Addison

Angelique leaned against the bar and watched Sara, the club owner, and a man she didn't know place the upright acoustic piano next to the slim black case housing her protoplasmic synthesizer. The Funky Piranha club looked forlorn with its empty tables in the dining room and the strings of tiny red and green lights blinking on the ceiling. The slight scent of beer wafted into the air from the wood floor. Later that night, the club would be filled with people who were in New Orleans for the music festival.

Angelique tapped the small, silver derm phone disk attached behind her right earlobe. "Phone on. Dial Brenda."

Her cousin's phone rang. "Damn," Angelique said as the message played. "Brenda, it's me again. I've been calling for days. Where are you? I just got into town and was planning on staying at your place. If you're holed up there with Clint, let me know so I don't embarrass myself interrupting your playtime. I can find another place to stay. Either way, call me."

She tapped the derm phone off, frowning. "Careful, don't lift it too quickly," she said to Sara. "Just place it at right angles. I'll adjust it."

They set the piano down gently. The man walked behind the bar to set up for tonight. Sara's cream-colored dreadlocks were sprinkled with tiny purple lights that flickered as she moved. She rolled her violet eyes. "Angelique, after five years, I think I know how to handle your equipment. I see you're still using the acoustic. I would have thought Milez would be enough." She gently patted the interface grid on top of the black protoplasmic container.

A soft gold light came on in the bottom of the tank. A tube of blue protoplasm snaked its way through clear liquid to the top, became a shape resembling a hand, splashed the inside of the grid, broke into round drops and folded back into the liquid. A deep, smoky male voice said, "It's all good. There's plenty of room for me and the wood."

Sara jumped. "Damn, I've never heard it talk like that."

"Brenda bioengineered a personal upgrade for me. It took longer to train it to speak everyday language, but I prefer that over 'System is functional'." Angelique changed the angle of the protoplas to the acoustic piano so she could comfortably reach the protoplas interface grid and the keyboard.

"How's that cousin of yours? Still doing hush-hush cuttingedge research over at Biolution?" Sara asked, standing next to Angelique.

Angelique nodded.

Sara wrapped her arm around Angelique's waist and whispered in her ear, "No one plays neo-bop like Tempus Fugit. Some folks were here last night asking if your group would be performing. I can't wait to hear you play tonight. Want to come upstairs for dinner and a little distraction before the show?"

Angelique gave her a quick hug. "I'm a little worried about Brenda." She smiled. "Maybe we can get together after the set tonight. I need to go to her place and find out why she hasn't answered my calls for the last couple of weeks."

"You know how that girl gets caught up in things. She's probably just working on some new project." Sara ran her fingers through Angelique's long braids. "I'd go with you to see her, but my skin's not too fond of afternoon sun. If there's any problem with a place to stay, you can always crash here."

"Thanks," Angelique said. She gently patted Milez' interface grid. "See you soon."

"You know it, baby," Milez said.

Angelique picked up her suitcase and walked out of the cool air of the club into New Orleans' humid, sunny streets. The corner vendors were setting up their food and drink booths. The wrought iron balconies were elaborately decorated with flowers and streamers.

It was easy to catch a taxi, since most people were at the race track for the afternoon concerts. Tonight the streets would be so full of people, no taxi would come near the French Quarter.

The taxi dropped Angelique in front of Brenda's apartment building. She walked to the second floor and put her thumb on the lock pad. The panel asked for a retina scan as a secondary security check. She sighed. Brenda used that lock only when she was out of town. The apartment door slid open.

Angelique walked in and pushed through an invisible membrane, the threshold of a strong protective spell. She frowned. A spell this intense had to be coming from someone nearby. She put the suitcase down.

"Brenda?"

The living room window shutters were closed, making the room night-dark on a sunny afternoon. Angelique turned on the light. The room was in more disarray than usual for her cousin, with plates of half-eaten food and stained cups on the coffee table and mantel piece. The plants near the windows were wilted, and the kitchen, dining area and guest bedroom were empty. She opened the door to the main bedroom at the back of the apartment and turned the light on.

Her cousin lay in the center of the bed as if asleep, her mocha-brown skin washed out, almost gray.

Angelique rushed over.

"Brenda, wake up."

She shook her cousin. Brenda radiated the protection spell, but didn't wake. Angelique checked her breathing and pulse.

"Damn it," Angelique said, sitting down on the bed. "What kind of trouble are you in this time?" She didn't like using magic, but there was only one way to get through to Brenda while she was in this state.

Angelique lay down next to her cousin and held her hand. After taking three slow breaths, Angelique chanted:

"We two,
both light and dark—
I, the shadow,
You, my kin,
Let me in,
Let me in."

Angelique closed her eyes and matched her breathing and heart-beat to those of her cousin. Within minutes she entered Brenda's dream state.

They stood back-to-back, looking out on hills covered in warm mist. Shadows moved in the mist. Still back-to-back, they grasped each other's hands. Suddenly a cold wind whipped through the air, taking their breath away, sending chills through them. They had to clasp hands tightly not to be separated.

"Who are you?" a mechanical voice asked.

Resisting the strong pull to say her name, Angelique let Brenda answer, submitting her will to Brenda's.

Brenda became rigid against Angelique.

"I am Brenda Wilson."

"Nosliw adnerb." The voice said Brenda's name backwards.

They lay in a container no bigger than their bodies. They could-n't move. There was a murmur of voices in the background, people chanting, their words indistinguishable.

Pins and needles pinched at their hands. Coldness spread slowly from the tops of their heads toward their feet. Angelique felt the life draining from their bodies. She melted into the numbing stupor.

"Show me what you found," the voice commanded.

Images swirled around them chaotically, moving faster and faster, until Angelique was so dizzy she thought she would black out.

A boom crashed in the air. Brenda's voice screamed a protective spell over and over.

They stood back-to-back, looking out on hills covered in warm mist. Shadows moved in the mist. Still back-to-back, they grasped each other's hands. Suddenly a cold wind whipped through the air, taking their breath away, sending chills through them. They had to clasp hands tightly not to be separated.

"Who are you?" a mechanical voice asked.

Each time Brenda screamed the protective spell, the dream re-peated.

Each iteration dragged Angelique farther from her own will. She pushed all her attention to the in-and-out movement of air through her lungs. Refusing to pay attention to the physical sensa-tions in their dream bodies, she concentrated on her breathing.

When the dream began again, Angelique turned to face Brenda. The voice that Brenda was fighting asked, "You are not her. Who are you?" Angelique screamed, "No," stretched her arms into a blanket shape around Brenda and, with a gasp, dragged both of them to consciousness.

Shadows in the bedroom seemed to compress and expand, as if taking deep breaths. One blink, and everything looked normal.

Brenda moaned, opened her eyes, sat up and looked around the room. "Angelique?" Brenda grabbed her hands, sending sparkling energy back and forth. "It's you, not the dream. You're really here?"

"It's me." The luminosity from her cousin burned her fingertips.

Brenda switched on the nightstand light, touched Angelique's face and braids, and started crying.

Angelique held her, letting her cry for a few moments, before pulling away gently. "What's going on here, Brenda? I had to go into the dream or nightmare or whatever that was to wake you."

Brenda sat back against the pillows. "They're after me, but now that you're here, it's going to be all right."

"What was all that?"

"You were in the dream?" Brenda asked.

Angelique nodded.

"I thought I was imagining you." Brenda rubbed her forehead with her fingertips. "Did you see them?"

Angelique shook her head. "I'm not sure what I saw. It was jumbled. Voices and images I couldn't make out. They said your name backwards with such power."

Brenda ran her fingers through her short-cropped curls. "I wanted to call you before now, but I was afraid they would go after you. This attack came while I was asleep. If you hadn't come in, I don't know how much longer I could have held out." She took a gulp of water from a bottle at the nightstand. "Remember how we combined our power when we were kids and saved Grandmom from that ghost?"

Angelique rubbed the tension out of the back of her neck. "That didn't feel like a ghost. It felt like a living person with a lot of power. Someone who knows how to use it. Does this involve the Order?"

Brenda nodded. "I think it's someone in the Order. You and Grandmom were right. Magic and groups of humans don't go together. Too much ego involved. I left them."

"What about Clint?" Angelique asked.

Brenda closed her eyes. "We're over."

Angelique breathed through the intense, tingling light coming from her cousin. "I'm sorry. You two were so good together."

Brenda shook her head. "Well, it's better this way. He'll be safer without me."

She slumped back against the pillows. "While I was in the Order, I met wonderful people. It was great being able to talk openly about magic with others. We had an influx of new members in the last six months, and there was a subtle change in the group's dynamics. Some underlying negative power.

"Clint and I talked about it, and he brought it to the attention of the executive board of the Order. There was an investigation. They found no evidence of magic being used in a dark manner." She stopped, and rubbed her forehead.

"Are you all right?" Angelique asked.

"No-no. It's hard talking about the Order, even to you. When I left, I had to accept a silence spell, to keep certain facts about the Order secret. We're so close, the spell doesn't detect you as a separate person. It's as though I was talking to myself. But even with that it's hard." She took another drink of water and chanted in a whisper:

"My mind is one.
I am alone.
The binding holds,
The binding holds."

"Maybe you shouldn't—" Angelique started to say.

"No, I'll be okay.

"So, the executive board didn't find anything wrong, but I was having strange dreams of being controlled and held. The more I slept, the more tired I became. My work began to suffer. I couldn't concentrate. I decided to leave the Order. Clint and I argued. It was terrible. He kept saying it was Gray Magic."

"Your magic turned negative back to you?" Angelique asked.

"Right, as if I haven't taken into account the repercussions of magic I've done. I may seem reckless, but not with magic. I'd know the difference anyway."

Brenda pulled her knees up and wrapped her arms around them.

"Anyway, the dreams became worse after I left the Order. I started losing the line between waking and sleeping. Even when I was awake, I felt like someone else was looking through my eyes. I began making mistakes at work. My latest project was suffering, so I took time off. I hoped to find out more about who was involved, but they're hiding too well." She shook her head. "I can feel them when I wake. Shadows, like birds, flapping in my mind. They're very strong."

"Do you have any idea who it is?" Angelique asked.

Brenda closed her eyes and took a deep breath. "I suspect a couple of people. I've looked all over for some sign of something placed inside my apartment, some kind of charm used to link them to me, but I haven't found anything. Did you pick up anything when you came in?"

"Just your protective spell," Angelique said. "Although, when I woke just now, I thought I saw something move in the shadows."

Brenda grabbed Angelique's hands. "What did you see?"

"Nothing I could describe. You know how we used to dream when we were younger, and could shape the shadows. I don't think it was someone else. There wasn't anyone else in here except me and echoes of you."

"Are you sure you didn't feel anything else in the apartment?"

Angelique held Brenda's hands in hers. "Nothing else," she said. "What are they after?"

Brenda looked away and then back at Angelique. "I don't want to say too much. It's better you don't know."

"Better how? They probably know I'm here, since I had to break you out of that dream. You might as well tell me."

Brenda fingered a bracelet of charms on her right wrist. "It's about my work. I've been doing genetic research, working on gene therapy."

"What's that got to do with magic?" Angelique asked.

"I've been working on a personal project at the lab." Brenda struggled to her feet, and stretched. She paced as she talked. "I've found something fantastic, Angelique. The thing I've been looking for."

"The magic gene?" Angelique asked.

"Something like that. Our team's been working with chromosome nineteen. Its network of genes controls the repair of DNA damage caused by pollution and radiation. You know how we've always wondered why some people have more power than others?"

Angelique nodded.

"I've found some sequencing data that implies chromosome nineteen makes repairs in DNA that increases the ability of people to access their power. I've been doing my own research on the side, looking at my chromosomes and yours."

"Mine, but how—?" Angelique frowned. "Oh, I guess you could have gotten a sample of my DNA from any of my visits. You should have told me."

"I'm sorry. I meant to tell you what I was doing. I've always believed there's a scientific explanation for magic. I think nature tries to fix us, and ends up making us different. The next question is whether we could manipulate someone's DNA to enhance or turn on their power. I'm afraid this is what they're interested in."

She stopped pacing and sat on the bed. "There was a break-in at the lab, but I don't keep the results there. I always download the data when I leave. Two weeks ago, there was a break-in here while I was at work. That's when I knew someone was after my research. Now they're trying to break into my mind and make me show them what I've discovered."

"I can't believe this." Angelique stood up. "You steal my DNA, do research I'm sure your lab didn't approve and now put us both in danger. I don't know how someone so smart can act so stupid sometimes."

Brenda shook her head. "You're right." She grabbed Angelique's hands. "But now that you're here, maybe together we can find out who's after me."

"And then what?" Angelique asked, pulling away. "There aren't any magic police to protect you. Do you at least have the information in a safe place?"

"Very safe. I'll figure a way out of this." Brenda looked at her watch. "Isn't Tempus Fugit playing at Sara's club tonight?"

"In about three hours, but—"

"I need to get out of here. Why don't you shower and dress here for tonight. We'll go to the club together. I'm starving. Sara's kitchen still makes the best po-boy sandwiches and onion rings around. By the way, how's Milez?"

"He's been fine."

"Good, I'll give him a quick checkup tonight, free of charge."

"You still haven't told me how you're going to handle this . . . attack," Angelique said, leaning against the doorway with her arms crossed.

"Don't worry, I will." Brenda rushed to the living room.

Angelique closed her eyes and massaged her temples. She was going to need something for this headache, and she had a feeling things were just going to get worse.

Angelique changed into the black bodysuit designed to communicate with Milez. Before they left for the Funky Piranha, Brenda stopped at the door. "Remember the protection spell you created when we were kids?"

Angelique nodded. They held hands and recited it together:

"Goddess of Day,
Complete the way.
Goddess of Night,
Surround us with Light.
I call upon thee,
I call upon thee,
To protect us two,
Protect us twice."

Warmth encircled them. Brenda gave her cousin a hug. "I'm so glad you're here."

When they entered the club, Brenda went straight to Milez. Angelique talked to Sara and the three members of her band as she watched her cousin talk quietly to Milez with her hand over his open interface panel. Tendrils of blue protoplasm moved over her right hand and wrist, and danced around her bracelet.

She walked over to Brenda. "So, what's going on?"

"Just catching up. I ran a quick check of his system, and he's in excellent shape." Brenda caressed his casing with her other hand.

"I'm always good around you, Brenda," he said. Lines of neon light fanned out of the interface panel, filling the ceiling of the club, as the protoplasm melted off her hand back into the container.

"Show-off," Angelique said, smiling. "Save the pyros for the show tonight."

"Don't worry, I've got plenty where that came from," he said.

Brenda sat at a small table next to the long bar opposite the small stage. The sound check didn't take long. Once Sara opened the doors to the public, the small club filled up quickly.

Sara turned down the lights. The band opened with "Combustion," a piece written by Angelique. Milez made his way to the top of his casing in slow, graceful, neon-bright blue drops, like rain falling up. Angelique rifted on the acoustic with one hand; the other hand lay over Milez's open interface panel. As the blue protoplasm touched her hand, it poured up and over her hand and arm, until she was spotted with glowing dots. Milez picked up the sounds from the piano and broke the chords into sharp, harmonic bursts to complement her playing. The bass, drums and violin danced in and around the main movement. The dots slithered and swirled into lines and patterns over her body. She played with her eyes closed, occasionally humming and scatting. Milez picked up her voice and morphed the sounds to play back against the original sounds. They teased back and forth, building and juxtaposing each other's harmonies. At the climax of the piece, Milez threw a rainbow of laser light into the air, the thin lines flashing into flame shapes overhead. The audience erupted into whoops and applause.

The rest of the evening went quickly. The band played two long sets, with a short break in between, to a standing-room-only crowd. The band finished well after midnight.

Brenda drank juice with her meal. In spite of being at the club all that time, her aura was brighter than when they had first arrived.

Sara locked the door after the band, bartender and bouncer left.

"How about we have some of my best scotch, to celebrate the three musketeers?" Sara asked, as they sat on the edge of the stage near Milez.

"The three of us?" Brenda asked, pointing to Sara and her cousin.

"No, silly," Sara said, laughing. "You, Angelique and Milez. I'll meet you in my office."

"You enjoy the scotch. I dig the juice in your club, Sara," Milez said, sending sparks into the dimly lit room.

"You can have as much electricity as you like," Sara said.

"Do you need me anymore tonight, baby?" Milez asked.

"No, you can sleep," Angelique said.

"Nighty-night, girls," he said. The soft glow of his suspension liquid dimmed and went out as his protoplasm settled into the dark base.

Someone banged on the front gate of the club. Sara pulled the curtain aside and peeked out. "It's the bartender. He must have forgotten something. You two go on. I'll be there in a minute."

"We'll pour one for you, Sara," Brenda said as they walked to Sara's office in the back of the club. "The band sounded better than ever."

"Thanks. It's been a long night," Angelique said, sitting on the small couch. "What are you going to do about your problem? You can't hide from them forever."

"I know, but I don't think I'll have to." Brenda sat in a chair next to the couch.

The office door opened, and Sara came in. Angelique started to speak, but the look on Sara's face stopped her. A large man and a tall woman came in behind her. Only after they shut the door behind them did Angelique see the guns. She began to rise when the Asian woman gestured with her weapon to sit down.

"Brenda, good to see you again," the man said. He had strong Native American features and wore his long hair in two tight braids wrapped in leather strips. Silver and stone charms hung from his multiple earrings. Power vibrated around him, like the sound of fine glass being gently struck.

"Mac, it's been you all this time," Brenda said.

"I had a feeling you knew that," he said, walking over to them.

"You know these people?" Sara said.

"Unfortunately we used to belong to the same club."

"Gun club?" Sara asked, sitting down at her desk.

"You're funny," Mac said. "Not many people can maintain their sense of humor with guns pointed at them."

"You should come to this club during Mardi Gras." Sara leaned back in her chair.

"Mind your manners, and you might get to see Mardi Gras this year," the Asian woman said.

Sara opened her mouth, then crossed her arms over her chest and glared at them instead.

Mac leaned over Angelique and caressed her face. "So, this is your cousin." He closed his eyes for a moment and took a slow breath. "The power runs deep in your family. Imagine the children you and I could make."

Brenda stood, and pushed him away from Angelique. "Did you come here to look for a wife?"

He grabbed her arms and pulled her close. "You know what I came for," he whispered. "We've played around long enough. I can't wait to get the information from you—even with my skills, you've kept me out."

"Why are you doing this?" Brenda asked.

He released her and laughed. "You can't seriously be asking that. The potential of your discovery is obvious. Everyone wants more of what they have, whether it's money, beauty or power."

"You're one of the strongest in the Order—"

"This has nothing to do with them." He leaned against the wall opposite her. "They're small-minded humans doing little tricks. I have bigger plans, which need bigger power. You've found the path, and now you'll share it with me." He spread his hands in front of him. "Why fight me on this? Your resistance can't keep me away forever. Why not work with me? I'm certainly a better match for you than that wimp, Clint."

"What's he got to do with this?"

"Nothing now." Mac smiled. "He has no more power than most people, making them very easy to manipulate. Like your albino friend here—a simple glamour spell, and she believed someone she knew was at the front entrance."

Brenda balled her hands into fists. "You influenced Clint to break up with me?"

"Should you be saying this in front of her?" the woman asked Mac, gesturing to Sara.

"Don't worry about her," Mac said. He turned to Angelique. "But you're worried about her, aren't you?" He nodded to the Asian woman.

She pressed her gun against the side of Sara's head. Sara

reached up to push the gun away, and the woman released the safety, Sara threw her hands in the air and slowly lowered them to her lap.

Angelique jumped to her feet. "Don't hurt her."

"Don't. I'm fine," Sara said.

"Yes, I thought so." He shoved Angelique back on the couch. "The air is thick with the attraction between you two. The thing is, I don't want to hurt anyone. I just want the information your cousin has gathered, and then I'll leave."

"What makes you think I have it here?" Brenda asked.

"Because if I were you, I'd keep it nearby, and we haven't found it anywhere else. We could search every inch of you—that might be fun—or we could go a more traditional route to convince you to co-operate. It's kind of low-tech on a magic level, but it can be persua-sive." He nodded to the woman. She took a slim laser knife from her jacket pocket, clicked it on and swiped at Sara. Two of her long, pale dreadlocks fell to the floor.

Angelique started to stand, but Brenda grabbed her hand and squeezed. A spike of electricity rushed between them.

"There's no reason to overreact," Brenda said.

"Then give me what I want," he said.

Brenda took a long breath and pushed out from the center of her body. The air in the room compressed.

"I was waiting for you to try something like this," he said. He waved his hands in the air, clenched his hands into fists and grunted. The pressure in the room disappeared.

Angelique squeezed Brenda's hand and took a breath at the same time she did, pushing out from her center. They worked to-gether, their power joining, and pushed the air toward Mac and his partner.

"Sara, run!" Brenda said.

There was a loud boom overhead. Lightbulbs exploded. Their ears popped as an invisible hand shoved them away from each other.

Brenda ran out the door, through the club and into the crowded street. She turned around and saw Sara but not Angelique. Sara stopped and looked back at the same time.

"Keep running!" Angelique's voice whispered urgently in her ear. She still didn't see her cousin, but grabbed Sara's arm.

"We have to get farther away," Brenda said.

"What about Angelique?"

"She's okay. Let's go." She pushed Sara in front of her. They shuffled through the packed streets. Sara ducked into an alley, and Brenda followed her, as they ran left and right through the alleys.

They climbed over a low fence, sprinted through a yard, and ran in the back door of a bar. The bar was an old neighborhood hangout, a safe haven for natives when the French Quarter was swamped with visitors. Sara grabbed Brenda's arm and led her through the crowd to the bar.

"Hey, Sara, what's up?" the bartender yelled over the jukebox.

Brenda looked at her and shook her head.

"Just out for a little downtime," Sara said.

The bartender poured two beers into frozen mugs and slapped the mugs on the bar in front of Sara and Brenda.

"We have to go back and get Angelique," Sara said.

"She's safe for now," Brenda said. "He'll use her to get the information from me."

"You know that for a fact?"

Brenda nodded and looked across the bar at the wide mirror. A shudder went through her.

She was back in the club, sitting in a chair. She tried to move, but ropes held her tight. A silence spell kept Brenda/Angelique from talking. Through Angelique's eyes, the images were warped and stretched.

"Brenda, I know you can hear me," Mac said. "It's fortunate that you and your cousin are so close. It saved her life."

Mac passed the laser knife in front of their face. "I can start carving your cousin up, or you can give me what I want. And just so you know, I'm serious."

He walked behind Brenda/Angelique. She heard the high-pitched sound of the laser coming on. They struggled in the chair, and screamed at the jolt of pain in her right hand. The pain dulled to a throb. Mac showed her a fingertip.

"I sealed the wound, so she won't bleed to death. Just the little finger, above the knuckle. Something that can be rebuilt. But I can do more, much more." He waved his hand in front of her face, and the silence spell lifted briefly.

"No, please, don't hurt her anymore," Brenda said, using Angelique's voice. "I'll meet you at the corner of Canal and Basin. Bring Angelique."

"I sincerely hope you're not going to try anything. I'd hate for you to experience the death of your cousin," Mac said. He shoved Brenda out of her cousin's mind.

"What's wrong?" Sara asked. "Are you all right?"

"Come on," she said, pulling Sara out of the bar.

As they walked to the meeting place, Brenda explained everything to Sara.

"I don't need magic to know that he's dangerous," Sara said. "Do you really think he'll just let us walk away after he gets the information from you?"

Brenda shook her head. "At the best, he'll use his power to scramble our minds, which could probably turn a normal person into a vegetable. You know what the worst case is. Angelique and I could probably fight off some of his power together, but I don't think we could protect you, too. In fact, you should go somewhere safe until this is over."

"No can do, not while Angelique's in danger. I've lived in New Orleans long enough to suspect there was something to magic, but I'm not sure I can believe all of this," Sara said as they walked down the street.

"I understand your skepticism," Brenda said. "If you won't leave, then you have to do whatever I say, whether you believe or not."

Sara nodded.

Brenda looked up at the entrance to St. Louis Cemetery Number 1.

"We'll meet them inside."

Sara hesitated. "Not that I'm afraid, but I don't think cemeteries and magic are a good mix."

"I'm hoping not." Brenda said a quick chant asking for the blessings of the dead before they entered.

They walked past the rows of stone houses. The full moon made the white stone crypts and concrete ground glow. Brenda went to a brick wall of arches, burial holes for the poorer community. A couple of the arch fronts had crumbled, leaving gaping openings. She laid her hand on the front of each small arch until she felt the vibration she needed.

"Someone in here died angry and betrayed."

"What are you doing?" Sara asked.

"Trying to get us out of the mess I got us into." She put her finger to her lips to quiet Sara.

She pulled a piece of red yarn out of a small bag in her pocket. Holding the yarn against the sealed burial hole, she said:

"With this knot I seal this spell.
You will not rest, you will not tell.
Knots of red, knots times three,
Bringing chaos and forgetfulness
From the rage within to thee.
So mote it be."

Each time she tied a knot, she said the spell, until she had tied three knots in the yarn. She bowed to the crypt, said a chant of thanks to the bones within and put the yarn in her pocket.

"Let's go," she said, running back to the cemetery entrance. They stopped within the borders of the grounds. "When they get here, I'll take care of Mac. You keep your eye on the woman."

A blue car pulled up slowly to the entrance. Mac got out with Angelique and the Asian woman. Mac walked with his arm around Angelique's waist and one hand holding the laser knife against her side. Angelique held her wounded hand tucked under her arm. She stumbled at the edge of the sidewalk. The woman held a gun down at her side. They stopped outside the entrance.

"Are you all right?" Sara asked.

"Don't worry, she'll be fine," Mac said. "A cemetery. Somewhat fitting, if you try to trick me."

"The information is in a memory rod in here." Brenda pointed into the cemetery.

"Then let's get it, and finish this," the Asian woman said.

"This way," Brenda said, leading them back to the brick wall.

Sara tried to talk to Angelique, but the woman waved her ahead with the gun. They walked past the sealed burial arches to one that was open. The concrete entrance had collapsed inside the arch.

Brenda put her hand inside, pushing aside chunks of concrete. "How do I know you'll let us go?"

"I didn't think you'd argue with sharing a forgetfulness spell between the three of you." Mac smiled.

"Okay." Brenda glanced at Sara and Angelique quickly. Sara stood next to the woman with the gun. Mac lowered the knife toward the ground. Brenda grabbed a chunk of concrete from inside the arch and threw it at the woman's head, hitting her in the face. As she fell backwards, the gun went off, the bullet grazing Brenda's arm. Sara jumped on the woman and slammed her head into the ground until she passed out.

Angelique grabbed Mac's wrist with her good hand and swung with all her weight, throwing him off balance. There was a crack as his wrist broke, making him scream and drop the knife. Brenda rushed in, and kicked him in the back of his knee. He crumbled to the ground. Sara grabbed the knife, sat on his back and held it to his neck.

"Don't move, Mac, or I'll activate the blade, and you won't care if the wound is sealed," she said.

Brenda pulled the knotted yarn out of her pocket and dragged the Asian woman next to Mac. She sat between them on the ground, placed her left hand on the woman's forehead and grasped Angelique's hand with her right along with the yarn. Angelique knew immediately what Brenda intended, and let the fingers of her injured right hand touch the back of Mac's head. Brenda said:

"With this knot I seal this spell.
You will not rest, you will not tell.
Knots of red, knots times three,
Bringing chaos and forgetfulness
From the rage within to thee.
So mote it be."

Electricity shot through the cousins into their captives. Mac's body stiffened, as did the woman's unconscious body. Brenda said it again. Mac moaned, "No." The third time Brenda said it, Mac's body went limp. The cousins closed their eyes.

They were falling in a dark sky. Thunder and lightning cut through the air. Four bodies tumbled in a circle, hands tightly clasped, as if fused together. The first word of Brenda's spell echoed in a strange voice around them, like the sound of a car crash. The screech of metal became winged creatures, their long beaks and tails ending in razor-sharp edges. On the second word, the creatures swooped at them, using their beaks and tails to cut and whip at the woman and Mac.

Mac tried to pull away, but the more power he gathered, the bigger the creatures grew. The woman screamed uncontrollably.

The voice continued reciting each word of the spell with building rage and poisonous anger. Thick blood splashed on the cousins as the creatures tore and ripped away at Mac and the woman. On the last word, Brenda and Angelique released their hands and opened their eyes.

"You don't have to hold the knife on him anymore," Brenda said. She took the knife from Sara and helped Angelique stand up. Brenda's upper arm stung and bled where the bullet had brushed it. She looked at her cousin's missing fingertip. "Let's get you to a doctor."

Angelique laughed weakly. "You need to have that arm looked at, too."

"So, we just walk out of here and leave them?" Sara asked.

"They won't bother us again. Their memory is in pieces, ripped to shreds," Brenda said.

"Where did you keep the information they were after?" Sara asked, putting her arm around Angelique's waist.

Brenda turned, and smiled in the moonlight. She jangled the charm bracelet in the air. "Mac was right. I always carry the data with me. But tonight I downloaded it somewhere even safer."

"Tonight?" Angelique asked, leaning against Sara. "You put it in Milez."

Brenda smiled.

Black Frontiers

Maurice Broaddus

Kansas, 1887

Govie Ikard had a bad feeling about the job from the start. She shoved a few drunken louts out of her way, cutting through the throng gathered in Old Man Stevens' barn. Fists clutching tattered dollars waved in the air. Some men stood on wood crates for a better view, the air thick with the stink of exhaled alcohol.

The commotion centered around a cleared dirt space, where two men circled each other. Rumors had circulated about how one of them was afraid to face the other in a contest to see who had the best hands, rumors probably started by the same fools throwing their money around now. A big country boy with straw-colored hair clumped to his red face looked to trade punches with a Negro built like an oak. The Negro stood six-and-a-half feet if an inch, and was every bit the man that had been described to her.

"The Ninth marched out with splendid cheer," the Negro sang to himself. His coal eyes radiated a disturbing acceptance, an unnerving calm. She knew from the moment she first set eyes on him that he was different. He stood straight and proud, with no hint of fear.

That country boy's face hardened. No more than a backwoods brawler, he rushed in. The Negro, not moving to evade him, stepped in, smashing the boy's nose. The blow landed like a clap of thunder. The boy grunted, a surprised look on his face, then walloped the Negro in the body. Years on the farm had given him hands like a slab of beef. Before long, they wrestled around, the spectators scrambling out of the way of their huge bodies. The dull-witted crowd roared with appreciation, but they didn't see what Govie saw. The two seemed a fairly even match, but the Negro moved too well. He was toying with that country boy. They tussled in the dirt, each trying to get the better of the other. The Negro clubbed the boy's gut so hard that even the crowd winced. The boy threw an off-balance blow to the Negro's jaw. Shaking it off, and having taken the boy's full measure, the Negro began to chop him down with powerful punches, any one of which would have sent any man in the crowd to sleep. The boy got an odd glint in his simple blue eyes, as if it occurred to him that he might lose this fight to a Negro. He picked up a wooden crate and crashed it across the Negro's backside, sending him sprawling to the ground in a cloud of dust and straw. The crowd cheered again. The boy turned to greet his supporters, whose back-patting cries choked short. He caught sight of their faces staring behind him. He turned in time to kiss the Negro's fist. He went flying past his supporters into the barn wall. He didn't bother getting back up.

"Didn't know you were that strong," a man said, clapping the Negro on his back before counting his winnings.

"Never had to show it before," the Negro said. He looked over at the country boy with something approaching pity. The boy's friends helped him out the door without so much as a backwards glance. None of the men who had won from his labors stayed behind long or offered even to buy him a drink. He picked up his shirt from the hay and buttoned it. That was when he first noticed Govie.

"Well, ain't you the fiercest buck I done seen in these parts," Govie said.

"I reckon." His thick lips barely moved when he spoke.

"Mind if I buy you a drink?"

"I don't drink."

"Then mind if you come watch me drink while I make you a business proposition?" she asked, the way that mothers did when they were telling their children what they were going to do. She cottoned to him mite fast. He had a swagger about him, almighty impressed with himself. The man was quite a sight. Pulling his suspenders over his hunting shirt, he clutched a dusty Union soldier's jacket. Govie noticed a buffalo insignia on the jacket. Neither the shirt nor the jacket made a lick of sense with his buckskin leggings and cavalry boots with Mexican spurs.

She pulled her wool cap snugly over her head, and fastened her coat by just the top button. She stood an even six feet tall, and the blue skirt was the only thing that gave a clue that she was, in fact, a woman. She was not exactly sure of her birthday, but Andrew Jackson had been president. All her years of living made her mean as a tripped-over rattlesnake, but she figured that she had a good twenty years left in her. Too stubborn to die, she lit a huge cigar while she drank.

"What's your name, son?" she asked only to be polite, since he'd already made quite a name for himself. A writer even spun a series of dime novels based on some of his misadventures.

"Bose Roberds."

"I'm Govie Ikard, but most folks 'round here call me Stagecoach Govie." She felt his eyes studying her, trying to make sense of her and gauge the legitimacy of any offer that she might make. He was a smart one, for sure.

"What's the job?"

"Escort a stagecoach. Some sort of special cargo they want guarded. I already hired a scout. Now I'm looking for another hand."

"Hand? You mean fist."

"Something like that. Things may not even come to that, but I could use the company, and I bet you could use the job."

"For who?"

"St. Peter's Mission."

Something in the air changed around him, like something left him. "We working for mission folks?"

"That gonna be a problem?"

"No man on a stick ever did anything for me. I make my own way."

"Shut your fool mouth," Govie said, half-offended, or leastways not wanting God to rain down any judgments on them. She wasn't what anyone would call a religious woman, but she had respect for it. Except for the time she spent as a slave, she'd lived a life under the stars, in the mountains, in view of sunsets and sunrises. God's creation taught her a religion of the heart. So she appealed to his practical side. "A job's a job, unless this whole bare-knuckle fighting's paying better than I think."

Bose's expression, which she assumed meant he was thinking, reminded her of a cow chewing its cud. The saloon doors opened to the murmurs of some customers. Govie cut a sideways glance before returning her eyes to Bose. He tracked the man approaching their table. She chomped on her cigar.

"Who's he?" Bose locked eyes on the man, who paid him no mind. She recognized the mild look of confusion in Bose's eyes. Few knew what to make of her traveling companion, whether he was Negro or Indian. The man took his place behind her, then crossed his arms.

"Daniel Gray Cloud, the scout I was telling you about. He doesn't speak much."

"Mute?"

"Naw. He knows English, Spanish and Seminole; maybe a couple others, but he won't tell. He just don't speak."

"Ever?" Bose asked.

"Only when he has something to say."

"That's the most damn foolish thing I ever heard."

"I wished more men had sense enough to shut up."

Govie kicked an empty chair out for Gray Cloud, but the stubborn cuss remained standing. He was handsome, with features like a European gentleman and smooth skin on a fearless face, except for the scar over his left eye. How he got the scar was never mentioned, but it grayed his eye to uselessness. Bronzed to the hue of tree bark, he had black hair that grew long and straight to his broad shoulders. He dressed like a Union soldier, except for his moccasins and a handful of feathers in a hat whose brim had been folded back.

"They ready?" Govie turned to Gray Cloud. He nodded. She turned back around, finished another heavy draught of whiskey and slammed her glass to the table. "You in?"

"I reckon. Nothing better to do," Bose said.

"then. Let's go."

Cascade wasn't quite a trail town, but it had its share of herders come through looking to blow off steam. It also served as a way station for Exodusters, freed slaves who moved into Kansas on their way to Cascade's sister town, Nicodemus, one of thirty Negro communities in Kansas. Govie feared for Cascade. She'd never seen a prosperous town so lifeless. Gray dust swirled about the streets.

Wind-battered frame buildings, with cracked paint and worn boards, greeted them. She watched the people of the town with their panic-stricken eyes grow pallid, ghostlike. They carried themselves like frightened children carrying a terrible secret. Her town was dying.

And that put her in a foul mood.

She spied the perfect person on whom to vent her frustration: a man who never paid her for his ride to Cascade. He was a Boomer, one of the white settlers trying to settle the Unassigned Lands, lands not yet designated for a specific tribe. He and his companion were walking along the opposite side of the street, trying to act as if they didn't see her.

"I thought I told you that I didn't want to see you tinhorns in my town."

"I don't care what some nigger bitch says. Trying to charge a white man to ride her stage."

"Uh, Bill, that's—" his companion offered.

"I don't give a right damn who that is."

Govie spit at the ground, then stepped to the man. Bose moved to back her up, but Gray Cloud stopped him. Govie stared at the man, hard eyes unflinching. He didn't have time to dodge. She knocked him flat.

"That's the last time I deal with you Boomer trash. Consider your bill 'settled'."

The Boomer rubbed his jaw, looking like he'd been sprayed in the face by a skunk.

"Those are the kind of antics that caused your dismissal from our employ the first time," a thin-chested, square-faced man with a bushy mustache and windswept black hair called to her. He carried a Bible the size of a small trunk by his side.

"As I recall, you fired me for defending myself in a gunfight." Govie's face drew down in hard lines, as if she had tasted some spoiled meat.

"Your assailant had already missed."

"He made the quarrel. And I let him live. Just fired close enough to let him know that I was letting him live."

"We don't tolerate . . . gunslingers."

"Yeah, unless you have a job too dirty for your pretty little church hands, Bishop."

"He don't look none too pleased to see you," Bose whispered loud enough for him to hear.

"It takes a while for Bishop Early to warm up to a lady," Govie said, then spat at his feet. The bishop, apparently not given to saying anything coarse, stood looking ugly, then hustled off with his back stiff, the way it got when he was mad. It was plain that he didn't like a woman who talked up to him the way she did. Govie's lips crinkled in a way that was meant to be a smile.

"Govie?" A soft yet firm voice caught their attention. Govie's eyes lit up with immediate recognition.

"Sister Mary?"

The nun barely came up to Govie's chest, but she had a stoutness about her. She had a big, easy smile with a sternness behind her green eyes that made people take to her right off. Sister Mary was an Ursuline nun for the St. Peter's Mission. When Govie had first arrived in Cascade, Sister Mary had helped convince the bishop to hire her to haul supplies from Nicodemus to the mission. Govie made such a name for herself—facing down Indians, fending off bandits, surviving blizzards and never failing to see her cargo to its destination—that she earned her nickname.

"People treat you like some sort of Negro princess," Bose said.

"Let me tell you a story about Govie that she's too humble to tell herself," Sister Mary said. "One time, the horses got spooked by wolves, and the wagon spilled on its side. Medicine that we badly needed. Govie kept the wolves away until morning, righted the wagon and reloaded it to finish her haul."

"They probably got a look at her ugly puss, and scattered." However, Bose's words lacked the conviction of insult. Govie noticed the slight furrow in the Sister's brow and the hint of sadness in her eyes. "What's going on, Sister? You seem mighty worried."

"Rumors, is all."

"It got anything to do with what's ailin' the town?"

"It seems like we spend too much time covering up the sins of men instead of dealing with them. And innocents pay the price."

"The bishop?" Bose was quick to ask.

"He doesn't know much more than me. He thinks he's helping." Sister Mary turned back to Govie, but there was something in her eyes. Sadness. Regret. Maybe disgust. "Men and their superstitions, letting their fears get the better of them."

"What, someone planning on looting the stage of its load?"

"I fear that the stage may not make it to its destination. That's why I fought to get you back on, over some people's objections."

"Where am I taking the cargo?"

"Far away from here. Fort Laramie, Wyoming, if you can."

That would take them across a lot of Indian territory. The job kept getting better and better.

Govie spent the morning preparing her stagecoach. Overnight, the bishop oversaw the loading of the cargo, free from prying eyes, and with specific instructions that it not be disturbed. She checked the modifications, since he had the coach windows reduced to slits and the doors reinforced, and loaded their provisions. She rubbed the noses of her horses, nuzzling them with her face, stroking them behind their ears the way they liked. Twin black horses, they were her "nightmares." Hers was a simple belief: take care of your horses, and they will always see you home. Rumor had it that she once clubbed a man near to death for beating his horse.

Bose set his pack atop the stage. Its weight shifted, and it tumbled to the ground, splitting open. A ribboned piece of metal spilled out. Govie retrieved it, but cradled the piece of metal in her hands.

"Congressional Medal of Honor." Bose grabbed it, tucking it into his pack.

"Is that real?" Govie asked.

"Real enough."

"How'd you get one?"

"Don't really like to talk about it."

"Then why keep it around?"

"A reminder. I rode with the Ninth Cavalry. Those days are behind me, but I don't want to forget." He had a deep sense of obligation written into his face. Govie was slow to make friends—she never had much use for them, plus she knew that she was a hard woman—but Bose seemed mighty alright.

"Gray Cloud will be riding ahead of us. You want to ride in back?"

"I'm a good shot. Thought I'd keep you company and ride shotgun."

"My jug of rye rides shotgun."

"Then I'll have to join it." Bose took a swig, then set it in his lap.

"I'll make a drinker of you yet."

They rode in silence, anything they said drowned out by the rumble of the stage, the crunch of leaves and the sound of rocks spitting from under the wheels. They passed nothing except grass and sky, maybe a buffalo wallow or occasional gopher hole. Thoughts of the cargo made them brood in the silence. Govie considered herself a professional, and no amount of curiosity would make her pull the stage over just to take a gander. Bose appeared to be a good man, with more than a grain of sense in his head. Still, the way he fidgeted with his Winchester, the more she suspected that he felt the same unease gnawing at his insides.

"You ever married, Govie?" Bose asked, but she knew the small talk was more to break the tyranny of their thoughts.

"Once. To my late Mason."

"He probably wished himself to death to get away from you."

Their half-hearted chuckles failed to alleviate the tension. Govie reached for the rye. "You ever think about hitching up with someone?"

"Can't do it. The way I figure, the West has too much that I want to see and do. A man's got to find his own way and be free."

"You don't ask much out of life."

"All I ever asked from life was a full belly, the *occasional* drink and some companions to share it with."

"And a good horse," Govie added.

"Damn straight." Bose took another swig from the jug, watching the land roll and tumble alongside them. She had the feeling all the rye in the jug wouldn't soothe their nerves.

Night settled on them, a slowly falling curtain, as they passed through a rocky promontory. Govie had planned to ride the horses to a spot out of the skyline where they could take a decent survey of the terrain before darkness fell. The horses gave a sharp whinny and reared up. Govie snapped the reins taut, but the spooked horses had ideas all their own. The stage overturned. Bose held fast to his rifle and the handrail. The jug of whiskey fell over the side, followed by Govie's curses. She scrabbled behind the still-spinning wheels of the stagecoach, soon joined by Bose, rifle brought to bear. She drew a Colt pistol, leaning on what she'd learned from hard living: when danger came, your Colt served you better in your fist than in a holster.

"Wolves?" Govie asked, scanning the shadows.

"This happen to you a lot?" Bose asked, trying to upset her, she guessed, to keep her focus off her fear. He needn't have bothered.

"Check the cargo. Make sure nothing's broken, but don't get all snoopy."

"Where's Gray Cloud?"

"Around. Trust me, he'll be here if we need him."

At first, Govie didn't notice the silence. She was so intent on listening for what might be there, she didn't right notice what wasn't. No rustling of leaves, no chirping insects, not even tree branches falling. It was like the world held its breath waiting for the next move. She had an awful lost-and-empty feeling inside.

"You might want to come see this."

Negotiating her footing with extreme caution—in part to not interrupt the silence, in part to avoid slipping on the stage or any of its contents—she made her way to the side of the coach. The spill had torn open the door, and the curtain inside had been pulled to one side by Bose. She peered in and saw a little white girl and an old man. Wide-eyed, cheeks dappled with freckles, the girl brushed strands of her red hair from her face. Thirteen, if a day, belied by her haunted, old eyes. Her dress was freshly smoothed and clean, like she was headed to church. She clung to the shadows. Dressed like a gentleman, the frail man, with his scholar's face and erudite eyes, coughed phlegm into his immaculately groomed brush mustache. He wrapped a cross on a string of beads around his hand, kissing it, then rocked back and forth, praying in some gibberish tongue. Govie couldn't shake the feeling of something malign and evil.

She spat.

Studying the terrain, she cursed herself for being a fool. Only half-concealed by brush, they were in a bad position: low ground, the perfect place for an ambush. The night filled her with a grave disquiet. Bose must've felt it, too, because a low, melancholy song sprang to his lips.

"The Ninth marched out with splendid cheer,
The Bad Lands to explore
With Colonel Henry at their head
They never fear the foe"

The night ripened with sadness. Govie hadn't noticed before how fine his voice was. He could be in a show or sing in a chorus.

> *"So on they rode from Christmas eve;*
> *'Til dawn of Christmas day;*
> *The Red Skins heard the Ninth was near*
> *And fled in great dismay."*

Her keen ears detected a sudden rattle of hooves somewhere along the trail. She scanned the surrounding terrain, the hair raised on the back of her neck.

"Get down," Bose yelled.

Before the old man could move, the sharp retort of a rifle rang out, leaving a spreading red stain sullying his vestments. Govie and Bose hunkered down behind the overturned stage. Shadows leaped from tree to tree. Bose fired a shot close enough to let them know they had been spotted. Moonlight glinted on a rifle barrel. A bullet whipped past Govie's ear. Bose replied with the roar of his Winchester. Heads emerged from behind rocks and trees, closing in around them. The men, whoever they were, didn't attack all at once. That meant that something had been taken from them that they wanted back, and maybe this would buy them some time.

"They getting set for a rush," Govie whispered.

"What are you planning on doing?"

"I'm not going to wait for my bushwhacking." Govie stood up, her Colt pointed to the earth, and yelled out. "You all too yellow to face me one-on-one?"

Bose pulled her down before the flurry of shots responded. "You're a damn shade of foolish, woman. You gonna get struck full of buckshot before you're done."

"Had to try and draw them out. I'd guess there are five of them—"

"Seven," Gray Cloud said, making them whirl and train their guns on him. He'd crept in like a carefree shadow. Sometimes there was no accounting for Indians, especially Seminoles. They followed their own unsettling notions.

"Three I think I recognized," Govie said.

"How?" Bose asked, scanning the darkness.

"Don't need much light to recognize ugly. The lead gun's got to be that piece of Boomer trash, Bill Downey."

"Guess he didn't take to your ladylike disposition."

"Two others looked to be the McCarty brothers, Wade and Josh. You can bet if he brought those wild coyotes, the rest are just as ornery."

"Got a proposition for you, Govie," a strained, high-pitched voice cried out with the strength of a bruised ego supported by bullying numbers.

"Go ahead with it, then, Bill."

"We only want your cargo. Make sure it gets to where it's supposed to. The rest of your outfit can leave without fear from us."

"And if I say no?"

"It's not like you have a choice."

She grew thoughtful when she heard that. They were boxed in but good. "They're stalling. Probably trying to get in position to rush us."

"They don't know what we're carrying," Bose whispered.

"You mean the girl?" Govie said. Gray Cloud threw her a quizzical look, but she gestured for him to check for himself. He scampered back.

"That's no girl," Gray Cloud said.

"What you say, Govie? We ain't got all night," Bill yelled.

"Wait a minute. We talking it over." She turned to Gray Cloud. "What do you mean?"

"You see for yourself, in the light of the moon."

Govie pushed the stage, angling the girl into the moonlight. The young girl's skin grew mottled like that of a corpse, the light revealing flesh torn from her body by her own claws. A feral gleam in her eyes hinted at madness, but she played with her doll without a care in the world. Staring at her made Govie's insides feel like worms burrowing through a rotted apple. She dropped the stage like it was scalding coffee.

"What the hell is that?"

"Nagual. An animal spirit forced into a person," Gray Cloud said.

"I heard tell of that," Bose said. "Mexican farmer spun tales of them 'round a campfire. I thought it was the tequila talking."

"You mean to tell me this here girl's been taken over by spirits?" Govie asked.

"Forced. Their true face is revealed by moonlight. Powerful magic's involved." Gray Cloud stared at the stage doors.

"What was the preacher for?"

"Keep her still until she got to wherever, I'd guess," Bose said.

"My men are getting antsy," Bill called out in a mocking tone.

"You know me, Bill. I've got . . . cargo that I've been charged with hauling, and I'm going to see it through."

" 'Fraid I can't let you do that. You see, these parts are crawling with red devils. And I aims to see that the cargo finds its way to them."

Only then did Govie realize that her job was meant to fail, that she was meant to be taken by Indians and the "cargo" to fall into their unsuspecting hands, like a disease-riddled blanket. A Boomer solution to the "Indian problem."

"Let's let them have her. Open the door, and let the moonlight take her."

"When the sun rises, the girl returns," Gray Cloud said with hesitance in his eyes. They turned to Bose.

"I don't know if that's a good idea, Govie," Bose said.

"If you're yellow, say so."

"The only thing yellow about me is my piss, which'll be in your coffee if you sass me again. I'll back your play," Bose said. "She'd distract them."

"Come and get her, Bill," Govie yelled. Hearing the snapping of tree branches behind them, she threw open the stage doors.

Govie, Bose and Gray Cloud ducked beneath the stage, their backs to its undercarriage. Wade and Josh McCarty stumbled out of the brush. Wade was a big, raw-boned man with coarse, black hair and a woolen undershirt that didn't quite cover his powerful arms or his thick neck. It was right smart of Bill Downey to bring along someone large enough to give Bose trouble. Josh, though wiry, was the meaner of the two and had an ugly ruthlessness writ into his face. They charged, strictly cover for the other, encircling men.

Govie started to recite the Lord's Prayer to herself.

The girl leaped from the stage with a snarl. Her lithe body belied the savagery with which she tore into the men. She landed on Wade like a mountain lion, rearing her right hand back, revealing talons that she buried in his throat. Her swipe reduced his neck to ribbons of flesh. The entwined bodies landed in a heap, with the girl burying her mouth in the rictus of his wound, snatching mouthfuls of flesh. She turned to Josh with her gore-stained face, his brother's body still spasming beneath her.

He had time only to scream.

Govie scuttled across the side of the stage, ignoring the loud, open-mouthed smacks and snapping bones. Bose and Gray Cloud moved out to either side. She heard the boom of a gun once she hit the ground, dirt jumping not an inch from where she landed. A second shot caused a searing pain like a branding iron to jab her in the left shoulder. Warm blood ran down her arm. That arm useless, her right hand belched fire into the night. A man fell from behind a tree. She found herself on her knees, catching a second slug, like a knife wound, along her ribs. A stream of curses followed. She pushed herself up, toward a cropping of trees. Examining every boulder, every tree, she caught sight of Bose turning loose his rifle, a tuneless hum on his lips. The man in his sights fell backward, the bullet blowing away the front part of his head. An unseen gunman fired once at Bose. A second shot soon followed from the same well-hidden position. Then the gun fell silent amidst the brief sounds of struggle. A silent Gray Cloud glided out from between the trees.

Govie stumbled across Bill Downey the same time Bose did. Bill fumbled with his irons, desperately trying to reload them.

"It's over," Govie said, covering Bill with her Colt. "Why don't you ride back into town and tell your Boomer friends that your cargo will be hauled off proper, but not ending up in the hands of no Indians."

"Why don't you drop your gun," a man with a shock of blond hair and bushy eyebrows said, his gun aimed square at Bose.

Govie glanced at Bose, then the gunman, then back at Bill. She started to lower her Colt.

A shadow fell upon Bose.

The gunman gave a sputtering cough, raising his gun and firing a wild shot in the air. Bose dove for cover. The man's shirt bulged, his body dancing in fits at the end of the nagual's arm. A man rarely surprised, Bose was startled to immobility, but his hands soon recovered their wits.

"Bose, no!" Govie yelled before he could draw down on the girl. Her Sunday-gone-to-meeting dress sprayed with dark splotches, and the moon's beams fully revealed her queer-colored flesh, like fruit rotting on the vine. Govie turned to Bill with the glare of an avenging seraphim. Bill, sick with fear, opened and closed his mouth. "You—run."

He recklessly sprang, with both guns bucking.

The creature stared at Govie with cold, penetrating eyes, then loped off into the woods. Govie picked up the nearly trampled doll from the dirt and dusted it off.

Footsteps echoed hollowly on the boardwalk. Bat-wing doors fluttered as they passed. The odor of stale whiskey mingled with lingering cigar smoke hit them when they walked into the all-white saloon. It grew quiet as a grave. A chair grated on the floor.

"My boys are mighty hungry," Govie said to the bartender, nodding toward Gray Cloud and Bose.

"Have a seat over there," the bartender said.

They took a table in the far corner, back against the wall. Facing a sea of uneasy stares, Govie massaged her still-sore arm.

"Something ain't right. I can feel it," Govie said.

"Must be them special powers of deduction that you have. Here I was thinking that three niggers in a bar wouldn't draw any attention," Bose said.

"What'll you be having?" the bartender asked.

"Steaks all around," Govie said.

"We're out of steaks."

She saw a man chewing on one glaring at them. Two men rested their hands on the hilts of their hunting knives. A hard-faced man with a weather-faded shirt slid over to the saloon door. Another moved to the end of the bar, close to their table.

Bose hummed to himself.

"I see how it is," Govie said.

"Why don't you just empty out your pockets?" The bartender rubbed his hands on a towel.

"We don't want any fuss. Let me tell you what. We ain't been paid yet, to haul our load up to Fort Laramie. Why don't I unhitch my horses, leave you my cargo and head out of town?"

The bartender looked over his shoulders. The hard-faced man shrugged. "Fair enough."

"This seem like the right place to you?" Bose asked, helping her unhitch their horses.

The young girl proved quite pliable by the light of the morning. Then Govie thought back to the face she saw under the moon's wan light.

"Always did hate these Boomer bastards. Heard some Exodusters settled in Boley, not too far from here."

So they rode.

Upstairs

Tananarive Due

Noelle Imani Bonner was not easily frightened. Her fearlessness was part of her family's folklore, the cause of more than one frantic trip to the emergency room. Last summer, at four, she'd knocked out two baby teeth riding on her brother's bicycle handlebars at the instant a fence greeted them at the bottom of the hill on Potter's Road. Noelle had also suffered stitches on her forehead and a tetanus shot, which, all told, were still mild compared to the consequences to her brother, though the crash itself had left him unmarred.

Noelle also had an affinity for insects that went counter to all myths about what little girls and boys are made of. With quick, unflinching fingers, Noelle could catch moths, caterpillars and a spindly-legged species of spider as big as her hand that her father called a daddy longlegs; the elegant spiders were her favorite plaything since her father had quashed her sister's claims that they were poisonous. Her bigmouthed brother gagged and swatted her away when she dangled a spider in front of him and dared him to touch it. Even as the youngest—a full three years behind Sierra and four years behind Victor—Noelle had no equal in boldness.

For all her parents' worry, neither of them took any joy from the thought of trying to teach Noelle fear. They remembered life at five—how much happiness came from small discoveries, and how foreign the concept of danger was—so they weren't in a hurry for their last child to grow up. She was old enough to keep her fingers away from light sockets, and she no longer tried to pour strange

powders from the kitchen cabinet into her mouth, so the consensus
was to let Noelle be Noelle, which was fine, of course, with Noelle.

Noelle's favorite spot in her family's two-story, wood-frame
house was the attic. All the other rooms, to Noelle, were lifeless.
But the attic! There were secret lives in the attic, things that scurried and rustled whenever she opened the door. Noelle made it her
business to try to discover what those things were—and, in fact,
she'd once chased a small black mouse until it vanished behind the
box of Christmas-tree decorations. A few of her long-legged spiders lived in the attic, too; in the main part of the house, they would
be attacked with a slipper or a newspaper, but no one bothered the
spiders in the attic. Noelle saw to this. She wasn't permitted to su-
pervise any other part of the house, even the bedroom she shared
with Sierra, but the attic and its inhabitants were *hers*.

The attic was just beyond the whitewashed door at the end of
the upstairs hallway, a door that was kept closed, but never locked.
Victor had accidentally locked himself in the attic when he was six,
screaming himself hoarse to be let out, so that was the end of the
lock's tenure on the attic door, as well as the end of any inclination
of Victor to spend time there.

Noelle, on the other hand, could spend hours in the attic. She'd
already decided that when she grew up, she was going to live there,
and she wouldn't have to come down even if it was time for dinner,
or church, and especially not bed.

She visited as often as she could.

The dull, wooden stairs leading to the attic, which were much
steeper than the carpeted steps to the first floor, required special
attention and a tight grip on the handrail. The light bulb had burned
out long ago, so the only light in the attic was natural, from windows facing four directions; three of the windows were swathed by
tree branches, which Noelle liked, because it made her feel like
she'd been swallowed inside a giant tree house.

And the space! Maybe that was the most important thing of all.
The attic was cluttered, yes—in the middle of the floor, there were
heaps of camping equipment, most of it still in boxes, and every discarded piece of furniture from the house—but the attic was the only
room that wasn't interrupted by walls, stretching endlessly from
one end of the house to the other. To Noelle, it was luxurious, mysterious, wonderful. An empire.

So, frankly, Noelle was not terribly surprised when she made her way up there one Sunday afternoon and happened to find a man lying asleep under the old dining room table. He was sleeping on a pile of blankets, and she could see newspapers peeking underneath that he'd spread for extra cushioning. The man was snoring very softly, not nearly as loudly as her father would. He was growing a beard that wasn't coming in right, so some parts of his face—which was very skinny, almost pointy—still looked pink and bare.

The man was sleeping here exactly the way Noelle had imagined she would one day, and she crouched down near the table to get a better look. Her heart flew with excitement. This was her finest discovery in the attic yet!

As if he could hear the cries of delight in her mind, the man opened his eyes wide. His eyes were blue, a clear kind of eye Noelle had never seen before. The eyes looking at her did not blink even once. In a hurry, the man scooted himself from underneath the table so he could sit up straight and give his broad shoulders more room. He was bigger than he'd seemed when he was curled up in a ball. His strange eyes squinted down at her.

"Hello," Noelle said. "Are you the man in the house?" The eyes narrowed more, and the man's head angled toward her, the way their neighbor's dog did when Victor opened his mouth wide and made his invisible dog sound, the kind only dogs could hear. "Mommy said yesterday she wishes there were a man in the house, because a bad thing happened, and I told her to throw a penny in the birdbath and it would come true. Are you the man?"

"Where's your daddy?" the man said. His voice was rumbly, like the sound a bicycle makes riding over rocks.

"He's on a trip. For his job."

"Oh, okay," the man said. He smiled at her for the first time. His teeth weren't white like Noelle's; they were the color of mustard. But, then, she remembered, he couldn't brush his teeth up here because there was no sink. "What bad thing was your mama talking about?"

Noelle shrugged. Something in the newspaper. Something on the television. Something her mother and the next-door neighbor, Mrs. Rigby, talked about in the kitchen that morning in their grown-up voices, the kind Noelle wasn't meant to hear. Besides, her mother's name was *Mommy*, not *Mama*. Strangers always got that wrong.

"I dunno," she said.

"Did somebody get hurt?" the man said. "Somebody right here in this neighborhood, about two blocks over?"

"Maybe," Noelle said.

"And did somebody do bad things to them? Ugly things?"

"I dunno," Noelle said again. Unlike Sierra, who thought she was so mature, Noelle wasn't interested in grown-up conversations.

"Well, since your daddy's not home and I'm the only man here, then I guess that makes me the man in the house," he said. He reached into his pocket for a cigarette and lit it with a red Bic lighter. The flame almost jumped up to his nose.

"No smoking in the house," Noelle said.

"Ain't in the house. We're in the attic. Besides, the window's open," the man said, pointing over his shoulder.

The window was not only open, it was broken, Noelle noticed. The tree branch from outside had stuck its way in and was rubbing against the window frame in a breeze with sad-sounding squeaks. There were big pieces of glass on the floorboards.

"Did you do that?" Noelle asked.

"By accident, I guess I did. I knew this was the house where the wish came from, and I climbed up the tree to get in, but then the window was locked. Hell of a thing. Guess I'll have to fix it when I leave."

"When are you leaving?"

The man touched the hair on top of his head, then ran his palm down until it reached his neck and then his shoulder. He had very long hair, almost like an Indian's, except it was light brown and curly. He blew smoke into the air. "When's your daddy coming home?"

"In three days," Noelle said. "On Wednesday."

"That's a long time to be gone. Your daddy always traveling like that, leaving you and your mama with no man in the house?"

"No. He had another job before," she said.

"Oh, yeah. It's hard getting work. People don't make wishes like they used to. I'm glad your mama did, because here I am. Just like that." He winked. "That bad thing had to happen first, but that's the way it goes."

"That's the way it goes," Noelle repeated. She liked the way the man had said that, with his voice flying up into singsong.

The man looked at Noelle very closely, as though he hadn't really noticed her before. "How old are you?" he asked.

Noelle held up five fingers. Victor told her she was too old to keep doing that, that she should just say it aloud, but she'd decided to wait until she was six for that. Fingers were easier.

"You ain't scared of me, huh?" the man asked.

Noelle shook her head.

He grinned. He put his cigarette back in his mouth, and the end of it glowed bright orange. "Imagine that," the man said, blowing smoke out of his nose. Noelle wondered if the smoke tickled his nose hairs. "Know what? That's the whole difference between devils and angels—not being afraid. Did you know that?"

Noelle shook her head again.

"What's your name?"

"Noelle Imani Bonner."

"Noel. Like Christmas?"

Noelle nodded. "Yep. What's your name?"

"Kris Kringle," the man said.

"Not-uh," Noelle said, giggling.

"Peter Pan."

"That's not a name for somebody in real life."

"Did you forget already? I'm not from real life."

"Your real name is Peter Pan?"

"No. Just Peter," the man said, and he reached out his hand for Noelle to shake it, the way grown-ups did. Noelle felt his big hand wrap around hers, with his skin that felt rough and scratchy. He held her tight. "Pleasure, little lady."

"Will you stay until my daddy comes back?"

Peter didn't let go of Noelle's hand, even though he wasn't shaking it up and down anymore. He looked straight into her eyes, and she knew he was about to say something important.

"I want you to pay real close attention, Noelle," he said. She could smell the smoke on his breath. "I'ma stay here as long as I can. But you can't tell anybody, and I mean *anybody*, I'm up here. If you do, the wish goes away; you won't have a man in the house anymore, and something bad will definitely happen here, too. I've got a very strong feeling about that. Ever get hunches?"

Noelle shook her head. She didn't. Or maybe she did, but she didn't know what they were.

"Well, we don't want that to happen. We want only angels in that attic, Noelle. Will you help me do that?"

Noelle said she would. She promised she wouldn't say anything about the smoking or the broken window, and she'd try to make sure nobody came to the attic but her. She was proud of herself because she'd thought of everything to keep the secret.

"I want you to do something for me, too," he said, finally letting go of her hand after she'd made her promises. "I want you to go downstairs right now and grab me a loaf of bread and a jar of peanut butter. Don't forget a knife."

"I'm not allowed to touch knifes," Noelle said.

"Not the sharp kind. The other kind. Don't let nobody see you. I want you to go down and do that right now. As you can see, there ain't no food up here. None at all."

Noelle didn't have a chance to tell him that she was going to move into this attic when she grew up, and when she did she would have a refrigerator full of food. She would tell him that later, she decided. For now, she wanted to turn around and go really fast to do what Peter said.

"Thank you very much, little lady," Peter said. "We're going to be good friends, you and me. You'll see."

"Okay," Noelle said, and she laid her index finger across her lips so he would be quiet before she got to the stairs.

Noelle had never kept a secret before, not a *big* secret, and she discovered it was hard work. At dinner, sitting at the table with Victor and Sierra and her mother, she couldn't stop thinking about how there was a man in the house right above their heads, eating peanut butter sandwiches, smoking cigarettes and sleeping under the old dining room table. Noelle's brain wanted to say it every time she opened her mouth, just to see how surprised they would be. Just to prove to her mother that wishes could work. To prove to Victor that the attic was special, like she said. And to prove to Sierra that she wasn't a baby, because how could she be a baby if she alone was in charge of the man in the house? The secret was making her bounce up and down in her chair until it squeaked.

"Stop that, Noelle," her mother said, and Noelle stopped bouncing because she didn't want to give the secret away.

Noelle planned to climb up and say good night to Peter before it was completely dark and she would have to go to bed, but her mother stuck her head out of her bedroom doorway just as Noelle was making a dash for the attic door.

"No, Noelle, it's too late to go up there with no lights," her mother said, and Sierra gave Noelle a look as she padded out of the bathroom in her Snoopy slippers. Sierra smelled like Crest. "You are too weird for words," Sierra said to her.

Victor leaped out of his room, across the hall from theirs, blocking Noelle's path in the hall. He was making an ugly face. "I'm gonna cut off both your arms! I'm the Mangler!" he said. He was curving his fingers like claws, slashing them near her eyes.

"What's a mangler?" Noelle asked him, not scared at all.

"Hush, Victor," their mother said, in a voice that meant business. When Noelle looked at her mother's face, she could see how worried she was—the same way she'd looked when she'd tossed a penny in the birdbath in the backyard, beneath the tree whose highest branches were now poking through the broken attic window.

"Mom, that freak's in Mexico by now, I bet," Victor said.

"I told you to hush. Go downstairs and double-check the doors, smart mouth. Don't forget the kitchen."

"Don't worry, Mommy," Noelle said before she kissed her mother's cheek. "Nothing bad will happen here."

When Noelle got home from school on Monday, the toilet seat was up in their hallway bathroom and there were little brown hairs in the sink. Noelle closed the toilet all the way and turned on the water in the sink to wash the hairs away. She sniffed the air to see if she could smell smoke, but she couldn't.

"Victor!" Sierra screamed from downstairs like bloody murder.

"What?" Victor was already up in his room.

"Where's my chicken? I told you I was saving it!" When Sierra yelled, her voice carried through the house. She'd had two wings left over from Popeyes yesterday, when their mother bought them lunch after taking Daddy to the airport. Sierra never ate all of her food.

"I didn't take your stank chick—" Victor started to shout back, but then Mommy's voice came loudest of all from downstairs, telling them to stop all that yelling in the house. Mommy was always in a bad mood on Mondays, especially the Mondays when Daddy was gone.

All day at school, Noelle had been afraid the man in the house would be gone when she came home, a make-believe dream. She didn't get up early enough in the morning to go say hello to him, so she'd had to wait all day long. Now, Victor was in his room, and Mommy and Sierra were downstairs. This was her chance! Noelle opened the attic door, closed it behind her and ran up the stairs so fast she nearly lost her balance.

Peter wasn't in his bed under the table, but Noelle saw the Popeyes box full of bones on the floor. She looked toward the window, to see if he'd fixed it, like he said he would when he left. It was still broken, but the tree branch had been pushed back outside. There were dry, dying leaves on the floor now, on top of the broken glass.

"That you, little lady?" the voice said from behind her.

He looked so different! His beard was gone, and he'd cut his hair much shorter than before. He looked like an angel for real. He was standing flat against the wall near the stairs, where he'd been hiding from her. Peter was taller than Daddy, taller than any man she'd known.

"I thought you left," she said, relieved.

"Wouldn't do that without saying a proper good-bye." He was holding something behind his back, but Noelle couldn't see what, since it was pressed between his back and the wall.

"You came downstairs," Noelle said, grinning.

"Sure did. Had to check the place over, get a bite."

"My sister's mad."

"About what?"

"You ate her chicken."

Peter made a sad face and sighed. "Damn. I'm sorry about that. I didn't know it was hers. I thought it was for me."

"It's okay," Noelle said, so he wouldn't feel bad. Peter didn't move away from the wall. She wondered why he was standing up instead of sitting down, like before. "You can't come out now. We're home," she told him.

"So I see. You and your sister, and your brother, Victor?"

"How'd you know his name?"

He didn't answer. "You got a nice family, Noelle," he said. He was speaking softly today, because the door was so close.

Noelle nodded. She wondered if the man was hot, because his forehead was full of sweat, and it was dripping down his face. Too bad there was no air-conditioning in the attic.

"You're taking real good care of me. Thank you," he said.

"You're welcome."

"You're a whole lot nicer than the last family I stayed with."

"Were they mean?"

"Very mean," Peter said. "Very."

"What did they do?"

"You would be shocked," Peter said.

"Not-uh," Noelle said, feeling certain "shocked" must mean the same thing as "scared," which she definitely would not be.

"Well ..." He sighed, staring up at the ceiling. Noelle stared up, too. She saw the beams crisscrossing above her, how the ceiling jutted upward into sharp points. "First of all, one of them hit me. Right in my face. I got a bruise, see?"

He turned his face sideways so Noelle could see better. Sure enough, she saw a dark mark beneath his eye. It was like the mark she'd had on her forehead when she crashed on Victor's bicycle, that time she got stitches. It looked like it hurt.

"Why did they do that?"

"Because they were scared," Peter said. "What did I tell you? It ruins everything when people are scared. You're just making small talk, keeping them company, looking out for things, and then they go and hit you. That's not very nice, is it?"

"No," Noelle said.

"I didn't think so either, Noelle."

"Did you hit them back?"

"That I did," Peter said. "I didn't want to, but with the position they put me in, well, that changed everything. Anyway, they said they were sorry. It took a little time, but they apologized just like they should."

Through the closed door below, Noelle heard Victor calling. She couldn't understand everything he was saying through the door, but she heard her name.

"That's you, little lady," Peter said.

"I'll be back," Noelle promised.

"Wouldn't do that if I were you. Not today. They'll think it's funny, you poking around up here. I'll be fine. Come back and see me again tomorrow. And remember, keep quiet."

Tomorrow was so far away! Tomorrow was the last day before Daddy would come home. Monday, Tuesday, then Wednesday. Noelle started to argue, but Peter was holding his gaze steady, so she knew he wouldn't change his mind, and he would think she was a baby if she started to cry.

"Can I see what's behind your back?" she whispered.

Victor called her again, this time closer to the attic door. He was saying Mommy wanted her, and she'd better come out.

"Go on, Noelle," Peter said. He wasn't smiling anymore. His voice, like his clean-shaven face, wasn't anything like it had been before.

Tuesday, for Noelle, was torture. She got up very early, before the sun was even shining very bright, but Mommy was up before her and wanted to braid her hair. That took all of her extra morning time. After school, Mommy took them to the mall because Victor needed a uniform for his band concert. Then, they shopped for groceries. Noelle got in trouble for being irritable; she sucked her teeth at her mother at the grocery store. It was almost time for dinner by the time they got home.

"Where are you going?" Mommy said from the kitchen when she saw Noelle climbing upstairs. "Not that attic. Come back down here and help Sierra and Victor set the table."

Noelle wanted to scream and stamp her feet like she used to when she was younger, but she didn't. Mommy wouldn't like that, and then maybe she wouldn't be able to see Peter at all.

Victor, who was watching TV in the family room instead of helping like he was supposed to, flipped from *Tom and Jerry* to the six o'clock news. The volume was too loud. "On Sunday, when a nine-year-old Magnolia Park boy and his mother were slain, and his father . . ."

"Mom, Victor isn't setting the table!" Sierra complained.

"Victor . . ."

Victor ignored Sierra. "They're talking about it, Mom!" Victor called into the kitchen.

"So? You still have to help us," Sierra said.

When their mother came out of the kitchen, Noelle couldn't tell from her face whether or not she was mad; she walked straight to the family room and stood beside Victor to stare at the television set. Her pinky was hooked to the side of her mouth. On the screen, between where her mother and Victor stood, Noelle saw part of a cartoon drawing of a man with long hair and a beard.

". . . any information, please contact the police . . ."

"No, Noelle," Sierra corrected her, tugging a fork out of her hand. "Forks go on the *other* side. You're not paying attention."

". . . considered mentally disturbed and extremely dangerous . . ."

"What's men-tally dis-turbed?" Noelle asked Sierra.

"*You*," Sierra said, probably because she didn't know herself.

Mom walked over to the television set and turned it off. She sighed, wiping her hands on the dish towel she was carrying. "I'm glad your father's coming back tomorrow," she said. "And here we thought moving to Magnolia Park would be safer than the city."

"Don't worry, Mommy, there's—" Noelle began, and she had to stop herself from saying "a man in the house," because she remembered her promise at the very last second. But Noelle also felt bad, because she wondered for the first time if her mother would be mad at her for keeping a secret, especially a secret about someone smoking upstairs, because she had allergies. What if Peter's cigarette smoke got in the air and made her mother's eyes start watering? Noelle hadn't considered that before.

"Let's just eat. No more talk about the Mangler," her mother said.

Noelle didn't ask again what a mangler was. Instead, she said, "Mommy, can I play in the attic after dinner?"

"Maybe for a little while, sweetheart, before it gets dark."

And Noelle was glad, but not as happy as she'd felt yesterday, or even when she'd first come running back into the house full of anticipation to see Peter. She didn't hurry as she ate her food. She wished Wednesday would hurry up and come.

"I've been waiting for you, little lady," Peter said. He was stretched out across a sleeping bag, his hands folded behind his head. Noelle wondered where he'd found the sleeping bag, until she saw the camping boxes thrown to the side, with Styrofoam and cardboard in the middle of the floor. It was a mess. She also noticed a box of crackers, two bags of potato chips and empty cans of tuna on the floor. Peter must have gotten this food from the pantry for himself, while they were gone. Noelle was surprised Mommy hadn't noticed. Mommy wouldn't like someone taking all their food.

"It's almost Wednesday," Noelle said.

"Absolutely."

"That's when my daddy comes home and the wish is over."

Peter grinned. When he sat up, Noelle noticed he didn't smell very good. Why didn't he take a bath while they were gone, too? She stepped away from him.

"You took our food," she said.

"Got hungry, little lady. Hope you don't mind."

Was that the same as saying he was sorry? Noelle wasn't sure.

"And you have to fix the window," she reminded him.

This time, Peter laughed; it was a laugh she didn't like, one similar to Victor's laugh when he was making fun of her. In fact, Peter was laughing as though she'd just told him a joke. He stood up, stretching out his long legs and reaching his arms high over his head. He could almost touch the ceiling, he was so tall.

"Got to fix the window. That's like the other house—the broken window. That's what woke everybody up. It was early, see. I was just stopping in to look things over, get some food. Seems like you can never get enough food, you know? You always need more. But I fixed the window, all right, Noelle."

Suddenly, Noelle felt something twisting inside her stomach, something that was making all of her skin feel thin and tingly. Right beside the empty tuna-fish tin nearest her feet, she saw three spiders. Three. Squashed, all of them. Dead. Their long, black legs were crushed and bent.

Before she knew it, there were tears in her eyes.

"What you lookin' at, Noelle?" Peter asked.

Noelle didn't answer him. She couldn't. Her mind was wrapped tight, and she felt as though she wouldn't be able to stand up with her knees straight for one more minute.

"Aw . . . Noelle . . ." Peter said softly, bending down to try to see her face better. He shook his head. "Noelle, Noelle . . . Thought you were going to help keep an angel in the attic. Angels, remember? No devils. I don't like to see you cry like that."

Noelle pointed at the floor.

"What? Tuna fish?" he said.

"You killed the spiders," she said. Her voice was shaking.

This man had come in the house and broken the window. And he'd eaten their food without asking first. And then he'd stepped on the spiders—*her* spiders—and killed them in the attic, where they were allowed to live. Daddy didn't even put bug spray in the attic. This was their place to be safe.

"You bet I did. Those big, creepy—"

"You shouldn't kill things," Noelle said. "You're not supposed to do that. They didn't hurt anybody." She'd never talked to a grown-up this way, in this big, bossy voice, but she couldn't help it. Besides, Peter wasn't a regular grown-up. He wasn't like any other grown-up she knew.

Peter's mouth was open, but he wasn't grinning or laughing anymore. He looked down at the spiders, then back up at Noelle. "Well, hell, little lady, I thought they were poisonous. You got to kill something first before it kills you. Right?"

Noelle didn't answer Peter. It was too late to explain to him what Daddy had said about these spiders, that they were just big and ugly to most people, but they were probably more scared of people than people were of spiders. And three of them were gone now. Noelle wondered if it had hurt when Peter's foot crunched down on them.

"My daddy will be here tomorrow. He's coming real early. He's taking me to school." This was a lie, only one of several Noelle had told in the past couple of days, because she knew very well that her father wouldn't be home until dinnertime. But Noelle didn't feel bad about lying to Peter because it wasn't the same as lying to her mother. It wasn't the same at all. "So you hafta go tonight, before he gets here. It's almost dark. You hafta go."

Peter leaned down and turned his head to look at her, as if he could see all the way through her like an X-ray machine. Noelle had seen X-ray pictures in the hospital. Peter was quiet for a long time. Then, he said, "You scared of me, Noelle?"

"*No*," Noelle said, because she wasn't. "But it's time for you to go now. 'Cause I say so."

With a sigh, Peter straightened up, shoving his hands into his pockets. "I'm real sorry about those spiders, Noelle." And he really did sound sorry.

"Okay," Noelle said. "Good-bye. You have to go."

Noelle didn't stay to hear Peter say good-bye back, or to see if he was going to clean up the mess he made; maybe it was the food smelling rotten, or because Peter hadn't had a bath, or the sight of the bloody spiders mashed on the floor, but Noelle felt very sick to her stomach. Her knees were acting up so badly that she had to climb down the stairs very slowly, because she was afraid she might trip. She knew she would be crying, really crying, by the time she got to the door, and she didn't want Peter to hear her.

"Well, kid . . ." Peter called after her. "If you say I gotta go, then I gotta go. Sure am sorry you're sore, though. I'm real sorry about that."

Noelle went to bed early, and her mother put a cold washcloth across her forehead and told her maybe the food she'd cooked had been bad. That night, before she went to sleep, Noelle listened to the trees and the wind, and tried to tell if any of the bumps against the house were footsteps or just tree branches. She didn't hear any breaking glass. She barely heard anything at all.

Noelle tried not to think about the man in the attic the next day. But that night, after she'd fought Sierra for a spot on Daddy's knee and told him what she'd done in school while he was gone, Noelle finally went upstairs.

The sleeping bag was still spread out on the floor, but the boxes were stacked neatly where they'd been, and the blankets and newspaper under the dining room table were gone. The food wrappers and empty tins had also been cleaned away. And, she noticed, the dead spiders were gone, too, except for faint bloodstains where they'd been. At the broken window, the tree branch outside was snapped at the end and hung limply, stripped of leaves.

Noelle sat in the middle of the attic floor. All she heard was the quiet, like last night in her bed. She didn't hear any of her hidden playmates rustling or scurrying around her, the way she used to. Maybe all of the mice and spiders had been scared away.

"Noelle!" It was her mother's voice, calling from near the door. She knocked twice, hard. "Lord, child, come down from there before you break your neck. It's getting dark!"

And it was, Noelle noticed. It was getting so dark, she couldn't make out any of the alphabet letters printed on the empty boxes around her. She couldn't see the lines between the planks of wood on the walls. She couldn't see the highest point of the ceiling, where it became a tip. It didn't seem like the same attic, in fact. It was ugly. Why had she ever wanted to live here? Noelle hadn't noticed exactly when all her plans and hopes for the attic first began to go away, but now they were just gone. She couldn't think of why she'd ever wanted to stay up here in a dusty, dark attic all alone.

Noelle jumped up toward the sliver of light coming from beneath the attic door. She didn't run, but she walked very, very fast. Looking toward her feet, she saw the fluorescent green glowing from her untied shoelace, which was flopping loose, and she reminded herself she'd better be sure to ask Mommy to tie it extra tight for her once she got downstairs, back inside her house.

She might trip and fall. She might break her leg.

Wishes didn't always work. Sometimes, bad things happened.

ABOUT THE CONTRIBUTORS

Eric Jerome Dickey, originally from Memphis, Tennessee, is the *New York Times* best-selling author of *Genevieve, Drive Me Crazy, The Other Woman* and several other novels. He worked as a computer programmer, a middle-school teacher, an actor and a stand-up comic before becoming a full-time novelist.

Lawana Holland-Moore lives in the Washington, D.C. metropolitan area. Considered an expert on the ghosts and hauntings of that region, she has also tracked supernatural occurrences in the Caribbean and Ireland. After spending a month in Senegal in 2001, she was inspired by the beautiful, unforgettable country and its people. She is currently working on a novel.

"It is the same sun bedewed with illusions,
The same sky unnerved by hidden presences,
The same sky feared by those who have a reckoning
   with the dead.
And suddenly my dead draw near to me."
                              —from "Visit" by Leopold Senghor,
                                    Senegalese statesman and poet.

Terence Taylor, in his own words: People ask why someone as nice, funny and kind to kids, animals and old people as I am writes horror stories, especially after years of writing wholesome and educational scripts for children's television. It's because horror can express truths about life in allegories people hear without judgment, layered with humor and insight.

In dealing with loss in my life, I've learned to explore the things and places that scare me, but also to find happy endings there, the lessons of loss. With horror, I try to give my readers a glimmer of hope in the darkness. For more, visit my website at www.terenc-etaylor.com.

B. Gordon Doyle, in his own words:

Born and raised in the Empire State,
The son of the son of a preacher.
A dark horse, a falling star
The last of the Dunbar Apache.

Knave of ravens, reluctant magician.
Out of the blue and bold as love,
I go walking after midnight along
The moonlight mile.

L. R. Giles is a Virginia native and an alumnus of Old Dominion University. His short story "The Track" appeared in *Dark Dreams*, and his serial novel *Necromance* has appeared on www.awareness-magazine.net. He regularly publishes fiction at his online home, www.lrgiles.com. He's hard at work on two full-length novels, *The Hourglass* and *Youngbloodz*, while maintaining two full-time jobs, as a systems analyst and a husband. Drop him a line anytime at lrgiles@ lrgiles.com.

An award-winning fiction writer, **Chesya Burke** has been writing supernatural/suspense fiction since 2001. In that time, her fiction has appeared in such venues as *Would That It Were*, *The Best of Horrorfind*, *Tales from the Gorezone* and *Dark Dreams*. Her chapbook collection *Chocolate Park* is available now.
"The Light of Cree" is an excerpt from her novel *Sylvia's Sun*. Look for more of her work at www.chesyaburke.com.

Brian Egeston is a writer living in Atlanta. The author of five published novels, Egeston has had work nominated for the PEN/Faulkner Award, Townsend Prize for Fiction and National Book Award. His work is used as a classroom text in schools from California to Maryland. *Granddaddy's Dirt*, his third novel, is currently in development as an independent feature film. His writings have appeared in nationwide publications, and he is a featured commentator for National Public Radio. He lives with his lovely wife, Latise.

Michael Boatman costarred for six seasons on the ABC comedy *Spin City* and for seven seasons on the HBO series *Arli$$* plus appeared in numerous other television and film roles. His fiction appears in print in *Horror Garage*, and in the anthologies *Razor-Edged Arcanum, Badass Horror, Daikaiju! II: An Anthology of Giant Monsters!* and *Revenant*, and in several online magazines. Currently, he is developing film and television projects in the horror/dark fiction genre featuring African-American protagonists. His second novel, *The Revenant Road*, is currently in development at Stan Winston Studios. He lives in New York with his wife and four children.

Leslie Esdaile-Banks, also writing as **L. A. Banks** and Leslie E. Banks, is a native Philadelphian and Dean's List graduate of the University of Pennsylvania, Wharton Undergraduate Program. Upon completing her studies in 1980, she embarked upon a career in corporate marketing and sales for several *Fortune* 100 high-tech firms.

In 1991, after a decade of working in the corporate environment, Esdaile-Banks shifted gears and began an independent consulting career assisting small businesses and economic-development agencies.

Esdaile-Banks soon found a hidden talent, fiction writing, which has led her on a successful trajectory toward becoming one of the nation's premier African-American authors capable of deftly crossing literary genres. Graduating in 1998 from Temple University's Masters of Fine Arts Program with a degree in film and media arts, she added the dimension of filmmaking and visual media (with a portfolio of strong documentaries) to her artistic and business endeavors. Drawing on her urban background, Esdaile-Banks uses both life experience and a vivid imagination to create new landscapes in print. Each of her many works, from classic horror to suspense/thrillers to women's fiction, and even within the romance genre, all contain a paranormal, otherworldly slant.

At present, Esdaile-Banks is broadening the scope of her work to include a series of projects for St. Martin's Press (the *Vampire*

Huntress Legend series, to be authored under the pseudonym L. A. Banks) and a series for Pocket Books (*Soul Food,* a novel series based upon the ShowTime/Paramount Television Show, to be authored under the pen name Leslie E. Banks). Esdaile-Banks lives in Philadelphia with her husband and children.

Anthony Beal is a thirty-year-old New York native whose passions include drinking aged tequila, eating Cajun food done right and writing dark horror poetry and short stories. A passionate fan of Edgar Allan Poe, Poppy Z. Brite, H. P. Lovecraft, Piers Anthony, John Skipp and Craig Spector, he feels that Brite, Poe, and Lovecraft have had the greatest influence on his writing style. Beal enjoys pressing his sweaty body against liquor-lounge wallflowers, and is believed to exist in more than one universe. It is said that he can distinguish between people closest to him sheerly by the taste of their sweat. When he isn't baptizing nude convent students with flavored oils, Beal enjoys collecting skulls, grilling dead animal flesh and achieving states of spiritual transcendence through inebriation.

Christopher Chambers is the author of the mystery thriller novels *Sympathy for the Devil* and *A Prayer for Deliverance,* as well as the Oxygen Network teleplay *Official Mischief.* He's written numerous short stories that have appeared in collections featuring authors such as John Edgar Wideman, Walter Mosley, Eleanor Taylor Bland, Grace Edwards, George P. Pelacanos and Gary Phillips. His first horror suspense story was "I, Ghoul," in *Dark Dreams.* His historical novel *Yella Patsy's Boys* is due in stores in time for Christmas 2006. He lives in Washington, D.C., with his wife.

Patricia E. Canterbury is a native Sacramentan, an award-winning poet, an award-winning short-story writer, a novelist, a philanthropist and a political scientist. Her first published novel, *The Secret of St. Gabriel's Tower,* is the first of a proposed five-book, middle-grade, historical-mystery series. It is part of *A Poplar Cove Mystery. Carlotta's Secret,* the first of her children's eight chapter-book contemporary mystery series, *The Delta Mysteries,* has been optioned by a major motion picture studio. Canterbury won the First Annual Georgia State Chapbook contest in 1987 for her poetry chapbook *Shadowdrifters: Images of China.*

Canterbury was the assistant executive officer of the Board for Professional Engineers and Land Surveyors. She lives in Sacramento with her husband, Richard, the author of the short-story collection *Snapshots on Hell Street,* and several pets. Canterbury has had short stories published in *Shades of Black,* an anthology of stories by contemporary African-American mystery writers, *Dark Dreams* and *Life's Spices from Seasoned Sistahs: A Collection of Life Stories from Mature Women of Color,* a 2005 anthology written by women of color from around the world. She received an honorable mention for her story "The Elderly Gentlemen" in April 2005 from the Elk Grove Writers' Conference. Canterbury is seeking new publishers for her series. She is very active with Sisters in Crime, Mystery Writers of America, Northern California Publishers and Writers Association and the Society of Children's Writers and Illustrators.

Born in Port Chester, New York, **Rickey Windell George** recalls having written horror since the tender age of five. Now internationally published, he is best known for his unique blending of no-holds-barred carnage and over-the-top sexuality.

George's work has been seen in a host of publications, including *Dark Dreams, Fantasies, Blasphemy, Chimera World # 1, Scared Naked Magazine* and *Peepshow* magazine. He is also the author of the 2005 collection *Sex & Slaughter & Self-Discovery.*

Linda Addison lives with writer Gerard Houarner in the Bronx, where they create strange dreams and collect fun artifacts. Her collection *Consumed, Reduced to Beautiful Grey Ashes* (Space & Time) received the Bram Stoker Award. Catch her work in *Dark Dreams, Dark Thirst* (Pocket Books), *Dead Cat Traveling Circus of Wonders and Miracle Medicine Show* (Bedlam Press) and *Dark Matter* (Warner Aspect). Her poetry and stories have been listed on the Honorable Mention list for the annual *Year's Best Fantasy and Horror* and *Year's Best Science-Fiction.* She is a member of CITH, SFWA, HWA and SFPA. Her Web site is www.cith.org/linda.

Maurice Broaddus holds a Bachelor's of Science degree in biology (with an undeclared major in English) from Purdue University and works as an environmental toxicologist. He has been involved in ministry work for well over a decade, and is in the process of planning a church. His horror fiction has been published in numerous magazines and Web sites, including the *Small Bites* anthology, *The Crossings* anthology, IDW Publishing's comic books, *Horrorfind* and *Weird Tales*. His television and movie reviews can be read at the Hollywood Jesus Web site (www.HollywoodJesus.com). Learn more at www.Maurice Broaddus.com.

Tananarive Due is the national bestselling author of *Joplin's Ghost, The Good House* and many other acclaimed novels. She lives in Southern California.

ABOUT THE EDITOR

Brandon Massey was born June 9, 1973, and grew up in Zion, Illinois. Originally self-published, *Thunderland,* his first novel, won the Gold Pen Award for Best Thriller. His other suspense novels include *Dark Corner* and *Within the Shadows*. He was also the editor of *Dark Dreams: A Collection of Horror and Suspense by Black Writers*.

Massey currently lives near Atlanta, where he is working on his next thriller as well as *Dark Dreams III*. Visit his Web site at www. brandonmassey.com for the latest news on his books and signing tours.